THE
Beloved
CAPTIVE

AMELIA DALE SMITH

authorHOUSE®

AuthorHouse™
1663 Liberty Drive
Bloomington, IN 47403
www.authorhouse.com
Phone: 833-262-8899

Published by AuthorHouse 11/09/2022

ISBN: 978-1-6655-7580-5 (sc)
ISBN: 978-1-6655-7578-2 (hc)
ISBN: 978-1-6655-7579-9 (e)

PROLOGUE

In the ethereal light of a crimson sunset, a solitary figure wandered slowly toward an endless horizon. The wind had died and the featureless sea of grass, known as the Staked Plains, grew silent, befitting a world of loss and vast loneliness. The girl named Wa Shana wanted to die.

She had shorn her dark hair as a symbol of grief. Her young husband had been killed by the white Tejanos, the Texans, during one of their punitive expeditions into the Palo Duro Canyon. Seven days later, she had been bit by a rattlesnake, gone into premature labor and her baby, a boy-child, was still-born.

Her people, the Comanches, believed Wa Shana was cursed, so no one had come to find her after she left the village that morning. Her clothes were loose and ragged. Her face smeared with charcoal and buffalo tallow, Wa Shana walked barefoot through the sage grass.

Men go out in the desert to find their puha—their power. Why can a woman not do the same? The girl wondered. She looked at her hands. *Maybe this is a dream*, she hoped. A medicine woman once told Wa Shana that if one could see their own hands in a dream, they could control their dream to learn many secrets. Wa Shana's hands were cracked and bleeding, from days of scraping buffalo hides and tending the cooking fires. Her whole life was one of toil, drudgery and scolding from the older women of the village.

The dizziness, this sense of being apart from her body, had started in mid-afternoon. Only a swallow or two remained in her goatskin bag; she needed to save it. Except for some pemmican and a small knife, she had no other provisions.

What little status Wa Shana had in the tribe was gone. A woman's power, her 'puha', came from being the center of a family—the power of drawing in a man, becoming the wife of a warrior, giving birth and raising children. Wa Shana no longer had any of that. She only had the reputation of humming strange songs to herself when she worked, which only intensified the tribe's belief that she was possessed by an evil spirit.

Facing the sun as it melted away in the west, the young woman sat down in the sage grass. She started keening; a mournful way of singing in Comanche. "Where are you? Where can I find you, the man I love? In the redness now, I seek you. I will run to the four corners of the universe to find you."

In the midst of her keening, some long-forgotten words came into her memory, yet they held no meaning. This only summarized the lost nature of her spirit. She took a short sip of her water. *If I am to die here, tonight in the darkness, so be it,* she thought,

The young woman stood to her feet and began walking again. For some reason, she felt she should walk north, with the sunset to her left. The strange words somehow were saying she had once come from the north.

Walking into grief, walking into pain and sorrow, even into some sense of guilt, the girl quickened her pace. She felt she should hurry, towards hidden places in her memory. Perhaps the Comanche widow was going out of her wits, but now her steps seemed to catch some lost rhythm.

The words, the meter became a song—a lost song, which made the girl sway. Wa Shana stepped back and swayed, facing north into a soft, new evening breeze. The long-forgotten music returned to her.

About a quarter-mile away, men on horseback watched the Comanche girl dance in the fading light.

"What is she doing?" one rider asked, in English. He was a southerner, a stranger to the west Texas plains. Other men spoke the same question, yet in Spanish.

They were all rough-looking men, except for their leader, who wore a black-leather coat, had a trimmed mustache and rode a fine, bay horse with a silver-studded Mexican saddle. He and the Spanish-speaking men were Comancheros, traders from New Mexico, who acted as middlemen between the Comanches and corrupt merchants from Santa Fe. The Comanchero leader grinned as he watched the girl step and sway, back and forth.

"Is she loco?" the Anglo rider asked. He was thin and angular-faced, wearing a frayed buckskin jacket and a gray Stetson. "What about it, Sergio? Why is she dancin'?"

"She is dancing the waltz, Señor Jack," said Sergio Ortiz. He turned to his men and told them the same thing in Spanish. Some of the Comancheros laughed.

"Well, I'll be damned," said Jack Jernigan. He was a fugitive slave hunter from Kentucky, who had come out west after President Abraham Lincoln had issued the Emancipation Proclamation. "She is crazy. I can't believe the chief wants us to bring her back to the tribe."

With a low cluck, Sergio Ortiz spurred his mount and led the six other riders forward. When the young woman heard hoofbeats, she stopped dancing, then she took off running,

This proved useless. A moment later, the seven horsemen surrounded the Comanche woman. Wa Shana pulled her knife out, then she realized the men were not Texans. Several of them wore wide-brimmed sombreros; two of them wore slouch hats with hawk feathers. They were mixed-race and Comancheros. Wa Shana dropped the knife, then the riders seemed to swirl around her vision. She fainted from exhaustion, the dancing and this sudden ambush.

When she regained consciousness, Wa Shana's hands were being tied with a leather strap. Two men picked her up and placed her on a spare pony. The Comancheros then tied the girl's ankles with a rope that looped under the animal's lower flank. An intense memory suddenly sparked in the young woman's mind; this was not the first time she'd been taken captive.

Sergio Ortiz studied the girl, then he turned to the Anglo and the other men. "Do not take her for yourselves, compadres," he advised. "She is a witch. If you lie with her, your manhood will wither and fall away."

CHAPTER 1

Lew McManus came in out of the rain, after failing to reach the El Paso livestock trading market in time before it closed that afternoon. Seeking a cantina that catered to Anglos, he found a saloon next to a house of prostitution in nearby San Elizario. McManus only wanted to drink in peace.

McManus was a dark-haired, black-bearded hulk. A young Mexican cowboy stepped aside to allow him a place at the bar counter. McManus took off his oiled, rain-resistant slicker before planting himself on a barstool; he ordered a whiskey. The barkeeper looked at him and asked, "What brings you to town, Mister?"

"I came to El Paso to buy some mules for my ranch," said McManus gulping his whiskey. "But the dang market was already closed."

The barkeeper asked Lew about his ranch. McManus explained how he and his partner, Jimmy Gray, had started with a thousand acres up in the Sangre de Cristo foothills, north of Las Vegas Grandes.

"Where ya'll from originally?" the bartender asked. This was a frequent question, for the Civil War was raging back East and people in the territories and west Texas wanted to know a stranger's loyalties.

"Tennessee," Lew said simply. He figured the barkeeper had already judged him by his southern accent. Lew hoped he would not pry any further, for he and Jimmy Gray had come west to avoid the Confederate Army and to someday strike it rich from finding gold. Thankfully, the barkeeper did not ask any more questions as he polished the glasses with a towel.

Lew ordered another drink. While imbibing his second tumbler, McManus heard a man cursing at the back of the saloon. He also heard a woman's voice, speaking swiftly in either Spanish or French; Lew couldn't tell. He glanced at the Mexican cowboy, who was now seated at the bar, ordering tequila. The cowboy seemed agitated. Lew hunkered over his own drink, not wanting to talk to anyone.

As the vaquero left with a bottle in his hand, the woman suddenly shrieked. Lew turned around and saw a white-bearded man, beating a young Creole girl with a short riding whip. McManus turned away to finish his whiskey. The señorita's cries became louder and more pleading.

"What's going on?" McManus whispered, leaning over the counter to address the barkeeper.

The barkeeper remarked that the old Texan provided prostitutes for the parlor house next door. Apparently, he was punishing the young woman for not collecting a fee from the Mexican cowboy.

McManus gripped his tumbler with his huge hand. He strode over and offered to cover the fee himself. The Texan proved to be a rough old cob. Red-faced from heavy drinking, the old man told McManus to "stay the hell out of my business."

Lew looked around to see if anyone else would help the young woman. She was a thin, light-brown girl with black hair. The beating continued. The girl waved her bare arms wildly, fending off the blows from the horsewhip, as the old Texan forced her back into a corner.

McManus cursed under his breath. *San Elizario is a cruel place*, he told himself. He downed his drink and crossed over to the back of the cantina.

Lew grabbed the old Texan's arm. "That's enough", he said. When the old man reached for the revolver on his hip, McManus grabbed his forearm. The Texan struck McManus with the short whip. In one motion, the Tennessean's huge hands grabbed the man's neck and Lew heard it crack. The old Texan fell to the floor.

Everyone in the saloon looked on in shock; this gave McManus time to throw a silver dollar on the bar counter, grab his rain slicker and back out of the saloon with his revolver drawn.

Escaping across the Rio Grande into Mexico, Lew McManus rode his painted gray and white horse through the rain-splattered streets of El Paso del Norte, later named Juarez. He hoped to find a cheap hotel or at least another cantina, where more whiskey might calm his nerves. Lew had not meant to kill the old man. "His neck snapped like a chicken for Sunday dinner," Lew told himself. Lew feared the dead Texan probably had friends on the other side of the river, who might try to avenge the white slaver's death.

As McManus was tying up his horse outside another small cantina, the Mexican vaquero he had seen in San Elizario rode up and hailed him. "Señor. *me amigo*, I followed you when I heard what you did for *mi novia. Gracias! Gracias!*" said the cowboy, as he dismounted. He was a lanky fellow who grinned cheerfully below a looping mustache. "You were right to come to Mexico."

"Do you know a place where I can hide around here?" Lew McManus asked. He thought for a moment and said, "If they put out a reward in Texas, word will get out over here and a big lug Anglo like me will stick out like a dance hall girl at an ice cream social. Better yet, can you get me back into the New Mexico Territory, Amigo? A way that don't go through Texas?"

"Si. You go around the mountain," said the vaquero, indicating they could go northwest. He introduced himself, "*llamo* Miguel de San Gabriel La Jolla. We can go to Mesilla. You can buy your mules there."

McManus realized this vaquero had listened to his conversation with the bartender. "Your name is too long for me to remember. "Miguel La Hoya, I'm Lewis McManus. You got any tequila left, compadre?"

The two men passed the tequila bottle back and forth as they rode out of the Mexican town, then away from the river. The rain stopped and a glowing sunset appeared below the pink-gray clouds in the west. Outside the village of Santa Teresa, McManus spotted. a hooded person on a thin pony, who waved to LaHoya when they approached.

Miguel waved back and quickened his horse's pace. When McManus got close, the person removed their hood. It was the creole girl. She and the vaquero kissed, while staying on their horses. "This is Senorita Rosa Amarilla Del Pais Rio," said Miguel.

"Heck. Another name too long for me to remember," McManus said. He grinned, once he realized the translation: "The Yellow Rose! Rosa Amarillo. I take it you two are sweet on each other?"

"Who would not be, Señor?" the love-stricken young man answered. LaHoya told McManus in Spanish that the girl's eyes were the color of pure honey.

"It's getting dark, but we need to ride on, Amigo." McManus said. He was glad to be free of Texas and felt lucky. Because Texas was at war with the United States, he might not be prosecuted for killing the old slaver. Although Lew McManus was a Southerner, he had just freed a woman from bondage. Now he only hoped that Rosa Amarilla would not become his responsibility.

Rodrigo and Jimmy Gray had worked on the roof all morning, removing spruce boughs from the section that had leaked all winter and replacing them with new lumber; now they were nailing down sheets of tin over the boards. Their ranch house had been abandoned for over a decade, before the Rim Rock partners purchased the property in February. The ranch property had once been part of the Duran Land Grant, granted to the Spanish settlers who founded the nearby village of San Geronimo.

Standing on the roof, Jimmy Carl Gray gazed westward, toward the shimmering peaks of the Sangre de Cristo mountains. "We ain't gettin' any rain or snow for a few days," he remarked, "so we can take our time and do more tomorrow. I need to go on into the village and mail a letter."

Rodrigo Red Water braced himself atop the ladder before climbing down to safe ground. A Mescalero Apache, Rodrigo was also part Mexicano, which helped him blend with the people in the village. "Si, I go with you," Rodrigo said, easing carefully down the ladder.

The adobe hacienda on the ranch had previously deteriorated to just a shell, consisting only of exterior and interior walls, a stone hearth, exposed beams and three-quarters of a roof. Gray and Lew McManus had added wood flooring, put in molding and glass in the empty window spaces and they had installed a wood stove in the main room of the house.

"Now we won't have to worry about rain drippin' down our necks," Jimmy Gray said, stepping nimbly down the ladder. Jimmy was lean and energetic, usually intent on getting as much work done in a day as possible. "When we get back, we can fix that break in the corral fence. Lew should have fixed it, before he run off to Old Mexico."

Red Water nodded silently. His mind seemed to be elsewhere and Jimmy asked him what was wrong. "I am not with my people, the *Nit'a hende,*" Red Water answered. He referred to the Mescalero Apaches, who were struggling down in the south-central region of the Territory.

"You talking about the Army and the New Mexico militia forcing the Apache onto that reservation?" Jimmy asked.

"Si. Yes, at the fort on the *Rio Pecos.*" Red Water replied.

Jimmy Gray leaned back against the adobe walls of the ranch house and rolled up a smoke. "Seems to me, General Carleton had no one to fight, after all them Texans were driven out of the Territory. That's all the more reasons why you should stick around here, at the Rim Rock. We are all equal partners."

Rodrigo kicked absent-mindedly at a pile of rocks. A small scorpion appeared, flicking its stinger in anger at the intrusion; Rodrigo and Gray watched it scurry away. "The Star Chief of the *Yanquis* had one of the great chiefs killed. Mangus Colorados. Now Cochise and Geronimo will never go to any reservation," Rodrigo told his friend. "How can I hide here under a fine roof, when my own people try to survive after a hard winter?"

Gray struck a match on the adobe wall and lit his cigarette. "By 'my people', you mean that woman called Broken Wing, I reckon," Jimmy replied. He grinned. "Bring her here! Maybe a feisty woman would make you less miserable."

"Aho. She is too wild a spirit—even for me," Red Water said. "She will never leave the land of the Mountain gods."

The local store in San Geronimo doubled as a post office. While Rodrigo loaded food and supplies on the ranchero's wagon, Jimmy Gray read the letter he had written one more time:

Dear Mrs. Jessica,

Much has happened since I wrote you before. Young Joe went back to Texas. He might have joined the Rebel army. Me, Lewis and our friend Rodreego did find gold on your late husband's claim. I am saving you your share. How are you doing in Denver City?

We bought us a ranch. Going to grow beans, corn and cows. Come to see us. I will buy you a piano!

Jimmy Carl Gray knew his spelling looked poor, yet he continued;

Our ranch is in North New Mexico. A town called San Geronimo. We call it the Rim Rock Ranch. It is nice. There are mountains and pretty sunsets here. You can see many stars at night. And less snow than Denver City.

Hope you and Ned are good. I have money for you. Want to hear you play music again.

Your Servent,
Jimmy C. Gray

P.S. Reason why we left the Black Range is because the Apaches are on the warpath. Come watch the stars with me.

Jimmy Gray wondered if he should have written more. He had not gone into detail about her older son—how Joe Piedmont had gone to Texas and joined the Fifth Partisan Rangers. Maybe it was better not to mention Confederate troop deployments. Back in 1862, Gray and McManus had been forced to become teamsters for the Texas Brigade; Jimmy still wore his Confederate forage hat. The hat had bleached from gray to white under the New Mexico sun. He glanced out the store window, where Rodrigo was waiting on the supply wagon. Red Water had ditched his buckskin leggings and moccasins, swapping them for trousers and Mexican huaraches, along with a multi-colored serape. His only Apache attire was a red bandana, which he used as a headband.

Jimmy felt grateful to have his friend working with him on the new ranch. Lew McManus could often be moody; he and Jimmy sometimes had heated arguments when they both drank. Red Water almost always refused liquor and hardly ever caused controversy. His knowledge of native medicine and his tracking skills were valued highly by the two rawhide ranchers; Red Water could also speak Apache, Navajo and Spanish. Over the past year, he had learned more English by staying with the former Tennesseans, although much of it involved curses and swear words from Gray.

"You must teach me to follow the tracks you make on paper," said Rodrigo, when Jimmy Gray came out after posting the letter. "Then other White men can not cheat me and my people."

"Ha, I'm not much good at it myself. And the way some lawyers write, I don't even think Mark Twain could understand it." Jimmy climbed up onto the driver's seat, tilted up his hat and grinned. "Now, when I go to Santa Fe next week, I can draw some of your money out for you. You are fairly prosperous, for a Mexicano Apache, muchacho. What do you want to buy, besides more beans and taters?"

"I want a stovepipe hat. Maybe these mestizos would respect me more, if I looked like your Great Father, Mr. Abraham Lincoln."

"Hey, he ain't my Daddy," Jimmy laughed. "Some Rebel or a Commanche might take a shot at you with that get-up."

"They will aim at the hat, but I will duck," Rodrigo said. Flashing his wide white-toothed smile, he added, "And I can fire back more truly."

"I reckon so," said Jimmy. He snapped the reins and hawed the two horses hitched to the wagon. "When Big Lew comes back, we'll all get top hats and be the sharpest tycoons in all of San Miguel County."

CHAPTER 2

Wandering through the central district of Denver, Trey Edgarton hoped to craft a story on the city's recovery from 'The Great Fire' in April. Thanks to a generous prospector, named Bradshaw, the young reporter had returned from the wilderness of Chalk Creek with gold in his pockets.

Many of the stores, saloons, hotels and gambling dens were now only charred ruins, but the sounds of hammers pounding and the smell of new lumber permeated the district. One main street merchant wasn't taking any chances; he had hired brick masons to reconstruct his hotel. Trey had left Denver City immediately after the fire and he was impressed by the frontier town's resilience.

At first, the young reporter had difficulty locating the former site of his favorite haunt, Billy Martin's saloon and dance hall. The Golden Slipper was still smoldering when Edgarton had left town three weeks earlier. Trey stopped; he looked around, then he saw two men amidst the ruins. Billy Martin and another man were tearing down a staircase that had once led to the upper gambling room of the dance hall. The other man held a crowbar, while Martin pulled nails with a claw hammer.

"I cannot believe that's the only thing of yours still standing," said Edgarton, upon approaching the pair. He carefully stepped over burnt boards and around destroyed stacks of furniture.

"She flared up so amazingly quick," said Billy. Martin was a short, thin man with angular features, who stood straight as a ramrod to maintain a maximum height. "They say the whole thing may have started in some chimney, putting sparks on a rooftop. Then the high winds spread the fire to other buildings."

"I knew I was indeed fortunate to pack up and get out of my hotel room in time," Trey agreed.

Billy Martin wore painter's coveralls over his regular clothing. He twirled the hammer and paced it in the loop in his hip. "This is Miles Porter," said Billy, introducing a man of average height, who wore a brocaded green vest and a white shirt. The man was also wearing a wide-brimmed pith helmet which resembled those worn by British colonial officers. "Miles, this is Trey Edgarton, who writes for the *Rocky Mountain News*."

"Ah, a journalist. I admire men who can make their living by use of a pen," said Miles Porter. He spoke in a southern accent, like Billy Martin. "I have only written advertisements and an occasional sonnet to the ladies in my lifetime." Porter dropped the crowbar and shook Trey's hand.

"Pleased to meet you, Sir," said Trey. He pointed to the stairs. "I used to ascend these steps quite eagerly, right Billy? To play faro or to try my hand at the roulette wheel. Of course, I often descended the same stairs in a much more somber mood."

This seemed to interest Miles Porter. "Is that so? I used to deal faro myself and engage in games of chance. You don't sound like a westerner—or even someone from back East, Mr. Edgarton."

"Trey is from Canada, "Billy Martin interjected, before Porter could ask. "He left here after the fire, to go prospecting. Did you find any gold, Trey?" he asked, reaching down to a pair of coats on the floor and pulling out two liquor bottles.

"As a matter of fact, I did. Yet not much." Edgarton remembered the prospector named Bradshaw had told him not to reveal the amount of one's gold strike to strangers. "Are you planning to rebuild, Billy?" Trey asked, changing the subject.

"It's all boom or bust in this city—and I'm busted, by God," said the saloon owner. "All I've got left from this spot is a bottle of Scotch and the last of my bourbon. Care to join us?"

"Yes, Sir. Bourbon, if you please, garçon," Trey replied, using a French accent. He smiled at Miles Porter. "I am from Ontario, not Quebec," he added. "I am always impressed by how you Americans face both triumph and disaster with humor."

"Equal parts of humor, fatalism, and alcohol," said Porter. "I guess the stairs to Nowhere will have to wait, eh, Mr. Martin?" Miles grabbed his black suit coat and sat down on the lowest step.

The three men discussed the war back East and other news while sharing the bottle. It was still morning, yet drinking seemed appropriate to Trey Edgarton, as they sat and drank in the blackened remnants of the once-lively saloon.

"General Grant is laying siege to Vicksburg," said Billy Martin. "They expect it will fall in a few weeks."

"Is that so?" Miles replied, acting like he was not interested. He handed the bourbon bottle to Trey Edgarton.

"My editor at the paper says that President Lincoln's emancipation of the slaves has only stiffened the Rebels' resolve," said the young reporter. "How do you gentlemen feel about that?"

Porter and Martin glanced at each other furtively, then Billy Martin spoke: "All the news is a mix of good or bad, despite which side one favors. For instance, the Yankees were whipped badly at

Chancellorsville, in Virginia. But the Confederacy lost their prize general, Stonewall Jackson."

Trey took a brief sip of the bourbon. He thought about asking how the two men, being from the South, felt in more detail; but he decided against it. Trey took a different tact: "Where are you from Mr. Miles?" Trey asked, handing the bourbon to Billy Martin.

"Alabama, Florida and many points in New Mexico. I've also sojourned in Texas, and floated along the Mississippi," the man answered. "When you're a professional gambler, you best keep moving on."

"You know, the overall bad news is that this damned war might really last a long time," Billy Martin said. "Thank God, the three of us are here out West." He stood to his feet. "And I am thankful that a beautiful lady is approaching, this very moment."

A two-horse, spring carriage drew up to the wreckage; a finely-dressed woman held the reins and a young boy sat beside her. The lady's navy-blue dress had puffed sleeves and she wore a wide-brimmed, ribboned hat to shield her face from the sun. Billy Martin sprang off the platform of the saloon's floor and helped her out of the carriage, as Mr. Porter and Trey walked over. As the woman undid the yellow ribbon that secured the hat, Trey believed he knew the lady.

"You'd better get busy and build me another performance hall, Billy," said Jessica Piedmont. "It's best if you use brick this time." Her eyes widened upon seeing Miles Porter. "Do I know you, Sir?" she asked, composing herself.

Mr. Porter introduced himself and said he had seen her act 'several times'. He began to introduce Trey Edgarton—until Jessica Piedmont said she already knew the young reporter. "Mr. Edgarton wrote an article about me for the *Rocky Mountain News*," she remarked. "He was very flattering about my piano performance at the Opera House back in February."

"Yes," Billy Martin agreed, "but it resulted in the Opera House stealing you away from me and The Golden Slipper."

"I had no intention of depriving you of this lady musician's fine talents," said Trey. "I only described Mrs. Piedmont as a splendid example of how women can come out West to lead productive lives," he told Miles Porter. "I sent my sister the article and it has inspired her. She is also a musician and hopes to join me here in Colorado."

Jessica Piedmont removed her hat, revealing her golden-brown hair and her rare, gray-violet eyes. She smiled. "I hope to meet your sister. It would be nice to have more women friends here. This is my son, Ned," she added, reaching over and rustling the boy's hair.

"Stop it, Mama," said Ned, yet he seemed to enjoy his mother's attention. Ned Piedmont was big for his age. He had blond hair and an impish grin.

The lady musician turned to Trey Edgarton. "Mr. Edgarton, I hope you don't always take breakfast in such a manner," she said, referring to the bourbon bottle in the reporter's grasp.

"Only on auspicious occasions such as this, Ma'am," Trey laughed. "We were talking to Mr. Martin about his plans for the saloon." Edgarton handed the bottle back to Billy Martin.

The boy stood up in the carriage. "Hey, Mr. Billy. Can I help tear down those stairs?"

"Knock yourself out, son. There's a crowbar over there. Mr. Trey, do you mind keeping an eye on the lad?" Martin requested. "To make sure the staircase doesn't collapse on him? Jessie and I need to talk."

Edgarton assented; he and Ned scrambled over to the staircase. "That young man is very handsome," said Jessica, watching them. "And he's very observant. But I don't believe he suspects anything. Do you?"

Miles Porter stepped over to the carriage and noticed there was a suitcase and other baggage stashed in back. "Where are you going, Jessie?" he asked.

Jessica Piedmont took the bottle Billy Martin now offered. She took a small sip. "Is it imperative I remain in Denver?" Jessica pulled a small envelope out of her bodice and slipped it to the gambler, along with the bottle. "That Treasury agent I befriended was a good resource of information. After a few drinks, he told me he has to leave town, when the mud from all the snow dries out. They will probably leave from Fort Weld, with a small cavalry escort. They'll take the Sante Fe Trail to Kansas. It's all in the note, so the rest is up to you, Mr. Wells. When did you change your name to Porter?" she asked the gambler.

Miles Wells, alias Mr. Porter, stashed the envelope into his inner coat pocket. "Why can't you stay and let Billy and I know exactly when the gold shipment is leaving?" he whispered, putting the bottle to his mouth.

Jessica Piedmont crossed her arms over her chest. "Because Adolphus Frankfort has gotten to the point where he wants me to do more than just twirl his mustache," she said.

Both men broke out laughing and Miles Wells spewed bourbon out of his mouth. Trey Edgarton looked over at the group and seemed to wonder what they were laughing about, but he could not leave Ned Piedmont. The boy was demolishing the stair steps with wild blows from the crowbar.

"I understand," Miles Wells told his fellow spies. "Billy, your man at Fort Weld needs to get himself attached as a scout to that cavalry unit. I am heading to Fort Washita, just as General Pike has planned. Telegraph your cousin, when the shipment leaves."

Billy Martin corked the liquor bottle. "Both of you must be careful," he advised. People here in Denver are saying Southern sympathizers set the town on fire, on purpose."

Jessica Piedmont fixed her eyes on the saloon owner. "Have you heard anything from your cousin, the colonel, about my boy, Joe? Better yet, Miles, can you check with the Texas Volunteers about him?"

"I will check on young Joseph," Miles Wells replied. "Where will you be?"

"I am going to Central City and will be at Billy's other saloon, The Golden Gulch, for a few days. After that, who knows? I will let Billy know." Jessica Piedmont knew it was best not to reveal all her options; she had received a letter from Jimmy Gray in the New Mexico Territory. These men did not need to know everything about her personal life.

Outside Denver, a Union lieutenant named Dave Bradshaw returned to the officer quarters at Fort Weld and found mail on his bed. The letter was postmarked from Buena Vista, a frontier town on the headwaters of the Arkansas River. The Lieutenant sat down on the bunk; he opened the envelope and discovered that his unpredictable older brother was actually alive:

May ? 1863
Buena Vista, Colorado Territory

Hello Davey,

Sorry I missed you at Christmas. Hope the New Year finds you, and your sweet wife safe and well. Guess you are a Papa now– Congratulations!

I took it upon God and a double load of blasting powder to deliver myself from the legal entanglements of the Miner's Court. Had scratched us out a side shaft to our mine, because us "Badgers" usually need a second way out of our predicaments!

Anyway, I was using an extra-long fuse that day. And I was praying for deliverance, but God must have mis-heard me––for he sent an avalanche! I was grateful that I used an extra-long fuse, or I'd be a ghost writer.

So, dear brother, I am now enjoying the second of my nine lives! As I dug myself out of the snow, I decided to head for the western slopes of the Rockies. Sorry to have to fool you, along with the authorities, but I feel I can make a new start here in the Lord's Wilderness. You can sell my share of the mine, if you want—to settle my debts.

I found color in a stream below the Sawatches. If you look up a greenhorn named Tray-or Trace? Edgarton, he can maybe tell you where it is. He is Canadian and works for the newspaper in Denver. I asked him to look you up and buy you a beer.

Take care of yourself, brother and give my love to Erica. Please write Ma and tell her I'm okay. Ha, and tell Charlie Lawson to lighten up a little! Don't be too mad at me Davey. I am heading over the Divide, to do more prospecting. Hope to see you again, on the far side of the summer!

God Bless!
Dirt Bradshaw

Dave Bradshaw shook his head. Dirt was once again dodging his responsibilities. Even though it was now spring, no one was working the Badger Hole claim up on Boulder Creek. Dave Bradshaw still owed the regiment another year on his enlistment. His older brother proving worthless, Dave decided to write back home in Wisconsin and tell their youngest brother to come out and work the mine.

Captain Downing, Bradshaw's commanding officer, knocked on the side of the open door and entered the room. "Lieutenant Bradshaw, there's a federal agent needing to talk with you. In my office," said the captain.

Dave stashed the letter under his pillow, stood up and saluted. "Yes, Sir. What for Captain?" he asked, fearful that the government was seeking charges on Dirt Bradshaw.

"He's from the Treasury Department and needs to interview you. Something about providing a military escort for a government wagon train. At ease, David," said Downing. "He told me he wants men of the highest moral character. I asked him if he was aware that most of us in the regiment were gold miners–but he didn't laugh at my joke. I recommended you, Lieutenant."

Dave Bradshaw put on his dark blue jacket and his gray, white brimmed cavalry hat with the acorn tassels. He wiped dried mud off his boots and headed for the captain's office.

Agent Frankfort rose from behind Captain Downing's desk and firmly shook the lieutenant's hand. Adolphus Frankfort was of average height, with a muscular build, even in his mid-forties, and he had thinning black hair and a thick mustache. The agent did not make small talk; he immediately began the interview:

"This expedition is under the authority of the United States Treasury," said Frankfort, "You will answer only to me–and you will be under orders not to reveal who I am, nor can you tell others the purpose of this mission. Can you do that, Lieutenant?"

"Yes, Sir. I can keep my mouth shut," said Lieutenant Dave.

"I will select each cavalryman, scout and teamster myself," said the agent. "Some of the soldiers may be men you're not familiar with. I do that to keep down gossip, and to maintain a direct chain of command. Understand?"

Bradshaw agreed. Frankfort explained that he himself would be the wagon train boss and that he would use an alias, pretending to be a Kansas City merchant named Frank Cooper. "For the record, we are hauling buffalo hides, high quality wood, furs, hops and trade goods to Kansas City. Understand Lieutenant?"

"Yes, Sir," said Dave. He looked straight at the older civilian. "May I ask what we are really carrying?"

"When the wagons are loaded and we join your escort, I will tell you. And ONLY you. No one else is to know."

"Yes, Sir, Mr. Cooper, Sir," Lieutenant Dave replied.

Something in the government man's condescending manner disturbed Dave Bradshaw. The fact that the lieutenant would not be leading his usual platoon did not bode well. Dave had met other leaders who demanded a direct chain of command, but did not follow a direct chain themselves. He had seen officers who dogged their immediate underlings, cultivated informants among the lower ranks and fussed over minor details. "I always follow orders, Sir." said Dave, "Whatever you decide."

Bradshaw thought the interview was almost over, yet Agent Frankfort followed up with many questions about the young officer's background. Frankfort verified that Dave had been married for a year, had a son, and had left a successful mining business to serve his country. He had accounted for himself well in combat, serving in the First Colorado Cavalry during battles in New Mexico. Frankfort questioned why Lieutenant Bradshaw had been passed over for promotion. Dave responded that he had no complaints; he had no disciplinary actions on his record, and he was always eager to prove himself. "I can think fast on my feet, when the unexpected happens, Sir," said Dave. "At the same time, I will defer to your decisions."

"Good. I will be back here at Fort Weld by the fifth of June. We will first travel to Fort Lyon, where we will join up with a livestock caravan. Understand?" Lieutenant Dave agreed. He felt relieved that the Federal Agent had not asked anything about his older brother.

CHAPTER 3

As Dirt Bradshaw stood atop a nameless mountain, he marveled at the fearsome magnificence of the Continental Divide. Shielding his eyes from sunlight on snow, his heartbeat quickened and he saw his breath crystalize in the cold air. Bradshaw wondered if it was the altitude or the reality of the unbound wilderness that made him somewhat dazed.

Bradshaw looked down at the green-forested foothills and the rugged reaches of an unknown canyon, where he heard the sound of running water. "Spring is here, Rosey" Bradshaw said to his burro. "It must be May, I do believe."

The High Country still held deep snow and Dirt felt lucky to have snowshoes. He stood for a while, caught his breath, then led his burro down the westward-facing slope. It was hard walking for the pack animal. Dirt kicked snow out of the way so the burro could follow in his path. The waters behind them flowed east, back toward the frontiers of civilization, back to war and the recriminations of Bradshaw's past. Dirt carried a pistol, a rifle, and powder for defense, but no tobacco or whiskey. These latter things provided little or no help in times of trouble.

Snow crunched, pots and pans clanged and clattered as man and beast descended down the mountain. Rosey, the burro carried mining tools, flour, beans, coffee, bacon, and venison jerky for the prospector's sustenance. A burlap sack of oats and barley would provide feed for Rosey when grass could not be found.

The prospector back-tracked several times before coming upon the remnants of an avalanche. The massive snowslide had cleared out huge trees and boulders, casting them aside like childish playthings in the path of an angry God. Crossing the snowfield, Bradshaw found a long, gentle sloping ridge that would lead him back below the timberline.

Dirt remembered a previous avalanche earlier that winter; one that allowed him to fake his death back in Boulder County and free him from criminal prosecution. Although the event had freed Dirt from his legal entanglements, it also severed friendships and family ties. Some who knew him would say Dirt Bradshaw was chased out of Denver

City; yet those who knew him best saw him as a man who often liked to go where no one would follow. Coming to a clearing in the evergreens, Dirt unrolled a crude map. Triangles, representing mountains, and squiggly blue lines denoting streams and rivers marked the way to the Black Canyon of the Gunnison. This was the land of the Ute People, fierce mountain warriors who lived west of the Divide, especially in the high valley that Bradshaw now viewed.

It took a whole afternoon and day of trekking until Bradshaw found Jim Taylor's river canyon. He found a game trail, made by large numbers of elk that led above the bluffs to an upland meadow. Dirt made camp for the evening, as he pondered his next move. *I need to lighten my load. And whiskey won't do it,* he resolved. He glanced around. Beyond the campfire he had noticed a strange rock in the shape of a long spearhead. Above the rock, a stately spruce stood out from the other trees. Dirt cleaned out a patch of snow, allowing Rosey to graze on the frozen grass underneath. He then carried his rucksack over to the spruce. He took his prospector's pick and marked the tree, making it look like a bull elk had rubbed the tree with his antlers during the rutting season. Dirt Bradshaw began to dig beside the spearhead rock. Taking a waterproof canvas bag out of his rucksack, Bradshaw stashed silver, his 'Double Eagle' coins and over a dozen nuggets of gold.

Dirt discovered many signs of wildlife in the high valley north of the Gunnison River; he noted elk, deer and bear tracks, yet he had no luck hunting his first few days in the region. Bradshaw wondered if his scent gave himself away. He hadn't bathed in two weeks; his hair, body and clothing also smelled of campfires.

The prospector turned south and came to a creek east of the main river. Here he stripped, and bathed with soap he'd stolen from a bathhouse in Salida. The water was ice-cold, so Bradshaw got out and built a big fire, to ward off the chill. Dirt decided to trim his winter beard. He heated water in his coffee pot, used the soap, along with a straight razor and a small hand-held mirror, and went to work.

The razor was too dull to trim Bradshaw's long hair by the time he finished. Dirt had shaved off his mustache and the whole beard. "Guess you don't recognize me now, do ye, Rosey?" Dirt said to his burro, which was eating the last of the oats and barley. Bradshaw tied back his hair with a blue bandana. His beans and bacon were gone, but Dirt had saved some grease to make fry bread. He still had coffee. "I reckon we can go another day or two, Gal," he said. "If I don't shoot something soon, we might have to head over the next pass, back to civilization."

Bradshaw had made camp beside the creek, on the edge of a meadow. Sleep came easily; days spent on long hikes up hills and searches along the mountain streams, panning for gold, had worn him out. Dirt passed out after gazing up at the brilliant white galaxy of the Milky Way.

In the pale light of morning when Dirt awoke, he spotted wild horses grazing about the meadow in the mist. He heard a sound–almost like a woman screaming, but it was definitely an animal, a wild cat of some kind. Dirt grabbed his rifle.

Rosey, the prospector's pack burro, had come untethered and was grazing with the wild horses. "It's a mountain lion," Dirt said to himself. He whistled for the burro. She ambled toward the camp; one of the horses followed her. It was brown, long-legged and lean, a descendant of the wild breeds which had escaped from the Spanish centuries earlier and multiplied by the thousands on the Great Plains. Dirt immediately wanted this horse.

He could tell it was a female, probably a young filly, yet it came no closer than thirty yards as the burro walked into the camp area. Dirt kept his rifle handy and stirred the remains of the campfire to make coffee.

The coffee pot was bubbling when three Ute Indians rode out of the nearby woods. Dirt was sitting with the Sharps carbine draped across his lap, yet he tried to act calm. He held up his open palm and grinned.

The lead warrior was mounted on a tall, red and white mare. His hair ran down in long braids on each side; he wore beaded buckskins and a short-brimmed hat with two eagle feathers. The warrior stared intensely at the lone white man. Perhaps he had not seen one without a bushy face before. The warrior spoke and Dirt thought he heard the word "kapi" spoken, sounding like it was part of a question.

Dirt swept his open palm over at the coffee pot, all the while holding the warrior's gaze with his own. "You want some coffee, Friend?" Dirt asked. "Kapi?"

The Ute swung himself off his horse and stood beside it. His face did not change expression. Dirt felt they were in a staring contest. Dirt looked away first and reached for the coffee pot. The handle was hot; Dirt yelped and cursed.

The other two Indians seemed startled. One had a bow strapped across his shoulder; the other grasped an old musket. The lead warrior laughed at Bradshaw burning his hand.

Dirt took a rag and grabbed the pot again. He was fortunate to have two tin cups and he poured the coffee. The Ute nodded and stepped closer.

"Sa-g'aru-mu ta' wa-chi." said the warrior. "I am Nicaagat." He touched the sheath of his big knife at his side, to show this white man he could defend himself in an instant. Bradshaw stood up and handed him a coffee cup.

"I am Dirt. Dirt Bradshaw," he said, blowing on his own coffee. "Do you know English?"

"Yes. Some call me Jack. When I was a young boy, I lived with Mormons. We sit down. Drink this."

The other two Utes eased their horses closer; they spoke to each other in their own language. Dirt realized that Nicaagat Jack was probably their leader and wanted to parley with him.

Nicaagat blew on his coffee and tasted it. He made a sour face. "Maru Kapi iyevu-pu-ni" said the Ute.

"Yes. My coffee is strong. Not puny, by any standards," Dirt replied. He reached for a small sack of sugar cubes and plopped two of them in Nicaagat's cup. Then he did the same in his own cup.

Both men drank. "Where you from, Ta'wa-chi?" the warrior asked. "Bradshaw, where you go?"

Bradshaw pointed east, toward the mountains he had crossed days earlier. He paused for a moment on the second question. "You see, I come alone. I bring no white men, no ta'wa-chi with me. Are you from around here?" Dirt used his hand to indicate the warrior and circled it around, indicating the high valley.

Nicaagat slurped his coffee. "This is better. We are Yamparika. We go to parley with the Uncompahgre. Talk with Ouray, 'the Arrow' who now is Uncompahgre chief."

Bradshaw understood. He had heard of Chief Ouray. Nicaagat Jack glanced over at Dirt's pack, pick and shovel. "No gold in the mountains here. You keep moving," the warrior warned.

Dirt Bradshaw grinned, showing his teeth. "I bring no other white men with me. Bring no whiskey or sickness. The Ta'wa-chi, back over the mountains, think I am crazy. I once lived with wolves myself and can speak their language."

The warrior's fierce look changed to amusement. "You ARE loco, Ta' wa-chi. You can not speak Sinaa-vi."

The prospector raised his chin, closed his eyes and gave a series of yelps and howls. When Dirt opened his eyes, he saw the other two warriors backing away on their ponies. Dirt's burro, Rosey, brayed and the Ute with the bow readied an arrow.

Nicaagat laughed loudly, slapping Bradshaw on the shoulder. "Aho, you not need whiskey to be drunk, Wolf Singer!"

The atmosphere in the camp changed. The other two Utes dismounted and Dirt gave one his tin cup to drink coffee. When Bradshaw pulled out two sugar cubes, he felt a horse nuzzle the back of his head. Dirt turned and it was the brown filly. She was not so wild after all. Bradshaw patted her nose and held out the sugar cubes in the palm of his hand. She accepted the treat.

Dirt wanted this horse. He instantly offered to trade anything for her. Then he realized the Utes would want his carbine. "The gun," said Nicaagat Jack, before Bradshaw could rescind his offer.

Bradshaw swallowed a breath of air. His rifle was needed to hunt game and he had little food left. Dirt still possessed his Navy Colt Revolver; it could be used for self-defense, but only at close quarters.

The lead warrior sensed Dirt's misgivings. "You come, go with us. We go to Conejos. They race horses there. This horse we give you is fast. Faster than all others. We get you back to your people, who are there." Nicaagat held out his tin cup. "More Kapi, por favor." he asked.

The other two Utes laughed nervously. Bradshaw handed over his Sharps carbine and poured coffee. He had made new friends.

Confederate agent Miles Wells came to Fort Washita, several miles above the Texas border, to meet with General Pike. After waiting several hours, Wells was finally allowed to see the Brigadier General in Pike's private office. Wells knew the Confederate General's history. Pike had resigned his commission as commander of the Department of the Indian Territory after the Battle of Pea Ridge in Arkansas, a battle in which Indian troops under his command scalped Union soldiers on the field of combat. Albert Pike still served the Confederacy, yet not in an "official" capacity.

When he stood up behind his mahogany desk to greet Wells, General Pike towered over the spy. Six-foot two, weighing three hundred pounds, he was in his fifties, with long hair and a full beard. "So you come from Denver, I hear," Pike remarked.

"Yes, Sir. It is an honor to meet you, General." Wells took a seat.

"Do you know why I summoned you back, Mr. Wells?"

"Only in vague terms." Wells knew that if information was kept to a minimum among the agents of subterfuge, the risk of one spy revealing the identity and actions of another would be lowered. "I don't have to know everything. I do understand, however, that I am to be involved in some 'fund-raising', for the cause. Is that correct?"

"Only on the front end. And maybe on the back end of the enterprise," said Pike, stroking his gray beard. "You are a good recruiter. Tell me, Mr. Wells, have you heard of the Knights of the Golden Circle?" The ex-commander referred to a secret organization, very popular in the South, that was being used for subversion in the Border states: Maryland, Kentucky, and Missouri,

Miles Wells coughed, then spoke, "Only the name, General, Sir. But I suppose they may have some influence...on the matters at hand?" Wells framed his answer as a question on purpose. Pike, a famous Freemason, had attained the highest rank of "Grand Commander" in the Scottish Rite. Wells had noted Masonic emblems on his gold watch chain and his ring bore both a star and crescent symbol.

"We need you to do some more recruiting," said the Confederate leader. "Chief Stand Watie and Colonel Martin's cousin both recommended you." Pike pulled out a rolled-up paper and unfurled it, like a scroll. "Here is a list of names from some of our master rolls. These men have proven their loyalty. Some of them are our Indian comrades-at-arms. They could prove useful, here in the Territory and elsewhere. We want younger men, if possible. Men that are impressionable—and also able to ride for days in the saddle. In addition, there are some code words, along with their meaning, on the list."

General Pike handed the scroll to the agent, but he did not fully release it into his hands. "Before you leave, I want you to write these names down, in your own handwriting. After you have selected the men you need, memorize the names. Then destroy your list." the General said.

"I understand, Sir." Wells walked around to study the list.

"Investigate the men, as much as possible. Determine their steadfastness, as well as their weaknesses. What line of work did you do, previous to the general conflict, Mr. Wells?" General Pike asked.

"I was a medicine salesman and owned a stagecoach service, taking passengers out West, Sir." said Wells. Miles did not mention being a gambler and losing the coach in a card game a year earlier. "That was before I served under General Sibley, as an undercover agent."

Pike released his hold on his end of the scroll. "Colonel Martin has his Partisan Rangers ready for action, doesn't he?" Pike asked.

Miles nodded; he studied the scroll. "Yes Sir, General. I brought him some new recruits a few days ago." Miles Wells referred to Joseph Piedmont and some other young Texans. "May I recruit one or two of them back, General? I will need some teamsters. Young men who can work with mules."

"Certainly." The General stood up and held out a massive hand. "We look forward to you ascending in the ranks, Wells. As a sort of Knight-errant and Templar to our cause. Let us smoke and have a drink if you prefer."

Miles agreed. Even though he sensed Pike was now gauging his habits and vices, Wells had come a long way, through a dry and thirsty land. One or two drinks could do little harm.

Pike took off his suit coat and donned a silk-lined smoking jacket with a red dragon on the back. "I bought this in San Fransisco years ago. Would like to visit there again, when California falls into our hands. Would you like bourbon, cognac, or a Napoleon brandy?" the General asked, walking over to a liquor cabinet.

"The Napoleon would seem appropriate," said Wells.

"Oh, lest I forget," said Pike. He reached into his pocket, then he pressed a half-dozen gold coins into the ex-gamblers' hand. Some were twenty-dollar gold pieces. "We may need your knowledge of the New Mexico Territory, as well as your experience on the Santa Fe Trail."

As General Pike unlocked the liquor cabinet, Miles Wells studied the coins. Three were twenty-dollar pieces. The other three each had a strange design: within a gold-edged circle, a five-pointed star hovered over an upturned crescent moon.

Pike handed Wells a snifter of the brandy. "Those first three are for your immediate expenses," the General explained. "You are to use the other three whenever certain key phrases are used. When you encounter other persons in our enterprise. Use them one at a time. When you give the other contact one of yours, they will give you one of theirs—along with instructions,"

"What phrases?" asked Wells.

"They are at the bottom of the list. Memorize them, but never write them down." General Pike lifted his glass, to raise a toast. "To our Conquistadors," he said.

"To empire," added Wells, clinking the snifter to Pike's.

Both men drank. Pike raised his rounded glass a second time. "And to our Native American allies," he said.

CHAPTER 4

Jimmy Gray and Rodrigo were repairing a fence rail, to keep their cattle out of Grays' vegetable patch, when Rodrigo spotted a group of horses and riders coming from the village. "Dog dammit, I don't need any more interruptions," cursed Jimmy. "You'd better go hide Amigo, in case it's the militia."

"No, it looks like Señor Lewis," said Rodrigo, squinting and shielding his eyes from the glare of the noonday sun. "He has two mules—and two riders with him."

Jimmy Gray dropped his end of the wooden rail and looked. He recognized the dark-bearded McManus, but he didn't know the Mexicano riding beside his partner. The third rider followed the men and mules at a short distance, on a pony. When the group drew closer, Gray noticed the person had their head covered by a hood or shawl. "Howdy, Fellers!" McManus shouted. "I brought us some help."

"We don't need help," said Jimmy, scowling, "and you're late." He almost let loose with a stream of invectives, yet hesitated when he saw the third rider was a woman.

"This here is Miguel La Hoya. And the girl is named Amarilla Del Rio," said McManus, getting down off his horse. The vaquero tipped his sombrero and the young woman removed her shawl. She had long, sleek black hair, and an olive complexion. Jimmy Gray figured she was a mulatto.

"There's always things that need doing on a ranch or farm," said McManus. "Miguel has worked as a ranchero and done cattle drives." Lew noticed Rodrigo was looking away, not wanting to seem impolite by staring, and Jimmy was obviously trying to determine Miss Del Rio's racial lines. "Amarilla here is creole—or criolla, to be correct. She can cook and speaks Louisiana French. That might come in handy, if we need a translator."

"Why the dagburn hell do I need to speak to some frog sombitch?" Gray replied. He reached down to grab the fence rail. The Mexican cowhand hopped off his horse and immediately hoisted the other end.

Rodrigo Red Water finally spoke. "Si, I heard the French people do cook food that is good. Better than the burnt bacon and beans we ate last night, Señor Jimmy." He smiled at the girl.

All four men went to work and the fence line was quickly repaired. Lew McManus pulled Jimmy aside. "Listen, I tried to palm the girl off at Eduardo Fazari's ranch," McManus whispered. "I thought Eduardo's wife could use her as a housemaid. But Francesca was jealous of her good looks—even though Amarilla is gonna marry Miguel here."

"Ain't my problem," said Jimmy. "We might could use the cowhand, but why did you bring that coon-ass French pastry?"

"Come on, Jimmy Carl. You gotta admit she's pretty." Lew crinkled up his nose and grinned salaciously. "Besides, our hacienda could use a woman's touch."

Jimmy Carl Gray studied the young woman. Rodrigo had offered her a drink from his canteen and they were both conversing in Spanish. Jimmy kicked at a rock that was embedded in the garden dirt. "You sure got a talent for complicating things," said Gray.

Lew McManus decided he would wait before telling Jimmy he had killed a man down in Texas.

Walking alongside a line of Confederate wagons, Joe Piedmont felt the military life was only a series of tedium and deprivations, punctuated by hurried marches and brief skirmishes. When Mile Wells first dropped the boy off at a supply station north of the Red River, Joe had expected to enlist as a soldier. Instead, he was made a stable boy, then eventually he worked his way up into being a muleskinner for the Fifth Texas Partisan Rangers.

Joe hated the Indian Territory. It was hot during the day and cold at night here in the Cross Timbers region. Walking along with another young volunteer, a Cherokee named Samuel Burningtree, the fourteen-year-old complained about the heat, and the red dust kicked up by the horses, mules and wagons of the caravan. "It don't look like I'm gonna get to shoot nobody," said Joe. "I ain't killed a Yankee since last summer. Up near the Kansas border."

Sam Burningtree was not impressed by his friend's bragging. Sam's uncle rode with the First Cherokee Cavalry, which led the Confederates as they advanced along a dry river bed. Days earlier, the Rangers had repelled a raid at a place called Webber Falls. "At least we're finally moving out. And seeing the rest of this country," Sam replied.

Joe asked Sam where the wagon train was heading. "My uncle said we're heading to the Creek Nation," the other teenager answered. "We might raid the Union supply wagons, heading to Fort Gibson."

"Hey, maybe we can get a rifle after all," Joe said." If the Colonel won't give us one, maybe we can steal one from the Yankees.'

All afternoon, the Cherokees and the Texans proceeded, traveling through the mix of savannah and post oak groves that formed the country between the eastern hardwood forests and the beginning of the Great Plains. The dust choked Joe Piedmont's throat and stung his eyes. Both he and Sam were fourteen; they were still considered too young to do actual fighting in this early stage of the Indian Territorial battles.

"Why are you fighting for us, Sam?" Joe asked his friend. He did not understand the various alliances and sympathies among the "Civilized Tribes", the Indians who had been transplanted west of the Mississippi River.

"T'was the U. S. government that sent my folks out West, to this dry Hell-hole. Uncle says we once lived in beautiful green mountains and forests, with clear, running streams and plenty of fish and game. And them dang Creeks helped General Jackson, that bush-haired bastid that sent us here!"

Joe shielded his face from the churning dust. "I bet we keep moving after nightfall," said the young Texan. "There ain't any trees no more. Where we gonna hide, in case there's an ambush?"

"Maybe we are better off back here. You know, Fort Gibson has changed hands twice now already, since the war started. My uncle says even some Cherokees have fought for both sides. First, for us Rebs. And now, for the Union."

"How the hell do you know who to shoot?" Joe Piedmont asked.

Sam Burningtree laughed. "I'm sure they will oblige us by wearing blue."

"If they don't, I'll just shoot anyone who aims a gun at me," said Joe. "I've gotta get a gun. Being with the wagons and mules doesn't guarantee we'll be safe. My Paw was killed by the Yankees while watching General Sibley's supply wagons. They were parked way back from the battle lines at La Glorieta." Joe was referring to the three-day battle in New Mexico, where the Texas Brigade's advance was halted by Colorado Volunteers in March,1862. "I ain't gonna die like my father," Joe declared.

Dirt Bradshaw now lived in a mountain paradise. He had hunted deer and other abundant wild game with his new friends, the Yamparikas, for several weeks. These Utes had no need for agriculture, gold or money; the Utes had freedom to go where they pleased, which appealed to Bradshaw's own wandering spirit.

The white prospector was now jokingly called 'Wolf Singer'. He accepted the name and now dressed like a Ute himself, wearing a beaded buckskin jacket and two wild turkey feathers in his hat. Shaving his beard every few days, he kept his hair long and traded away his mining equipment. In order to keep his rifle, Bradshaw also gave Nicaagat Jack his burro, in exchange for the brown filly he now rode. Dirt named the horse "Waukesha', a Potawatomi Indian name adopted by a town in Wisconsin, Bradshaw's home state. She was sturdier than Dirt first thought: fast, yet able to endure over a long distance in these high altitudes.

Bradshaw also felt that breathing mountain air, sleeping under the stars and running free had given him a new lease on life.

Gazing down from the heights of the fourteen thousand-foot San Luis Peak, Dirt surveyed the upper headwaters of the Rio Grande and the magnificent San Juan Mountains. "How can I imagine God's Heaven, when here it is?" Bradshaw wondered. He felt uncivilized and free, having escaped the boundaries of his old world and rejoicing in this new one. "I want to forget the ways of the white Ta'wa-chi," he told Nicaagat, who stood beside him.

Nicaagat pointed to a half-dozen, thin lines of smoke trailing up from the valley below. "There is the Uncompahgre camp," he said. "Ouray, the Arrow should be there. He is going to meet with a treaty group of the Ta'wa-chi. Before we and the Uncompahgre go to hunt buffalo and fight with our new enemies, the Sioux."

"I look forward to meeting Chief Ouray. I heard he speaks both Spanish and English and is a learned man," said Dirt. "Aho, Jack! I'll race you to the bottom!"

That evening, Nicaagat introduced Dirt Bradshaw to the chieftain at his lodge. A heavy-set leader in his mid-thirties, Chief Ouray told Bradshaw he was half-Apache and half Tareewach Ute. "So tell us, Wolf-Singer, why are you here in our mountains?" he asked.

"You already know my new name, Chief. So, you probably also know that I once sought gold," Bradshaw said, sitting down across from Ouray and his wife. "But your people have taught me something of far greater worth. Living off the land and being free are all a man needs." Dirt nodded toward the Chief's wife, who seemed particularly pleasant. "And of course, the love of a good woman," he added, smiling politely.

"You do not have much to trade, Bradshaw," Ouray observed. "Each Spring, more white men come down from the east, to dig for the gold and silver metal. How do we know that if we allow you to pass through our mountains, you will not bring more whites to settle here? To build their houses, cut down our forests and plow the earth?"

"No towns or cities follow my tracks," Dirt promised. "I travel alone."

"Your cities stink and hold disease. We do not want them here." The chieftain signaled to some warriors outside the lodge. "We are going to trade with the Americans in the Mexican towns of the Rio Grande. And we will meet with men from your Governor. To tell them your people must live on the other side of the high mountains. Do you know of this man, named Evans?" Chief Ouray referred to John Evans, the new Territorial Governor, back in Denver.

Dirt grinned. "He is a lawyer and a politician. My Father wanted me to be a lawyer. But I thought I would have more self-respect emptying cuspidors in a Chicago cathouse." None of the Utes laughed or grinned. "I beg your pardon, Ma'am," Bradshaw said to the Chief's wife, then he continued:

"These lawyers will speak big words about how great you are, Chief. Smile at these, but do not believe whatever they say next. And what they put down in writing is always more dangerous. They have a way with written words that can even fool me."

"I can see you have a way with words, yourself, Wolf Singer. So, you can read their English, as well as you speak it?"

"Well, yes. I reckon so," Dirt admitted. "However, I have seen how their written words can be bent, later on, into new shapes. Different meanings."

Ouray nodded. "You come with us, then. Aha, you can be my lawyer!"

28

CHAPTER 5

J essica Piedmont heard a violin playing in the hall next door. Perhaps Central City had some sort of culture after all. *Perhaps I can find work here*, thought Jessica. "Stay here and watch the carriage, Ned," she told her son. "I am going into the tavern, but I'll be out in a minute."

The saloon looked better inside than Jessica had expected, judging from the exterior. Gas lights, linen tablecloths and a tile floor made it seem more like a fine restaurant than a tavern. A long bar with brass foot rails and large mirrors above the rows of many-colored bottles dominated one side. Behind the bar counter, a red-headed woman was drying wine glasses with a hand towel. Jessica assumed she was a cook, because there were only four customers in the establishment.

"Pardon me, Madam. Do you happen to know how I may contact Mr. Owen Singletary? Or Alvin Reynolds?" Jessica asked.

The lady seemed surprised. "And who might you be?" she inquired. She seemed younger than Jessica first thought.

Jessica tried to think of a false name, one that did not have an association with Denver. Miss... Mrs. Gray," she stammered "I'm a friend of your employer, Mr. Martin. Have you heard from Billy?"

"Billy disappeared," the woman said simply. She put down the towel. "What'll ya have?"

Jessica was stunned. "What? What do you mean?" Then she realized she needed to make this meeting more of a business transaction, in order to draw more information from this lady bartender. "May I please have a small whiskey and water? Do you have soda water?"

"Whiskey's two bits. If you want a big glass, with soda, it's thirty cents. I am not sure why, but the Sheriff is looking for Billy."

"Well, I guess you know about his dance hall in Denver burning down. Don't you? I used to play piano there for Billy," said Jessica.

"That's where I've seen you before," the woman remarked. She slid the whiskey and soda over to Jessica. "But didn't you go by a different name?"

Jessica realized she'd been caught in a lie. This conversation was already awkward. "Ahem, Gray was my maiden name. I performed as Jessica Piedmont. Mr. Piedmont was my late husband's name. And you are?"

"Christina Jones. I'm a widow, too, Honey." Mrs. Jones smiled. This eased the tension between the two women.

"I'm sorry. We're both too young to be widows," said Jessica.

"Yes. Let me guess–the War?" Christina Jones asked.

On this question, Jessica always had a ready answer. Jessica knew Mrs. Jones had already picked up on her southern accent, so she told the bartender that her husband had died in a mining accident; instead of being killed by a Yankee at La Glorieta. "So Mr. Jones was killed in battle, I assume?" Jessica asked.

Christina Jones nodded and looked down in sorrow. Mrs. Piedmont sipped her drink and decided to change the subject. "That is lovely music coming from next door. Who is the man playing over there?" The musician had changed to a more sweet, plaintive tune.

"She's a lady," Christina Jones said. "From Canada. She's already famous, and she's giving a performance tonight. Miss Jane Edgarton."

Jessica's mouth dropped open. Trey Edgarton had told her his sister might come out West. Jessica felt jealous, but she hid this reaction. "Oh, I have met her brother." she said. "Trey should have introduced us. So, have you met her?"

"Yes. She raises money for the Soldier's Aid Society. She helps Union widows. My husband was a captain. He was killed at Fort Craig a year ago, down in New Mexico."

Jessica avoided looking at Christina Jones. She took another drink. Henry Piedmont had fought at Valverde as well. Somehow, seeing her own grief reflected in the eyes of another widow, Jessica's recent desire for vengeance seemed trivial—even pointless. "I am... sorry, Mrs. Jones. Now, about my reason for asking you about Misters Singleterry, or Reynolds. When does the stagecoach arrive?"

On a cool spring morning on the Conejos River, a group of Ute leaders and warriors came to negotiate treaty terms with representatives from the Federal government. Indian Agent Lafayette Head lived in Conejos and he was sponsoring the event.

Agent Head was also sponsoring some horse races. He owned a track along the Guadalupe bend of the river. The Uncompahgre, the Yampas and other Utes were eager to race the white soldiers from Fort Garland and Santa Fe. Lafayette Head was on good terms with Chief Ouray, who had once been his interpreter when Head was appointed Special Agent to the Ute and Apache nations in 1859.

Soldiers, men and women in civilian clothes, including townsfolk strolled about the field, checking out the horses and making bets. Chief Ouray and two of his warriors accompanied Agent Head and his delegation over to the group that was preparing for a three-quarter mile race.

The field contained a variety of horses, ponies and riders. A young white corporal tended to a quarter horse, while a short Mexicano soldier from Santa Fe spoke in Spanish while holding the bridle of a black Navaho gelding. Chief Ouray pointed out three of his Utes next to their wild horses. Another chieftain, Colorow of the Muache tribe, stood with his jockey and the chief's finest horse, a long-legged chestnut Morgan.

Several people in Head's group seemed to favor the Morgan; others expressed confidence in the horses of the military. Agent Head and his party strolled on, when they spotted an odd-looking contestant. He was dressed like a mountain man or prospector, in fringed buckskins, yet he wore moccasins instead of boots. The man wore a weather-beaten flop hat, with turkey feathers stuck above the brim and he sported a brown pony tail. He was stooped over, knocking some dried river mud off his horse's hooves. The mount was a sturdy-looking mustang, brown, with lean features.

"Are you racing for the United States or the Ute Nation, sir?" Agent Head inquired.

"Neither," said Dirt Bradshaw, looking up and revealing a tanned, clean-shaven face. "I got twenty bucks says I can beat all your boys in blue, that Mexican and the Chiefs' warriors." Dirt had lost weight over the past month, while his filly had grown stronger.

"Count me in," said one of the Americans, a tall gentleman wearing a suit and short tie. He was a lawyer, an explorer, and the ex-governor of the Colorado Territory, William Gilpin. "Dirt, I'll wager you don't even place in the top three. And I'll raise it with a postmaster's position if you do win. Gilpin grinned and extended his hand. "You're looking well, for a dead man, Bradshaw."

"I'll be danged, if you don't get around even more than me, Bill" Dirt laughed. They shook hands. Gilpin told Dirt that he would be surprised to see Bradshaw win with such a wild mount.

"Just watch. We couldn't beat that corporal's horse in the quarter-mile, so I didn't enter. But my filly's got more wind and endurance, from roaming and hunting in the Rockies. Waukesha can take 'em all." Dirt scratched his chin, "A postmaster's job, heh?"

"Yeah, Dirt. How much you think that's worth?" Gilpin asked.

"About five bucks. You and I can talk about it later," said Dirt. "We're putting gold and silver coins in the kitty. But we'll take your federal green-backs, if that's all you've got."

Gilpin chuckled. "I can't leave evidence of gambling away Federal resources," he said, then he turned serious. Waiting until agent Head and the others moved on, Gilpin added," Dirt, you know you're in trouble, back in Denver City, don't you?" Something about selling worthless stock to some British investors?"

"We can talk about that later, as well," said Dirt. Bradshaw swung himself up on Waukesha's back. He had no saddle; only a folded Indian blanket lay underneath him.

Bradshaw studied his competition as the nine horses lined up. The race was two laps around an oval race course. Dirt figured to let the Utes set the pace in the first lap, yet he needed to gauge the race as it went along. He whispered some encouragement to the filly, then drew a deep breath.

The pistol shot rang out and the race began. Dirt's young filly started out slowly, but the prospector was not alarmed. The race was for seven furlongs. The black pony led at first, with the Mexicano in the saddle. A Yampa Ute, one of Nicaagat Jack's warriors, ran a close second. Dirt kept his filly close to the Union quarter-miler, which gradually gained ground on the pack.

By the time they reached the back bend, the chestnut Morgan took the lead. Three Indians all war-whooped as they rounded the bend, challenging the new leader. "Yee-hah, fellers!" yelled Bradshaw, as he overtook the Quarter-Miler and the black pony. As the horses raced closer to the crowd of spectators, composed of soldiers, Indians and civilians, Dirt spotted a young white woman in the gallery.

Some of the horses faded at this point, but not Bradshaw's filly. It was just Dirt and the Ute warriors now, He had not been much of a horseman before now, but Dirt felt like a man transformed. His long hair trailing wildly behind him, he leaned forward to the filly's black mane and shouted, "come on, my Beauty! You can win!"

Here was the second lap. The strong legs of the wild-bred filly did not falter. Dirt was sure she had Arabian blood in her. They soon rounded the back bend once again; now they passed the chestnut Morgan, whose flanks were foaming. As Dirt and Waukesha raced toward the gallery, the wind from the mountains was at their back. They overtook the Utes and drew neck-to-neck with the Yamparika's horse.

With a last burst of energy, the filly crossed the finish line a nose ahead of the Yamparika's horse. Dirt and his Native American friends hollered and whooped at the soldiers.

"Damn it, you should have let the Indians win," said Agent Head, when Dirt brought his horse back to the gallery. "It would have put them in a generous mood!"

Bill Gilpin stood behind the agent and laughed, "Spare the diplomacy, Lafayette," said the ex-governor. "A Colorado man won the damned thing, after all." Gilpin slapped Dirt Bradshaw on the back, after Bradshaw dismounted.

"Glad to take your money, Bill," said Bradshaw, as his old friend doled out four five-dollar bills. "You weren't serious about that postmaster's job, were you?"

Before the ex-governor could answer, a familiar voice sounded out from the crowd. "Och! Och! Dirt Bradshaw, it is really you!"

Dirt turned around and saw his former mining partner, Charlie Larsen, looking tall, blond and tanned in a blue Union uniform. "Well, I'll be—" Before he finished, Dirt's response was muffled by Larsen's tight bear hug.

"You're alive. Alive!" Larsen exclaimed, in a heavy Swedish accent.

Dirt felt many people looking at him; he was embarrassed by Charlie Larsen's effusiveness. At the same time, Dirt was glad to find Charlie, whom he hadn't seen since his friend had enlisted in the Colorado Second Infantry. "So you came here from Fort Garland?" Bradshaw asked.

"Yah, we are here, with the treaty party." Larsen wore two stripes on his jacket.

Agent Head announced that members of the delegation were now invited to his home in Conejos. "Ladies and gentlemen, please follow me," said the agent. "Food and refreshment will be provided and you all are welcome."

"You heard that, Dirt? Refreshments means liquor," Governor Gilpin remarked, as he followed the crowd,

Dirt hesitated, holding the reins of his horse. He noticed a young woman approaching; she was the same woman he had seen during the race. Wearing an aqua dress and a wide-brimmed straw hat, the young lady smiled. "Congratulations on your race, Mr. Bradshaw," she said. Dirt was surprised she knew his name.

"This is a fine animal," the lady added, patting Waukesha's neck.

Bradshaw looked her over, admiring the curve of her derriere and her golden blonde hair. "Yes. Very fine," said Dirt, grinning and giving Charlie Larsen a wink. "Do I know you, Miss?"

"Jane Edgarton," said the lady. "My brother, Trey, pointed you out when you flew past us the first time around. He told me how you gave up your gold claim to him. We want to thank you." Miss Edgarton pointed back to the crowd, where a brown-haired man was speaking to the ex-governor. "There's Trey. He's been too busy chasing a story to introduce me, I suppose." She waved to her brother, catching his attention.

"This is Corporal Charlie Larsen," said Dirt, remembering his manners. "Charlie and I go way back. He and my brother were my partners in a mining operation on Boulder Creek."

The young journalist, Trey Edgarton, strode up, wearing a brown-checked suit and a derby. "Mr. Bradshaw, excellent to see you again. I didn't recognize you, at first, in your frontier attire."

Dirt and Edgerton shook hands; when Dirt introduced Charlie, Trey said that he and Corporal Larsen had met on the caravan from Fort Garland. "I am covering a story about the treaty with the Utes," Trey Edgarton explained. "I'm sorry. If you will excuse me, I need to see

Chief Ouray back there. There is a rumor that the Chief may relinquish the mineral rights to the western slopes. Maybe I can confirm that."

As her brother rushed off, Jane Edgarton asked Dirt, "How long have you lived with the Indians, Mr. Bradshaw?"

"You can call me 'Richard" or 'Dirt' if you prefer. I first met up with the Utes a month ago. They traded me this fine filly, who has trained me, more than I trained her. I still can't believe we were lucky enough to win."

"I believe one makes their own luck," said Charlie Larsen.

"Yes, though Trey was indeed lucky—that Mr. Bradshaw gave him that claim! That yield enabled my brother to wire me enough money so that I could join him out West." Miss Edgarton smiled at the prospector. Dirt detected an amber glint in her eyes, like the color of a fine bourbon, held up to the sunlight.

Trey Edgarton returned, having little luck in getting the Ute chieftain to talk. "Shall we go join the delegation?" he suggested, proffering his arm to his sister.

"Sure thing," Dirt agreed. "Let me buy the first round, okay, Miss Edgarton?"

"Keep your winnings, Richard. And please, call me 'Jane'. Mr. Head would not be much of a diplomat, if he charged us for our drinks, would he?"

Dirt agreed. Leading his horse toward the town, Bradshaw walked with Charlie Larsen, as they followed the Edgartons. Most of the crowd had dispersed and had headed off to the village, while the politicians and soldiers were getting into carriages, or retrieving their horses. Dirt Bradshaw hesitated, turned and looked back at the racecourse, where his friends, the Uncompahgre and the Yamparika, still lingered. Dirt felt himself being pulled away by his own people once more. He felt he was abandoning the Utes, but seeing old acquaintances once again and meeting Miss Edgarton was luring Bradshaw back into the society which the world called 'civilized.' Dirt Bradshaw took a deep breath and walked on.

CHAPTER 6

Deputy Marshall Edward Fazari dreaded this summons from the Union Commander of New Mexico. General Carleton was having severe Indian troubles in the late Spring of 1863, but Fazari believed that should be the military's problem, not the U. S. Marshall's Service. The brief telegram from Carleton had not specified which tribe would be discussed; Fazari figured it was either the Navahos or the Apaches.

The United States Army was struggling now in a Civil War to end slavery, yet out here in the New Mexico Territory, Indian peonage remained prevalent. As recently as late 1862, a Navajo child could sell for as much as four hundred dollars in Albuquerque or Santa Fe. Colonel Kit Carson himself, the commander of the New Mexico Militia, owned several Navajo children. In addition, the Mexicano soldiers and the Ute scouts under Carson's command often took Native American children in their attacks on the Navajo villages. So Fazari felt Kit Carson should be the man to solve the problem.

As he walked across the Santa Fe Plaza to the Territorial Governor's headquarters, Fazari resolved to express this opinion. General James Carleton was a fierce-eyed, humorless New Englander, who had recently led his army of two thousand men from California through Arizona and into New Mexico. Carleton's army had fought Apaches and driven a Confederate Texas force out of the Territory, yet Edward felt General Carleton was out of his element as a government administrator.

The General was sitting at his desk, finishing a letter to Washington City when the Deputy Marshall entered the room. "Have a seat, Mr. Fazari," said Carleton. "I am recommending that we move the Navajos out of their old homeland and into the protection... and control, of the Federal government. That should break the cycle of war parties and retaliatory raiding."

"Yes, Sir, General. I heard you are already doing that with the Mescaleros," said Fazari, taking a chair.

"Yes, Deputy. Colonel Carson has herded most of them to the Bosque Redondo." The General referred to a new camp, on a desolate section of the Pecos River, where the Native Americans could be concentrated and controlled. "I expect that once all the older Indians die out, the younger ones can be 'Christianized' and be trained to become farmers. Let me read this last statement."

"As time elapses, and these races die out, these islands, or reservations may become less and less. Until finally, the great sea of white men will engulf them, one after another, until they become known only in history—and at length, are blotted out of even that, forever."

Edward Fazari thought this was both grandiose and cruel. Originally from Louisiana, he was reminded how the British had run his Acadian ancestors out of Canada. "That's splendid, General, Sir," he commented, choking down his resentment. "May I ask why you wanted to see me?"

"Colonel Carson is taking a thousand men to move the Navajo people," Carelton continued. "That leaves our other troops rather thin, being spread out along both prongs of the Santa Fe Trail." The General turned and pointed to a map of the American Southwest Territories which hung behind his desk. "We have to keep things safe—from Texans, Kiowas and the Comanches." Carleton folded his letter and placed it in an official brown envelope. "We have a lot of problems to solve," he added.

Edward grinned slightly, feeling glad he did not have the military governor's headaches. "Yes, Sir. And of course, then, you have those peace efforts with the Chiricahua Apaches, as well." Fazari tried to hide the sarcasm in his voice with an expression of concern. Carleton's troops had started an all-out uprising among the Chiricahua and other Apaches, by the assassination of their great chief, Mangas Colorados, back in January.

"You should be protecting the Overland mail!" Carleton shouted as he scowled and struck his fist upon the desk. "Mr. Fazari, you are indeed fortunate that I have not reported your laissez-faire attitude to Washington City! It seems your ranching interests take precedence over your duties as a U.S. Deputy Marshall."

"I am here and at your disposal, General, Sir," said Fazari, trying to remain calm. Edward half-hoped the Territorial Commander would relieve him of his law enforcement duties, for it was Spring and the Fazari-Martinez ranch now required Fazari's full attention.

"Since you do have knowledge of livestock, I am ordering you to take action on the livestock raids we have experienced lately. I want you to deal with the Comancheros. You have heard of them, I presume?" Carleton asked.

"Yes, Sir. The New Mexicans and half-bloods, who trade with the Comanche Nation. I have researched them, and how they trade guns, whiskey and goods to the tribes in Texas, in exchange for stolen cattle."

"We had sixty mules stolen from the U.S. Cavalry over at the Penasco River," said the General. Carleton turned around; he pointed to the map on the wall. "More recently, the Comanches raided and stole cattle near Fort Union and Fort Sumner. Those beeves were meant for our soldiers and the reservation at the Bosque Redondo. They need to be recovered!" The Territorial Commander was at his wit's end; down at Fort Sumner, the Army had recently bought back the very cattle stolen from Fort Union. "What has your research shown?" Carleton asked.

"The Comancheros use a route through the llano Estacado, close to the Canadian River. If I may, Sir?" Fazari walked over to the map and pointed to midway on New Mexico's eastern border. "First the cattle smugglers run the herds out of North Texas-either at the Arroyo Saldito, or north of the Mescalero Ridge here. They head northwest, to Santa Fe, or Las Vegas, where they sell the beef at those markets."

"So they come back through the canyons and the draws in the Caprock region," said Carleton. The General stood up; he was taller than Fazari by several inches. "You must make preparations to take an expedition that way, post-haste. Intercept the Comancheros at the places you described, then bring back the stolen cattle. Understand?"

"Yessir, General. I am fixin' to recruit some good men, who know the area."

"Fixin' to? I want you to just DO it. What sort of men are you talking about?"

Fazari knew Carleton liked to fuss over details, yet he also knew how to handle leaders like this Yankee general. "That is where I need your astute foresight and permission, Sir. The men I'm talking about have had some run-ins with the law. Minor things, over in Kansas and down in Texas. But they are good trackers, know how to survive in the wilderness, and can fight. They were gold and silver prospectors before the war."

The General's face lit up at the mention of gold. He believed the New Mexico Territory held vast amounts of hidden treasure, yet to be discovered. Like California, this would eventually lure in white settlers and a prosperous civilization into this backward region. "Yes, yes, I see where you are going with this, Marshall Fazari," Carelton agreed. "Tell your men they shall be granted full pardons upon their success. I would like to speak with them someday. These are the very type of men we need now—to boldly move New Mexico into an honorable future!"

"You need to quit your whore-mongerin' and whiskey drinkin' ways, dog-dammit!" Jimmy Carl Gray said, scowling at Lew McManus. "We got ranch work to perform."

"I do as much work around here as anyone," said McManus, stepping over to a firepit. The burly Tennessean grabbed a branding iron out of the fire, while Jimmy Gray held a young calf down. Gray's ranching partner stuck the sizzling iron on the animal's rear flank. The calf bawled and struggled; the number '3' and an 'R' on his haunch stood for the Rim Rock Ranch. Lew and Jimmy's property comprised nineteen hundred and forty acres, in view of the southern Sangre de Cristo Mountains. The two Tennesseans had started with seventy-two head of cattle, four horses and two mules, along with some chickens and a pregnant sow.

The former miners had spent almost all of their gold earnings on this venture and they still owed the Fazari-Martinez ranch a share of future earnings on the beef cattle. Don Pablo Martinez had instructed Jimmy to run an irrigation ditch from the narrow creek nearby, for a drought had plagued the region the previous two years. Jimmy agreed; the land was too arid to support many crops, so he and Red Water had dug the ditch, in order to grow several acres of corn and alfalfa.

Since the adobe ranch house was almost a half-day's ride from Las Vegas Grandes, Lew McManus sometimes spent a night in that town. The girl, Rosa Amarilla Del Rio, now lived in Las Vegas Grandes. She and Miguel LaHoya were having problems, so Rosa Amarilla had talked McManus into taking her to "Our Lady of Sorrows of the Great Meadows," as the town was called in Spanish. Rosa Amarilla found work at a hot springs hotel outside Las Vegas Grandes, in a place called Montezuma.

"You show up today at noon, just like last time. And then you say you work as hard as me? That's bullshit," Jimmy complained. He let the calf loose. "I ain't trying to preach to you. It's just that your entanglement in some love triangle might jeopardize our operation here. Especially, if your heathern ways results in some dang disease."

McManus laughed. "Don't worry about me, Maw. I can take care of myself. Hey, why ain't Rodrigo back? You should never have let him go hunting up in Blue Canyon this morning."

"If he brings back an elk, or a Rocky Mountain Bighorn, that's one less cow we'll have to eat," said Jimmy. "Don't sass me, when your mouth's all full of gravy."

The vaquero, LaHoya, rode up. He had gone out to bring in the last group of young cattle, but returned with no steers. "They broke through the west fence and are in the woods," said Miguel.

McManus and Gray hurried to their horses. "Hell, Jimmy, maybe we'd be better off cross-breeding these dang wild-ass Longhorns with buffalo. Then just let our Apache go out and shoot one when we need meat."

"Heh, so they can range like you, into Las Vegas to jump a pretty heifer now and then," said Jimmy. He had a new horse, sired by a captured mustang and a Kentucky mare. "Bring your branding irons with you, Lew, and we'll build another fire." He and McManus hoped to sell beef to the Army at Fort Union by the end of summer. After that, they planned to take up the life of "cibeleros," hunting buffalo in eastern New Mexico in October, when the buffalo hides were in their prime. Both men loved to hunt.

As the three cattlemen rode up toward the west end of the ranch, Jimmy told McManus they might want to talk with Lucien Maxwell, the land grant baron Jimmy had met the previous summer, up at Cimarron. "Maxwell has the finest breed of cattle in the Territory," said Jimmy. "Like the King Ranch, down in Texas. If we got a young bull from him, there'd be no stopping us."

"Nobody but the blasted Comanches," Big Lew replied. "Eduardo Fazari tells me that they're stealing cattle everywhere. He wants our help. Hey Miguel! Have you ever fought Comanches?"

"No. I am not loco." said the young vaquero. "We shot at them, but they got away. When men try to track them down, after they steal the cattle, they will lose their lives in *la emboscada*."

"Well, I mis-spoke. Fazari says we would actually be the ones doing an ambush. On the Comancheros," Lew explained. "He proposes we track them down and wait at the border for them to bring the stolen herds out of Texas."

"If Fazari wants that done, he should do it himself. " said Jimmy. The thin Tennessean still harbored resentments against the Deputy Marshall, for stealing a young woman, Francesca Martinez, away from him and thus gaining the Martinez ranch at Bernalillo.

Lew McManus slowed his horse to a walk as they entered the pine woods along the Tecolote' Creek. "You ain't thinking this through, Jimmy. Suppose we pick out a few choice heifers we take from the Comancheros and use them to increase our herd? The Army will never know."

Gray and McManus looked at each other and both men grinned. It reminded Jimmy of the time he and Lew had first decided to come out West, when they left hard times in Tennessee, for a new adventure. "Let's do it. Hunt down the Comancheros. We got a renegade of our very own, who can track a flea across a rock," said Jimmy. "When Rodrigo gets back, we'll talk to him."

CHAPTER 7

Up in Blue Canyon, Rodrigo was having a difficult time finding his way back to the ranch. He had hunted down and shot a bighorn ram high up on the mountain, but now the ranchers' two dogs had led him astray. Rodrigo thought they were on the scent of their back trail, but the dogs were actually just tracking a group of deer. Lew's scruffy Airedale and the Red Bone coonhound loved to chase deer on the far-flung ridges. Clad in a tattered long coat and armed with Lew's Sharpshooter rifle, the Mescalero stepped cautiously along the rocky canyon's rim. The pack mule he was leading by a rope was acting skittish; the mule did not like a dead, wild animal being strapped across its back.

Red Water came to a high point overlooking a green conifer forest and a winding creek below. He realized he was on or near Hermit's Peak. Over to the east, the edge of the southern Great Plains gleamed in the afternoon sun.

This was good land, teeming with wildlife and lower Alpine pastures. Rodrigo sat down to rest and take in the view. He thought about his homeland, in the south-central Sacramento Mountains, and his people, the Nit'a hende. They were not being allowed to live there anymore; most of the Mescaleros were being herded to the dry bend of the Rio Pecos, to the concentration camp set up by the Anglo Americans.

So now, Rodrigo Red Water felt like a refugee, a *refugiodo*, in his own region, the Southwest. Being part Mexicano, Rodrigo was now using the last name of "Rojas" over at the village of San Geronimo. Up here in the mountains and forested foothills, he could at least feel connected to a wilderness, like he had done before with the Deer People.

Turning his gaze back to the side of the mountain, Rodrigo was surprised to see the strange figure of a man standing on the edge of a rock ledge. The man waved to him. Wearing what looked like a brown frock and a short-crowned hat, the man looked like some sort of Padre, or a ragged monk—except for his bush of long hair and a gray beard. Red Water realized this man was the "Hermit Priest", a holy man from Europe. who lived in a cave upon the mountain. The villagers in San Geronimo said the Priest was a wandering monsignor, who had walked here all the way from a place called "Boston", refusing to ride on any wagon, horse or mule along the way. They said he may have been doing penance for some past misdeed—and though banished from the Vatican—he could tell the future and cure leprosy.

Rodrigo did not believe such superstitions, but he felt the hermit Priest was at least a man worth talking to; so he began hiking up to the padre. "Hola. Donde vas?" Rodrigo called to the priest, once he drew closer.

"En camino a la salvación," said the Priest, meaning he was on a journey to salvation.

Rodrigo liked the answer. He had always thought life was a journey toward eventual redemption, rather than salvation being something you could put in your pocket and carry around like a badge or a weapon. As he stepped out onto the same ledge as the holy man; however, the Priest said something loco.

"Are you the Good Shepherd? Bringing me a lost sheep that strayed from the ninety-nine?" the Priest asked in English.

"More like the Foolish Shepherd, who cannot find his way back home," said Rodrigo. "I am called Red Water."

"Ah. I am Giovanni Augustiani, un Padre disonorato della compagnia. Si, I have walked many miles to these mountains."

"Tell me Padre. Where are you staying?" Rodrigo asked. Like most white men in the wild, the hermit seemed hapless.

"God uses the foolish things of the world to confound the wise. Perhaps there is hope for the both of us. Follow me. It is not far from here," said the Priest.

As they walked up the trail, the Hermit Priest babbled on, in a weird mixture of Italian, Latin, Spanish and English. Rodrigo wondered if the padre had gone mad, from living too far from civilization and not talking to another person for months at a time.

From what he could gather, Rodrigo learned the man had once been a priest or even a bishop. The hermit said something about his station with the Church "falling amongst worldly thorns" Somehow there was a woman involved. "A woman encompasses a man," said the Priest. "I do not know the heart of a woman, except for Mia Mama. And I will never know."

"Si, they are all different, but we men treat them all badly," said Red Water. He thought of "Broken Wing", the Apache woman he still loved, but whom he had abandoned. For some reason, he also thought about the exotic creole woman, the one named Rosa Amarilla Del Rio, whom Lew McManus had brought from Texas.

They came to a small cave. Rodrigo immediately took pity on the man, who appeared to dwell in absolute poverty. There were remains of an old fire, but little else to show a human being lived here. Rodrigo saw a crude crucifix at the cave entrance. It was fashioned from a mesquite bush and still held thorns. On the flat side of a boulder, the words "*Capri*" and "*Gesu Mari*" were written in white paint. The melted remains of a white candle stood atop the rock.

"Padre, I have the sweetbreads, the liver and the heart of this ram with me," said Rodrigo. "Let me build a fire, so we may eat. I also have some fry bread in my pack. While the meat is cooking, will you take my confession?"

The Priest refused at first, saying he was no longer worthy to take confession, yet Rodrigo insisted.

"Forgive me, Padre, for I have sinned," Rodrigo began a short time later. "It has been twenty-two years since my last confession. Which was also my first, my only confession."

"Go ahead, my son."

Red Water decided rigorous honesty was the best course. He described his upbringing. First being raised as a Mescalero, Rodrigo was later schooled at a Catholic mission. He abandoned Christianity a few years later, returning to his Mescalero father. "I became a *curendero*, a Medicine Chief," Rodrigo explained, "Which means, to the Mexicanos, that I am a male witch—or wizard. I know that is forbidden to your faith. Oh, and I have also killed a man. A white man."

"Go on." said the Priest, sensing this was the most troubling thing on Rodrigo's heart. The holy man looked aside from Rodrigo as they both knelt, as if there was an invisible confessional screen between them.

"He was a Yankee soldier, who had killed some of my people." Red Water described how a Union officer, Captain Dunhill, had set a trap for a group of Mescaleros at a treaty gathering the previous year. "I did seek to avenge many deaths," Rodrigo added.

"Si, was this *un acto de guerra*?" asked the Hermit Priest. "An act of war?"

Rodrigo nodded but kept his eyes closed and his head bowed. "*Ub acto de Guerra*," said the priest. After speaking some words in Latin, he told Rodrigo to say three Ave Marias. "If you are now at peace with the Army soldiers–and yourself—kill no more of them. For our salvation, the Lamb of God was also slain." Augustiani made the sign of the cross once more, then held out his palm, instructing Rodrigo to rise. "Now let us eat mutton." he added, with a grin.

Red Water felt strange, to have this act of redemption end with a joke, yet he did feel like a burden was lifted from his heart. He glanced over at his pack mule and the two dogs milling about. Rodrigo decided to give the Priest an additional quarter of the bighorn and advised him how to smoke the meat.

As they broke bread and ate the meal, Red Water told the Priest about the captivity of the Mescalero people. He asked what steps he could take to free the captives, without killing any more soldiers. "What do the scriptures say about such a thing?" Rodrigo asked.

The Priest stared up at the sky and stroked his long beard. "*Pacencia.* A tincture of time," said the religious hermit. "Such things as these must be endured. For a time and a season. Remember the Hebrews, who were held captive, at Babylon? There are men who say, 'all things must pass', yet first, they must be endured. To work out the mighty grace of God."

Rodrigo almost replied, yet he paused to consider what the hermit said. Avenging the deaths of the *Nit' a hende* people had not brought peace. Confessing his act of retribution and receiving forgiveness brought some solace—-yet it would not stop the onslaught on his people by the U.S. soldiers and the hatred of white settlers. Here he was, hundreds of miles away from his own land and people, while hiding out as a mestizo.

As the priest cut slices of the ram's heart and ate, Rodrigo Red Water considered the things white men were doing, by seeking the destruction of all the native peoples. Red Water rose to his feet. "A seeker has to be certain that his heart speaks truth to himself," he declared. "I am a *Curendero*. I am one who gives healing to the body and spirits of my people. I can no longer hide myself, due to the tiny fears of my own death."

CHAPTER 8

The treaty delegation left Conejos and headed back to Fort Garland, with Dirt Bradshaw trailing along. Dirt was mostly following Miss Jane Edgarton, wherever she went; in addition, the prospect of a postmaster's job also appealed to him. Jane and her brother, Trey Edgarton, rode ahead in a carriage with ex-governor Gilpin, while Dirt and Charlie Larsen followed on their horses. An escort of two dozen other Union soldiers rode at the front and rear of the entourage.

Bradshaw had learned that the young lady was an ardent abolitionist, who was touring Colorado and other towns out West, in order to raise money for the Soldiers Aid Society. After the delegation reached Fort Garland, the Edgartons and Governor Gilpin were traveling on to Taos and Santa Fe, to drum up support for the Union cause.

"Why don't you join our regiment?" Charlie Larsen asked Dirt, as they neared the Army fort.

"And lose this fine horse to some envious lieutenant?" Dirt responded. Bradshaw rode beside another carriage, where several dignitaries from Taos were passing around a bottle of Kentucky bourbon. "Bill Gilpin told me about a postmaster's job in San Luis," Dirt added.

Colonel John Fransisco overheard this conversation. "You may have to petition Washington City to be a postmaster," the Colonel told Dirt. He passed the bottle to Bradshaw.

Dirt took a good swig out of the bourbon, leaned over to the buggy and handed the bottle to Judge Henry Daigre of Taos. "Well, Gilpin bought a huge parcel of land on the eastern slopes of the Sangres Mountains. And he wields some influence around here," said Dirt. Bradshaw gazed ahead and saw Miss Jane talking with the ex-governor and a blue-clad Union officer. He hoped the young lady would look back his way, yet she did not pay him any attention. "Excuse me, gentlemen," said Dirt, urging Waukesha into a quick trot.

The Edgerton's carriage was going over some rough ground and Jane Edgarton held on to her straw hat to keep it from blowing off her head. "How are you, Miss Jane?" Dirt asked. "I hope you're enjoying this sunshine today."

"I am fine, Mr. Bradshaw. This is a lovely country we are passing through." Miss Edgarton wore a blue dress, a white cashmere shawl, and she seemed vibrant in the high mountain air.

"Me and Charlie came through this region a little over a year ago. When there was several feet of snow on the ground," said Dirt. "Hello Trey. Hello Governor."

"Hey, Dirt," William Gilpin simply responded. Holding the reins of the four–horse carriage and sitting up front in the driver's seat, he was not acting friendly today. Like many politicians, Gilpin was more animated when he wanted one's vote, yet he could also be non-committal, when sensing a supplication in the works.

"What do I have to do, to get that postmaster's job you promised, Bill?" Dirt asked.

Gilpin shrugged, thought for a moment, then a bright smile appeared on his face, "Actually, Bradshaw, I think it would help if you started with the Overland Mail. They need drivers and gregarious men like you to guard the stages from Santa Fe. You know, with your past history in Denver, maybe you shouldn't work in Colorado."

This greatly mortified Dirt Bradshaw. He felt embarrassed to have Gilpin say this in Miss Edgarton's presence, but he also wanted to appear agreeable. "Sure thing. That sounds fair enough." Turning toward the Edgartons, he asked, "And whither goest thou, young Missy?"

"Trey and I are going on to Sante Fe, as well," Jane replied. She smiled and turned to a young lieutenant, who sat beside her. "We're going there with Mr. Gilpin and Lieutenant Soule," Jane added, clutching the officer's elbow.

Dirt was taken aback. The lieutenant studied Dirt's wild appearance and seemed unimpressed. Soule was sharply-dressed in a starched uniform and he sported a neatly-trimmed mustache. The officer reminded Dirt of his own brother, Dave Bradshaw, yet Dirt already hated him. "Silas Soule, Lieutenant of the Colorado Cavalry. Pleased to meet you, Mr. Bradshaw," the lieutenant said.

"Oh, please forgive my manners," said Jane, "I should have introduced the two of you. After we go to Santa Fe, Silas and Trey are escorting me to play in Albuquerque, some places in Kansas and then we go on to St. Louis. While we are in New Mexico, we are going to speak out against the slave code in the Territory. They enslave Indians, you know."

"So you're going back East? It seems you just arrived out West recently," said Dirt. This news and the loss of the postmaster's position felt like a double disappointment.

The caravan was now in sight of Fort Garland. Charlie Larsen rode up to bid farewell; his platoon was going to another fort in Colorado. "Please, join our cause, Dirt, we need you," Charlie Larsen pleaded. "Your brother is doing what he can."

"That's well and good, Charlie. I am sorry, but the U.S. Postal Service is calling me. I appreciate what you're doing, Friend," said Dirt.

At the fort, Dirt Bradshaw stayed with the carriages and horses, while the Treaty delegation dined with the high-ranking officers of Fort Garland. It was a sunny, blue-skied late afternoon, with high, alto-cumulus clouds gleaming above the mountains. It felt cooler at this higher elevation, so Dirt buttoned up his fringed jacket and munched on some venison jerky by a clear running stream. Dirt missed the days of prospecting for gold and he missed the Utes.

Jane Edgarton appeared, out from behind a wagon. She held a tin plate, covered by a cloth napkin. "I brought you supper, Richard," said Jane, surprising Dirt by the use of his Chrisitan name. "It was not fair that they did not invite you."

Dirt Bradshaw fell instantly in love with this young Canadian lady. For her to come out, unescorted and offer him a meal seemed the height of kindness. "My God, Miss Jane, you are a beautiful saint," Dirt smiled, taking the plate. It held roast beef, potatoes and baked carrots.

"If you don't mind, walk with me just now," said Jane.

Dirt set the plate aside; he and Jane sauntered along the stream bank, enjoying the early evening air. "Why are you in such a hurry to go back East?" Bradshaw questioned, "with the war going on?"

"I'm sorry, Richard, but that's precisely it. I have much work to do. I am a member of The Women's National Loyal League. It's a women's anti-slavery organization, which holds concerts, lectures and fairs, to raise money for widows, and medical supplies for our troops. We are also petitioning the government, for total emancipation of all slaves—in all of the United States. Not just the ones in the Confederacy." Jane pulled her shawl up over her shoulders. "Mr. Lincoln did only half his job. His declaration only freed those captives in the states of rebellion. So I am going to Kansas and Missouri."

"Kansas and Missouri are pretty dog-gone dangerous right now," said Dirt. "There are bushwhackers and southern sympathizers all about. Maybe I should accompany you." Dirt offered Jane his arm, for he and Jane now walked on some uneven ground.

"I have my chaperones. Trey and Silas will escort me. I wish you had spoken more with Lieutenant Soule. He and his family worked on the Underground Railroad–much like my family in Canada. He worked closely with the martyr, James Brown, helping slaves escape."

"You mean that fanatic? The one who started all this mess?" Dirt asked. Like many westerners, Bradshaw was confused how the hot-heads in the eastern states had forced the nation to explode in a Civil War.

Jane Edgarton continued and Dirt listened as she explained how her parents had worked with the Canadian Mission, assisting freed Blacks and fugitive slaves in Ontario. Trey Edgarton now hailed the couple; he stood over by the carriages and wagons. Jane and Dirt turned and started hiking back to join Jane's brother.

"I understand your zeal," said the Colorado prospector, "but why are you so concerned with the Indians in New Mexico?"

"Don't you see, Richard? We struggle not with the South, but against powers and principalities. We are at war with the Kingdom of Slavery, here in this New World. Doing battle against the same forces that plagued the Old World for centuries—that denied freedom to all common men and women," said Miss Edgarton. "Slave, serf, or unwilling servant, it makes no difference."

Dirt recognized the religious fervor in the young woman's eyes. They burned with a desire, sparking a different sort of fervor within himself. Before Bradshaw could express himself, Trey Edgarton joined them.

"I see you've met my sister," Trey Edgarton said, making a joke. "I hope Jane has not frightened you with her passion."

"The recruiters could use her," said Dirt. "She makes me want to hop on my horse and go strangle Jeff Davis personally." He turned to Jane, "May I write to you, Jane? Is there an address where I can reach you? Sometime?"

Jane smiled tenderly. "Why yes. My new home in Cincinnati. But do not expect a rapid reply. I will be very busy this summer. What about you, Richard? Have you given thought to our struggle?"

"Well, yeah. I want to help you anyway I can," Dirt murmured.

Jane Edgarton touched Dirt's shoulder. "So many of our women are mothers of soldiers, or wives, who have encouraged their husbands to join the Army." Her eyes gleamed, the same bright color as the bourbon Dirt had been drinking that afternoon. "Can you be encouraged, Richard, to risk your life for liberty?"

"Heck, yes!" Dirt said impulsively. "You'd certainly encourage me, if you were my wife."

The three stood awkwardly—until Trey Edgarton laughed out loud. "Aha! Yet another proposal," said the Canadian. "Dear Jane has practically gotten one a day, since arriving in Colorado. Yours is quite original though, Dirt." Trey glanced over at his sister, to see how the offer affected her. "My Lord, you did a miracle, Mr. Bradshaw. You did render her speechless!"

"Excuse my manners," said Dirt, feeling flushed in the face and seeing the blush reflected on Jane's features. "I did not mean to offend either of you!"

"We should be moving along. The officers and the delegation are waiting for Jane's performance this evening," Trey remarked.

"I am sorry," Dirt apologized again. "I guess there's still a lot of the mining camp in me."

"No, there is a fine heart within you, Dirt," Jane said softly, placing her palm on his chest and looking up at him in earnest. "Please, have your dinner. Then come and hear me play my music."

Fourteen wagons left Fort Weld in mid-June of 1863, destined for Fort Lyon and points eastward. These wooden wagons, the standard freight carrier for the U.S. Army, were fitted with iron wheels and could carry loads between three to five thousand pounds. They had slightly curved bottoms, to prevent the loads from shifting while traversing hills and mountains. Some of the wagons carried buffalo robes, leather, extracted minerals, lumber and grain. Five of the wagons held far more valuable cargo.

Custom-built bottoms on four of the five wagons carried stacked ingots of refined gold, each one weighing thirty-five pounds. The fifth wagon actually carried two chests of gold and silver coins from the Denver mint. The caravan's official trail boss, "Frank Cooper," did not tell Lieutenant Bradshaw which wagons held Federal treasure, but Dave Bradshaw guessed which ones held gold ingots. Bradshaw surmised that buffalo hides and wool do not ride that low. Agent Frankfort was driving one of these wagons, which was also pulled by oxen, not mules. So much for secrecy, thought Lieutenant Dave.

Thirty-nine men and soldiers drove or accompanied this government caravan, as it journeyed southward alongside the South Platte. They would meet another caravan, that was transporting cattle and horses from New Mexico, at Fort Lyon. In order to avoid encounters with the Arapaho and Cheyenne, the wagon train stayed close to the settlements on the South Platte River, then swung southeast, to Colorado City and Pueblo.

Lieutenant Bradshaw had confidence in most of the men Frankfort had selected, with the exception of one soldier and a teamster. Alvin Reynolds had also served under Union Colonel John Chivington and he had a reputation of snitching on the junior grade commissioned officers to the Colonel. Dave Bradshaw considered Reynold a long-tailed rat. Reynolds was also friends with William Todd, a teamster from Denver. During the Colorado gold rush, Todd had the reputation of being a petty thief.

Adolphus Frankfort, the Treasury agent, demanded that all the soldiers stay out of the settlements during the first part of the expedition. "Keep them out of the saloons," he told the Lieutenant. Frankfort did allow one or two men to buy extra provisions in the towns. At Colorado City, he granted both Todd and Reynolds this privilege.

Determined to win loyalty from his new platoon, David Bradshaw let the soldiers take turns hunting wild game ahead of the caravan; it provided meat and gave them an opportunity to hone their marksmanship. At night, everyone ate well, their beans and hardtack supplemented by venison, antelope and buffalo.

At Fort Pueblo, the Federal caravan turned due east, alongside the upper Arkansas River. Agent Frankfort was now stretched tighter than a piano wire, for he had received reports of Confederate subversives in the region. A Denver City saloon owner was being sought as a spy. "From now on, Lieutenant, I will need a report on how your men are doing—and what they are saying," the agent declared one evening, after summoning Dave Bradshaw to his tent.

"Yes, Sir, Mr. Cooper. I assure you, they are proving to be good men. Some of them have fought Texans down in New Mexico," said Dave. "I have no doubt they can take on any Indians or bushwhackers as we head into Kansas."

"You need to designate someone as a scout, Mr. Bradshaw. No more hunting. It might alert our enemies. In addition, I am recommending we stay somewhat away from the river. Too many woods, in which the Indians may hide"

Corporal Alvin Reynolds appeared at the tent entrance. "Everyone's settled in, Mr. Cooper," said Reynolds. "Lieutenant," he added, acknowledging his superior officer, yet neglecting to add 'Sir'—or even salute.

"I will be out shortly, to check the wagons. You are dismissed, Corporal," said Frankfort.

This greatly irked Bradshaw. He was the corporal's immediate superior, not the treasury agent. "When you check the wagons, be sure and look underneath. To make sure the axles are holding out, Corporal," Bradshaw instructed.

"Yes, Sir, Mr. Todd is checking them now." Reynolds gave 'Cooper' a furtive glance, then he finally saluted.

After the corporal left, Lieutenant Bradshaw asked Agent Frankfort if he could take on another non-commissioned officer for the escort at Fort Lyon. "Since we're adding more wagons, I think we need to add some men. I know a sergeant, who fought beside us at Glorieta."

"I'll take that into consideration, Mr. Bradshaw," the Treasury agent replied.

CHAPTER 9

The four riflemen rode hard after leaving Las Vegas Grandes, across a wide-open country of mesas and rolling plains. On the third day, they looked upon an area called the Caprock, a prominent line of three hundred-foot cliffs, marking the edge of the Llano Estacado. With summer's arrival, heat waves shimmered on these high plans and dust kicked up by the horses permeated each man's clothing, gear and face.

This was the Rim Rock outfit, searching the desert and arroyos for any sign of the hidden route the Comancheros used to smuggle stolen cattle into New Mexico. Deputy Marshall Fazari was not with the group; he was still at his ranch north of Albuquerque. According to Fazari, the Comancheros traded guns and whiskey to the Quahadi tribe, in exchange for cattle stolen from central New Mexico ranches.

Rodrigo Red Water, the Apache, discovered cattle tracks and old wagon ruts coming out of the Arroyo Saladito. "You must back-track now," he told Jimmy Gray. "Make your camp back at that sunken creek, that last waterhole we saw. For when they come, the herd will need water."

"Suits me. I'm ready to call it a day, after frying out here in the sun for hours," Lew McManus complained.

"I will keep going, on foot," said Rodrigo, "to see if they are near. Stay in the wagon ruts, try not to leave any tracks yourself. We'll take them at the creek crossing."

"Okay, we'll each stake out a vantage point," Jimmy Gray agreed. "Be careful and try to get back before daybreak," he added.

The two Tennesseans and Miguel LaHoya rode back to the shallow creek, which had dried up in places. They unsaddled the horses and set up camp; however, Gray insisted they not build a fire, lest it be spotted by the cattle smugglers. He took the first watch, while his friends slept.

Jimmy felt too anxious to sleep anyway. He rolled cigarette after cigarette and wondered how well-armed the Comancheros might be; he hoped his group would not be greatly outnumbered. Fazari had told McManus that if all went well, Lew could be pardoned for killing the old Texan down at El Paso months earlier.

Rodrigo returned shortly after midnight. He said the Comancheros and the herd were resting up on the plateau. "It is a big herd, over two hundred head, maybe," said the Mescalero.

"How many men?" Jimmy asked.

"I snuck close to their campfire and counted seven men. Do not know how many were watching the herd."

An hour before daybreak, Gray and his fellow gunmen took cover in the trees and cat-tails of the creek bottom. They watched and waited as first daylight appeared and the earth took color. Hiding up in the tangled branches of a bodock tree, the thin Tennessean watched as the high palisades of the Llano Estacado could now be seen in the distance. Jimmy Gray clutched a Henry rifle.

About a hundred yards to Jimmy's right, Lew McManus had staked out a blind in the cat-tails, where the old wagon trail crossed the trickling stream. Lew was armed with a double barreled twelve-gauge shotgun and his two Army Revolvers. McManus pulled the brim of his cattleman's hat down low, to block the bright rising sun. This is like a deer or a duck hunt, he thought, except it's a sight more dangerous.

McManus glanced over to his far right, where Red Water waited with Lew's long-barreled Sharpshooter rifle. On the north side of the line of shooters, the young vaquero, Miguel LaHoya kept all the horses sheltered in a high-banked bend of the creek bottom. Miguel held a Sharps .52 caliber cavalry carbine, loaned to him by Deputy Marshall Fazari.

The young cowhand held strong doubts about this foolhardy venture. He thought about Rosa Amarillo Del Rio, how much more splendid it would be to be holding her in bed this morning; rather than hiding in this wilderness, awaiting possible death and destruction. Miguel still wondered about the two Anglo ranchers. Why did they agree to this? Why are they compadres with an Apache medicine jefe? LaHoya did not want to be an outlaw, hunting other outlaws.

Jimmy Carl Gray gave a low whistle and the hunters all looked to the southeast. Just below the distant bluffs, clouds of dust rose and drew closer. The low rumble of the herd soon followed; one could hear the cattle lowing and the steady sound of hoofbeats.

The Comancheros rode behind the herd, letting the cattle run free toward the creek. Jimmy Gray worried that Lew was going to be trampled by the stampede. The beasts thundered closer, their long horns gleaming in the morning sun. Six Comancheros now milled about behind the herd, shouting and yelling, attempting to spread the cattle out along the creek bottom. Jimmy spotted a lone covered wagon some distance beyond the group. Two men, one wearing a black leather jacket, sat on the driver's bench.

"Now!" Jimmy Gray shouted.

McManus fired first with a revolver, in order to keep from being trampled by the first clump of longhorns. The lead Comanchero shot into the cattails; he then fell from Lew's shotgun blast. Rodrigo purposely missed another horseman, but made the rider wheel his horse around and flee. With his Henry rifle steadied against the bodock trunk, Jimmy Gray shot the man holding the wagon reins at a hundred yards' distance. The wagon veered off the trail, with the four hitched horses running wildly.

With two men down, the cattle smugglers drew their revolvers and returned fire. The alarmed cattle ran here and there, causing still more confusion. Jimmy made a second shot and dropped another Comanchero.

This backed the outlaws off; they spurred their horses and retreated. Lew McManus rushed out of the cattails, firing both of his Smith and Wessons, while running to retrieve his horse. Miguel LaHoya provided cover, downing still another Comanchero. One smuggler, a brave fellow, rescued the wounded man, by riding back and lifting him up on his own horse.

Jimmy Gray scanned the field while reloading his rifle. One Comanchero halted at a slight rise, took aim with a rifle and fired. Jimmy saw Miguel LaHoya tumble back down into the dry creek bottom. McManus, who was now mounted on his own horse, charged out in the open to do battle. Jimmy suddenly wondered, where in the Hell is Rodrigo? Revolvers quick-fired; riderless horses and stampeding cattle now raised so much dust that Gray could not see anything more. Climbing down from his tree stand, Jimmy stayed low, using the creek bank as a means of cover as he rushed off to help Miguel. As the dust cleared off, Jimmy looked out. He saw the wounded wagon driver being assisted onto a spare horse. A quarter mile away, the runaway wagon had overturned in a gully, with the horses having broken the hitch.

Jimmy finally spotted Rodrigo Red Water. The Mescalero stood out by the wagon, inspecting the wreckage.

"They got Miguel!" McManus shouted. Lew still sat astride his gray and white gelding. "I'll tend to him. You and Rodrigo need to round up the herd. We ran them bastards off! Whee-hah!" the big Tennessean whooped.

Sure enough, all the remaining cattle smugglers were now riding back to Texas without their cattle. The ambush was a success, Jimmy thought—unless the vaquero was mortally wounded. Gray sat down on a dead stump. Gunpowder smoke stung his nostrils and he rubbed the dust out of his eyes.

When McManus reached the creek, he was surprised to see Miguel standing. The vaquero seemed stunned; he was hunched over and embarrassed. "Caramba! I am shot in the culo!" Miguel declared, then he cursed in Spanish and dropped his trousers.

Lew dismounted and checked out the wound. "It grazed you. There ain't no bullet hole," he said. "Ow, but I got hit, too."

Miguel looked down. Lew's right boot was covered with blood. "Well damn, they winged me," McManus said, in a matter-of-fact manner.

Jimmy Gray retrieved his own horse and rode out on the plain to check on Red Water. The Mescalero stood at the top of the gully, looking at something. As Jimmy drew closer, he was surprised to see a figure climbing out from the wagon. It looked like a boy, a young Negro, and Gray figured he was a slave, or a captive of the Comancheros.

The captive took one look at Jimmy, saw the faded Confederate fatigue hat on Grays' head, and took off running! "Ha! He won't get far. He's barefoot," said the Tennessean. "What else is in the wagon, Rodrigo?"

"Jugs and kegs of whiskey," said Red Water. "Maybe a Comanche chief did not want them."

"Or maybe those outlaws robbed a caravan," Jimmy replied. "Go help Lewis round up those dang cows. We need to get the Hell out of here! Them outlaws might come back, with a bunch of Comanches helping them."

McManus and LaHoya rode up, leading two of the outlaws' horses. "We are rich in cattle now, Señor Jimmy!" Miguel shouted, leaning sideways in the saddle to relieve the pressure on his wound.

"Not yet, we ain't," said the thin Tennessean. "Not until we herd them cows north, back to the Rim Rock. Here you go boys," Jimmy added, tossing a ceramic jug to McManus. "There's more where that came from."

"Who is that?" Lew asked, gazing out toward the lone figure standing out on the vast plain.

"They had a captive with them. Either a slave, or some Comanche captive that they planned to sell in Santa Fe. The Comancheros do that, you know," said Jimmy. "Dang, what's Rodrigo doing?"

The boy captive was now sitting down by a group of tumbleweeds and Red Water walked toward him. As Jimmy Gray climbed back up on his own horse, McManus took a big swig of the strong whiskey to ease the throbbing in his foot. "I hope we don't have to take that hostage back to some town," Lew told Miguel. He handed the jug to the young vaquero. "Drink up, Amigo." It stings, but not as bad as a pain in the butt."

As Jimmy Gray approached Rodrigo and the captive, the boy sat stoic and still, staring out at the horizon and awaiting his fate. Dressed in grimy buckskin leggings and some sort of long shirt made of tattered, old blue and white striped bed ticking, he was covered with grease. The boy was thin and the shirt was far too large and loose on him; Gray figured he was half-starved, maybe fourteen or fifteen years of age. His hair was short cropped and brown—or just dirty. The boy looked more Indian than Negro.

"Steady, boy, we ain't gonna hurt you." Gray held his open palm up as a sign of peace. The captive did not seem to understand English. "Speak to him in Spanish, Rodrigo," Gray suggested.

Red Water asked the boy's name. It did not work; the captive muttered something unintelligible in some strange language. His wrists were bound by rope.

"I do not know los Comanche," Red Water admitted.

Jimmy Gray pulled out his Green Tree hunting knife to cut the boy's rope. The captive's eyes widened in fright; Jimmy stepped back, when he noticed the eyes were bright blue. "My God, he is part White," said Jimmy.

"Mien Gott," said the boy.

Jimmy cut the rope. Using sign language, Rodrigo and the youth communicated some basic facts. The freed captive pointed to himself, then pointed to the northeast. He crossed his wrists, indicated to himself, then lowered his open palm to a height of three feet.

"I think.... he was taken by los Comanches, when he was young. North of here," said Rodrigo.

The boy made more hand gestures. He stroked the side of his head, like he once had long hair, then cradled an imaginary child in his arms.

"Mama? Or, you had a sister?" Jimmy asked.

The youth seemed frustrated. He spoke Comanche, then some other language, using more signs. "Ich bin....qus..Qua-ha-das. Terk-wa-shana."

"Quahadis? The Quahadis are one of the Comanche tribes in Texas," said Jimmy. "Fierce warriors. Ask him his name again."

Rodrigo pointed to himself. "Red Water." He pointed to the child. "You? Como se llamo?"

Tears started streaming from the blue eyes and the child's mouth trembled in despair. He sat back down in the sage grass and looked up at Jimmy and Rodrigo. For a moment, it seemed like the youth could not even remember his own name. Catching a breath, the captive finally spoke. "Nee..Neek...Neek..Claws."

"Nicholas," said Jimmy. "Well, we will call you Nick, I guess, for now." He smiled at the boy. "Come with us Nick. Okay?"

As Jimmy Gray and the boy walked back to the wagon, Rodrigo rode out to help round up the cattle. Lew McManus and Miguel were slowly urging the strays back to the creek.

Later that afternoon, the group drove the cattle herd north, toward the Canadian River. Jimmy gave 'Nick' one of the Comanchero horses and saw that the boy could ride proficiently. 'Nick" stayed close to Jimmy Gray, but he seemed to shy away from Big Lew.

McManus and Gray had repaired the covered wagon and recovered the horses that pulled it. "We got us a Prairie Schooner," said Lew, hopping up to take the reins, "I gotta rest my foot," he explained, yet Jimmy figured his partner wanted to steal a drink from the whiskey jug now and then.

"These cows and steers are mostly just hide and tendon," said Jimmy. "Once we get 'em to good grassland, we'll not move them so quickly." Gray sniffed the air. Dang, Nick! You stink in those rags. We'll make you take a bath when we reach the river."

They reached a bend of the Canadian the next afternoon. By then, all the men said they had enough; Jimmy and Lew insisted that Nicholas shed his lice-infested clothes and dunk himself in the river. Nicholas was reluctant; but McManus caught him, carried him to a swimming hole, then threw the lad in.

The youth seemed embarrassed. He could not swim, but the water was only three to four feet deep. McManus stood on the riverbank, urging the youth to take off his rags. He threw the boy a bar of lye soap. Nick removed his leggings and began scrubbing.

"Now the shirt. Take off the top...!" McManus hollered, grabbing the hem of his own flannel shirt.

The former captive dunked his head under the water again. He wrestled the tunic off, then crouched in the water, so that only his face and shoulders were revealed. Nick threw the tunic up on the bank.

The Comanches had smeared buffalo tallow and charcoal into the captive's skin and hair, disguising the youth as one of their own. It took hard scrubbing, with soap and a wash rag, but gradually, the youth's face, hair and skinny arms took on a more pinkish tone.

"Dang, if he ain't halfway White, at least," McManus observed, sitting on the bank and sipping from his whiskey jug.

Jimmy Gray walked up, carrying a folded bundle. "I've got an extra Union suit and some other trousers that might fit him." said Jimmy.

Lew McManus cursed. "Whoa-damn! Look, Jimmy Carl. Lookee there, dammit!" As the freed captive rose naked from the water, white breasts were exposed. There was only a patch of blonde hair, where the youth's manhood would have shown. 'Nick' attempted to cover this spot. "Haw! Haw!" Mcmanus boomed, as Jimmy dropped the bundle. "We was all blind, Jimmy Carl! He ain't no Nick. We got us a Nicole!"

"Wa Shana!" the girl shouted.

That evening, Gray and McManus sat by the campfire and argued over the captive girl's fate. "Rodrigo tells me she was probably taken by the Comanches when she was a young kid. They raised her as one of their own and called her Wa Shana," said Jimmy Gray.

"Or made her a slave. You can tell she's not been fed well." Lew McManus remarked. "At first, she couldn't even handle eating beans and bacon. She threw it up, 'cause it made her sick." Lew had unplugged his whiskey jug.

"I think it wasn't the Indians, but the Comancheros who were not feeding her," said Gray. "From what Rodrigo could gather, she was what they call a 'beloved captive.' The Quahadis adopted her." Jimmy stood, threw some wood on the fire, then he looked over at the tent he had put up, to give 'Wa Shana' Nicole some privacy. After a hard day's ride along the south side of the Canadian river, the girl was sleeping soundly inside the shelter.

"Either way, she's ruined. We can't take her back to live with White folks," said McManus., He tilted up the jug of whiskey and took a long draught. "Aah, that eases my aches. Those cattle smugglers were probably gonna sell her into whoring."

"Which is why we can't take her to Las Vegas. She'll only wind up that way anyway," said Jimmy. "I'm taking her back to our ranch first."

"Hah, I see where this is going," Lew McManus said. "You believe she might be pretty, once her hair grows back and you put her in some fancy frills." Lew took another drink.

Jimmy scowled at his partner. "Take it easy, Claw. We can't make Miguel and Rodrigo watch the herd all night by themselves. I don't need you shit-faced, with you hogging that jug."

"Well, hell, then you take a drink. Help me out," said Lew. He offered the Jug to Gray.

Jimmy took the whiskey. He slurped a portion, gargled with it then spit it out onto the fire. The flames shot up higher. "Dammit, that's almost pure alcohol!" he shouted.

"Taos Lightning," said McManus, referring to a popular moonshine produced in the region. "I plan to sell it in Las Vegas Grandes."

"I already told you! We ain't goin' into Las Vegas. We're following the Mora River, up to Fort Union and returning the herd. Well, most of it, anyway."

The two ranchers continued to argue; McManus declared he could sell the untaxed alcohol in the Mexican villages along the Mora Valley. Jimmy Gray countered that would only cause more trouble and the military governor might not grant any pardon. Rodrigo Red Water walked up out of the dark night and warned them their loud voices would awaken the girl.

"Silencio. The girl must rest. Has she not had enough trouble?" Red Water questioned.

Jimmy Gray found the cork to the whiskey jug laying at Lew's feet. He picked it up, put the plug in the jug and set it out of his partner's immediate reach. "What else did you learn from her today, Amigo?" Jimmy asked Rodrigo.

Red Water explained how the girl was beginning to remember some English. As they rode together, Rodrigo pointed out things along the trail and named them. Gradually, WaShana recalled her family being on a wagon train, when Comanches attacked. She remembered her father being killed by the warriors and her being strapped to a horse. She lived with the Comanches, worked with the women and she played with the other Comanche children.

"She said they named her 'WaShana.' Her new mother was good, but all the other women were bad to her. If a girl is young enough to not be a woman, but old enough to learn their ways, the Quahadi people take her in."

"Thanks for working with her, Rodrigo," said Jimmy. "Go ahead and sleep now. Me and Lew are taking the next watch."

"She also speaks another language, which I do not know."

Red Water stared into the fire. "She should not return to the ranch with us. She should go back to her first people. What remains of her family. You must take her there—I cannot."

"And just where the Hell is that?" Lew asked. "Who is her family? How can we find them, if she doesn't even know her own name?"

A rustling sound over at the tent drew the men's attention. The girl stuck her head out. "Nicole Klausman," she said. "Ich bin Deutche. Mein Zuhause war in Kansas!"

CHAPTER 10

The Federal caravan reached Fort Lyon a few days after the Fourth of July in 1863. Soldiers at the fort were jubilant. News of the enormous battle of Gettysburg in Pennsylvania, a Union victory, had reached Colorado by telegraph in Denver. Lieutenant Dave Bradshaw also heard about Vicksburg finally falling to General Grant's forces in Mississippi.

Dave was eager to get more details; he asked Agent Frankfort if he could go into the nearby town and retrieve a newspaper. The Treasury agent allowed him a half-day's leave. The lieutenant was reading about the astonishing victories in *The Rocky Mountain News* at a tavern in La Junta, when the stagecoach from Colorado City arrived.

Passengers from the station next door hurried into the tavern to purchase food and drink. Lieutenant Bradshaw was surprised to see "Shanghai Bill" Hickock among the group. "Hey, Bill! How are you doing?" Bradshaw asked, putting down the newspaper and kicking out a chair for Hickock.

"Feeling glorious," said Shanghai Bill, grinning and stroking his long mustache. He grabbed the chair and set it against the wall before sitting down. "I see you're reading about Gettysburg. These are heady days, aren't they?"

"Yes indeed," said Dave. He had once played cards with Hickock, down at Cimarron. Hickock was a former teamster on the Santa Fe Trail; an ardent gambler, who was also fond of whiskey, Shanghai Bill had come close to having a gunfight with Bradshaw. "Bill, do you remember the last time we played poker? I was not cheating. You were drinking pretty heavily at the time. Just because I wasn't didn't mean I was cheating, okay?"

"Fair enough," said Hickock. He signaled the barkeeper, telling him to bring a bottle. "I guess you wish you were fighting back East. Instead of wet-nursing wagon trains, heh?"

"I do what I can," said Dave. Bradshaw suspected that Hickock might be a scout, or a spy, for the Army. Bill had once used the Alias of "James Haycock" the previous year. "So, what's the other news from Denver?" he inquired.

Hickock waited till the barkeeper brought him whiskey. He poured a shot, then downed it. Leaning over the table, he whispered. "I know you got some delicate cargo on your caravan, okay?"

"And how do you know that?"

"I have my sources." Bill Hickock leaned back against the wall and took his ease, putting his boots up on the table. "Have a snort, Dave. The barkeep brought two glasses."

Although he had to report back to the wagon train before sundown, David complied. He poured Hickock another drink first, then one for himself.

"Jessica Piedmont. You've heard the name, right?" Hickock asked, after both men took a drink. "She caught the stage going to Denver last year?"

"You already knew that. My unit escorted the coach as far as Fountain Creek. And she was quite the rage in Denver, wasn't she?" Dave remarked. "She played piano at the dance halls, I mean. She seemed like a respectable lady."

"Well, she disappeared," said Shanghai Bill. Just like your brother. Sorry about your loss, in that instance."

"No, Dirt is alive, he's out in the San Juan Mountains. Digging for gold, I guess," said Dave. "He doesn't have any connection to Mrs. Piedmont." Dave Bradshaw paused for a moment. "Does he?"

"No, no." Shanghai Bill slid his boots off the tabletop and leaned forward again. "But SHE has a connection to Billy Martin. The saloon owner. You know who I'm talking about right?"

"Well, yeah. Everyone in Denver and Central City knows Billy. Everyone who drinks, gambles and enjoys the ladies, that is. Including you," said Dave. Bradshaw wondered where this was going.

Hickock laughed. "There's a warrant issued, claiming that Martin is a Rebel spy. He will surely hang for it." Hickock leaned back in his chair again, with his hands behind his head. Two Colt revolvers gleamed in their holsters. "You got time for a hand or two of poker?"

"Wish I did." Now, Bradshaw was worried. Sliding his chair around the table, the lieutenant leaned forward and asked, "Is our expedition compromised?"

"You tell me," Hickock said softly.

Lieutenant Bradshaw said he needed to get back to the wagon train. He needed to ask Adolphus Frankfort if he had ever met Jessica Piedmont.

"Don't forget your paper," said Hickock. "It's funny, how that news about Gettysburg reached us so fast. They say President Lincoln runs the whole War Department from the telegraph room at the Capital. It will make the Overland Mail obsolete, one day soon. Just like the railroad will put you cavalrymen out of the escort business."

Dave Bradshaw did not comment. He was thinking about how anyone could send a message by telegraph—even a southern sympathizer, using code words.

The next day, Lieutenant Bradshaw was relieved to see the other wagon train arrive from the New Mexico Territory. This meant more guns. Dave's former sergeant, Geniero Mikowski, rode with the escort. As he shook hands with the stocky coal miner, Lieutenant Bradshaw vowed that he would persuade "Mr. Cooper" to keep Mikowski on for the trip to Fort Leavenworth. "For once, the man has to listen to me," said Dave. "I can't tell you why, just yet—but the wagon boss must do what I recommend."

The second caravan consisted of twelve wagons, a herd of beef cattle, mules and a good number of horses destined for Fort Leavenworth. The Union Army was in dire need of horses and mules in Missouri and back East, for the Federal forces were now relying more heavily on cavalry regiments. "We added the cattle herd at Trinidad," said Sergeant Mikowski. "Our trail boss says he knows you."

Bradshaw and Mikowski rode out to meet the main cattleman, who had camped with his men down by the Arkansas River. Daniel Colburn had once been part of the Colorado Gold Rush himself; he knew both of the Bradshaw brothers from their Central City days. "Good to see you again, Davey," Colburn said, in a Midwest accent. "What about your no-count brother? Is he still prospecting?"

"Dirt ran off to the western slopes—chasing rumors, I imagine," said Dave. "You remember Charlie Larsen too, don't you? I married his sister. And Charlie joined the Second Colorado Infantry. They've gone off to fight in the Indian Territory."

Dan Colburn operated a ranch west of Trinidad. He was taking steers and a few cows to Fort Larned on the Santa Fe Trail. "How many men have you got, Davey?" he asked.

"With these new soldiers, twenty-seven. Think that's enough, with the Comanches and Kiowa hunting buffalo this time of year?"

"It ain't Comanches I'm worried about," Dan Coburn said.

"Me too," David replied.

CHAPTER 11

On the fourth night of the cattle drive, the Rim Rock outfit made camp on a mesa above the Mora River. Earlier in the day, McManus had to put down a steer that had broken a leg in a prairie dog hole. He and Jimmy Gray were now cooking the tenderloin and haunch of the unfortunate beast, while other members of the group watched the cattle herd.

Rodrigo Red Water and the girl sat on their horses, listening to the Mexican vaquero sing some high, lonesome Spanish love song a short distance away. Miguel was serenading the cattle, keeping them settled down; their black shapes milled about, some grazing, others laying down. It was a moonless night. A million stars glimmered in the night sky, while the Beloved Captive recounted her sorrows. Although Red Water did not understand all her words, when the young woman lapsed into German, he still listened as she spoke.

Nicole Klausmann said her mother and father were German. They were on a wagon train in Kansas when the Comanches killed them. The Comanches strapped Nicole to a horse and she remembered riding non-stop, going south for days on end. She was given no food and only a little water. When the Quahadi warriors finally reached their village, Nicole was treated horribly by the women.

"But after some moons pass, they give me a new family," WaShana Nicole continued. Her remembrance of English was returning. "They name me 'WaShana'. I sleep on buffalo robes. I work hard, skinning buffalo, cooking and making tallow. They rub me with the tallow—and coal ash from the fires-to make me one of them."

"I have heard the Comanche do these things," said Rodrigo. "But why did they give you to the Comancheros?"

"Not give. Sell. Before... I was to be the woman of a warrior. They pierce my ears and braid my hair. And give me silver earrings. I was...promised? To a son of a chief. But he die. From the White man's sickness."

"My people, the Mescalero, have suffered too. From smallpox and the hog cholera." Rodrigo said. "Go on."

"More moons later, I become the wife of another warrior," said WaShana Nicole. "But he die too. The Tejanos, the men from Texas, kill him. The Quahadi women call me cursed. They say, since I am born white, I bring death to their warriors. Some say I am a witch. So they sell me. For.. two guns, kettles and a milk goat. And they take away my earrings, my robe with beads, and put me in rags." WaShana sniffed and rubbed her eyes; she was crying now. "And they make my face black and tell me. 'since you will now be a slave to the Mexicanos and White men, we make you Black'."

Rodrigo handed the young woman his bandana. "You are not a witch. You are not a slave now," he said softly.

"The Comancheros wanted me to be sold as..." WaShana hesitated. "As a slave woman, to many men at a time. Are you and your friends.. going to do the same thing?"

"No, no. You are free to go now, to go as you please. Do you know where your people are living now?"

"They are in Kansas. Will you go with me? To find out?" WaShana asked. "Por favor?"

Rodrigo felt much pity for the girl, so he immediately agreed. "Si, yes. I will," he said, yet he himself was very far away from his own homeland. He did not know Kansas, Lew McManus had told Rodrigo that 'Kansas is nothing but Jayhawks, who poke soiled doves.' Red Water did not want to encounter such strange birds.

Gazing at this girl, this young woman in the starlight, Red Water realized that she, like him, had grown up in two vastly different worlds. He figured she was seventeen or eighteen years of age, but years of hunger and deprivation made her look fourteen. The top of her Union suit was partially unbuttoned, revealing she was indeed a young woman, and the men's trousers she wore were shrunken enough to grace her bottom. Rodrigo did not fear the idea of going to Kansas; he worried this girl would not do well there. "I will speak with my friends," said Rodrigo. He rode off toward the campfire.

Leaning back on his saddle by the fire, Lew McManus was drunk again. The big Tennessean gnawed on a rare chunk of beef tenderloin. Red juices dribbled onto his black beard. "Hey Rodrigo!" Lew hailed. "You been pokin' that new girlfriend of your 'un?"

Red Water ignored him and turned to Jimmy. "She wants to go to Kansas," he announced. "And I cannot go back to the ranch with you. I am not respected in the towns around there."

"But we've got to take this herd in with us," said Jimmy. "To Fort Union. After we drop a few heifers off at the ranch."

"Yeah, Rodrigo. Take that young heifer to the Rim Rock and bed her there, then she won't even think about Kansas," said McManus. He poured moonshine into a pewter cup.

"Will you shut up, dogdammit?" Jimmy shouted. "Ain't none of us respected in Las Vegas," he told Rodrigo, "and that's saying a lot! What about Cimarron? We could take her there."

Rodrigo Red Water grew angry. "No, she is not that kind of girl! If you do not want to help her, I will. Dogdammit!"

Both Gray and McManus were startled by the Apache's zeal, his fierce countenance and his actually blurting out a cussword.

Jimmy Gray now laughed. He snatched the whiskey jug away from McManus. "I think we've got a man who has fallen in love, Claw. You'd better watch yourself and steer clear. Besides, you've already got that whore angel in Las Vegas."

Lew McManus almost uttered another snide remark, but he held back. Perhaps, realizing he had crossed a line—and was getting too drunk as well—he took off his wide-brimmed hat and ran his fingers through his matted hair. "I'm sorry, Amigo," Lew apologized. "Haw, I'll go with you. I want to see how this turns out. Jimmy, why don't we go and sell them heifers to Lucien Maxwell in Cimarron? Or trade 'em for a choice bull? Then you and Miguel can handle the steers and take them on to Fort Union."

Gray told his partner he would think about this option. He turned the spit, to see if one side of the beef was cooked enough. "We should have cooked this under hot coals," he said. "Rodrigo, why don't you carve off a bunch of slices, then take them and some beans out to Nicole and Miguel?" Gray suggested.

"Yeah. That Mexican cowboy might be singing to HER now," McManus added, getting in one last jibe.

"I trust Miguel. He is a good man," said Rodrigo. The curandero looked the big Tennessean square in the eyes. "Like you used to be, Amigo," he added. "You drink too much."

"I apologize again, Amigo," said Lew. "I did not know you had strong feelings for the girl."

"It is the part we keep hidden that rules us," said Red Water.

Lew fell silent as he considered this. Was Rodrigo talking about himself? Or me? Is he talking about the stuff I keep stuffing down inside of myself?

"I hear something," Jimmy Gray said suddenly. "Down by the river."

All three men listened. Above the sound of the crackling fire, there was the sound of horses, or maybe mules, and the clacking sound of a wagon. They also heard men's voices.

"It's just some travelers on the Trail," said McManus. The Santa Fe Trail crossed the Mora River not far from their campsite. "Hey, maybe they will buy the rest of that steer meat. The beef will go bad by tomorrow evening."

"Hush, there's something else," said Jimmy.

Down in the river bottom, there came the sound of men laughing and someone singing.

The overland Mail stage still had a hundred more miles to go before a change of mules. This section of the mail route proved very rocky and rutted, but the stage hands knew going off the old Trail would risk sinking the coach's wheels in sandy soil. Dirt Bradshaw rode ahead of the stagecoach on his horse Waukesha, while carrying a lantern to show the road.

The brightly painted stagecoach ran from Santa Fe to Independence, Missouri twice each month. This was Dirt Bradshaw's first time to go this distance; however, he had already run a shorter route, from Santa Fe to Trinidad, Colorado in late June. Pulled by six mules, the mail coach was normally escorted by six stage guards, but two men had quit at Las Vegas Grandes.

Dirt knew this trip would be grueling. The mules were exhausted, after running 'hell bent for leather' all day. The stage would change to fresh draft animals at Wagon Mound, twenty-two miles away from the Mora River crossing. After this stop, the mail carriage would take the Cimarron Cut-off, also called the 'Dry Route', passing through the Indian Territory, and continuing into southwest Kansas.

Although it was shorter and quicker than the northward Mountain Branch Route, the Cimarron Cut-off was much more dangerous. Comanches and Confederate partisans threatened this Federal mail service more than ever this year, but General Carleton and other Military commanders did not want any interruptions in their correspondence, or the delivery of payroll for the troops at Union forts.

As he searched in the darkness for the river crossing, Bradshaw decided to sing a ditty he had learned in the mining camps:

"Oh, Mormon girls are fat as hogs
And the Mormon wives fight,
Like cats and dogs—
Oh, Bring 'em Young!"

"Hush that infernal caterwauling!" a deep voice boomed from atop a nearby mesa. "You'll stampede our damn cattle!"

Dirt Bradshaw looked up and saw flickering lights atop the mesa. He caught the scent of woodsmoke and roasting meat and it proved very tantalizing. "Whoa! Whoa, boys!" Dirt called to the stagecoach, so it would not run him over. "Hello, the camp!" he shouted, "I will stop singing, if you give us some of that bison meat."

"It ain't bison, it ain't buffalo. We've got Texas beef! Come on up, if you've got money, or somethin' to trade," declared the man standing up on the rocks.

"What is it, Dirt? Why are we stopping?" asked the stage boss. He was an older man, named Clancy.

"I don't think we should stop," said Brent Osgood, the stage driver. "They might be bandits."

"Hell, bandits don't take the time to set up a barbeque," Dirt laughed. Osgood was a dull-witted sort. "And they don't go announcing themselves, like that big yahoo up yonder."

The man atop the bluff was now silhouetted by the firelight; Bradshaw could tell he was huge, practically a giant. "I'm coming up!" Dirt shouted, dismounting and lifting his lantern in search of a path.

"Hey, Dirt! Ask them if they got any whiskey!" one of the hired guns on the stagecoach hollered. "We is powerful thirsty."

"Dirt? Dirt Bradshaw?" questioned the big man. "Are you Dirt Bradshaw of the Badger Mine?"

"As long as you aren't one of my creditors, the answer is 'yes'. It's me. Who be ye?" Dirt asked.

"Haw, haw, I'm Lew McManus, from Tennessee. You're supposed to be dead, you Yankee bastid!"

"I ain't dead yet, you Rebel hog-farmer," said Bradshaw, lighting a trail up the steep slope.

"Dirt, we don't have time for this," said the stage boss. "You can't leave. It's a dereliction of your duty."

"You're the only derelict, Clancy," said Dirt. He noticed William Clancy was already following close behind. Gaining the top of the bluff, Dirt viewed the cattlemen's campsite, the beef haunch suspended on a spit, and two other men, standing in the shadows, beside a covered wagon.

Lew McManus grabbed Bradshaw's free arm and hoisted him up, like lifting a bale of straw. He and Dirt shook hands. "What are you doing here on the Mora?" Dirt asked him.

"We were driving cattle up to Fort Union," said the Tennessean, "and one of our steers broke a leg. So we're barbecuing him. Do you remember my partner, Jimmy Gray?"

Dirt recognized the thin Tennessean at once, then he squinted at Rodrigo, the Indian he had last seen on a rooftop in Santa Fe. "Why, Mr. Gray! And Mr. Red Water, is it?" The last time I'd seen ye, you both had hammers in your hands. It's been over a year, ain't it?" Dirt shook Jimmy Gray's hand, but Red Water stayed over by the fire. He seemed suspicious of the men down below.

Huffing and puffing, Will Clancy appeared at the bluff edge. He was thin and wrinkled in the face, from years in the sun, and he was bare-chinned, except for a neatly-trimmed mustache. "You have beef for sale?" Clancy asked.

"You and your men are welcome to all you can eat," Jimmy Gray offered. "Keep your money. There's more where that came from—we can't eat it all."

Clancy's face lit up. He also spotted the whiskey jug lying beside Lew's saddle. "Thank you, I will," said the stage boss.

Lew picked up the jug and handed it to Dirt Bradshaw. Dirt took a drink, grimaced and passed it to Clancy. "I see you're still drinking that swill from Taos," said Dirt.

McManus pulled Dirt aside. "I've got a lot more in my wagon. Hoped to sell it in Cimarron. But if you're interested, I'll sell you and your friends a keg or two."

Dirt Bradshaw told McManus that he could not risk any trouble from the government, by selling untaxed liquor. "Especially from a U.S. Postal Service vehicle," he added.

Will Clancy, the stage boss, overheard this conversation "I know the quartermaster at Fort Larned," he piped up. "He'd pay good money for this."

Lew McManus invited the stage boss over to the covered wagon, to show him the whiskey kegs. This gave Jimmy an opportunity to talk to Bradshaw in private. "Can you trust that fellow?" Gray whispered, indicating Clancy.

"Far as I can throw him," said Dirt.

"Keep this to yourself," the rancher said, "but are you allowed to take on passengers on that stagecoach?"

Dirt Bradshaw nodded, but said this was rare now, because few people wanted to risk the Cimarron Cut-off. He noticed that Rodrigo had slipped away into the darkness. "Who is it?" Dirt asked.

Jimmy told Bradshaw about Nicole Klausman, that she was a white girl from Kansas, who had been taken by the Texas Comanches when only a child. To Jimmy, this looked like an opportunity to palm his new problem off on another man. "We don't know much about her, except for her name and she wants to go to Kansas, but we don't know where. She doesn't speak English very good. Just Comanche and some other tongue. We think it's German."

Dirt Bradshaw put his hand to his chin. "German, you say? Back where I come from, there were a lot of German immigrants around Milwaukee. At New Berlin. I learned to speak die deutsche sprache— well at least enough to order beer, I guess. Could I speak with her?"

"Si, you can," said Red Water, causing Bradshaw to flinch, when he stepped back into the light. "Por favor, come with me."

Dirt grinned at Jimmy Gray, "Dang, your scout could sneak up on a Giraffe in inch-high grass," he said with a nod and a wink, then he and Rodrigo walked off toward the cattle.

They found WaShana perched on a flat boulder, watching the herd. To Dirt, she looked more like a boy, yet as Dirt came closer, he noticed the girlish facial features. "Guten Abend, Fraulien Klausman. Durfeen.. wir reden?" he asked, trying to gain her trust.

The girl looked startled. She frowned, her mouth opened, yet then she had to think, for a moment. "Wer...bist...du?" She asked. "Who are you?"

Dirt said he was Rodrigo's friend. "Ich bin Dirt Bradshaw." In a mixture of halting German and English, Dirt offered to help Nicole help find her family. After some brief attempts and failures, Dirt decided to name a few towns in Kansas and he asked Miss Klausman to remember if she had ever lived in any of them. Dirt listed the towns he knew— Council Grove, Topeka, Westport, McPherson. He grew frustrated, when the girl did not remember any of them, but he continued. "Great Bend. Lessee, Fort Leavenworth, Lawrence?"

"Ja! Das ist es! It is my home!" the girl shouted. She looked at Rodrigo; tears welled in her eyes and she hugged the Mescalero. "Yes, Danke mein Herr," she said, thanking Bradshaw. "You can call me WaShana. Will you take me home?"

"WaShana? So that's your Comanche name?" Dirt realized the girl was really quite intelligent. He also felt very sorry for her. A White girl, who was raised by Indians, would not be fully accepted back in White society.

As the night wore on, Dirt and WaShana Nicole discussed her time with the Quahadi people. Rodrigo grew disheartened to see the young woman converse so freely. Rodrigo wondered if the Colorado man had his own self-interest in mind; in addition, the teasing from Lew McManus earlier had discouraged the Mescalero. Although she had been raised as a Quahadi, WaShana Nicole was still White. Red Water was an Apache, a fugitive and a refugiodo. Maybe I should just go live in a cave, like the Hermit Priest, he thought, while trudging back to the campsite.

The stagecoach men were now all gathered around the fire. Eating beef and drinking whiskey, they were no longer in a hurry to resume their journey. Rodrigo kept his distance. These men were strangers; they would soon be drunk. Red Water could tolerate McManus, when the big Tennessean got foolish by himself, but a rowdy group of Anglo drunkards could cause harm. Rodrigo worried what they might do to WaShana, so he hurried back to her.

Dirt Bradshaw was returning back to the campsite and Red Water stopped him. "Your friends are drunk," said the Apache.

"Really? Well, then. They need to sleep it off," Bradshaw remarked. "Can you stay with the girl, Amigo? I'll bring you both some food in a little while. She shouldn't be around those yahoos tonight."

Rodrigo was reassured by the prospector's good sense. "Gracias, you and I know she has suffered too much trouble, and does not need any more."

"Well, yeah. Listen, I can take WaShana on to Kansas," said Bradshaw, "but someone in your outfit needs to go along with her. In case her folks don't accept her back, okay?"

"It must be big Señor Lewis. I am Apache and do not fit in either."

"You can pass for a Mexicano, since you know Espanol, my friend." Dirt grinned slyly. "Let me make sure Mr. Clancy gets snookered. I know how to work him. In the meantime, you and the rest of your outfit need to make Miss Nicole look more like a boy, understand?"

Circled around a blazing fire of mesquite and pinon, the Overland stagecoach crew passed the whiskey jug around and around. Only Dirt and the thin rancher, Jimmy Gray abstained. Both men sat on a log, away from the group.

"So, where is Lawrence, Kansas?" Jimmy asked Bradshaw.

"It's clear across the state, close to Missouri," said Dirt. "The girl's got a hard journey ahead of her."

"Keep an eye on her for me, will you?"

"Yeah, I will. I'll keep her away from the stage hands," Dirt replied. "And I'll say she's your nephew."

Jimmy Gray extinguished the stub of his cigarette on the log. "It ain't just them. It's Claw." This was Jimmy's nickname for McManus. "He talked that Clancy feller into taking him and his whiskey stash to Fort Larned. That's fine with me. Dammit, I hate dealing with a bunch of drunks."

"Me too, when I'm not drinking myself," said Dirt. Gray stood up, went over to the covered wagon and took out his bedroll. "I'm going out to watch the cows," he said. "I'll leave you to watch the drunkards. See you at sunrise."

As the rowdiness continued around the campfire, Dirt thought about his frustrated desires and broken dreams. He was not drinking, because he blamed drinking for most of his past failures. A year earlier, hopes of a wonderful marriage to Christina Jones, a young Union widow, had gone bust. More recently, meeting the lady abolitionist, Miss Jane Edgerton, had spurred Bradshaw into limiting his use of alcohol. Dirt believed he could better his chances with good women, if he did not drink. Dirt had heard Miss Jane play the violin, both at Fort Garland, and later, at the Governor's Hall, in Santa Fe. Both times, Bradshaw had been transported to what seemed a higher dimension by the young Canadienne's music. She seemed so unattainable, unless Dirt himself resolved to make more of a mark in the world.

CHAPTER 12

Carrying coal, wool, hides, lumber, grain and the hidden gold cargo, the twenty-six wagons of the Federal caravan were accompanied by a herd of cattle and a remuda of horses and mules. As the wagon train moved slowly along the north side of the Arkansas River, trail boss Daniel Colburn yielded his command to the wagon master from Denver, Mr. Cooper.

Lieutenant Dave Bradshaw hated this decision, for Cooper was actually the trifling U.S. Treasury agent, Adolphus Frankfort. The Federal agent's knowledge of leading a caravan wasn't worth a damn, in Dave's opinion; his orders and tirades grew worse as the wagons and men headed east.

"Why are we stopping here?" Frankfort questioned, on the third day out from Fort Lyon, when Colburn and Bradshaw stopped the wagons and told the livestock men to picket the horses and mules.

"There's good grass and water here—and the animals must rest and graze," said Colbun. He knew this section of the Trail.

"Nonsense Mr. Colburn. We should go on for a few more miles. Those mules will never make it to Missouri, growing fat and lazy in the midday sun. Lieutenant Bradshaw, have your men saddle back up and search for a good encampment further up the road. Meanwhile, conduct an inventory of our food and check the water barrels and refill them if need be. We will continue on for several more hours."

Dave glanced at Dan Colburn, who looked somewhat amused. Bradshaw hesitated; counting beans and bacon was not one of his duties. This was all just a power play; the Federal agent used these sort of tactics to show his authority to the whole caravan.

As the cattleman and the lieutenant walked away, Colburn muttered, "I'd tell him to kiss my arse. He doesn't run the War Department."

"Mr. Colburn, we need to talk!" Frankfort shouted, as he stood up in the driver's seat on the lead wagon. "I have a few complaints about your Mexican cowhands."

Now it was Lieutenant Dave's turn to smirk, "Go on, Danny boy, he chuckled. Bradshaw told Sergeant Mikowski to check the mules and cavalry horses. He noticed teamster Todd and Corporal Reynolds hanging around, waiting to rat out one of his soldiers to Agent Frankfort. "Todd, Reynolds! Don't just stand there!" the lieutenant barked. "Go check our food supply and fill the water barrels!"

Jimmy Gray was already up and making coffee, when Dirt Bradshaw climbed out of the covered wagon. The sun had not yet risen, yet it was first light and a faint fog covered the river bottom. Three of the stagecoach workers were strewn about the campsite, having passed out from too much whiskey. "You did right, sleeping in that wagon," Jimmy said, "It's better than sleeping on hard ground."

Dirt rotated his shoulder and stretched. "Where is Clancy? And Lew?" he asked.

"Your boss and that other stagehand, the mean lookin' one, said they were sleeping in the coach. Claw has gone to fetch the girl."

"So she's going on with us?" asked Dirt. He knelt down and poured himself some coffee.

"Yessir, but get this—Rodrigo is gonna go with you all too. WaShana insisted. She won't go without him. You need to convince your boss to let him go along." Jimmy took a shovel and spread the hot coals of the fire out, in order to kill the flames.

"Okay. I'll bribe Clancy, by saying I won't report him to the postmaster—about him getting drunk and delaying us a day," said Dirt. "Also, it might be best if Lew and them bring their own horses. We've been short two guards anyway."

Lew McManus stumbled up to the campsite. His black hair was all matted, his eyes looked bleary and he was in a foul mood. "I almost dragged your arse out of that wagon last night, Yank," Lew told Bradshaw. "I'd planned on sleeping up there, but Jimmy said I didn't need to mess with you. On account of you taking us to Kansas."

"Well, that was right neighborly of you, Lewis," said Dirt.

"You ain't makin' bacon?" Lew asked Jimmy.

"Hell no, eat some more of that damned beef." Gray scowled. "Me and Miguel gotta get goin', since you and Rodrigo are traipsing off to damned Kansas. I'll have to hire a couple of Mexicanos at Watrous. Can hardly see how I'll make any money from this gambit."

"Well, shee-ite," grumbled McManus, squatting down and pouring his pewter mug half-full of coffee. "No good sleep, no bacon—and hardly any coffee left, you sombitches!"

Dirt Bradshaw held his palm to his mouth, to keep from laughing. "I can see why you're reluctant to let Lewis go away, Mr. Jimmy," Dirt said. "I hate to break up a happy marriage."

After loading up the whiskey barrels on the Overland Mail coach, Dirt and Lew saddled up on their horses. Rodrigo and WaShana Nicole had ridden on ahead, hoping to get a head start.

Will Clancy sat next to the new driver, a stage guard named McCluskey. Other than Dirt Bradshaw, he was the only Overland employee who was not experiencing a severe hangover; hence he held the reins. "When we get to Cold Springs, we can take 'Aubrey's Cutoff', and shave fifty-two miles off our route," Clancy remarked. He looked at Dirt Bradshaw, "That way, we'll make up for our lost day of travel. For the time already wasted, when we stopped to pick up your friends."

"Journey on then, Boss-man," Dirt replied. "Anything that puts less wear and tear on my backside and less time in the saddle, is much appreciated." Dirt urged his filly, Waukesha, forward; he was eager to start the day's journey before the day grew hot.

With six sturdy mules pulling the coach, the Overland Mail team rumbled on to Wagon Mound, where they caught up to WaShana and Rodrigo. The girl was now dressed as a boy again, with a slouch hat and an oversized jacket. Red Water wore Miguel LaHoya's sombrero, a gift from the vaquero.

After a change of draft mules at Wagon Mound, the stage continued on, to the Rock Crossing of the upper Canadian River. Here, the Cimarron Route turned in a more northeasterly direction, into the dry, short grasslands of the southern Great Plains. Not stopping for another overnight camp, the travelers rode on, The mail carriers took turns sleeping in the coach, during the journey.

Suffering from too little sleep, Lew McManus wondered if he should strap himself to his horse, in case he fell asleep on the Trail. Up ahead, Lew could make out the swaying light from Dirt Bradshaw's lantern; Bradshaw was lighting the path ahead, to ensure the group stayed on the main road. Rodrigo and WaShana now rode inside the stagecoach, with their horses tethered behind the carriage. Lew figured the couple weren't getting much sleep; this section was rocky and rutted, causing the stagecoach to bounce and lurch as it rumbled on.

Sometime after daybreak, the mail stage entered the Indian Nation Territory, a dry and dusty region of sagebrush, mesquite and tumbleweeds. Around midday, it finally stopped at Cold Springs, where a road ranch allowed for a brief rest and another change of draft animals. The stage guards were swapping out mules for horses; the ground would be less rugged from here on, and horses ran faster.

Lew McManus went into the dugout sod and log structure of the stage stop, to see if he could sell the station keeper some whiskey. Rodrigo and WaShana, the freed captive girl, sauntered down to the rocky springs that gave the station its name. WaShana was teaching Rodrigo words in the Comanche language. The two had grown close. After drinking from the flowing waters of the spring, they sat down in the shade of a cottonwood tree. Rodrigo asked WaShana Nicole what she would do if she did not find any relatives in Lawrence, Kansas.

"I will have to find work," said the young woman, who kept her jacket on so she could stay disguised as a boy. She took off her hat; her hair was still short, but now it looked more blonde, with slight curls at her temples and the nape of her neck. WaShana gazed up at Red Water and her blue eyes seemed to reflect the sky. "Or, I will have to take a husband."

Rodrigo Red Water's heart swelled. Hopes that he had kept hidden, that cried out for expression, could not stay secret forever—yet, before Rodrigo could reply, Dirt Bradshaw appeared on the walkway to the spring. The gold miner from Colorado was leading his horse down to the water's edge for a long drink.

"Howdy, Miss," said Dirt, tipping his hat to WaShana Nicole. "Hope I'm not interrupting you two." He grinned at Red Water.

Rodrigo looked away to hide his anger. WaShana admired Dirt's horse, patting its brown and white muzzle. "She is a good pony," she said, "Would you let me ride her, when you take a rest in the wagon?"

"You sure can," said Bradshaw, smiling. "Waukesha and you are a good match. As long as you give her back," he laughed.

WaShana laughed, but Red Water remained silent. There was only the sound of the water, bubbling out of the spring.

Sensing the awkward moment, Bradshaw changed the conversation. "I've heard you've done some gold mining yourself, Mr. Rodrigo. Big Lew says you're a hard worker and reliable friend. If things don't work out well, for either you or Miss Nicole in Kansas, I would be happy if you came to Colorado. My brother and I have a mine in the foothills of the Front Range. We could all live at Boulder Creek—that is, if my brother still wants anything to do with me."

WaShana Nicole smiled, yet stayed silent. Bradshaw handed her the filly's reins. "You two ride together and talk it over. I am heading back to the stagecoach, because I'm ready to saw some logs."

When they returned to the stagecoach, Rodrigo and WaShana found the horses were all hitched up and the stagecoach was ready to roll on. Dirt Bradshaw climbed into the coach and arranged himself atop the mail sacks in order to rest. Lew McManus now sat up in the driver's seat and held the ribbons. He seemed more energized, for he had sold one of the kegs of Comanchero whisky to the station master. "I'm eager to get to the Arkansas, People," McManus announced. "Hold on to your hats and hair-pieces! Because I'm gonna show you all how we did it on the Butterfield Line. Haw, haw!" he shouted.

The stage took off in a mad rush. The remaining whiskey barrels strapped on top of the stage almost broke their bonds at first. Inside the coach, two half-kegs in the upper storage compartment rolled over on top of Dirt Bradshaw, just as he reclined to sleep. Dirt yelped and cursed the driver, but Lew McManus just laughed. McManus was in his element, having shared a sample of his own wares with the station master.

Full of purpose, the Overland Mail group left Cold Springs and headed for the North Fork of the Cimarron River. The other stage guards now had fresh horses, but WaShana and Rodrigo did not. As Lew McManus hurried the stagecoach on ahead, the pair gradually fell further and further behind the stagecoach. Dirt Bradshaw had told them they would all rendezvous at the Middle Spring of the Cimarron. Rodrigo and WaShana rode on at a steady pace, leading their friends' two horses along the way. As night fell and the evening wind blew softly on the waving short-grass prairie, WaShana Nicole Klausman finally returned to Kansas.

The Colorado plains stretched far and wide on the northern section of the Santa Fe Trail. Stark and treeless, below the great expanse of blue summer sky, the plains seemed endless, with low grasses as far away as the eye could see. Only a cloud of dust marked the line of twenty-six freight wagons, mules and cattle, as the Federal caravan plodded slowly eastward along the Arkansas River.

Shortly after noon, the wagon train came upon a mounted band of Arapaho Indians, who asked Lieutenant Bradshaw if they could trade for food. Dave knew the elder chief of the Arapaho from his previous forays on the Trail. The chieftain's full name was 'Walks Yellow Like the Sun'. Using various words and sign language, Walks Yellow told Bradshaw what lay ahead on the Trail.

The Chief held two straight fingers near the outside edge of his right eye, then pulled them back towards his ear. This was the sign for the Kiowa people, whose warriors trim their bangs to prevent a drawn bowstring from catching in their hair. Lieutenant Bradshaw felt this news was important enough to bring to the wagon master's attention, so he found Dan Colburn and they walked with the Chief, back to Frankfort's wagon.

"Why are we stopping again?" the Federal agent asked, when he saw the Arapaho. Frankfort scowled at the leather-faced, old Chief.

"The Chief says the Kiowa are camped nearby. And they are watching our every move," Dave Bradshaw explained. "He also asked if he could trade for some of our cattle."

"We have no time to waste on these vagabonds," said Frankfort. "We are responsible for every item in this caravan. And I count every penny, every animal wasted. The cattle are designated for Fort Larned."

"I think my herd is still my responsibility," said Colburn. "The Araphoes are starving, because the Kiowa are keeping them from hunting buffalo. I don't mind giving them a few head."

"They are considered government property, Mr. Colburn. Tell them to move aside, Lieutenant—or I'll have your troops shoot them down." The agent gestured toward the cavalry soldiers, making sure the Arapaho Chief understood this threat.

Walks Yellow stared back without showing fear. By the tone of his voice and the whites of the government man's eyes, the Chief could tell this was a petty, cowardly man who tried to act tough.

"A little good will goes a long way, Mr. COOPER!" said Lieutenant Dave Bradshaw, emphasizing the agent's pseudonym. "These Plains Indians do talk with each other."

"I have not come to barter, trade, or bandy words with these savages. Tell this Indian, if the Kiowa show themselves north of the river, they will be destroyed. Now, get these wagons moving, Lieutenant!"

As he and Colburn walked back to the front of the line with Chief Walks Yellow, Dave Bradshaw shook his head, made a couple of signs and pointed back to the Federal agent. Colburn also made a gesture, signifying that the wagon master was crazy in the head. The old chieftain grinned, then he left to rejoin his warriors.

"What do you think the Chief will do?" Dan Colburn asked Dave.

"He and his band will tell the dang Kiowa we don't want to be friends," Lieutenant Bradshaw replied. "Then the Kiowa will go tell their friends, the Comanches, that we've got plenty of fresh beef."

CHAPTER 13

Miles Wells was now branching out on his own. Many of the Confederate Cherokee and the Chickasaws had no immediate prospects, so Wells began recruiting them for his new mission. He sat at a small table outside his tent and began enlisting recruits. Joe Piedmont and Sam Burningtree had already signed the muster roll and stood off to one side, while the other young men stood in line.

"I have to pick from the remnants of the Indian Partisans. And the pickings are slim," Miles Wells told Joe. "Some of these Indians were privates in Drew's Regiment. If I don't sign them up, they might abandon our cause and go over to the other side—the Indian Guards, with the Yankees."

Wells and the volunteers were encamped on a high bank of the North Canadian River. Joe Piedmont looked around at the Native Americans soldiers who had already mustered in with Wells. Joe knew the Cherokee Corporal named Path Killer, who had fought alongside him at Cabin Creek. As the new recruits signed up, Joe grew amused at some of their names: Private Archie Peach, Private Musk Melon and Private Deer in the Water, all in their late teens or early twenties.

A spindly, shabbily-dressed man of undetermined age and race stepped up to the table. Joe could not tell if he was full Indian, or if his skin was dark red from a "whiskey tan," from drinking too much alcohol. "Name," asked Miles Wells, still gazing at his sheet of paper.

"Drunk," said the recruit. Wells looked up and repeated the question. "Drunk," said the enlistee.

"Whose company did you serve?" Wells asked, glancing at some older muster rolls. The recruit did not answer. "Do you have any special skills? Or experience?" Miles questioned.

"Drunk" The recruit began to sway, but he saluted.

"Okay, Private Drunk. Sign, or make your mark here," said Wells, exasperated. "We'll make you a teamster."

Joe Piedmont leaned forward. "Make me a scout," he whispered, "Captain, Sir. Not a private, or a mule-skinner. I can't serve directly with some of these fellers."

"War makes strange bed-fellows." Wells simply answered. Wells was thinking about the Confederate contacts he was supposed to meet. He knew about Dick Yeager, from Missouri. The Confederacy had also made an alliance with a former slave hunter, a Comanchero from Texas and New Mexico, who was named Sergio Ortiz. Such was the nature of General Pike's orchestrations and plans. Joseph Piedmont did not know that his own mother, Jessica Piedmont, had first alerted the Confederate spy network to the Federal Gold shipments. Of course, the General was correct in keeping all contact parties operating separately at first. *One cannot be too careful,* thought Miles. He had received word that Jessica's main contact, Billy Martin, was now revealed as a spy, and Martin was forced to flee Denver. Miles yearned to know Mrs. Piedmont's present whereabouts. *I hope she's safe,* he prayed.

Miles Wells also hoped to be promoted to a captain's rank, for he was still under the authority of Lieutenant Crabgrass Smith, the Cherokee. Smith had more knowledge of the Cherokees' role in this operation; he also knew the Indian Territory more profoundly than Wells; however, Miles felt he himself was more creative and determined to make everything a success. After he had finished signing up the men for his new platoon, Wells sought out Joe Piedmont and told him he would make the boy a scout.

"You acquitted yourself well in our recent fights, Joseph," Wells told the youth, "It will take great resourcefulness, stamina and determination to make a difference in the weeks ahead. Along with some double-quick running away. I'll do the quick thinking. You will be my eyes and ears, my forward scout and maybe a great warrior, like Achilles of old. Yes, you can be our Achilles—and I will be the cagey Ulysses."

"You mean like that Yankee—General Grant? I hate that bastard." said Joe.

Miles laughed. "Well, then you can call me Odysseus." Joe gave Wells a blank look and Miles realized the boy had no knowledge of the Greek classics. "Just get the Cherokees to teach you how to read tracks, Joseph," said Miles, then he strode off to talk with Lieutenant Smith.

Joe Piedmont returned to his good friend, Sam Burningtree, who was trying to repair the broken stock of the Enfield musket Joe had given him. "Mr. Wells says I'm gonna be a scout and a real Ranger now," Joe bragged.

Sam Burningtree was wrapping wet strips of cowhide around the musket's stock and didn't look up. "You're supposed to call him 'Lieutenant' now. Did he tell you where we are heading?"

"Up the river here, then into Kansas and the Yankee front lines," said Joe, acting as if he really knew. "We finally get to fight, like men! Instead of being hunkered down like groundhogs."

Lieutenant Crabgrass Smith studied the muster list that Miles Wells had delivered. "So you want Private Piedmont as your scout?" he questioned. Isn't he too young?"

"He's fought well. And Piedmont has experience on the Santa Fe Trail," said Wells.

"Ok, then I'll take Corporal Path Killer and the Muskogees," said the Cherokee lieutenant.

Miles Wells realized this would take some of the best men from Drew's regiment. "Leave me Private Burningtree as well. You can have Ned Moler and Private Drunk," he said.

Smith grinned, his white teeth showing against his dark features. "I will give you the boy, Burningtree. He is good with the wagons and horses. You will need him. Make the older man, Moler, your Sergeant. He is true to our cause and will keep the younger men in check. Now then, here are your orders."

The Cherokee lieutenant handed Miles two maps, with instructions in the lower right corners. "The first one shows the Forks of the Canadian River. We will all travel together, then you will go north, to meet our bushwhackers. They should be traveling along the Cimarron River. I will go west, to the upper Canadian River, in north Texas.

You shall head northwest, eventually following the Cimarron River, until you come upon the mouth of Crooked Creek in Kansas. That is shown on the second map. You must wait several days to meet the men with the gold."

"So I will be meeting Ortiz?" Miles Wells asked, "What if Ortiz doesn't show?"

"By all means, either you or I must meet—or find him. The Comanches will not have any dealings with any Texans, that is why we need the Comanchero. Sergeant Ortiz has to go with you, as your guide and interpreter. He and your whole party will be disguised as traders. It is why you are transporting cornmeal, food, guns, ammunition, wares and whiskey. To trade with the Comanche or the Kiowa. Perhaps we Cherokee can make peace with the Plains Nations, once the Federals are ousted from the Southwest."

"Perhaps," said Miles. He did not have much hope in this regard. "How can we be sure everyone will do their part?"

"There are ways that order will be enforced. There are many hands in this.... this adventure."

"That's what I'm afraid of. The hands that will hold the gold, they may also hold the knife," said Wells.

"More information will be revealed to you along the way," Lieutenant Smith repeated. "Just keep your Private Drunk out of the whiskey stash."

The United States Treasury man had complete charge of the wagon train now, yet Frankfort continued to act as if he was always being wronged. After the federal caravan crossed over into Kansas, the agents' tirades and recriminations grew worse. Lieutenant Bradshaw was ordered to move the wagons at a faster pace, leaving Dan Colburn's cattle herd behind on the Trail. Frankfort said that Colburn's need to graze the cattle only slowed the whole expedition down. Now the government caravan was three days into Kansas and Lieutenant Dave Bradshaw felt the draft animals were being pushed too hard.

Bradshaw's cavalrymen were herded the cabellada, the group of extra horses and the mules. Only one of Colburn's vaqueros was left to assist with these duties. He was just a boy, sixteen years of age, and his name was Juan Villareal. Sergeant Mikowski had befriended the youth, who had been wounded on another caravan the previous year. The young vaquero walked with an obvious limp, but he could still outride any of the cavalrymen.

From a hidden ravine, a half-mile away, a band of Kiowa warriors and some other men on horseback surveyed the long line of wagons that moved slowly eastward. The war party was led by a chieftain named Iron Shirt. The Kiowas were strong allies of the Comanche Nation; both tribes had been encouraged to attack and disrupt Union supply caravans.

The Kiowa traditionally migrated with the American bison herds, moving from the Texas panhandle into Kansas and eastern Colorado. They were a mounted warrior nation, who roamed in bands and sometimes raided for horses, livestock and other plunder. The war chieftain, Iron Shirt told his warriors this supply train would be a fat prize.

Two dozen warriors, armed with lances, bows and arrows, and stolen rifles, waited for the chief's signal. Their faces and upper torsos were painted red and black and their hair was cut in the ancient style, horizontally, from the outside edge of the eyes to the back of their ears. Iron Shirt extended his forearm from his chest, to his right after the wagons passed. Lying low on their horses, the warriors kept to the ravine, as they followed the caravan on a parallel course.

CHAPTER 14

With the sun setting low on the flat horizon, Lieutenant Bradshaw's troop got busy making camp. Everyone had to hurry, for the caravan's leader had once again demanded that the wagons travel as long as possible, before halting for the day. The teamsters set to work circling up the freight wagons before it got too dark.

Adolphus Frankfort stood on the driver's seat of his ox-drawn wagon, barking commands and overlooking the work of the teamsters and soldiers. The teamsters lined the wagons up, end-to-end, so that they could chain the outward facing wheels together to make a crude fortification. Dave Bradshaw sent some of his men off to get wood for the cooking fires. "Hey, Juan, go ahead and picket the mules," Dave instructed the young Mexican vaquero.

"No, boy, un-yoke these oxen, before you picket the mules," said Frankfort. He did not want to leave his wagon, which carried gold bullion, until he was sure all was in order.

"He will, as soon as we get the other wagons in place, Frankfort," Lieutenant Bradshaw muttered. "I mean, Yes Sir, Mr. Cooper." David hated this mustachioed bastard.

"What are those lights off to the south?" asked the Treasury agent. "Is there another caravan, camped down by the river?"

The lieutenant turned his horse; Dave saw spots of orange light glowing on the plains. He noticed the wind had shifted as well. The lights lengthened, then suddenly merged together. The lieutenant caught a whiff of some new scent: smoke.

"Indians!" Bradshaw shouted. "They've set the prairie on fire! Set up firing positions, men!"

"Stay here, Lieutenant!" Frankfort commanded, standing on his wagon.

Escorting a caravan was one matter, but Dave Bradshaw was not going to let this government man tell him how to fight. Bradshaw turned around to tell Frankfort to get off the wagon, just as he saw the agent lurch backwards. An arrow struck Frankfort–right in the throat! The agent's eyes widened. Blood gurgling from his mouth, Frankfort tumbled head first from the driver's seat. Shots rang out and the frightened oxen bolted.

The warriors attacked, using the smoke and the wind-swept fire to cover their advance. Lieutenant Bradshaw drew his Colt Army revolver and spurred his horse. The incoming fire panicked the mules. "Let them go, Juan!" Dave told the Mexicano boy. "Get behind a wagon!" Lieutenant Bradshaw raced along the perimeter of the circled wagons, summoning his cavalrymen to mount up for a counter-attack.

Shots and shouting and the thunder of horses intensified, as warriors and the fire swept into the encampment. The teamsters fired back from the half-completed circle of wagons. Several warriors rode with their bodies hidden behind the front flanks of their war ponies, in the manner of the Comanches. Shooting their rifles and arrows from under the neck of their horses, at full gallop, they presented impossible targets. A wagon caught fire in the confusion.

Now a second wave of warriors attacked from the west. Dave Bradshaw and a dozen cavalrymen rode out to meet them and protect the caravan's right flank. Riding headlong through the flames, shooting their carbines and revolvers, the soldiers broke through the Indian line.

The fire had already burned through this section of the prairie, but the grasses still smoldered. Two of Bradshaw's soldiers went down; Dave stayed close to the men, protecting them. Out of cartridges in one revolver, Lieutenant Bradshaw drew his second pistol and shot a warrior.

Sergeant Mikowski and more Union cavalrymen now joined the affray. "Get these soldiers back to the wagons!" Dave shouted, then he turned away from the wounded men to keep on with his counter-attack.

Suddenly, feeling the hot ground, Dave Bradshaw's horse reared back on its back legs. Dave was thrown free. Stars exploded in his vision as he hit hard ground. Then everything turned black.

When Bradshaw regained consciousness, the Indian warriors were retreating. Other men; whom Dave did not recognize, were firing rifles and shotguns, routing the attackers. Lieutenant Bradshaw assumed they might be Dan Colburn's teamsters. From out of the darkness, one burly man reached down and pulled Dave up off the blackened ground.

"Well, if it ain't my old mining partner!" Big Lew McManus bellowed. "Haw, haw, we can't let you have all the fun now, can we?" McManus turned and fired a last shot at the retreating warriors with a long-barreled hunting rifle.

The back of Dave's uniform was smoking, so he took off his jacket. "What are you doing here?" he asked McManus.

"I'm with the Overland Mail Stage," said Lew. "It's funny, who you can meet up here on the Trail. At least we ran off those dang Comanches."

"They weren't Comanches. If they were, we'd still be fighting them. No, they were Kiowa," Dave replied, looking down at the red and black-painted body of a dead warrior.

"Your brother said we might come across the Kiowa on this part of the Trail," Lew agreed.

"Dirt's with you? I thought he was in the San Juans."

As they walked back to the wagons, McManus told Dave that his brother and the mail stage would arrive sometime soon. "After we rendezvous, we're going on to Fort Larned, Council Grove and Fort Leavenworth," he added. They returned to the enclosure of wagons, where the men were regrouping and putting out fires.

The Union lieutenant was basically in charge of the caravan now; Dave needed to immediately take stock of the damages. Three wagons, which were not yet joined to the circle, were still ablaze. The teamsters attempted to extinguish the fires, by tearing off canvas and emptying the water barrels on the vehicles. Dave saw Sergeant Mikowski and another soldier tending to some of the wounded. "How many casualties do we have, Sergeant Mike? David asked the enlisted officer.

"We lost two men. Private Hanson and our scout. The teamsters lost three men, including Mr. Cooper," said Mikowski. "We're still assessing the wounded."

"We may have been lucky," Lieutenant Bradshaw remarked. "They caught us unprepared. Thanks to that meddlesome Treasury agent. Now that the bastard's dead, I can tell you—his name wasn't Cooper. He was a federal agent, named Frankfort."

Juan Villareal brought Lieutenant Bradshaw's horse back to him. The Mexican boy also informed Dave that two of the escort wagons were stolen during the skirmish.

"Which ones?" asked Dave, fearing the worst.

"The ones with the oxen—they weren't chained up yet," Juan replied. "Señor Cooper's was one. I think those warriors wanted the animals for food. And the barley, on the wagons."

"Damn it all to Hell!" Dave shouted. "We have to get those wagons back!" Lieutenant Bradshaw calmed himself; acting like Agent Frankfort would not help the situation. "I'm sorry, Juan," Dave added. "But if the Kiowa only wanted beef, they would have waited for Dan Colburn and his herd."

Dave Bradshaw ordered several of his cavalrymen to mount up and quickly reconnoiter the area. "The rest of you, round up the stray horses and mules." Turning to McManus, he added, "I might need your help, Lew. I have to stay with the caravan."

"I might have to head out with the stagecoach, when it gets here. What's so important about a couple of loads of grain?" McManus wondered.

"Come with me," said Dave. He told McManus they needed to speak in private. Walking away from the camp, Dave told the Tennessean that the two wagons should be easy to track. "The wagons have iron wheels. If we're lucky those Kiowa warriors will only unhitch the oxen and take them off. Without checking the barley. You and my men can take our mules, some harnesses and chains and go hitch them up to the wagons."

"Haw, that might be suicide, riding off into the dark and risking another ambush. I can think of harder ways to get scalped," McManus argued. "Maybe after you get all your horses and mules together, some of your troopers can go scout and see where the Indians crossed the river. Then they can follow them in the morning."

"I cannot wait that long. If the Kiowas abandoned the wagons—if they didn't look in the hold, my men won't have to go after them," Dave reckoned. "Yet. I cannot wait. We have to find out."

Sergeant Mikowski came running from the camp. "Lieutenant, Sir, we have a problem," he said. "I was going about, checking to see who was wounded—when I discovered that Todd and Corporal Reynolds are missing."

Dave took a deep breath, shook his head in exasperation, and clenched his fists. All his suspicions were confirmed. "Chuck-a-Luck" Todd was a thief who hadn't changed his ways. Reynolds knew what was hidden in the secret compartments.

"This is urgent. Someone has to go find them. Now!" Dave said. The three men walked back to the wagons.

The sound of horses and a heavy wagon alerted the camp. Soldiers grabbed their rifles. The Overland stagecoach appeared on the Trail; three riders on horseback accompanied the mail carriage.

Dirt Bradshaw, looking hale and hearty, rode up on his brown filly. "By God, it looks like I missed the party!" the miner declared. Dirt gazed around at the battlefield: the destroyed wagons, the burnt ground, bodies covered with army blankets, and his brother, whose face and coat were covered in soot. "Who did this? Comanches or Confederates?" he asked.

"Kiowas," Dave replied. "They set the prairie on fire and swooped in just after dusk. Stole two of our wagons, as well." The lieutenant suddenly felt exhausted; he sat down on the ground to rest. "How are you doing, Dirt?" Dave asked.

Dave's older brother dismounted. "Better than you, Brother," he said, tying Waukesha to the wheel of a wagon. "How can I help?"

"I need you to help us recover those stolen wagons," said Dave, struggling to his feet. "Sergeant Mike, come with us."

Hiking once more out onto the burnt prairie, Lieutenant Bradshaw did not speak until they were well away from the camp. He pointed to the southwest, toward the river. "I need you to be steady this time, Dirt," said Dave. "We first need to find where the Indians crossed the river. We have to get the wagons back."

Dirt Bradshaw asked what was in the wagons, so his brother explained how the Federal caravan was carrying an enormous fortune in gold.

"What about Lewis? Can we take him with us?" Dirt questioned.

"I'm not finished," said Dave. "I am in charge of this escort and the whole wagon train now. I have to continue with the caravan. And you have to keep everything a secret. Understand?"

"Sure thing, Davey," Dirt replied. "Sergeant Mike, Mikowski, isn't it? I believe we met once, back at Fort Lyon last year." Dirt shook Mikowski's hand.

"Be careful what you tell Lew McManus," said Dirt's brother. Dave Bradshaw was looking back at the camp, where a few of his soldiers were talking with the big Tennessean, and probably discussing the Indian attack. "I don't think you really know the man."

"Big Lew comes and goes as he pleases," said Dirt. "Guess you think I'm like that too, huh? Leaving on a whim now and then, I mean?"

"Yeah, I've got some God-awful mining partners, haven't I? It feels strange, winding up here. Away from our mountains and our home," said Dave. "Who is that Mexican, over by your stagecoach? And that Indian-looking boy?"

"Hah," Dirt laughed. "Well, the Mexican is actually an Indian. And the boy is actually a girl. She's going east to find her family. It's a long story. Anyway, Rodrigo, the Apache, is a great tracker."

"Do what you must. Take him. And take Lewis," Dave advised. "Sergeant, how many men do you need?" he asked Mikowski.

"We can check down by the river with a half dozen." said the stocky enlisted officer.

"Good. Bring back the wagons, if the Kiowa ditched them. If they are not abandoned, I think it means that Todd and Reynolds took them, because they are not deserters—but traitors. Dirt, do you want to hire on, as our new scout? It pays thirteen dollars a month. Ha, and all the beans you can eat."

Dirt thought for a minute. "That depends on what we find down by the river. Let's go, Sergeant."

As they returned to the camp, Lew McManus asked Dirt if he was going on with the stagecoach, "Your boss, Mr. Clancy, needs to know."

"Davey has a better offer for me. I'll draw my wages, if Clancy's got 'em," said Dirt.

Dirt glanced over at his brother, who nodded. "Why don't you come scout with us, Lew? And check things out, down by the river? Hell, the mail can wait, and our draw horses are exhausted. Tell Clancy they need to rest overnight."

"You tell him yourself," said Lew. He looked at the two Union officers. "So what's going on? I reckon whatever's on those wagons must be worth more than your penny-ante job, ain't it?"

"You don't know half of it." Dirt grinned "Lieutenant Dave says we're going to need Rodrigo for a little while, as well."

When it reaches the western border of Kansas, the upper Arkansas River has wide, shallow, sandy banks, lined with cottonwood trees. The searchers found wagon tracks, the hoofprints of the oxen, and marks of many horses on a large sandbar, showing where the Kiowa warriors had crossed the river.

"Be careful. There are pockets of quicksand in this section," Sergeant Mikowski cautioned Lew McManus, who led the way.

McManus ignored him and guided his horse, Duke, across the shallows and onto another sandbar. He waited for Rodrigo Red Water to cross, then they continued up the opposite bank. Dirt Bradshaw, the sergeant and three cavalrymen followed.

Beyond the riverbank, the ground was thick grassland, much like the terrain on the north side of the river. With only a quarter moon now overhead, tracking would be more difficult. McManus told the soldiers to keep back, until he and Red Water located the wagon tracks. "Look for where the grass is flattened," Rodrigo advised Lew. They both got down off their horses and scoured a sixty-foot half-circle, looking for any kind of signs.

Rodrigo shouted when he found a dead body.

Off in the tall grass, there lay one of the missing teamsters. The man's corpse was stuck full of arrows. "He has so many arrows in him, he looks like a porcupine," said McManus.

Dirt Bradshaw dismounted and turned the body over; he recognized the teamster. "Why, it's old Chuck-a-Luck Todd! One of the Bummers gang. I knew him back in the Gold Rush days. Back in Denver City."

"He may have been cooperating with the Indians," said Mikowski.

Dirt and Lew McManus exchanged glances. "This is all too suspicious," said Dirt.

"Yeah, Yank. The Kiowas usually travel with hundreds of Comanches around them," McManus remarked, "and why did they steal a few oxen and the wagons, when your brother tells me there's a whole herd of beef cattle coming up behind the caravan?"

Dirt and Seargent Mikowski now looked at each other. "Should we tell him?" Dirt asked. Mikowski nodded. "Lew, the reason those wagons were stolen is that they hold more gold bullion than you can imagine in your wildest dreams," Dirt said.

"Ha, I figured as much," said McManus. He shouted at Rodrigo, who was still searching for more tracks out on the grassland. "What about it, Rodrigo? Did you find any more dead bodies?"

Red Water shook his head silently. He had reluctantly left the girl, WaShana Nicole, back at the camp.

"It's getting late," said Mikowski. "My men and I are tired and muscle-sore, from a day's hard ride and the skirmish we had with the Kiowa."

Dirt and McManus agreed. They had ridden the previous night and all day with no sleep. "So let's get a few hours rest. And we can start out at daybreak," Dirt suggested. "I guess we'll haul Mr. Chuck-a-Luck's body back to the camp."

"Haw, more like Mr. Out-of-Luck," said Lew McManus.

CHAPTER 15

The Overland Mail stagecoach, parked outside the enclosure of wagons, was close enough for Will Clancy to do some quick profiteering. Lew McManus had gone off with the search party, so Clancy was selling shots of Lew's whiskey to the eager teamsters. Freed from the Treasury Agent's strict control, the wagon drivers decided to reward themselves for surviving the Kiowa attack. The stagehands were also drinking, after they had taken a half keg to their own campsite.

Inside the passenger compartment of the stagecoach, WaShana Nicole stayed low, hoping she would be overlooked. She did not trust these white men, whose voices grew louder and rowdy as they drank Lew's whiskey.

One of the express guards, Alex McCloskey, was talking with Brent Osgood, the young stage driver as they drank. "Be glad we got this break," said McCloskey. "We've still got a lot of Kansas to go through."

"We'd better hurry and finish this, before that big feller gets back, and sees us drinking his wares," Osgood told the guard.

"Heck, I can handle him," McCloskey bragged. Alex McCloskey was the best shot and fastest gunman among the stagehands. Lean and cruel and originally from Kentucky, he had lately taken to disregarding the stage boss, Will Clancy. McCloskey tapped the two revolvers that hung from his belt. "If that big galoot comes at me, I have a right to defend myself. Then all of the whiskey will be ours."

Another guard stumbled over. "Say, where's that boy? I ain't seen him all evening—and he ain't done no work today."

"You mean our passenger?" Brent Osgood asked. "We should consider this whiskey our extra wages. For hauling the little slackard."

The three men kept talking, but now Nicole could not hear their conversation. Quietly as possible, she moved the mail sacks around and tried to hide under the passenger seat of the stagecoach.

"There's something strange about that boy," said McCloskey. "He don't talk at all. And has any of ya'll seen him go off and take a leak, like the rest of us?"

"No, but he has pretty curls. And I spotted that half-breed getting pretty close to the sprout, like they was in love," the other guard laughed.

"I don't think he is a HE, dammit," McCloskey declared, throwing his empty cup aside.

"Let's go find out!" Brent Osgood shouted. "If she's a girl, I get first poke. Hee-yah!"

WaShana figured her only chance of escape was to go find the Lieutenant, Dirt Bradshaw's brother. She tried to slip out the other door of the stagecoach, but she was too late! The stage driver tackled her. WaShana shrieked and Will Clancy, over by the campfire, shouted for his men to stop. McCloskey pulled one of his revolvers and told Clancy to stay out of it.

Brent Osgood's rough hands pulled at WaShana Nicole's trousers, while the other stagehand covered the girl's mouth and knelt, with one knee on her chest. "She's a gal, alright," said Osgood. "Let's take her out past the woodpile."

WaShana could not catch her breath. The other guard kept his hand on her mouth, as he and Osgood carried her out into the darkness, away from all the wagons.

It was the Mexicano vaquero, young Juan Villereal, who intervened. "Alto! Alto! What are you doing?" the boy yelled, running over to stop the drunken men. When Juan reached for Brent Osgood's arm, Alex McCloskey struck Juan on the back of the head with the handle of his gun. Juan Villareal went down, unconscious.

Juan's attempt alerted others at the encampment. "What's going on out there?" Lieutenant Bradshaw shouted, just as Osgood and the other men dragged WaShana over to the far side of the woodpile.

WaShana, the former Comanche captive, decided to fight with all her strength. As Osgood unbuckled his belt, she kicked him right below the buckle. He crumpled like a shot duck. Free for only a second, WaShana tried to get away. The other guard caught her by the ankle. Now Juan Villareal was back, but McCloskey held Juan at bay with his revolver. The barrel glimmered in the moonlight.

"You thieving bastards!" Lew McManus challenged. Lew and his friends had returned to the camp. As McCloskey turned and took aim, Rodrigo swung a shovel at the gunman's head, knocking him down and making McCloskey drop the weapon. The brawny Tennessean tore into the other two stagehands like a raging grizzly. As Rodrigo pulled WaShana away from the fracas, Dirt Bradshaw grabbed McCloskey's revolver and told the gunman to avoid any foolish moves.

WaShana wept in Rodrigo's arms as Juan Villareal brought back her trousers. In a loud and brutal rage, Lew McManus now pummeled Alex McCloskey. "Kiss the ground, you bastard!" Lew shouted, shoving the man's face into the dirt.

"Looks like your stagehands and you better hit the road," Lieutenant Dave Bradshaw advised Will Clancy. Both men could only observe; for all three of Clancy's men were now subdued. Brent Osgood lay curled in a fetal position; Alex McCloskey was spitting turf out of his mouth and his right eye was closed. The third stagehand's face was now unrecognizable. "Dirt, you and Red Water take the girl to the camp," Dave Bradshaw told his brother.

"You all better hope you never see me again!" Lew McManus shouted, as the mail carriers struggled to their feet. "Get your wormy arses outa here!"

Not wanting to experience Lew's wrath, Will Clancy handed the Tennessean some money. "Take this, Mr. Lew. I'm glad none of you were hurt," he said.

Lew's knuckles were red and bleeding. He looked at Juan Villareal, who stood by Lieutenant Bradshaw. "You did good, Amigo," McManus said, tapping the boy's shoulder.

After unloading most of the whiskey kegs, Will Clancy climbed up on the stagecoach's driver's seat and bid Dirt Bradshaw and Lew McManus farewell. Clancy apologized once more. "Keep that girl safe," he advised Dirt. The mail carriage creaked off into the night, as the vanquished stagehands moaned and groaned, in a sorrowful dirge of defeat.

The sun was already shining, when Dirt Bradshaw awoke to the sound of Waukesha snorting and grazing on an unburnt section of prairie grass. For a moment, Dirt thought he was back with the Ute Indians, in the San Juans; yet here the terrain was all flat. The clink and clatter of the caravan breaking up awakened him further, along with the scent of bacon. Bradshaw sat up.

The morning was cool, yet Dirt sensed it would soon grow hot, for the sun was well up over the horizon. He had settled down for the night a good distance from the encampment, for he wished to be alone. Hanging around the wagons would only have tempted him into more drinking.

"Wake up, sleepyhead," said Dave Bradshaw, bringing out an enamelware coffee pot and two cups. "It's checkout time."

"Thankee kindly, brother," said Dirt, appreciating Dave's thoughtfulness. Dirt yawned, rose to his feet and stretched; his back ached from sleeping on the ground. "Darn, I'm getting too old to camp out under the stars."

"Your friend, Lewis, is gone," Dave announced.

"What? Maybe he's just out scouting or hunting," Dirt wondered. "Are you sure?" He sat back down with his coffee cup in hand.

"Dammit, yes. He left almost all his whiskey, but took two of our mules." Dave Bradshaw's goodwill had vanished. "You went ahead and told him about the gold, didn't you?"

"Well...yeah," said Dirt, sipping his coffee. "The Sergeant and I thought it would be for the best."

"You never could keep a secret. Always gotta tell things," said the younger brother, hovering over him.

"Don't be hateful this early in the morning. It's bad for your digestion," said Dirt, propping himself up on one elbow.

"We ain't talking breakfast," said Dave. "You missed it. I've already spoken with your Indian compadre. Red Water's going with you to track down the big yokel. You'd better get moving." Lieutenant Bradshaw squatted down and poured himself half a cup of coffee. He told Dirt that Sergeant Mikowski would lead the recovery mission, along with a small squad of cavalrymen. "I'm staying around here for a day or two, Dirt. I am waiting for Dan Colburn and his men to meet us with their cattle herd.

"So, I'm just a scout, like Rodrigo?" Dirt asked. Then he remembered the events of the previous night. "Oh, the girl, Nicole. I'm supposed to take her to Lawrence, Kansas. I promised her."

"She insists on staying with Rodrigo," said Dave. "Look at me, Dirt. She's grown up wild—like an Indian! She can't go back to white civilization. Other women will never accept her."

Dirt paused to consider this. "I might know of one," He murmured, thinking of Jane Edgerton. "Okay, WaShana goes along too. But when this thing is over and done, I'm taking her on to Lawrence."

"Suit yourself," said Dave, finishing his coffee and standing up. "Come on, Dirt. Get cracking now."

As he and Dave walked back to the camp, Dirt saw the teamsters repairing several wagons. Some of Dave Bradshaw's cavalrymen were digging graves alongside the Trail. Sergeant Mikowski sat by a dwindling campfire with Rodrigo Red Water and WaShana Nicole. Hiding her embarrassment from the men in the encampment, WaShana covered her head with a brown wool army blanket. "You folks waiting on me?" Dirt Bradshaw asked, for all three of their horses were saddled and geared for travel.

"I want you to take six mules with you, along with some harness and the Mexicano boy, Juan," said Lieutenant Dave. "He's worked with the mules. When you find either or both of the wagons, hitch them up. If by chance you do find both wagons, bring back the gold in one wagon. Rodrigo, you and Dirt will be our scouts. Maybe you can teach my brother a few things."

"What about those barrels of whiskey, Davey?" asked Dirt, pointing to three kegs, what was left of the Comanchero moonshine. Lieutenant Dave shook his head and replied that since it was untaxed liquor, he would destroy it all.

"Well, you're no fun anymore," Dirt laughed. He saw a coffeepot sitting on the coals and poured himself still another cup. Turning serious, Dirt said, "You're making this sound all too easy. There's the matter of some well-armed Kiowas standing in our way. How many of us are going?"

"I am getting to that," said Dave. "Sergeant Mikowski is bringing four cavalrymen with him. Sorry, that's all we can spare. After we get our wagons repaired, we're only traveling half a day, then making camp and waiting for Colburn's cattle herd. After that, we'll be at Fort Larned, okay? Try to meet us there."

Lieutenant Bradshaw turned solemn, as Juan Villareal and the Union soldiers arrived with the mules. "I am depending on all of you to work together. Dirt, you and Sergeant Mike are in charge, but listen to Red Water and take his advice."

"I want to go, too." the girl, WaShana spoke up. "I stay with Rodrigo and Juan."

"It may be dangerous, girl," Dirt objected.

Dave Bradshaw disagreed. "We already discussed this, Dirt. Rodrigo says she can speak both Kiowa and Comanche. And she can ride as well as any of us."

Rodrigo Red Water stood up and spoke: "I will find Señor Lewis. He will be tracking the gold, I know." Seeing that he now had the group's attention, Rodrigo added, "There are other White men with the Kiowa."

Lieutenant Dave was impressed. "How did you know?" he asked.

"Three or four of the riders are Comancheros—or Confederados. Their horses have shoes. Some of the boot tracks have spurs. The Kiowas do not want gold, I think. They will trade it for guns, powder and bullets, maybe even whiskey."

"One of them might be Alvin Reynolds, our deserter," said Sergeant Mikowski.

"Listen up, people," said Lieutenant Dave. "There were spies back in Denver, who knew about our shipment. Bill Hickock told me there was a woman who compromised the Treasury agent," Dave Bradshaw pointed over to one of the graves. "When I asked Frankfort, he denied knowing her—just to protect his own arse, I reckon."

"Fat lot of good that done him," Dirt muttered.

"Don't trust anyone you meet along the way. Anglo, Indian or Mexicano. That includes Lew McManus. Treat him like a lone wolf."

"Señor Lewis is our amigo," said Red Water.

"Maybe he was," Lieutenant Dave said, "but you all don't know what the lure of gold will do to a man."

"It will get a man killed," said Dirt Bradshaw.

CHAPTER 16

Jimmy Gray and Miguel LaHoya brought the recovered cattle herd to the Mexicano village of Valmora, where they hired a couple of additional drivers. "Pick out ten or a dozen choice heifers," Gray told LaHoya, "for here is where we split up. Me and these new boys will take the rest of the herd on to Fort Union, as planned."

Miguel agreed. He would take the cows on ahead to the Rim Rock, where McManus and Gray could use them to breed more stock. LaHoya was a valuable employee; Jimmy felt he deserved a break. "After you've got the new cattle settled in, go ahead and see your señorita in Las Vegas Grandes," Jimmy suggested.

The vaquero acted like this was not a good idea. "No, I will stay at the ranch," he said.

Jimmy wondered why Miguel and Rosa Amarillo were not yet married. "What's the matter? Ain't you and your Creole angel still in love?"

Miguel looked saddened at this mention of the young woman's name. "She is always angry with me, yet it is she who might be unfaithful. When I ask her if there is another *hombre*, she almost cut me with a knife."

Jimmy did not comment. He knew that his partner, Lew McManus, had sometimes gone to the Hotel de Montezuma, north of Las Vegas Grande, where Rosa Amarillo resided and worked as a hostess. Jimmy was worried that if the vaquero found out Lew McManus was his competitor, things would get prickly at the ranch. He didn't know how to fix this situation. Rosa Amarilla was obviously keeping things a secret, yet eventually, Miguel would discover why McManus was going to Las Vegas Grandes so often.

The next day, after he received some money for delivering the stolen cattle, Jimmy paid his hired cattlemen and rode back south. On the way, the Tennessean decided it was time to settle the matter. He would ride into Las Vegas Grandes himself. Jimmy figured the reason why Rosa Amarillo and McManus were together was because Lew McManus had land and money, whereas Miguel LaHoya was only a hired hand. He imagined that the girl might even be wanting Lew to marry her. "Claw" McManus was not marrying material; however, so Jimmy decided he would intervene and individually talk sense to both parties. The first task was to talk with the Creole woman, maybe even give her some money and tell her it was from Miguel.

The Hotel de Montezuma was built next to a hot spring, where cottonwoods and tall cedar trees provided cool shade from the late afternoon sun. The hotel's irrigated gardens scented the air with flowers. As he hitched his horse outside the entrance, Gray caught the aroma of roses, sage and blooming jasmine. Meat was grilling in a carniceria next to the hotel. Jimmy realized why McManus enjoyed visiting this establishment.

Up on the second floor of the hotel, Gray's leather boots clomped down the hallway, searching for Rosa Amarilla's room. Many of the guests kept their doors open, to let the cool evening breeze from the mountains circulate. Jimmy Gray averted his eyes, to respect their privacy. Room 210 was at the end of the hallway. He knocked twice, waited, then knocked once more.

"¿Quién es?" a woman's voice questioned.

"Es Señor Gray," said Jimmy. "I'm the rancher, the one with Señor Lewis. And *un amigo de* Miguel LaHoya." Jimmy did not know if he was speaking correctly.

The scent of patchouli and yellow-flowered musk wafted from the room when the black-haired girl opened the door. Rosa reminded Jimmy of Francesca Martinez, the young Spanish woman Eduardo Fazari had stolen from him—only darker, more exotic. She wore a floor length, violet dress with thin straps and a ruffled hem; Jimmy could see what drew men's attention. Rosa's eyes were yellow-brown, like clover blossom honey. She had full, African lips and graceful, golden-brown shoulders.

"*Pourquoi?* Why are you here, *Monsieur* Jim-may?"

Hearing this young woman speak French confused the rancher; Gray temporarily forgot the speech he had prepared while riding down to Las Vegas. This Rosa was not the mute, meek girl in a shawl that McManus had brought up from El Paso two months earlier. With a wave of her hand, Rosa Amarilla invited him in, then she closed the door.

Jimmy Gray found his tongue and told the young woman that he was here to give her money from Miguel LaHoya. Then he stated his true purpose: "Señor Miguel is in love with you. You should not reject him," said the rancher, holding his hat with both hands at his waist. "Señor Lewis likes you—but he will not take you as a wife. It is Miguel who wants to marry you, Señorita." Gray blurted this out quickly; he was never comfortable discussing personal matters with women.

"Who says that I wish to marry?" said Rosa, appearing angry. She stepped over by a small couch in one corner of the room.

"It's just...see—well, you are very beautiful. You will cause my *compadres* to fight each other, see?" Jimmy tried to explain, as he followed her over to a corner of the room.

Rosa Amarilla smiled at the compliment. "*Merci*, you say I am pretty?" she whispered, gliding closer.

"You don't wish to see Miguel get hurt, do you?" the rancher asked, drawing himself back from her approach.

The young woman pursed her lips, breathing softly on his ear, as she whispered, "Why don't you speak for yourself, *Monsieur* Jeem-Mey?"

"This ain't what I planned," Jimmy Carl Gray said. "It's just, well…" He halted when Rosa took his hand. She squeezed it; Jimmy pulled it away, and dropped his hat.

"Oh," said the Señorita. She stepped back and reclined on the couch. Arching her back, she lifted the ruffled hem of her gown, showing one of her long, bare legs, Rosa Amarilla reminded Jimmy of a tawny lioness. She was like a wild cat, hypnotizing her prey with her bright golden eyes, waiting to pounce at the first sign of movement.

Jimmy Gray put his cattleman's hat back on, like he was leaving. "I want you to stop seeing Big Lewis," said Jimmy.

Rosa Amarilla de Pais Rio had watched these men her first few days at the ranch. She admired Lew McManus for his strength, his bluster. Miguel LaHoya was generous with his affections—maybe overly affectionate sometimes. This third man always seemed taut—like a bowstring; or maybe he wanted to go his own way, free, like a mustang. Either way, Rosa Amarilla wanted to break him.

"*Je suis libre maintenant*," the young woman murmured. "I am free to do as I choose. As are you, Señor Jeemy?"

The way Rosa Amarilla alternated between French, English and Spanish confused the Tennessean. Now he wondered why he had really called on this woman. He knew what she was doing—and it was working on him.

"Why else are you here?" Rosa Amarilla beckoned.

Jimmy felt there was only one way to answer all her questions. He threw his hat aside and approached the couch.

Millions of American bison roamed the Great Plains in 1863. Each Spring, the vast southern herds migrated toward the new green grass in the north. By the middle of summer, much of the prairie grass was turning dry and brown, so the bison spread out, in search of water and pasture.

Lew McManus lost the trail of the Kiowas among the many tracks of these colossal herds. The buffalo seemed to be proceeding generally from a northwest to southeast direction. Trying to think like the Kiowas, who probably wanted to hide their own trail, McManus headed south by southeast. He had been following the horse tracks, oxen hoofprints and the iron-wheeled wagon tracks at a pretty good clip the first day; but now McManus had to slow his pace, in order to search for the tracks.

Lew dismounted off his gray and white gelding and led his horse by the reins. He had picketed the two mules a hundred yards back. Limping from his recent wound as he scoured the flat, brown prairie grass for any sign of the wagon wheels, Lew assumed the Kiowa would stay behind the herd. He wished the Mescalero or the Rim Rock's Redbone coonhound was along for this quest; that would make this so much easier.

McManus had learned to read the fine points of tracking animal signs on his hunting forays back in Tennessee. Following the path of Native Americans was an entirely different matter than tracking a deer, bear or wild turkey; however. Here in the West, Lewis could rapidly go from the hunter to being the hunted.

When the sun eased low in the west, the Tennessean climbed back in the saddle, retrieved his mules, then he headed due south. He rode until the imprints of the buffalo gave way to unmarked ground. The herd had turned to the east. Riding parallel to the pock-marked trail, both westward and then eastward, he finally found signs of the war party.

He saw many lines of horse tracks, but only one set of wagon tracks. Where is the other wagon? Lew wondered. "Oh, heck, they split up!" he said aloud. Looking more closely at the various tracks, Lew made another discovery; some of the tracks were horseshoe-shaped. White men. The Kiowas had met up with American or Mexican riders.

Lew marked the area by sticking a picket stake in the ground and tying on a red bandana. He doubled back, hiding his own trail now amongst the thousand marks of the buffalo. Without making a fire this evening, Lewis set up his crude camp and kept his weapons close at hand.

As he sipped strong whiskey from one of his jugs he had packed along, Lew McManus figured the Union soldiers would be several hours, maybe even half a day behind him. Ordinarily, they would have more difficulty tracking—unless Red Water was with them. "Hah, but Rodrigo would never leave WaShana," he declared.

Exhausted as he was, Lew had difficulty falling asleep. He worried that he had made a huge mistake, by heading out alone. Eventually, his thoughts became more jumbled. He felt he was still in the saddle, riding in the desert.

Rodrigo Red Water found the big Tennessean's tracks quite easily; he determined McManus was on the right trail of the war party. As the hot afternoon wore on, Rodrigo and Dirt Bradshaw rode ahead of the search team, which was encumbered with the mules and wagon gear. "You reckon we can catch up to Lew?" Dirt asked his Apache friend.

"Si, but I hope we do it before the Kiowa come back and ambush him," said Rodrigo.

They rode on, with Red Water tracking McManus through the countless prints of buffalo. Just after sunset, when Dirt wanted to turn back, the Mescalero halted, climbed down off his horse, then he walked in a circle, with his head bent down. Dirt knew it was best to stay back, so Rodrigo could investigate something more thoroughly.

"The wagons have separated." Rodrigo announced. Dirt rode over to look for himself. Sure enough. The heavy, iron wheeled freight wagons' tracks diverged in separate directions. One set went more eastward, the other set turned due south.

"Which one do we follow?" asked Dirt.

Red Water took off his wide sombrero, fixed it in a place with a small rock. Then he told Bradshaw they should return to the other searchers. "Señor Lewis is following the wagon that goes toward Texas," he said. "The other wagon is staying with the buffalo." Rodrigo looked down, picked up some soil from one of the horse tracks and sifted it in his hands. "They are a half-day or so ahead of us."

Dirt gazed off to the south; this expedition was now at a crossroads. The Kiowa had not abandoned the gold wagons; they weren't just stealing beef. A long, dry and dangerous journey lay ahead. "We have to go back and parley with the Sergeant," said Dirt. "I think we all have to separate as well."

"The wagons going south are now pulled by mules. Look here," said Rodrigo. "There are many boot prints. They switched animals, so that they can move faster. And they are not Kiowa."

Dirt and Rodrigo rode back to join the rest of their search party, which had picketed their mules and horses for the evening. The five U.S. cavalrymen, Juan Villareal and WaShana were making camp. Juan had gathered some driftwood along the banks of the Arkansas earlier that day and he built a fire.

"I'm glad I'm not eating food cooked over buffalo dung." Dirt told Juan. "That's some good forward thinking."

The scouts and the Union sergeant sat by the fire, discussing strategy. Red Water explained what he had discovered. Sergeant Mikowski agreed that the group should split up in the morning. "I'm familiar with this part of Kansas," he said. "The buffalo will head east by southeast toward water—to the wet forks of the Cimarron River, or to Crooked Creek".

"So you take your men that way," said Dirt. "What do you think, Rodrigo?"

Red Water was studying a map, given to him by Sergeant Mikowski. This was a new and wonderful tool, yet the Mescalero would need Bradshaw to read the names of the different places on the paper. "Señor Lewis goes that way. It is more likely he will join with us, rather than you soldiers."

Sergeant Mikowski put his fingers on his chin and thought. "I see what you are saying. He does not trust us Yankees. Also, if he does join you, there will be five men in each group. Well, four men and a girl in your group, that is."

"WaShana is no less than any man who can ride a horse for days on end," said Red Water. "And since we are heading south, there will be *los Comanches*."

Sergeant Mikowski pointed to the map. "It is best if we plan to rendezvous later. The best bet is Wagon Bed Springs, on the Cimarron River. Tomorrow evening or the following morning, understand? It is the lower spring and the first reliable source of water below the Arkansas."

Dirt looked at the map, along with Rodrigo. Bradshaw pointed to the spot, the Lower Spring. "What if the wagon we're following doesn't go that way?"

"Then men and beasts may perish," said Mikowski. "Trust me on this."

Lew had ridden since daybreak, with few stops and little water. His horse and both of the mules were exhausted, so now McManus ceased his tracking and searched for a place to camp, somewhere with either water or shade. It was still afternoon; he had to stop; going any further in this heat might kill the poor mules.

The wound in his foot, from the Comanchero fight, had not entirely healed. Lew's foot throbbed with pain after being in the stirrup so long. He stopped, and looked around. The land was flat, here and everywhere, with dry grass, sagebrush, but no trees. Shielding his eyes from the glaring sun, Lew looked to his right; he spotted a slight dip in the terrain. Lew swung himself out of the saddle and led Duke over to a small arroyo. The gully had been eroded by heavy rain. McManus limped down and started digging in the sandy soil, hoping to find any source of water. Finding none, McManus walked back out and unsaddled his horse. The mules had found a place to graze, so Lew picketed them there.

His canteen was half empty. Taking out his pewter drinking cup, Lew gave Duke some water, then drank a half-cup for himself. For the second evening in a row, he built no fire. He just chewed on the last of his dried beef jerky, then he dozed off, with his head resting on the saddle.

McManus awoke to the sounds of his horse and mules snorting and pawing the ground. The moon was setting off in the west, amid some thin clouds and the wind was up. Lew hoped it would rain the next day.

The Tennessean almost went back to sleep, until he heard another noise. A lone figure moved slowly in the grass, toward the three animals. *It's a damn Kiowa,* thought Lewis. He glanced around; his long rifle was out of reach.

McManus eased up on his feet. Crouching low, he took a few steps. The stranger had his back to Lew, so Lew decided to rush him and snap his neck.

Just as the horse thief reached out to touch Duke's muzzle, McManus pounced. "I got you, you dang bastard!" he said.

"So you do, Lew!" said a familiar voice. McManus held Dirt Bradshaw in a headlock. "Why did you let me sneak up on you like that?"

McManus laughed and released his hold. "Who snuck up on who, huh? What are you doing, trying to steal my horse?"

"I was going to let Duke sniff my hand, so he'd recognize me," said Bradshaw. "You are crazy to be out here alone. You're lucky I saved you."

"Yeah, I feel a lot safer, with you around, Yank," Lew said sarcastically. "The Kiowas might shoot you first."

Rodrigo and WaShana Nicole appeared. Out on the grassland there was another person on horseback, leading more horses or mules. "Who's with y'all?" asked McManus.

"You remember the Mexican boy—Juan—don't you? He helped Nicole out two nights ago," said Dirt. Bradshaw glanced around the campsite. "Hey, you reckon it's safe to build a fire, Rodrigo?"

Lew McManus was glad to have company. Bradshaw had shot a buffalo and they had fresh meat. More importantly, the crew had packed jugs of water, flour, coffee, trail food and gear. "Thank you," said Lew, when Dirt handed him his canteen. "I've got whiskey, but didn't dare drink it, knowing it would only dry me out."

WaShana and Rodrigo built a fire, using dry grass, buffalo chips and the last of Juan Villareal's firewood. Dirt Bradshaw told McManus that a group of Union soldiers were also part of the search team, but they had all gone off in another direction, to look for the other freight wagon. "Sergeant Mikowski and his men might meet us at the Lower Spring of the Cimarron. We stopped there on the way up to Kansas, with the stagecoach."

"What makes you think those Kiowa are going to head for the Santa Fe Trail?" asked Lewis.

"Because the men with the wagon you're following are not the Kiowa. Rodrigo says they're either Comancheros or Anglos."

WaShana had kept the meat from the buffalo tender by rolling it up inside the buffalo hide. Juan Villareal built up the campfire and dug a hole beside it, in which to shovel hot coals for roasting the meat, along with some potatoes and onions. "Damn, y'all came prepared," McManus observed. "How about some Taos Lightning, Dirt?"

While the meat was roasting in the ground, McManus and Bradshaw drank and entertained each other with their past exploits and tall tales, from Tennessee and Colorado. Juan Villareal and Lew listened as Dirt Bradshaw recounted a 'true' story from the Rocky Mountain mining camps:

"Do you know, there are streams high up in the Rockies that are so cold, that only fur-bearing trout can live in those waters?" With his eyebrows arched high, Dirt's expression looked wild in the blazing firelight. McManus guffawed, but young Juan listened intently.

"There was an old trapper I know, by the name of Wolverine Wilson. From Flapjack Creek in the Sawatch Range. Ol' Wolverine tried to set a beaver trap for them trout. Well, you might know, a beaver trap works by drowning the animal. But you can't drown a fish! So Wilson, he set his traps up above the water—about five or six inches above the surface on some overhanging branches, using live crickets and fat horse flies as bait."

"Why didn't he just use a fishing pole?" Lew McManus asked. He took a pull from the whiskey jug.

"You can only hold one pole at a time," Dirt continued. "Wolverine was after profits, not dinner. Anyway, this old trapper set his traps, waited overnight and came back the next morning. He discovers he caught fur-bearers all right—but they's all a bunch of bats!"

"*Caramba!* That is *loco!*" said Juan.

"No, Señor Dirt is loco," McManus told the Mexican boy.

"I'm not finished," said Dirt. "Wolverine Wilson still made a profit!" Dirt pulled out a piece of string, pantomiming what the trapper did next. "The bats were still alive, so he tied strings to their back legs, sewed the other ends of the strings onto hats, and sold them down in the towns and saloons in Texas, as personal fly and mosquito catchers."

"Haw, haw!" laughed McManus, spewing out his moonshine. "That sounds just like some scheme you would hatch, Yank! I can just see your drunk ass, walking into a saloon, with that chamber pot of a hat you wear—with a buncha bats circling around your noggin!" Lew handed the jug to Bradshaw. "Now, where did Rodrigo go off to?"

"He slipped off with WaShana," Dirt whispered. "I think we'd best leave them alone."

WaShana and Red Water had walked some distance away from the fire. Carrying a Navajo blanket and an army blanket, they wanted to share some time alone. WaShana Nicole was curious about Rodrigo's people—the Apache. "Where are the *Nit'a hende?*" she asked, as they spread the blankets and sat down.

"They have been herded to a place under the White man's guns. What used to be called the *Bosque Redondo*," said Rodrigo.

"Why?" asked the Beloved Captive of the Comanches.

"Why do the White Eyes do anything? Because they always want what other people have—even if they themselves have more than anyone," Red Water said bitterly.

WaShana Nicole did not want to dwell on sad things. She was happy to be free from the Comancheros and the rough men from the stagecoach. Staring up at the sky, she said, "Out here on the prairie, it looks like we could reach out and touch the stars. There are so many."

Rodrigo Red Water held his open palm up to the myriad lights of the Milky Way. "My grandfathers of long ago came from the Star People. Very long ago, when the earth was young. And now, I have more spirit relatives than family in this world."

The young woman had not known Comanche men to be this mystical or somber. They were usually noisy, competitive, mischief-loving warriors. Who liked to boast, gamble, sing and dance. Red Water was strange, even for an Apache. "What was your life like, as a child?" she asked.

"I am only half-Mescalero," Rodrigo said. "I was raised partly as a Mexicano, and was taught things at a mission school. Until my father brought me to the *Nit'a hende.*"

Having a sad childhood herself, WaShana Nicole felt drawn to this man, who now protected and cared for her. "So your people are the Star

People, the Deer People and 'Those that Live Against the Mountain'," she said. "Aho, you are even more mixed up than I am! The Comanche do not give much thought to creation. We are just here. Like you and I, now. We became mighty warriors, when the Great Spirit gave us the horse."

"What about your White people? The Germans?" Red Water asked.

"I remember.... sour cabbage. And cheese and sausage," said WaShana Nicole. "And baked bread. And sweet..." WaShana struggled for a second. "I remember apple strudel!" Her eyes lit up at the memory.

Red Water admired the faraway look in the girl's eyes. Though her face was once more blackened with charcoal, this made her light blue eyes shine more distinctly in the starlight.

"I know you want to be back with your people. Here in Kansas," said Rodrigo. "I am sorry we took you off the path you wanted."

WaShana looked straight into Rodrigo's eyes. "No, I would rather be here—now, with you, Rodrigo. I only want what any woman wants. To laugh, to have joy, to be wanted. To dance! Do your people dance?" the young woman asked suddenly. "Our young men dance, more than do the women. They seek the spirit power, by doing the Eagle dance. Come, I will show you!"

"Our women may sometimes dance more than the men," said Red Water, "except when we go to war." He smiled at WaShana. "If you were to dance for me, Young One, your face would be painted with the white shell. For you are much younger."

"No, for you are not so old, as you pretend to be. Like you are the grandfather to the Star People," WaShana teased. "We dance when there is an offer of marriage. There is feasting and dancing." Touching Rodrigo's hand, she squeezed his palm. "And I remember the *Deutch* people dancing." WaShana Nicole stood up and moved in a three-stepped dance, humming to herself. "If you dance more, you would be happy! Look over there, by the fire."

Over by the campfire, Dirt Bradshaw, the prospector, was in the middle of a story, gamboling about to demonstrate some strange event. "We can dance better than that!" said WaShana, taking Red Water's arm and urging him up on his feet.

Red Water tried to copy the young woman's steps, but he soon changed to his medicine chief's rhythmic strut. WaShana taught him the Eagle dance, then she tried to teach him the Waltz. "No, I do this!" she said, making a curtsy. You bow, like this—oh!" They struck each other on the head, stumbled on the blankets and fell on their backs.

"Aha ha ha!" WaShana laughed, gazing up at the stars. Then she turned toward Red Water and looked serious. "I am not a maiden, Rodrigo. I even had a baby—who died."

"I am sorry," Red Water said softly, feeling a rush of affection, as tears streamed down the young woman's face.

WaShana's eyes grew big and full of life. "I am scared to go alone in Kansas, Señor Rodrigo," she said. "I do not want to be Nicole again. I want to be WaShana. Your WaShana! I want to be your people," she sighed.

Red Water kissed her, awkwardly, at first, yet the slight young woman responded in a manner that a woman who has known a man responds. For a moment, Rodrigo worried he was the one who was not experienced. WaShana was like the wild, little fox of the desert, quick with her movements. With her bright eyes urging him onward, Rodrigo felt a sense of power he had not felt in years. They kissed passionately, rolling and rocking back and forth on the grass, then they embraced more lovingly, longingly, beneath the starry night. *White men can have their whiskey,* thought Red Water. *This fox of the desert is all I desire.*

CHAPTER 17

In mid-July, Jimmy Gray was summoned to appear before a military tribunal in Santa Fe. Under orders of the Territorial Commander, General James Carleton, Gray was being charged with Malfeasance and Harboring a Fugitive. *This is all the crap I need,* thought the rancher, as a blue-uniformed lieutenant read out the charges. These stated that

Gray had failed to return all of the recovered Army cattle and he was accused of giving safe haven to a Mescalero warrior named Red Water.

The quasi-judicial proceeding was governed by three other military officers—two captains and a major in blue uniforms. Major Aurthur Morrison presided over the hearing. Jimmy did not know one captain, yet he did recognize the other officer. This was not good. James "Paddy" Graydon was a former saloonkeeper, and Irishman. He had once been lauded as a hero at the Battle of Valverde; but Jimmy knew Graydon had also assassinated leaders of the Mescaleros at what was supposed to be a treaty session.

"Are you James Carl Gray, of San Geronimo, in San Miguel County?" asked the prosecuting attorney, when Gray was put on the witness stand.

"Yes, Sir," said Jimmy. He saw Eduard Fazari, the U. S. Deputy Marshall enter the courtroom. Jimmy could not help but grin, for he expected Fazari would defend him. When the Deputy Marshall took a seat at the prosecutor's table; however, the rancher's smile vanished.

"Did you not, Mr. Gray, agree to recover certain beef cattle for the United States Army last month?" the lieutenant questioned. Gray nodded and said 'yes'. "And these cattle had been stolen by the Comanche Indians, correct?" the lieutenant asked.

"That's what the Marshall told me," said Jimmy, nodding toward Fazari. "Yep."

"Who assisted you in this recovery?"

Jimmy Gray turned to the presiding major. "I guess I'm gonna need a lawyer," he said. "Or at least a drink of that cactus juice Captain Graydon hawks as whiskey."

Several people in the room laughed. The Union Major pounded his gavel to restore order. "Please understand, Mr. Gray," said Major Morrison, "this is not a trial. It's not even an arraignment. The Territory is under martial law. Just answer the questions. Repeat the question, lieutenant."

"Who assisted you in recovering the cattle, Mr. Gray?"

"The men Marshall Fazari and I talked about" When his answer did not suffice, Jimmy said, "Lew McManus, Mr. Fazari's former employee."

"Who else?" asked the prosecutor.

"A Mexican cowboy, named Miguel LaHoya. And we had a part Indian scout, named Rodrigo Rojas."

"Was this 'Rodrigo' also known as Red Water?"

Jimmy reluctantly answered in the affirmative.

"Major, if it pleases the court, may I state that the Mescalero Apache, Rodrigo Red Water, is a war chief. He killed a U.S. Army captain, Robert Dunhill, down at La Placita last year." the lieutenant announced.

"Were you aware that Red Water is a fugitive from justice, Mr. Gray?" the Major asked.

"I wrote General Carleton a letter two months ago," said Jimmy. "You see, I was the town constable down at La Placita back then. Captain Dunhill was killed by a warrior named 'Long Legs'. In retaliation for Dunhill slaughtering several chiefs at a treaty negotiation at Fort Stanton. Much like Captain Graydon did also."

The hearing room buzzed with conversation. Morrison pounded his gavel again. Jimmy noticed Eduard Fazari was now whispering in the prosecutor's ear. "Captain Dunhill killed the Indians under a flag of truce, your Honor," Jimmy added.

"You should have answered just 'Yes' or 'No', Mr. Gray," said the Major.

"I want a lawyer," said the rancher.

"The lieutenant stood up. "Major, Sir, we have the letter. At this time, I would like to ask if the U.S. Deputy Marshall, Eduard Fazari may continue questioning Mr. Gray? In a related manner?"

The Major agreed. Fazari stood up, adjusted his waistcoat, and asked, "Do you know Mrs. Jessica Piedmont?"

"Not any more than you do, Eduardo," Jimmy replied. "I ain't seen her since she was part of your wagon train last year."

This made Fazari flinch. "Have you had any communications with Mrs. Piedmont?" he asked.

"No," Jimmy lied. "Lookie here, I ain't got time to tangle with no woman."

"Where did she go?"

"Back to dang Texas, for all I know—or maybe on to Denver City. Listen, I contracted to herd steers, not womenfolk! Are we through here?" Jimmy asked the tribunal.

"We're going to take a short recess," said Major Morrison. He tapped the gavel twice. "Marshall Fazari, see me in my chamber. You've got some explaining to do."

Jimmy Gray chuckled as Fazari passed by, looking sheepish. The rancher was told to wait outside of the hearing room.

As he lingered in the lobby outside, Gray realized the questioning about Jessica Piedmont was a fishing expedition. He knew Jessica had once volunteered to spy for the Confederacy, but he knew nothing beyond that fact. Jimmy hoped Jessica was not in trouble; he also hoped no one would ask about Miles Wells.

Eduard Fazari walked out of the hearing room and told Jimmy that the tribunal had reached a decision. ""I have to deputize you," said the Marshall. "You can prove your loyalty by bringing in the Apache, Rodrigo Red Water."

"What? He and Lew are supposed to be pardoned," Gray sputtered. "That was the deal, if we recovered those stolen cattle."

"You will take him to the Bosque Redondo. Just be grateful they ain't arresting you," Fazari whispered. "Or making you join the Army. You've heard of the Conscription Act, haven't you?" Fazari referenced the Federal Conscription Act, which now drafted able-bodied men for the Union Army.

"Which one?" asked Jimmy. There was also a Conscription order from Confederate President Jefferson Davis.

Eduard Fazari laughed. "Well, you haven't got three hundred dollars to hire a substitute for the Yankee Army, do you?" And if you go to Texas, you cannot be exempted, unless you own at least fifteen slaves."

"That's why I left Tennessee, dog-dammit," said Jimmy Gray. "I wasn't gonna fight for the same rich planters who caused me to sell my farm. Did they give you Hell in there?" asked Jimmy, referring to Fazari being summoned into the judge's chamber.

"They made me so angry I wanted to go back and fight for Louisiana," said Fazari. Eduard Fazari was a Cajun, and he was getting fed up with the military authorities in the Territory.

As Dirt Bradshaw's search party journeyed south, the short grass prairie turned to sagebrush and salty soil. The wagon tracks eventually joined up with the ruts and relics of the Santa Fe Trail. Rusted kettles, broken wheels and the sun-bleached bones of horses and oxen now littered the path.

"I can see why they call this the Dry Route," said Dirt, feeling the hot, dry wind on his face. As he and McManus crisscrossed the Trail, looking for any fresh sign of the iron-wheeled freight wagon, the brown grass crackled underneath their boots.

"The ground's so hard, there ain't no tracks," Lew McManus remarked. "Have we lost 'em?"

Bradshaw said their only option was to keep on the Santa Fe Trail and follow it to the Lower Springs. "It should be just a few more miles, I hope," he said, wiping the sweat off his brow. "Let's rest a bit and wait for the others."

Rodrigo, WaShana and Juan came along with the four mules a short time later. The group pressed forward, on a southwestern tack. Horses and mules now struggled against an overpowering sun and a constant thirst for water.

Red Water had taken the lead and was gone for about an hour. When he returned, the Apache pointed off in the distance, where vultures circled overhead.

"I found the Springs. Along with two dead men on the Trail," the Mescalero said. "They are Confederados."

Lew and Dirt followed Rodrigo back to the bodies. Both of the dead men wore the gray trousers of the Rebel Army. They had been shot in the chest and head. "You think the Kiowa, or the Comanches did this?" Dirt asked McManus.

"No, they ain't scalped or mutilated," said Lew.

"Look at this," said Dirt, inspecting the dead men more closely. He pointed to one man's temple, where red and black paint had been applied and only partially washed away.

"I saw that same war paint on a dead Kiowa, back at the wagon train," said McManus. "The Rebs were in on this from the beginning."

"Sure enough. Thank God, whoever did this did not dump them in the springs there," Dirt said, pointing to a stand of willow trees. "It would have poisoned the water. They don't know they're being followed."

McManus waved to Juan Villareal and Washana, instructing them to stay away from the sight as they led the mules to water.

"They came a long way," Dirt observed, studying the worn boots and ragged clothing. "And their associates didn't even take the time to give them a Christian burial. But we will. Grab our shovels."

The gold miner, the Tennessean and the Mexican boy took turns digging the shallow gravesites. Dirt turned his shovel to Juan and took off his hat to wipe his forehead. "Hey, Lew, we came out west to dig for gold and silver. Now we are scratching the earth, to plant dead Rebels. We're going downhill fast."

McManus did not reply. Already exhausted, he sat down on the pile of dirt beside the hole. Juan Villareal pointed to a patch of mature sunflowers beside the spring. "If we plant the seeds from those sunflowers on top of the graves there will be flowers growing here next Spring," said Juan.

"Well, I pray we don't have to plant this giant Tennessee man further down the Trail," said Bradshaw. Dirt tried to draw McManus into a philosophical discussion.

"You best pray for yourself, Yank," said Lew. "You'd be sproutin' a field of cockleburs, with your luck."

When they finished digging both holes, they placed the dead men in their graves and covered them with earth. WaShana and Rodrigo watched from a distance. Dirt and Juan took their hats off, while Dirt spoke some words: "Lord, these men were people, just like us. We do not know them, but ye do. Have compassion on their souls," said Dirt. "You know how we are. We are like dust. Our days are like the grass beneath our feet. It flourishes, like a flower of the field—the wind blows over it, and is gone."

Bradshaw glanced over at McManus, who was washing his face and hands in the pool by the spring. Closing his eyes again, Dirt continued, "Bless the Lord, Oh my soul," he added. "Amen."

Rodrigo walked up to Bradshaw. "I see you speak to the Great Spirit," he said. "WaShana cried when you spoke. She remembers—her father was a man of the Christian God."

Dirt placed his hat back on his head. "A preacher? Most likely Lutheran, if they were German. But I'm no preacher. Listen, Amigo. You stick close to her, no matter what, okay? If those gold thieves turned on their own, they are doubly dangerous."

Rodrigo, WaShana and Juan Villareal stayed at the Lower Springs the next morning to wait for the Union soldiers, while Lew and Dirt scouted on ahead. Red Water and WaShana built a fire of mesquite and were using it to smoke strips of the buffalo meat to eat on the trail, when the Federal cavalrymen arrived at the Springs exhausted. The soldiers had ridden all night, after failing to recover the other stolen wagon. Sergeant Mikowski told Red Water about tracking the wagon all the way to a Kiowa village. "We got as far as Crooked Creek, where there was a large encampment of Indians. With well over a hundred—maybe two hundred tepees!"

Mikowski's mouth was cracked and bleeding from the sun, the heat and not being able to quench his thirst. He and Red Water stood by the springs, while the soldiers' mules and horses drank long and hard. "There was no way we could get that wagon back. So we got out of there, before any of the Kiowa saw us."

"Did you see any white men—any Confederados—in the village?" Rodrigo asked.

Mikowski took a long-handled gourd ladle that was left at the rock-bordered pool of water. "Not that I could see," he answered, then he drank deeply. "Aah, I needed this," he sighed. He scooped another ladle-full and poured it over his head. "What are those graves back there?" the Sergeant asked.

"They were Confederados. Their own hombres shot them."

"What? That makes no sense. Why are the Rebels killing each other?" Mikowski sat down on a flat rock to rest.

"Bradshaw says they steal the gold for themselves," said Red Water. "He says he has seen men go crazy for the oro and its shiny power."

"Well, I aim to take that other wagon. We've all gone three days now. After I rest my men and our horses, we'll resume the chase."

Red Water squatted down beside the sergeant. "Why do you do this thing? Is the gold part yours?" he asked.

"It belongs to our people, in a way. To the Union. I am just a soldier. Just a warrior—you understand that. I follow the orders of my war chief—Dirt Bradshaw's brother, the Lieutenant. He follows the orders of our other war chiefs. Dirt said you were once some kind of chieftain. Is that not true?"

Red Water scraped some lines in the sandy soil beside the pool with a stick. "Si, I was once a medicine chief," he said.

"Go on," said Mikowski. Looking down, he saw Rodrigo drawing a circle.

"I was a curandero, a healer. My grandmother taught me these ways. Her people were called the Opata. From down in Mexico. She taught me that flowers are tears of the Great Spirit," said Rodrigo, pointing to some tiny blue and white flowers growing by the spring.

Sergeant Mikowski dipped the gourd into the water and handed it to Rodrigo. "Then, there will be many flowers growing everywhere— after this war is over," he said.

Several miles northeast of the Middle Spring, Dirt Bradshaw and Lew McManus came upon two dead horses and a pile of grain. The gold thieves had obviously made camp on the north side of the Dry Cimarron. A circle of blackened rocks and gray ashes indicated a campfire; boot prints and matted grass showed where men had walked and slept. "I don't get it," said Dirt, kneeling by the remains of the campfire. "These ashes still have some warmth from this morning—but these horses are bloated, like they've been here a couple of days."

McManus inspected the horses. "I think they foundered. Probably got into the barley overnight and the men put them down."

"But why dump the grain? Their other horses might need the extra sustenance," said Dirt. "Unless they did it to lighten the wagon. Those bricks of gold weigh quite a lot, I imagine."

"Oh yeah. They can't be too far ahead," Lew McManus agreed.

"So what do we do now?" Go after them?" Bradshaw wondered.

"It's best to go back and have more guns on our side," said McManus, "but I don't always do what's best."

"Okay, but keep alert, in case those bandits double back on their trail." Dirt climbed back up on Waukesha.

"Yep. You don't want to get yourself killed all over again, Yank," McManus said. "You and I can track 'em easy enough now, by ourselves. Besides, Red Water won't leave that girl alone long enough to be of much use right now."

Dirt laughed. "He and WaShana haven't done anything, except for making googly-eyes at each other since last night," he said.

Two gunshots sounded out across the prairie, followed by a rapid volley of rifle fire. Lew McManus had just mounted up; he quickly drew his Sharpshooter rifle out of its saddle boot. "It came from across the river," Lew remarked.

"You think our Union Boys have found them? How many shots was that?" Dirt asked.

"About nine or ten. Maybe they're shooting at each other. C'mon, Dirt!"

McManus and Bradshaw rode quickly, but they kept on the north side of the river, where willows and brush hid their approach. Dirt kept his eye on the wagon tracks, expecting to see where they crossed the dry riverbed. "Keep your distance, Lew," he advised, "maybe if we let those bushwhackers thin themselves out, our task will be easy."

"I think they crossed around here," said McManus. He pointed to a section that still held water, with a sandbar on the opposite side. "You see where the water is muddied?" He eased his horse down the higher bank, across the shallow pool and onto the sand bar. "Sure enough, here's a buncha horse tracks!" Lew shouted.

Bradshaw hesitated up on the higher bank. He was confused, for the iron-wheeled wagon tracks continued on the north side of the river. "Hold on!" he called to McManus. "The wagon went this way.! They split up."

McManus dismounted and kept studying the horse tracks on the sand bar. "One rider crossed here," he said, "and all the others crossed a little ways downstream. Come look."

Bradshaw argued that they should keep following the wagon. He remembered his promise, to his brother, that he would persevere on this quest to retrieve the gold.

Lew McManus kept following the line of tracks, walking about forty to fifty yards away from the river. The lone rider's tracks now became enmeshed with the others. "I think they are chasing this one rider!" Lew remarked. He waved for Bradshaw to join him.

Dirt reluctantly forded the river on his Ute filly, then he climbed off and looked for himself. "This is a fine kettle of fish, dammit," he cursed. "They might have divided up the gold and separated."

A series of pistol shots, rifle shots, men yelling, and the boom of a shotgun punctuated Dirt's remark. "I don't think they're being too agreeable with each other," said McManus. He was anxious to give chase. "Let's check it out. Mount back up. We can always come back to this spot and wait for the others to get here."

The miner from Colorado checked the loads in his revolver. "Dang it, I guess we do need to investigate. But be careful, Lew." Bradshaw drew out his Spencer carbine.

McManus led the way, following the tracks away from the river. They heard more shots up ahead. Coming into an area of gullies, scrub brush and small, sandy hillocks, they halted. "They're right ahead of us. I see some of 'em," Lew whispered. "We can follow this ditch and flank 'em."

The ditch turned out to be a long arroyo, a dry watercourse cut out by erosion and heavy rain. McManus and Bradshaw eased up off their mounts and stayed out of view, leading the horses up the long gully.

"Easy, Girl," Dirt whispered to his filly. They followed McManus up the wash, towards the sounds of gunfire and men cursing.

"Hold here," Lew whispered, holding a palm out to his partner. He and Dirt could now hear what the gunfighters were saying to each other:

"Give it up, Lee!" shouted one of the men. Dirt peered out from the scrub bushes and saw four or five dismounted men, apparently facing off with a sixth man, who held them at bay from behind a clump of rocks. Some of the five wore faded gray trousers and jackets, others wore the butternut trousers used by Confederate cavalrymen. "We've got you out-numbered, Lee!" the first man continued. "You can't get away!"

"You are all fools, staying with the wagon," the man behind the rocks replied. "Them Yankees will be on your tail real soon!" He shot once with a revolver, but the other men stayed hunkered down in a ditch, fifty or sixty yards away.

The ditch basically ran perpendicular to the deeper arroyo in which Dirt and Lew were hiding. "I think we can take 'em," Lew McManus whispered. Dirt shook his head.

"Leave go of that gold, Sixkiller!" one bushwhacker shouted, his head rising slightly above the trench. "Leave go of it and we will leave go of you, dammit!"

Sixkiller answered with a rifle shot, killing the bandit who spoke. The other thieves fired back with pistols.

Dirt turned around to whisper something to McManus, but Lew was now back up on his horse and brandishing one of his Smith and Wesson revolvers. "What are you doing?" Dirt asked.

"You get the gold. I'll take out the guns," Lew replied. Putting his horses' reins in his mouth, McManus spurred Duke out of the wash. He rushed the bushwhackers and his Army revolvers boomed away, in quick-fire succession.

McManus totally surprised the four remaining robbers. Hurrying up the gully without his horse, Dirt Bradshaw came around to catch a view of the man named Sixkiller. Out of the corner of his eye, Dirt saw two of the other men fleeing the gunfight on their horses.

Bradshaw heard cursing in a language he didn't understand. As he stepped out of the wash, Dirt saw the lone gunman was wounded; he was attempting to climb up on his horse. Bradshaw clicked the firing hammer back on his Spencer and approached cautiously. "You need help, fellah? Don't go for your gun!"

The wounded man was shot in the left arm. Although dressed as a Confederate soldier, he looked Indian. "Yes. Those men tried to kill me," he said in English.

Dirt kept his carbine pointed at the Confederate Indian. "What for?" Dirt asked.

"In my saddlebag. There is gold that they stole. We can share—I'll show you."

The Indian reached for the saddlebag, as Lew McManus rode up. Bradshaw told the man to stop and raise his arms. "Or at least, your good arm," Dirt added.

CHAPTER 18

McManus and Bradshaw rode on to the Middle Spring, with Lee Sixkiller as their prisoner. Sixkiller was a Cherokee; he kept telling his captors he was no bushwhacker. "I was only hired to bring a team of mules up from the Cold Springs station," he said. "You see, I am on the same side as both of you."

"So why are you wearing those butternut trousers that the Rebs wear?" asked Dirt. "And why were you carrying four bars of pure gold in your saddlebags?"

The Cherokee did not answer immediately. His hands were bound together as he rode between Dirt and Lew McManus. A moment later, Sixkiller decided to explain; "The men I met did not tell me at first what they were hauling. They were led by two men—a Mexicano, named Sergeant Ortiz and another man—a Southerner. I was forced to go with them. And later, I learned they had stolen the gold from the Yankees. That's it, I planned to return the gold to the Union. I have cousins who fight for the Yankees—at Fort Gibson."

"We found two dead Confederates back up the Trail," McManus told the Cherokee. "Did you kill them?"

"I did not do that. Senor Ortiz and a man named Reynolds. A deserter from the Northern Army. They shot those men. That was when I knew they were keeping the wagon for themselves."

Dirt Bradshaw laughed. "See, it's like I told you, Lew. The robbers may have once been secessionists, but I knew they did not plan to share their plunder with Jeff Davis."

"Is that all you know?" Lew McManus asked the Cherokee. Sixkiller nodded. McManus gave him a hard look, then he turned to Dirt Bradshaw. "Yeah, I don't think we need to keep a prisoner in tow. He's only gonna slow us down."

Lee Sixkiller's eyes widened, for he believed these strangers were getting ready to shoot him. "You keep the gold. Just set me free and I will not tell anyone. Honest!"

Dirt Bradshaw grinned. "Naw, we'll take you back to the Yankees. They can decide, if they want to reward you—or hang you," he said.

The Cherokee decided to take a different approach. "No, I can go with you. To get the wagon. I know where they are going."

"Thanks, but we already have an Indian scout," said McManus. "He can track that wagon sure enough."

"But does he know Texas? Does he know the Comancheria?" Sixkiller referred to the vast wilderness ruled by the Comanche Nation.

Dirt and Lew looked at each other. Dirt rolled his eyes and Lew broke into laughter. "Let's just say our scout is learning more Comanche every day," said Dirt.

Bradshaw and McManus were glad to see the Federal cavalrymen when the search parties reunited at the Middle Spring later that afternoon. Dirt Bradshaw told Sergeant Mikowski about the skirmish with the gold raiders. "This is Cherokee Lee. He says he wants to join the Union Army," Bradshaw added, climbing off his horse.

"The Hell you say. Then why are his hands tied?" Sergeant Mikowski asked.

"We thought it best to give him some time to think about it. Before we give him his guns back." Bradshaw reached into the Cherokee's saddlebag. "And we found these on him." He lifted out a heavy ingot of refined gold. "They were slowing him down."

"Whoa! Where are you going with that, Buddy?" the Sergeant asked the Cherokee.

"To Hell with you, Buddy," said Sixkiller, angry at this turn of events. He feared that the soldiers were going to hang or shoot him now, for they had all gotten down off their horses.

Dirt admired the young man's spunk. He decided to speak up for him. "Mister Lee says the bushwhackers are indeed taking the gold for themselves. And he knows where they are headed."

"Well, he had better start talking. He seems a bit insubordinate to become a cavalryman." said Mikowski.

As he considered his words, Lee Sixkiller studied this search party. There were five Federal soldiers, well-armed and ready for battle. The Sergeant was telling the Yankee named 'Dirt' about not recovering the other gold wagon. The giant with the black beard was not talking now; Sixkiller sensed he could go from moody to mean. At the back of the group, the Cherokee noticed a Mexican boy, with a group of mules.

The two Indians in this group confused Sixkiller. The older man scowled at him. The silent boy beside him had to be only part Native American. He was slight and the face looked almost pretty under the blackened charcoal war paint. "You are a strange group of warriors," said the Cherokee, "but I will help you. Both wagons were supposed to rendezvous downstream on the Cimarron River. With officers of the Confederacy. A man named Yeager was in charge at first. He relied on a Comanchero, the man who brought the Kiowas into the raid on the wagon train. But the Comanchero killed the two Rebel soldiers near the Lower Spring and took off on his own."

"Why did they decide to have the wagons separate?" Dirt Bradshaw asked.

"The two boss men made that decision, to make it harder for the northern soldiers to track us all down. They told the Missouri Rebels to go with the Kiowa, to their village. Some of them stayed with us, to keep the Comanchero honest. After killing those Rebels, Ortiz told the rest of us we would be next, if we did not do well. I was on guard duty one night, when I fell asleep and let two horses get into the barley."

"So what's your part in all this?" Sergeant Mikowski asked. "How do we know you're telling us the truth?"

"I am just a muleskinner, I swear," said Lee Sixkiller, holding up his right hand. "When I messed up, I feared they would kill me. So, I decided to run the Hell away."

"He does not speak the whole truth," Rodrigo Red Water told the Sergeant. Rodrigo had been studying the prisoner's mannerisms as he spoke. "I can see it in his eyes."

"And I can see your boy is not a man," the Cherokee said, scowling back at the Apache. "SHE is not even a boy, you old fish-eater!"

Red Water drew his knife, but the girl stopped him. Lew McManus burst out laughing.

"Ain't this the craziest bunch of kaka?" Lew exclaimed. "Indians wantin' to kill Indians. Bushwhackers killin' bushwhackers. Here I am, a Tennessean, helping out a bunch of Yankees! Haw! Meanwhile, that damned second wagon is getting' further and further away from us."

"He's right," said the Sergeant. "Mount up and let's get moving, men!"

"And ladies," Dirt Bradshaw added, grinning at WaShana.

Miles Wells and his Native American Confederates waited for a full day at the juncture of Crooked Creek and the Cimarron River, yet the bushwhackers did not show. Miles had been instructed to wait at least two days before moving up the Cimarron, but he felt this was not a good place to tarry. This was Kiowa country and the Kiowa were allies of the Comanche Nation.

Joe Piedmont was also anxious to keep moving, so he went to the Confederate agent's tent that evening. Wells was sitting at a makeshift desk, constructed of wooden crates. "How much longer do we have to wait?" Joe asked.

"Ah, the wonderful enthusiasm and impatience of youth," said Wells. He showed Joe the map he'd been studying. They were now close to the Kansas border. "I know this country, having traversed it several times in the past two years," said Wells. "Tell the men we will break camp early tomorrow morning."

A dozen horse soldiers, most of them Native Americans, were encamped between the two streams. Wells and his Confederate rangers had left Lieutenant Crabgrass Smith's company two days earlier. After riding due north as instructed, they were now camped facing the Cimarron River, using a series of sand hills as a fortification.

Wells believed this whole expedition to be ill-conceived and poorly communicated; the logistics were being developed as they went along. "I am going to have to be my own Sergeant-Major and take charge," he told himself, so he decided to venture out on his own.

Although he did not hold a definite rank within this polyglot platoon, Wells felt he could throw his weight around. He was the senior white man in the group. Gazing out of his tent, past the sandhills, Miles viewed the sunset and the dry, flat landscape to the northwest, where the narrow but wide-banked Cimerron flowed out of the high planes. Miles Wells believed the Cherokees needed to follow the river upstream, in case the gold raiders missed their rendezvous point.

The CSA agent looked quite polyglot himself, with his gray confederate jacket, wide-brimmed hat, butternut trousers and his two-day whiskers. The evening was still hot, so he shed his jacket and rolled up the sleeves of his shirt. The southwestern heat was brutal out here in mid-July. Miles Wells sat back down and began writing a message to his immediate commander. He spoke out loud as he wrote:

"We need to take action!" Wells wrote the Cherokee lieutenant, Crabgrass Smith. He paused, with pen in hand, wondering what to say; then he explained his intentions. "We will follow this river upstream. And try to meet the escort along their projected path." Wells pulled off his hat and wiped his brow. "If they are not coming down the Cimarron, we shall search for them along the Santa Fe Trail."

Miles grew flustered. "But I have no guarantee of that. We all seem to be operating in different spheres," he continued. The agent grinned; he unfolded his worn-out map once again. "My men must go northwest." Wells wrote. He was quoting Smith's own instructions. "Will proceed with haste, going all the way to the Santa Fe Trail, if necessary." Miles folded the map back. "Best of luck with all your future endeavors—signed, CSA Lieutenant M. Wells."

Wells thought for a moment, then he added this postscript: "Vaya con Dios. Hope to see you at the Texas border, as you instructed."

Miles Wells hurried out to tell his rangers. He now had wings to his feet, for he considered himself in full command of his platoon. "Look alive, Joseph!" Miles shouted, upon finding Joe Piedmont with Sam Burningtree. "Rouse yourself, Samuel," he said to Joe's Cherokee friend. "I am leading our people out of this wilderness."

"Yep. To even more wilderness," Burningtree said, aside to Joe Piedmont, as Wells strode away to give his message to one of the other Cherokees. Sam was not impressed with this former medicine salesman's leadership qualities.

Rosa Amarilla Del Rio dawdled in the main room of the adobe ranch house; she felt lackadaisical and bored with waiting for the men to return to the Rim Rock hacienda. Amarilla hated her new home's dirt floors, the heat of summer and all the animals that needed tending. The cattle could fend for themselves; the dogs should go catch a jackrabbit, she thought.

As for the horses and mules left behind by the ranch owner, Amarilla felt too sick to feed them just now. She wished she had not left the Hot Springs hotel, north of Las Vegas Grandes—but Jimmy Gray had insisted on her moving to the Rimrock.

The young woman had expectations of marriage; however, she now felt the rancher only wanted as a housekeeper. It was now mid-July; the late morning sun shone with a blinding brightness outside as Amarilla looked out the window.

The meager garden needed watering; the thin stalks of corn and pole beans were turning brown. Hungry chickens pecked at the front door, for Amarilla had not fed them yet. "Go away! Vamoose!" she shouted. In another hour or so, it would be time for a siesta.

The pecking and clucking continued, so Rosa Amarilla put on a wide-brimmed straw hat and stepped outside. She trudged to the henhouse. Coyotes had decimated the ranks of the hens and roosters at night, and lately, desert snakes were stealing the few eggs that were being laid. Loading a bucket of coarse corn meal from a covered tin barrel, Rosa Amarilla scattered the meal haphazardly, then she simply dumped the whole bucket on the ground. Five or six hens rustled their wings and pecked wildly at the pile. Amarilla flung the bucket back toward the henhouse, where it clattered and bounced. "These ranchers think they can keep a Señorita living this way in Tennessee, but thees is no way to court a lady from New Orleans!" Rosa Amarilla declared. She wore a white, lace-bodice blouse and multi-colored Spanish skirt.

Amarilla marched back to the shade of the front porch and sat down in a wicker rocking chair. She knew she was pregnant, for her monthly time had passed. "*Oh mon Dieu! Je ne peux pas attendre,*" she said in French, meaning she could not wait. "This is too much!" Amarilla Del Rio did not believe the baby would be Jimmy Gray's, nor did she know if the child was fathered by Lewis McManus or Miguel LaHoya. Because of this uncertainty, she now decided that whoever of the three men showed up first, that man would be told of her pregnancy. "I will say el niño is his," she said. "They will have to marry me."

Satisfied with this thought, Rosa Amarilla lounged in the wicker chair. As this late morning heat radiated to a swelter, the young woman dozed off.

The sound of horses approaching roused Amarilla from her nap. *This may be him. Whoever he is*, she thought. The arid ground reflected waves of shimmering heat, but Amarilla could make out two riders as her eyes adjusted to the bright sunlight. The figures appeared to be riding through shallow water. One rider was taller than the other, so Rosa Amarilla would have to choose between the Tennessee men. This was good—they both owned the ranch.

Shielding her eyes with her hand, Rosa Amarilla gazed out again. Both riders were strangers. One was only a boy, the other, a woman. She wore men's trousers, but her hair and the way she rode was definitely female.

The woman was Jessica Piedmont; her son, Ned, rode beside her. Mrs. Piedmont had dyed her hair black in Trinidad, Colorado, just before she fled to the New Mexico Territory.

"I am looking for Mr. Gray. Jimmy Gray," Jessica announced, riding up to the house in a cloud of dust. "This is the Rimrock ranch, is it not?" she asked the woman on the porch.

"Oui. But Señor Jimmy, he is not here. Qui êtes vous?"

The Confederate widow was taken aback by this tawny girl's strange mixture of French, Spanish and English. She thought how her tone sounded somewhat arrogant. Descending from her horse, Jessica handed the reins to her son. "When do you expect him back? Is there anyone else here I can talk to?" she asked.

"Non. Je suis ici. What do you want?" asked Rosa Amarilla.

Jessica stepped onto the porch. The dark girl held no weapon. "Well, I guess we can wait for him, if you don't mind. Who are you?"

"I am Rosa Amarilla. Rosa Amarilla Del Pais Rio." Rosa Amarilla detected the tinge of a Texas accent in this haughty woman's speech. "I am Meester Jeemy's woman," she said defiantly. She smoothed the back of her dark hair and lifted her chin.

Mrs. Piedmont thought this young woman too airy and affectatious to be of any real consequence. "Oh, really? I don't think that is true. You're just a servant, his housekeeper, I bet," she challenged.

"I carry his child," said the Criolla woman. "And thees is my property, too."

Jessica was surprised, but undeterred. "Well, I own a share of this ranch," Jessica said. "If we were in Austin, I could whip you for your insolence." Turning to her son, Jessica said, "Hand me my riding crop, Ned."

"No, Momma, that ain't right," Ned Piedmont replied. "She's a free person, ain't she?"

Rosa Amarilla's eyes widened, showing fear. She remembered Texas and the old slaver's cruelty at San Elizario. "I have his baby," she repeated. "I am no longer in Texas. And I am free."

"Mr. Lincoln only freed the slaves in the Confederate states that are fighting him," Jessica Piedmont declared. She reached her hand back. "Ned, the crop."

The boy refused. "You said we went to Colorado to be free, Momma. She left Texas too. Maybe I don't understand freedom—or maybe Mr. Lincoln ain't that bad, after all."

Jessica was amazed by her son's logic. If Joe Piedmont had taken after his father, Ned was definitely her son. Jessica touched Ned's shoulder. "Never mind, then," Jessica said softly.

Rosa Amarilla rushed inside the ranch house, slamming the front door shut.

"Well, so much for manners," said Mrs. Piedmont. "Have a seat, Ned. We are staying, until Jimmy Gray returns."

CHAPTER 19

Miles Wells sent two scouts out at daybreak to search for the other Confederate group. Joe Piedmont and the platoon's sergeant, Ned Moler, left the camp and rode out along the Cimarron River, westward into Kansas.

Just before noon, Joe discovered a Missouri bushwhacker on a wooded bend of the river. 'Who you with, boy?' the bushwhacker asked, drawing down on the youth with his gun as Joe approached the Confederate. The sound of pistol hammers clicking back in the woods stopped Joe in his tracks.

"I'm Confederate," said Joe. "Come on out, Sergeant," he yelled to Ned Moler, who was hiding in the bushes. Joe held up his hands and grinned in a friendly manner. "We've got more fellahs coming up the river, to meet you-all."

One by one, the guerilla fighters emerged from behind the trees. Some were mounted on fine horses, some were on foot and did not look much older than Joe. They did not have full beards, but their hair grew long out under their slouch hats. The men on horseback looked colorful, with red and brown hunting coats, orange or red bandanas and ammunition belts on their torsos. They each carried two to four revolvers on their belts or in holsters, and they each held carbines. This was a real force to be reckoned with, thought Joe.

A man in his mid-twenties rode up; he was Dick Yeager, a well-known highwayman on the Santa Fe Trail. Yeager introduced himself as the group's captain. He was square-jawed, with short-cut hair and icy blue eyes. "Do you know the whereabouts of Mr. Miles Wells?" Yeager asked.

"He's our Lieutenant. And commands a bunch of Indian Partisans," said Joe. He remembered to salute. "Yes, Sir, I know him."

The Cherokee named Ned Moler stepped out into view. He was older and more cautious than the Texas youth. "I am Sergeant Moler, Captain," said the Cherokee. "I will take you to Wells and our Cherokee warriors. Where are the wagons, Sir?"

"We left our wagon with our Kiowa friends. It only slowed us down. And we don't take mules or slow-footed infantrymen," said Yeager. Unlike the younger bushwhackers, who were mostly farm boys from Missouri, Dick Yeager was an experienced outlaw. "The freight wagon we had taken carried gold coins, not heavy gold bricks. We're taking these down to the Red River, on the Texas border, and some of it to Missouri, to aid in our fight with the Jayhawkers."

Joe Piedmont now counted fifteen raiders in the group. "Can I join you?" he asked Yeager.

"Only if you can ride fast, shoot true and love a hot fight," the robber captain declared, impressed with Joe's enthusiasm.

Five more bushwhackers emerged from the willows along the riverbank. As Joe rode with Yeager's rangers back toward the Cherokee platoon, one of the Missouri men introduced himself. Jim Anderson said he had joined Quantrill's raiders after his family had been treated harshly by pro-Union forces. "Leave them Injuns and ride with us, Joe," Anderson offered, after Piedmont had told him his own father had been killed by Yankees in New Mexico. "They murdered my Paw, too. After this, we're gonna go to East Kansas and wreak some real vengeance," Anderson added.

Joe Piedmont seriously considered this. These men were active fighters and he had little faith in Miles Wells and his Indian Partisans. Joe looked around; all these bushwhackers were White, with the exception of a tall, serious scout, who carried a long rifle. He was older, looked part Indian and he wore buckskin trousers and a fringed buckskin jacket without a shirt.

Later that afternoon, the Confederate guerillas found Wells and his Indian Nation partisans. Miles Wells sat in a folding chair, under a lone cottonwood beside the river. Yeager told his men he wanted to speak with the Confederate agent privately.

"Where are the gold wagons?" asked Wells.

Yeager explained that his men were carrying sacks of gold coins on their horses. After riding to the Kiowa village, he had given the Kiowas his wagon and the oxen, along with rifles and ammunition as a peace offering. "And to guarantee our safe passage through their hunting grounds," Yeager added.

"But where is Sergeant Ortiz?" Miles Wells asked.

Yeager's face turned red, not from embarrassment, but with anger. "That damned Comanchero sergeant has double-crossed us! After we separated, he did not rendezvous with us at the North Fork of the Cimarron, as we had agreed."

"Maybe you shouldn't have let him out of your sight," said Miles.

Dick Yeager scowled. "We knew we were being followed. That is why we split up," he said. "And why I abandoned those slow-moving oxen and the freight wagon. It's easy for you to second-guess us, Wells, while sunning yourself like you're on a holiday picnic."

"I did not choose that Mexican sergeant for this mission," Miles Wells declared. Noticing Dick Yeager's expression and the four revolvers the robber captain carried on his person, Miles decided to soften his tone. "And I guess you did not either, Sir. What do you suggest, Captain?"

"I'm sending some men to north Texas. The rest of us will go east, to meet Bill Quantrill," said Yeager. The Confederate leader was reluctant to give up the gold his men were carrying. "You must give chase to Sergio Ortiz, Mr. Wells. He is dangerous, mind you. I had sent two of my best men along with him. When I sent my scout to check at the Lower Spring, he came back with the news that Ortiz had killed them—and some Yankees were burying them."

Miles Wells asked Yeager where he thought the Comanchero sergeant was heading. "One would think he would go to Texas, as planned," said Yeager, "but I bet he takes the Trail, to the New Mexico Territory. Either to the caprock bordering the Llano Estacado, or the desert. Find him, Mr. Wells. Kill him and all who are with him."

The Confederate agent stood up and pointed to the southwest. "Wish it was that simple, Sir. Are they sticking to the Santa Fe Trail?"

"Ortiz hates Texans. And he knows the New Mexico Territory," said Yeager, walking with Wells to view the Indian Partisan encampment. Yeager's bushwhackers moved about the camp, trading stories and equipment with the Cherokees. Joe Piedmont was introducing the younger men to Sam Burningtree.

"I will trade you two of my raiders for your young Texan there," Dick Yeager said. "He told me he wants to go with us when we raid the towns in Kansas."

Miles noted the admiration Joe Piedmont was showing for the revolvers the bushwhackers were carrying and the quality of their horses. "Who are you giving me in return?" he asked Yeager.

"Robert Allison. Over there," said Yeager. He pointed to a dark-haired young outlaw with a brooding look. Allison seemed agitated, sitting atop a black horse.

Yeager's lean scout, an older man in fringed buckskins approached the two group leaders. "And this here is Will Dare, the Chickasaw," said Yeager.

Miles thought the scout looked more White than Native American; buckskins and Dare's long rifle made him seem like a contemporary of Daniel Boone on the Appalachian frontier. "I hate to lose my young warrior apprentice," Miles told Yeager and Dare. "I told Joe's Momma I would look after him."

"This ain't no country for Momma's boys," said Will Dare, then he walked away.

Miles Wells realized he had little to bargain with, for Yeager held the rank of captain and Miles was not even officially a lieutenant. Yeager's notoriety for causing mayhem and terror on the Santa Fe Trail was well established. He and his bandits had gone out in groups of three or four men before the war, robbing stages, travelers and Federal payrolls. "I was in Arkansas this past winter—and met the General," Yeager told Wells. "Pike introduced me to Mr. Dare. Will knows how to follow turkey tracks."

This phrase was one that Miles Wells had memorized; it meant "The Golden Circle" was still guiding this mission. It demanded a response. "Yes, Sir, and when hunting turkeys, always aim for the head," said Miles.

Dick Yeager reached out and shook Miles' hand. He slipped the Confederate agent a gold coin. "Good luck to you, Mr. Wells. The Chickasaw will guide your steps along the way."

Miles walked off to tell Joe Piedmont the news about him joining the bushwhackers. Joe had already pinned up the front brim of his new hat, like the other raiders, and he was showing Sam Burningtree a shiny new Colt revolver.

"You're staying with us, Samuel," Miles told the young Cherokee. "We strike for the Upper Spring of the Cimarron. So fill up all the water barrels. We're breaking camp now and we'll head due west, not following the winding course of this river."

"Thank you, Mr. Miles, for letting me join the Missouri boys," said Joe.

Miles gazed off at the red and orange sunset. "We need to start riding at night from now on," he remarked, "when it's cooler. Good luck to you, Joseph."

★   ★   ★   ★   ★

From the Middle Spring of the Cimarron and the Point of Rocks in Kansas, the Santa Fe Trail followed the river upstream, into the southeastern corner of Colorado. This grim territory of shortgrass prairie and rock canyons was frequented by both Kiowas and Comanches, so Dirt Bradshaw's group hurried along with little rest.

At one point, they lost the trail, but Rodrigo searched the riverbanks and discovered the gold robbers had routed the wagon through a shallow section of the Cimarron to hide their tracks. Rodrigo found where the wagon had crossed a large sand bar. "The Trail runs from here into the Indian Nation Territory," said Sergeant Mikowski.

Dirt Bradshaw rode beside the Sergeant. "I would think we'd run into other travelers on the Trail by now."

Mikowski explained that raids by the Comanches had frightened most caravans into taking the "Mountain Route," further north in Colorado. "We're about a half-day's ride from the Upper Spring," he added, "but I suggest we rest soon. All our horses and mules are about to give out—from the heat and all the riding we've done today."

Bradshaw agreed with the Colorado Cavalry sergeant's assessment, but Dirt also felt it would be cooler traveling at night. "Once we reach the Cold Springs station, some of us could get fresh horses."

About an hour before sunset, the search party stopped along a bend of the Cimarron, where willow trees lined the riverbank. While the animals grazed on the meager grass, the searchers slept for several hours. Although he was exhausted, Lew McManus took the first watch. Rodrigo Red Water joined him about an hour before midnight on the river's edge.

"What do you think, Rodrigo? Is it safe for you and WaShana in New Mexico?" Lew asked the Apache.

"Si, if we stay with these soldiers, they will speak well of us." Rodrigo did not add to his statement. The moon was obscured by clouds and the glow of Lew's cigarette was the only light. After a few minutes, Red Water sighed and broke his silence. "But we cannot go back to your ranch again. It will put our amigo in trouble."

"Dammit, that ain't fair, Rodrigo. You and I worked just as hard as Jimmy to buy the ranch. You worked the digs at Tierra Blanca, just the same as him," McManus said. The Tennessean lit another cigarette with the burning nub from the previous one, then he flicked the nub into the river, where it sizzled and floated away. "Ain't it strange? Now here we are, chasing someone else's gold—and taking chances at getting ourselves killed."

Red Water did not reply. As Lew puffed on his smoke, he looked over at the Mescalero Apache. Rodrigo's expression was one of despair; he was not dwelling on chasing outlaws. "Hey, Amigo, I know you want to go where your amorita goes," Lew said, referring to WaShana. "You've helped us enough, compadre. Maybe you and her can start a new life somewhere."

"We have circled through the land like *tontos perdidos*. Like lost fools," said Red Water. He noticed a shadowed form walking up along the riverbank. It was Dirt Bradshaw, leading the Ute filly.

"Here's another perdido," McManus laughed. "Que pasa, Yank?"

"I'm riding on ahead," said Bradshaw.

"Why are you doing that? Are you tired of living?" McManus asked. "Or do you want that gold for yourself?"

"Naw, neither one. That Cold Spring stage stop is only a day's ride from here. Remember? We stopped there over a week ago. Maybe we can get fresh horses and some provisions," said Dirt.

McManus stood up. "Huh, and maybe some of that whiskey is left, too. Heck, I'll go with you. Care to join us, Rodrigo?" McManus asked.

Red Water hesitated. Dirt Bradshaw picked up on his reticence; Rodrigo did not want to leave the girl, WaShana Nicole, alone without his protection.

"I got an idea," said Dirt. "Let's take Juan with us. The young fellow's been itching to do more than just tend the mules. If we find any new developments, we can send him back, with a message for the others. You stay here, for now, Rodrigo."

Bradshaw and McManus woke up the cavalry sergeant and told him about the plan. Mikowski agreed with the idea. The young Mexicano, Juan Villareal, roused slowly at first; however, he was eager to join the two men on this scouting adventure. Juan checked his pistol and saddled his bell mare. The mules were trained to follow this horse when traveling along steep trails or at night. "I don't think you should carry that bell along," Dirt Bradshaw advised the boy. "It's dangerous."

"*No tengo miedo,*" said Juan. "I ain't scared."

"It's just that we might need to sneak up on some feisty banditos," said Dirt. He noticed the bound prisoner, Lee Sixkiller, was also awake. "Should I take him along, too, Sergeant Mike?"

"We can babysit him a little longer. Mr. Red Water is keeping a good eye on him," said Mikowski. "Don't go any further than the Upper Spring just yet. We'll join you directly, then we can all go to the stage station together."

As the two men and the boy rode for several hours in the pre-dawn darkness, the clouds thinned out overhead. Light from a half-moon illuminated the wagon tracks and made for easy tracking. Dirt Bradshaw rode at the front, keeping an eye on the trail. Glancing up at the silver moon and the stars of the Milky Way, Dirt thought there were few things more wondrous than the night sky on the high plains of the American Southwest.

Lew McManus took the lead next. A little while later, the horses began snorting and Lew spotted a faint glimmer in the distance. "Stop, that may be them," he said.

The light up ahead appeared to be a fire. The scent of wood smoke wafted on the morning breeze. McManus climbed off his horse. "Hold Duke for me," he whispered to Juan Villareal. "I'll stalk ahead on foot and see if it's the bushwhackers." McManus pulled out one of his Army revolvers and vanished noiselessly into the dark landscape.

"Damn. He's pretty sneaky for a big man," Dirt whispered to Juan. They waited in a sandy draw, away from the main road.

As McManus snuck closer, he also listened, hoping to hear men's voices. He heard nothing, saw no horses or any guard keeping watch. This seemed strange.

Lew found the burning remnants of the freight wagon a few minutes later. Only the charred bed, the axles and the iron wheel rims, glowing in the blaze remained. This meant that tracking the outlaws would not be easy from henceforth. As the fire crackled and sizzled, McManus detected the smell of kerosene. He quickly scanned the area for any dead bodies or other signs, but found nothing. Putting two fingers in his mouth, Lew whistled loudly to his friends.

When he came upon the scene, Dirt grabbed one end of a piece of oak board from the fire and used it as a torch. Searching more intently, he found horse and mule tracks going away from the destroyed freight wagon. Following several sets of tracks, Bradshaw grew discouraged. He felt their chances of recovering the gold shipment had now slipped away—in three different directions!

"What about it, Yank?" McManus asked the Colorado miner.

"They scattered, like a covey of quail." Pointing to some tracks, Dirt added, "One group is staying on the Trail, heading to New Mexico, I reckon. Another took off toward the south—for Texas. Then this third group is heading ...southeast, I guess."

"They vamoose with the *Oro*? And make it hard to find?" Juan Villareal wondered. He put his pistol back in its holster.

Dirt said there was no sense going onward for now. He sat down by the fire, his face glowing with disappointment. Lew McManus pulled out a rolled cigarette and lit it on some of the glowing coals.

"How much gold are they carrying? It's got to slow them down," said McManus.

"Rodrigo said they had mules pulling the wagon. They can use them as pack animals," said Dirt. "And I guess a horse could carry four bars of gold pretty easily. We might as well wait for daylight and the Federal boys to get here, with Rodrigo."

Lew McManus puffed on his cigarette and stared into the fire. "Damn, we will all have to split up, too," he said. "I'm hoping that maybe the bastards will rendezvous later. We'll need both Red Water, and maybe that other Indian, to help us track the three groups."

Dirt's face brightened. "The Cherokee! Yes, Sir. Mr. Sixkiller hasn't told us everything, I bet—but he did say he knows where they are going."

CHAPTER 20

Gaining the crest of a high rocky hill overlooking the valley of the Cimarron, Rodrigo Red Water scanned the landscape, looking for signs of any dust cloud on the far horizon. Sergeant Mikowski had lent Red Water his spotting scope, the "magic eye" that would let one see faraway objects as if they were close at hand. "What are you looking for?" asked the Sergeant.

Rodrigo knew that a contingent of men on horseback would kick up dust in this area of the high plains desert. Before the bushwhackers had separated, there were at least a dozen men with the freight wagon. "The four men who took the three mules will not be far off," said Rodrigo.

"That is likely. And their leader, the Comanchero named Ortiz, would likely go with that group," Mikowski agreed.

"If what the Cherokee says is true, that may be so," said Red Water. He turned to look down at the Santa Fe Trail. Adjusting the lens of the scope, Rodrigo focused on the former captive, WaShana Nicole. WaShana had quit disguising herself as a dark-skinned boy. Though she still wore trousers, she now covered her head with a red bandana rather than a slouch hat; her hair was also growing more blonde from days in the sun. WaShana sat beside the spring-fed pond, talking with young Juan Villareal. The Mexicano muleskinner was only a year or two younger than WaShana and she seemed to act more friendly toward the youth.

On the other end of the pond, the U.S. Cavalrymen were watering their horses. Lew McManus and Dirt Bradshaw were busy, talking with their prisoner, the Cherokee.

"Okay, Mr. Lee. Here is where we decide to either shoot you, or let you live," McManus threatened. The black-bearded hulk adopted his fiercest expression. "Where exactly are those outlaws taking that gold?"

Lee Sixkiller gulped. This southern giant was the man most likely to shoot him. "To the river that flows into Texas. It is called the 'Rita Blanca'."

"I'll be damned," Lew muttered to Bradshaw, "I have been there before. With Jimmy Gray and a shady bastard named Miles Wells. That's south of here."

Dirt Bradshaw nodded, yet he wanted more information. "We need to know our foes," he said, "Who is this Sergio Ortiz? What's he like—and who are the men with him?"

"He is the boss man, the leader, the only man who can safely guard the white Confederates through Comanche country. But there is another man," said Sixkiller. "His name is Jack Jernigan and he is to be feared. He used to hunt slaves who escaped from Kentucky. He is their best shot." The Cherokee turned to Lew McManus. "You chased him away, when you bravely attacked the men who were shooting at me. I wished you had killed him, too."

McManus walked off to speak to Red Water, while Dirt Bradshaw asked for more information. He learned that Ortiz was a shrewd tactician, for he had recruited men from different towns, territories and races. Each of the gold thieves was suspicious of the others; it was unlikely they would band together against Ortiz and Jernigan.

"I'm surprised he decided to give some of his bandits the chance to go their separate ways," said Dirt. "Maybe, since they know we're following them, he and that Jernigan fellow decided to split up."

"Will you free me now?" Sixkiller asked. "This rope is tearing up my wrists as we ride over hard ground."

"Not up to me, Amigo. Wait till we get to that stage station, at Cold Spring. We're going to follow the main group for now," said Dirt. "After we get fresh horses, then I might let you go back to your people—the Cherokee."

The search party rode on, with the intention of taking on provisions at the Cold Spring stage stop. Once they swapped for fresh horses, Bradshaw and Mikowski planned to track down each robber group separately.

Several hours later, their plan struck a major obstacle. The searchers found the station deserted. The station keeper was dead, lying in a pool of blood inside the sod and log structure. All of the draft animals, horses and livestock had either been taken, or run off by the bushwhackers. Dirt told Rodrigo and Juan to keep WaShana out of the station, so the girl would not see the grisly scene. "By God, it's every man for himself, out here in the sagebrush," said Bradshaw, as he and McManus searched the station house.

Lew McManus seemed surprised that the thieves had left some whiskey. He helped himself to the dead man's keg. Rodrigo entered the room and told them that the robbers had taken another wagon from the station.

"Yep. Along with food and all the horses, it seems," said Dirt. He searched around for shell casings. "Lew, don't drink too much of that rotgut. We aren't that far behind them. This blood hasn't dried."

"That leader of theirs runs a tight ship, if he's not letting his men have whiskey," said McManus. "He's a cold-blooded killer, too."

The other searchers milled about outside; some led their horses and mules to water. Behind the station, Sergeant Mikowski and another soldier walked over to some limestone bluffs that were known as "Inscription Rock." Traders and travelers on the Santa Fe Trail often stopped here, writing their names and the year they passed through in the limestone.

Sergeant Mikowski had found a chisel by the stage station's barn and he was hammering his own name into the rock, when Dirt Bradshaw came out to discuss the search party's next move. He told Mikowski that Sixkiller had said the outlaws will meet up again, down on the Rita Blanca. Mikowski paused and wiped his brow. "There's no guarantee they will do that," he replied. The Union sergeant had already chiseled out 'G. Mikowski' in the limestone. "My men and I will follow the new wagon's trail. I suggest that McManus and Red Water try to track the other groups." Mikowski went back to chiseling.

Lew McManus and Rodrigo walked up to give their advice. They had decided to follow the tracks that led southeast, rather than going southwest into the New Mexico Territory. "We'll take Juan with us," said Lew, pointing to the Mexican boy. "The young pistolero's itchin' for a fight."

Dirt gazed over at the stage stop's barn, where Juan and WaShana were chasing some stray chickens in the yard. "That leaves me and the girl. Do we go after the third group?" he asked.

Mikowski stopped chiseling again, "No, you two should wait here at the station, Dirt. You might still be considered an employee of the Overland Mail Service. It's best for someone to stay here, in case the stage comes back through, or if any caravans or Army troops arrive."

"Now hold on a minute," Dirt protested, but the Union sergeant went back to hammering and did not hear him. "I need to do more than wait. I promised my brother I would chase those rascals and recover the gold."

"Señor Dirt, the Señorita will be safer with you here," said Rodrigo. Red Water trusted the Colorado prospector.

"It's too dangerous for her out there in the wilderness. You can protect her," McManus argued.

Dirt took off his hat and slapped the dust off against his knee. "Yep. And if any Comanches come along, I guess she can talk them out of taking my scalp," he said, sarcastically.

Mikowski had now added 'USA' and a date to the rock edifice. "This is as immortal as I'll ever be," he told Dirt. The Union sergeant seemed strangely serene. "Do you want to carve your name?" He offered the hammer and chisel to Bradshaw.

"No thanks, my brother told me I already have a marker, up at Left Hand Canyon. They can just change the end date, when I shuffle off this mortal coil." Dirt studied the sergeant's work. It read: 'G. Mikowski USA, 7-24-63.' Bradshaw told Mikowski he had inscribed the wrong date. "Today's the twenty-second, if I figure correctly. You're two days ahead of yourself."

Lew McManus asked about Lee Sixkiller. "What do we do with the Cherokee?"

"Keep him tied up at the station house. We can deal with him when we get back," said Mikowski. "Unless you and Rodrigo want to take him as a guide."

McManus and Red Water both shook their heads.

Jimmy Gray wished he had gone with Lew McManus to Kansas. Gray had returned from the tribunal in Santa Fe several days earlier, only to find Mrs. Jessica Piedmont at the Rim Rock. One contentious woman was enough at the ranch house; two women, often in disagreement with each other, was more than Jimmy could stand.

Jessica Piedmont had peppered Gray with the same questions over and over again. She asked why he had not tried to find her son, Joe Piedmont. She harangued him over and over again about Rosa Amarilla Del Rio. Jimmy Gray responded by staying away from the ranch house as much as possible during the day; he rose early, before sunrise, and took off to check fences, dig irrigation ditches or tend the cattle. Sometimes he rode over into San Geronimo and drank at the village's lone cantina. This only seemed to intensify the Texas widow's interrogations.

Neither woman shared a bed with the rancher. Some nights Jimmy slept out on the porch; one night he had even taken a bedroll out to the covered wagon he and McManus had taken from the Comanchero cattle smugglers. Here he was, not able to sleep or relax in his own home.

One day, Jimmy and Miguel LaHoya rode out to capture wild mustangs on the plains east of Las Vegas Grandes. The rancher returned late in the afternoon and found no supper on the kitchen table. Standing, with her arms crossed in the living room, Mrs. Jessica Piedmont once again accosted Gray;

"That first day I arrived your young mulatto greeted me with news that she was with child. For the last time, is the baby yours? Or is it your partner's—Mr. McManus?"

Gray stayed silent for a moment. He sat down in a cushioned rocking chair, leaned back and said, "I don't know, but if the young 'un comes out with black hair, holding a whiskey glass, it's definitely Lew's baby."

Judging by the hardened look in Jessica's eyes, Jimmy could tell she was not amused. The young woman in question was out by the corral, watching Miguel LaHoya train Ned Piedmont on how to break a wild mustang.

"So, once again, what do you plan to do with her?"

Jimmy rocked back and forth; the only response was the squeaking of the chair. Jessica tried a different approach: "Do you have any idea, how many men approached me in Colorado? With both honorable and dishonorable intentions?" She fixed her violet eyes on Gray, looking at him intensely. "I did not consider any of them and waited to get back with you. Apparently, you could not wait, however. You took up with the first harlot you could find, didn't you? Even brought her up here from El Paso. Isn't that right?"

"Lew brought her—I didn't. She came with Miguel, dammit," said Jimmy. Now he was angry at McManus, for being absent, and angry at Jessica because of her accusations. Jimmy Gray bounced up from his chair and crammed his hat on his head. "I've got work to do, woman! Okay, I admit it! I'm a prowlin' tomcat—a heathern hound dog! So, what do you aim to do with that?"

The widow faced him with her hands on her hips. "Ned and I can help you run this ranch. You just get Mr. LaHoya to marry that churlish wench—and take her to Las Vegas, or Santa Fe, or wherever."

Jimmy was surprised; although he had promised Jessica a share in the ranch, he did not think she had any interest in ranching. Jimmy did not know where he stood with the woman personally. While she was gone, Jimmy had carried an idealized image of her. Now, she only made him feel guilty and confused. "I can't let Miguel go. He's too good a worker," said the rancher.

"Miguel can stay—as long as that girl goes back to Las Vegas. Then you can go and bring my Joey back," said Jessica, referring to her older son.

"I ain't going nowhere. I just got back and I've had my fill of wandering in the dang desert," said Gray.

Jessica Piedmont sat down; still weary from her own travels and tired of this conversation that was going nowhere, she sighed. "I thought you were different, Jimmy Carl Gray. I see now that I should have put my trust in Miles Wells instead. He'd get my Joe for me. Where do you think I might get in touch with Mr. Wells?"

"Ha, I think you know better than me. I don't deal with spies," said Jimmy. He turned and walked away.

CHAPTER 21

WaShana Nicole and Juan captured four stray chickens while the men were off talking. After placing the birds back in their cage, Juan hurried off to find a hatchet. Everyone was tired of eating buffalo jerky. Dirt Bradshaw walked into the stage stop's barn, looking for a place to tie up the group's prisoner. Lee Sixkiller, looking contrite and still bound by a rope, stood beside Bradshaw. "I'm gonna tie Mister Sixkiller up inside this evening," said Bradshaw when WaShana entered. "Then in the morning, I'll go out and search for any cattle the bandits might have left us, so he can have company."

"I thought we were all leaving in the morning," said WaShana.

"Let me tie the Cherokee up first, then I'll explain," said Dirt. After binding the Cherokee up to a central post beam, Bradshaw told WaShana about the other searchers going off to track the separate trails of the gold robbers. "You and I will hold down the fort, okay? It's just for a few days, until they all get back," he said.

"Rodrigo is leaving us? Why can we not ride together?"

Dirt understood her misgivings. "He'll be with Big Lew—and Juan. The soldiers are going after the really bad man, the Comanchero named Ortiz."

"Oh, no, he is the man who bought me from the Comanches! He was going to sell me—as a sex slave! Until Rodrigo and Jimmy and Lewis rescued me." WaShana Nicole trounced around in a circle, with her hands held to her chest. "No, no, he might kill us all!"

Rodrigo saw the girl was in a panic and rushed up to the barn. "What is wrong?" he asked.

"Sergio Ortiz! The man you fought back in New Mexico is the man we are tracking! No one told me until now," said WaShana, beginning to cry.

Rodrigo embraced her. "One of the Comancheros with the cattle?" he questioned. "One of them that got away?"

"Yes, the one who drove the wagon I was trapped in," the girl sobbed.

"We stopped him before. The soldiers will shoot him when they find him," said Red Water. "And Señor Dirt will keep you safe here."

"I told her that." Bradshaw added.

Lew McManus and Sergeant Mikowski walked up "What's all this?" Lew asked.

Dirt Bradshaw explained the situation. All the men reassured WaShana that they would protect her, that the gold robbers would not come back to the Cold Spring station. "I found the station master's shotgun," said Dirt. "We'll let you use it, Okay, Missy?"

Juan Villareal came running out of the station house, wielding a hatchet. Lew McManus laughed. "Haw, look there Miss Nicole! Juan Boy is even ready to scalp them sombitches."

Promising to return soon, Red Water and McManus left with Juan Villareal at first light the next morning. They were going back to the Upper Spring, to resume tracking the robbers who had gone south. The Federal cavalrymen left shortly thereafter, heading west on the Santa Fe Trail, in order to catch Ortiz and the new wagon. They left one of their mules behind, in case Bradshaw needed a pack animal.

"Let me show you how to use this twelve-gauge," Dirt told WaShana, after everyone had departed. Bradshaw held a side-by-side shotgun with external hammers. "You can either fire one barrel at a time—or let loose with both of 'em. Trust me, no one's gonna want to come near you when you're wielding this goose gun."

"Where are you going?" WaShana asked, for Dirt had saddled Waukesha.

"I found cattle tracks beside the spring this morning," Bradshaw explained. "Deer tracks too. We might have us a barbeque when the others return. Just keep watch on Mr. Sixkiller and I'll be back before noon."

After Dirt Bradshaw left, the former Comanche captive took some buffalo jerky and a bowl of oatmeal out to Lee Sixkiller. WaShana held the long shotgun under one arm. The Cherokee prisoner sat on a pile of straw at the foot of a post. Even though the man was strapped in, with both hands bound, WaShana was cautious when she set the tin plate beside him. "Where is your man, Girl?" Sixkiller asked.

"He will be back. Mr. Bradshaw is at the house," WaShana replied. "You eat now."

"You lie, Girl. I heard him ride off. So, you once lived as a captive of the Comanches? Did they keep you tied up like this?" Sixkiller spread both of his legs out wide.

WaShana ignored the insult. "No, I was free to do as I please. I was treated like one of them."

"You are not Comanche. You are White. I have some Anglo in me, too." Sixkiller grinned and leered at the young woman. "You marry me and we'll have strong, blue-eyed children."

WaShana pointed the shotgun at him. "You shut up and eat. I am Rodrigo's woman," she said.

"Ho, that gray-balled turkey buzzard? You need a young brave. Like me."

WaShana had grown used to taunts and boasts from young warriors, but she frowned and aimed the gun at Sixkiller's lap. "I will make YOU someone's woman, Fool—if you don't shut your mouth!" she threatened.

Lee Sixkiller acted afraid, then he gave her a sad look, "You should know how I feel, being a prisoner. That black-haired, buffalo-headed giant will kill me, when he comes back." The Cherokee spoke softly now; "Please, set me free and I will just go away."

"No, you will try to kill us and steal that gold again."

"You keep the gold. Buy yourself some earrings and a pretty dress." Sixkiller then noticed the girl's eyes seemed saddened; she may have been crying all night. "I am sorry. You are beautiful—even without those things. You are like the dawn in the high mountains. Like the sunlight on the spotted fawn." Sixkiller was trying every approach possible. "I would never hurt you. Please, set me free now."

WaShana refused and told him to eat his breakfast.

Dirt Bradshaw tracked the lost cattle back toward the Upper Spring and found a half dozen of them feeding below a rocky hill. As Bradshaw approached on his Ute filly, the cows bolted, running toward the spring. "We didn't plan on becoming vaqueros, did we, Girl?" said Bradshaw. He'd developed the habit of talking to his horse. Waukesha was proving to be a nimble range horse and Dirt enjoyed giving chase. As he rode, Dirt moved further and further away from the Cold Spring station.

Bradshaw did not halt until he saw clouds of dust further up the Trail. By now he had reached the Upper Spring of the Cimarron. *Is it McManus and Red Water returning?* Dirt wondered. He listened; the sound seemed to come from many horses, approaching from the east. Bradshaw wondered if a wagon train or the Union cavalry might be coming his way. Taking caution, Dirt trotted his horse up the high, rocky hill that overlooked the Upper Spring. He hid his mount off in a small grove of scrub pine, then he crouched low on a hidden ledge.

Fourteen mounted soldiers rode up to the wide pool of the Upper Spring. Some wore Confederate uniforms, but they appeared to be Indians, with hawk or eagle feathers in their slouch hats. As he watched, Dirt feared this was an advance guard of the Rebels. The Confederate rangers climbed off their horses and let them drink from the pool.

A freight wagon pulled up behind them and a White officer in a Confederate uniform climbed out of the driver's seat. Dirt heard him telling the rangers to rest a while. Gazing back toward the west, Bradshaw spotted the cattle he'd been following earlier. The six cows were about a mile off, ambling back to the Cold Spring station.

Crouching low, Dirt Bradshaw eased back to Waukesha, climbed back up on the filly and slow-walked away. He used the hill as cover. "We're in big trouble," he whispered. After gaining some distance, Bradshaw hurried his pace.

Back at the stage stop, Lee Sixkiller had worked his way around the thick support post of the barn. He stood on his tiptoes and was rubbing his ropes on a rusted nail in the post. The Cherokee had to hurry; if the girl brought lunch too soon, she might catch him trying to escape. While jerking up and down and pulling sideways at the binding ropes, Sixkiller also gnawed at the ropes around his wrists with his bare teeth. Sixkiller wondered if he should take the girl hostage and make her tell him where the White men had hidden the gold. Maybe he could carry her off and make her his woman.

When the strands around his wrist were separated enough, the Cherokee twisted around and used the nail to break the rope. Now he quickly worked on the knots that tied him to the post. Minutes later, Sixkiller was free.

Walking over to the closed barn door, Sixkiller peered out through the cracks. He did not see or hear the young woman. Over at the road ranch's small corral, Lee spotted his own horse. He waited and listened. Reckoning that WaShana was in the station house, the Cherokee opened the barn door just enough to allow passage. He stepped outside. There, at his feet, lay an iron chisel. Sixkiller picked it up; he could use it as a weapon, to use on the girl.

"Go ahead and git!" said the girl's voice, startling the Cherokee. Perched up on a boulder, WaShana Nicole took straight aim with the double-barreled shotgun. "Go away from here—or I will shoot you," she threatened. "This gun will blow those oats right out of your belly!"

Sixkiller dropped the chisel. "Don't shoot me, Girl! Can I take my pony?" he raised both hands in the air.

"That's all you're taking. It's already saddled. Don't you dare come back," WaShana demanded.

"You won't shoot me," said the Cherokee. He grinned, still trying to bargain with the young woman. "I think you set me free, because you've fallen in love with me. Right?"

"Wrong!" WaShana clicked the hammers back on the shotgun. "Dead wrong—if you don't leave!"

Lee Sixkiller vaulted over the corral fence and jumped up on his horse. The gate to the corral was unlatched; the Cherokee and his mount bolted away.

Sixkiller did not look back until he was out of shotgun range. He saw the girl now held a pistol straight up in the air. She fired it—once, then twice. The Cherokee decided to head for the Cherokee Nation, for the shots were a warning, to summon the White man back to the station. As Sixkiller galloped away, he heard the girl laughing scornfully.

Maybe she is part Comanche after all, thought Sixkiller.

Discovering the remnants of the burnt freight wagon, Miles Wells pondered his next move. He and the Chickasaw scout were bent over, studying the multitude of horse tracks leading away from the wreckage. "What do you suggest, Mr. Dare?" Miles asked.

"Most of the tracks continue down the Trail," said Will Dare. "Yet some of them might be Federals, giving them pursuit."

Miles Wells agreed with this assessment. "We not only have to track Ortiz—we also have to dodge the Yankees while doing it. Surely, they will break off from the main route. Eventually, right?"

"There is no guarantee with Ortiz. He was supposed to meet the others in Texas, but I told Yeager not to trust him. Any man who deals with the Kiowa or the Comanches is ruthless," said Will Dare.

Will Dare had grayish, blue eyes and his short-trimmed hair made him look White, yet his complexion was deeply tan and he had the high cheekbones and demeanor of a Native American. The Chickasaw spoke more distinctly and deliberately than most White men Miles knew, yet there was a strange agitation about the tall scout. Miles felt it sprang from years of navigating the world of Anglos and the various tribes in the Indian Nations Territory.

"I will go south," the lean frontiersman announced. "You take the wagon and the Cherokees along the Trail, going west by southwest. After you reach McNees' Crossing, in the New Mexico Territory, follow the first group of tracks that veer south of the main Trail." The scout stared intently at Miles Wells, to make sure he understood. "McNees' Crossing is very apparent, it crosses a rock-bottom creek in a wide-open terrain with no trees."

Miles Wells stated that he knew the place. "What will you be doing?" he asked.

"We will meet up again, Lieutenant. I most assure you," said Dare.

Wells was surprised at the Chickasaw saying he could foresee future events. "Yes. Certainly—I hope," he said. "But what about the third group, that goes southeast from here?"

"If they do not turn south, like these other ones, they will be....." Dare searched for the appropriate word. "Annihilated. By the great Comanche horse warriors –the Quahadi." The frontier scout's visage turned grim. "Unless the Comanchero, Ortiz, is with that group. I chance he is not."

"Take Mr. Allison with you," Miles suggested. Besides Wells himself, the trail hand was the only other Anglo in the platoon. Clay Allison was ill-tempered and often contentious with the Indians, yet Dare could keep him in line.

The scout shook his head. "No, I will take young Burningtree. I can teach him to follow signs, for he is willing to learn."

"Alright then," said Miles Wells, hiding his disappointment. "Are you sure he's the only one you need?"

Will Dare simply walked away, without answering. He did not seem to like wasting any more time.

CHAPTER 22

Dirt was angry when he returned to the stage stop and learned the Cherokee had escaped. He told WaShana she should have kept a better watch on the prisoner. WaShana decided not to reveal how she had let Sixkiller leave. "I saw he got loose," said the girl, as Bradshaw looked at the sheared ropes. "I shot at him, but he was too far away. I am sorry."

"It looks like he gnawed, or cut his way free somehow," Bradshaw observed. "Durn it, girl—but this is the least of our worries now. We've got Indians coming up the Trail. Confederate Indians, of all things. Pack up what you can. Hurry!"

WaShana followed Dirt out of the barn. "We cannot leave without Rodrigo. He will not know where we go," she said.

"He'll just have to figure it out," said Dirt. "Pack whatever you can on your horse and let's skedaddle. I will go dig up the gold."

Bradshaw took a shovel and the group's remaining pack mule over to the far end of the corral; he began digging at the base of a fence post. The gold bullion lay at the bottom of the post hole. Dirt pulled the heavy bricks out one at a time and placed them in an old Pony Express mailbag on the mule, then he walked over to a small tool near the station house. There he found a small army tent, which he packed on the mule.

Inside the sacked trade store, WaShana sought any other items they might use on the Trail. Red Water had given her a knife, a pouch with various medicines and a canteen. WaShana grabbed some cooking utensils and cotton cloth, for bandages.

Dirt Bradshaw walked in and searched behind the store counter. He found a pencil and paper. "We will follow the soldiers west, on the Trail," said Dirt. As he wrote, he said the message out loud: "Dear Amigos. WaShana and I have gone West on the Trail. We have seen Indians. Be careful—we hope to see you in New Mexico. We will wait for you at the 'Rabbit Ears' camp. Signed D. Bradshaw." Dirt looked up. "Anything you want to add?" he asked.

WaShana peered over the counter at the message. "I do not remember how to write," she said, ashamed at the fact. "And Rodrigo cannot read."

"Well, Lew McManus can. Come here and hold the pencil. I will guide you,' said Bradshaw. "We print first."

Guiding the girl's hand, the miner added a postscript:

Rodrigo, Come find me. I will wait for you.

Love,
WaShana Nicole.

Tears watered in the girl's eyes, as Dirt Bradshaw guided her into signing her name in cursive. Overwhelmed with gratitude, WaShana thanked him. Dirt walked over to the wooden whiskey keg and tacked the note to the side of the barrel. "That's so Big Lew will find it." said Bradshaw. He can read it to your Apache Romeo. Now, let's get out of here!"

Later that afternoon, Miles Wells and his Confederate rangers arrived at the Cold Springs station. The Cherokees scoured around for provisions. Miles Wells noted a recent grave outside the store; he looked for traces of the renegade gold robbers and for any clue as to who was following them. Private Drunk went inside the store; when Wells entered a few minutes later, he found the Cherokee drinking from a whiskey keg. The ranger held his mouth under the spout, slurping up the contents.

"I scout for you," said the private, when Miles told him to quit. Private Drunk handed him a piece of notepaper.

"Yeah, you're scouting out how much liquor's still in the barrel, I can tell," Miles Wells muttered. The Confederate agent scowled as he read the message. The first part gave vague directions; there might also be soldiers following Ortiz and the robbers. The bottom of the letter was a love note. "Rodrigo?" Miles questioned. "Can it be Red Water?" Miles Wells knew the Mescalero from the brief war in New Mexico.

"Nah, that's impossible," he said, crumpling the note and casting it aside. The ball of paper bounced over to a section of the floor that was stained with dried blood.

"Ortiz was here," said Miles. "The Federals wouldn't have shot the station manager. That's whose grave that is."

Sergeant Ned Mole appeared in the doorway. He told Wells that the rangers had captured several chickens and a steer had wandered into the barnyard.

"Cook 'em up," Wells ordered. His Confederate detachment had ridden hard the last few days and nights. They deserved a good meal and rest. "But make our camp up yonder, below those bluffs and post a guard atop one of them. We don't want a Union patrol coming back and surprising us tonight."

That evening, the Confederate Cherokees made merry, roasting a side of beef and two chickens on makeshift spits. Miles Wells enjoyed the luxury of sitting by his tent and sipping whiskey while smoking a cigar. "I might as well be like General Grant," Miles told Sergeant Moler, who sat beside him. "At the battle of Shiloh, General Sherman was upset at the Confederate victory that day. General Grant said, "That's alright, we'll get 'em in the morning."

"How do you know these things?" asked Moler.

"I read the Yankee papers when I was in Denver," said Miles. "You know, if I had been in charge of this whole operation, it would have all been a lot less sloppy." Wells puffed on his cigar, sipped his whiskey, then made a face. "And we would have a finer quality of libations."

Later that evening, as Miles was preparing to carve a roasted chicken, the guard atop the bluff shouted that a rider was approaching. The horseman was waving a white cloth. When the rangers brought the man over to their commander, the rider said he was a Cherokee, named Lee Sixkiller.

"If you seek the stolen gold, I know where the robbers are going," said Sixkiller. "And I know who is chasing them. Five Union soldiers. And some strange people."

Miles Wells was unimpressed—and annoyed. He desired to feast on roast beef and chicken breast. "How do we know you're not a spy?" he said. "Because it's strange you know both sides of the situation. Take him prisoner, Sergeant."

"No! Listen to me first," Lee Sixkiller protested.

Miles put down his tin plate. "Alright, let me ask you a question. Is there an Indian named Red Water with them?"

"Yes, yes! Rodrigo is his first name. And there's a girl—and a big man, a southerner, like you. The big sonuvabitch tried to kill me."

Wells told his men to release their hold on the Cherokee. Picking up his plate again, he asked, "Who was the big man?"

"Mack—McManus," said Sixkiller.

The Confederate agent put down his fork. "Lew McManus? What? I thought he was prospecting way down in the New Mexico Territory."

"I told you. He is chasing the men you were supposed to meet—the men I was riding with. Sergio Ortiz and Jack Jernigan." Sixkiller eyed the beef and chicken the ranger officer was eating. "If you feed me now, I will guide you, Sir."

"Tell me more first. Where is Sergio Ortiz going?"

The five cavalrymen journeyed west all day and well into the evening. Sergeant Mikowski figured they were probably in the New Mexico Territory by now. He and his soldiers came to a shallow, rock-bottomed creek crossing, where some travelers on the Santa Fe Trail had once camped. Mikowski stood on a small rise, overlooking the crossing. McNee's Crossing was named for a young trader and scout, who was killed by Comanches in 1828.

Mikowski studied a series of worn caravan ruts on the east side of the crossing. Two of his men rested on flat rocks beside the almost dry creek; two other soldiers took the horses and the three mules slightly downstream, to a spot where they could drink. Still on the trail of the mercenaries who had deserted the Confederacy, the Union sergeant wanted to press on, yet now it was too dark to track. Although previous wagon trains had used this place as a campsite, Mikowski feared the terrain was too flat and open; a campfire could be seen from over a mile away. He and his men were bone tired; however, so the Sergeant decided to make camp anyway.

"Go ahead and get some sleep, fellows. We'll start out early tomorrow," Mikowski said, when the soldiers returned with the animals. "I will take the second watch. Burton, you take the first. It's just hardtack biscuits and jerky tonight. We can build a small fire before daylight, to make coffee before we head on."

The soldiers grumbled about having a meager meal. After eating fried chicken, scrambled eggs, hoecakes and beans, supplemented by draughts of whiskey the previous night, they missed the cooking and camaraderie of Dirt Bradshaw and Lew McManus. One of the soldiers was from Denver; his name was Gregory Abramson and he knew the Bradshaw brothers from the mining camps. Two cavalrymen hailed from Colorado City. The fourth soldier, Corporal Jack Burton, was a Cornishman. Like Mikowski, he had worked in the coal mines at Trinidad before the war.

"If only we had slayed a rabbit or two along the way," said Burton. "That would have made a very fine supper."

Sergeant Mikowski sat on a rocky knoll above the creek while his men slumbered. The moon was almost full now; he could see his shadow. Although he felt exhausted from physical exertion and little sleep, the cavalryman's mind was active and somehow strangely attuned to the natural world around him. Water trickled in the stream and a soft wind blew in from the northwest; after a full day in the summer sun, this was a welcome respite.

Shortly before sunrise, Mikowski decided to take a short walk. He had noticed a small grove of cedars and other trees a half-mile away; perhaps he could gather a little firewood for coffee this morning. As the earth took color, he hiked along a creekside trail, until he discovered a vivid spread of wildflowers.

Varied sorts of red, gold and blue-purple wildflowers, interspersed with Queen Anne's lace, grew beside a wide sandbar. The cavalryman remembered Christ's description of flowers being more brilliantly arrayed than King Soloman's finest robes. He also remembered Red Water, the Apache medicine chief, telling him that flowers were the tears of the Great Spirit. Mikowski took off his boots. Moments later, he stood in his bare feet like a child, feeling cool water running between his toes. Gazing back at the flowers, he imagined God as a wind-swept spirit, laughing as he scattered wildflower seeds along this rare oasis.

A sudden force spun the soldier around. Hot fire seared in his chest as he heard a rifle's report. Sergeant Mikowski's heart leaped wildly; he fell back into the water, then rolled over on his side. He saw red, yellow, blue and purple; the flowers were like a shimmering rainbow. Now the Sergeant's vision darkened and narrowed, like looking into a tunnel.

The face of a man now hovered over the dying cavalryman. Mikowski noticed how the man's face appeared angular, with a sharp jaw, beak nose and square forehead. He was White and held a rifle.

"Is he dead, Jernigan?" another man asked. Mikowski turned his head to look. It was the traitor, Alvin Reynolds.

"Pretty much. Let's get out of here," said Jernigan, then he disappeared.

The sergeant heard the muffled sounds of men shouting, calling his name. His soldiers were coming to find him—but it was too late. The flowers beside the stream swirled about in different colors, like an Aurora Borealis, then everything turned black. Sergeant Generio Mikowski died there among the flowers, shortly before sunrise, on the twenty-fourth of July, 1863.

Two days earlier, he had chiseled this date into Inscription Rock.

CHAPTER 23

Lew McManus and the Mexicano boy remained in their saddles as they watched Rodrigo ford the North Canadian River. The Mescalero told his compadres to remain on the other side. Walking in a crouch, he searched the area, looking for tracks. Humps of sand, piled up by a past flood, dotted this section of the river. Every so often, Red Water disappeared among these low sand mounds.

"Go ahead and let your horse and the mules drink," Lew McManus told the boy. Juan Villareal held a rope that tethered the two mules the searchers had brought along. McManus scanned the horizon and kept guard with his Sharpshooter rifle in hand.

When Red Water returned, Lew asked the scout what he had found. "There is a strangeness here," said Rodrigo. "Other men on horses have joined the Confederados, from downriver. They are going west now."

"That's not so strange. That Cherokee told us the groups would join back together." McManus pulled out his tobacco pouch. "Eventually, they should turn south and head for Texas."

"You do not understand. There are signs of a battle. I found blood and a man may have fallen off his horse, then he was dragged into the river."

McManus rolled a cigarette. "These are Judas-kiss bastards we are tracking," he said, "their treachery knows no bounds."

"*Si los hombres es loco,*" Juan Villareal agreed.

The Tennessean struck a match and lit his smoke. "Yessir, amigos. If they keep killing each other, we may outnumber them yet. I just want you both to know, I have no interest in keeping that gold for myself. Giving it back to the Union government might help get Rodrigo a pardon."

Rodrigo frowned. He was ready to head back to the Cold Springs station, but instead he asked, "So, we keep following these men?"

McManus nodded and puffed his cigarette. He suggested they take turns riding the mules to give their horses some rest along the way. "I think we can overtake the robbers before they reach the Rita Blanca—if we ride on into the night."

The three searchers followed the tracks along the river, reaching the two forks of the North Canadian by nightfall. Rodrigo guided them westward, onto the high plains of New Mexico. McManus became perplexed when he realized the raiders were not aiming for the Rita Blanca. "Huh, what gives?" McManus wondered, when Rodrigo pointed this out. "So, they're not going to Texas—but back to the Santa Fe Trail?"

"Si, to join back up with the hombre named Ortiz," said Red Water.

"Or maybe not. If Sixkiller lied, there's no telling where they are heading," McManus replied.

"The tracks do not lie," Red Water insisted.

The Tennessean agreed. He told his friends he had enough riding for now. They were now in the grasslands; it was best to rest, for they had gone eighteen hours without sleep. Seeing no reason to build a fire, the three men picketed their horses and mules where the animals could graze. Lew McManus and Juan went to sleep immediately, using their saddles as headrests.

Rodrigo Red Water kept watch. Judging by the angle of the three-quarter moon, it was almost midnight. The coyotes were yipping to each other. Rodrigo thought about WaShana, the former Beloved Captive, who had captured his own heart. Gold or no gold, he wanted to go back to her at the Cold Spring station. He did not need the Territorial government's forgiveness and WaShana might not do well living back in a White man's world.

Lew McManus took the second watch in the wee hours of the morning. He tried to stay alert, smoking cigarette after cigarette and listening to the summer night sounds of the prairie. Crickets chirped, the wind blew softly, and once in a while, Lew heard the coyotes talking to each other. A desert owl called to its mate. McManus wondered about Rosa Amarilla Del Rio; he half-hoped she would take back up with Miguel LaHoya, due to his own absence. The Tennessean also thought about his family back home. His older brother, William, had joined the Confederate Army. Nashville and most of Tennessee had been taken by the Federals. With the war still raging back in the South, McManus wondered why he was helping the Union here in the Southwest.

Juan Villareal had agreed to take the third watch, yet McManus decided to let the Mexicano boy sleep until daybreak. Despite the danger in building a fire out here in the open, Lew had packed some kindling and he wanted coffee. The three men had halted only a half-mile west of a creek, so Lew decided to walk back and fill the canteens for the next day's ride. It was best to keep busy, lest he fall asleep.

The walk took longer than Lew expected. When he reached the draw that led to the river, it was nearing daybreak. McManus hurried, filling the canteens and gathering some driftwood. Suddenly, far off in the distance, Lew thought he heard a gunshot.

Dropping the firewood, McManus rushed back to camp. "No time for coffee, dammit." he growled.

Rodrigo was already awake and he also heard the rifle shot. "There was only one," he stated. "Perhaps a hunter, but we should go see."

They awakened the boy and quickly saddled their horses. Looking off to the southwest, Lew noticed a lone mountain and a butte that looked familiar. "That's the Rabbit Ear Mountain. We saw it on the stage route two weeks ago. We've made a big circle, back towards the Trail."

"Yes, I remember a crossing, where there is a campsite," said Red Water. "Slow down, we must ride more quietly."

Parallel ruts in the shortgrass revealed the Santa Fe Trail. Lew drew out one of his revolvers, and Juan did likewise. Rodrigo held a Springfield Indian Carbine they had confiscated from Lee Sixkiller. It had been converted from a musket, having a cut-down barrel and the stock was decorated with brass tacks.

When they came upon McNee's Crossing, Rodrigo's heart fell. Four of the U.S. soldiers were assembled on a grassy knoll and the blue-clad body of a fifth cavalryman lay draped upon one of the horses.

"It's Sergeant Mike." said Lew, confirming Red Water's worst fear. "What happened, you-all?" he asked the soldiers.

"Och, we think it was the gold robbers," said Private Abramsen. "Our Sergeant was on guard duty last night."

"They ambushed him?" McManus asked.

"He had gone out to gather wood, when the hellions blasted him," Corporal Burton replied.

Lew McManus hung his head. This Scandinavian and the Cornish coal miner seemed green to the ways of the frontier; the group should never have encamped in such an open area, unless they were part of a large group. Then again, he and Red Water had done the same thing that night, due to their exhaustion.

"Show me where you found him," said Rodrigo.

Abramson led the Mescalero upstream to the bend where the sergeant had fallen. Searching around, Red Water noticed how some of the wildflowers had been trampled. Two bootprints, different from the footwear of the ones on the creekbank, appeared fairly fresh on the sandbar. This man wore the narrow-toed high-heeled boots of a cattleman, with spurs attached. Rodrigo had seen the same prints along the North Canadian River.

Rodrigo and Abramson walked back to the crossing where McManus and the Cornishman were digging a grave on the grassy knoll. "The men we were following shot your Sergeant," Red Water told the cavalrymen. Rodrigo held a cluster of wildflowers in his hand.

Lew McManus handed his shovel to Private Abramson, to give him a turn at digging. "This is the first of our own to fall, Amigo. And I am tired of grave digging. If you want to go back to Miss WaShana, I can't blame you."

Red Water paused to consider this, then he replied, "First, we must learn where the banditos are going."

Private Abramson stepped over onto the pile of dirt beside the grave, when the Mescalero Apache noticed something. Red Water bent down to look at the soldiers' boot print. "Aho, those are the same as the other tracks I saw yesterday. At the river—and again, up on the bank of this creek. Where our friend was shot."

"These are Army issue," said Jack Burton, the coal miner from Cornwall. He pointed to his own black, round-toed boots. "That means it was Alvin Reynolds, who deserted us, back in Kansas."

After placing Sergeant Mikowski in his grave and covering it with earth, Red Water dabbed wildflower seeds into the soil. "We sprinkle these seeds, the tears of the Great Spirit, for you my friend," he said. The medicine chief stood and raised his hands up to the sky. "This is a wide world we travel over. Now, there are shadows cast between us. There are steep gullies between us. You died on this trail we are on, but now you must go, Sergeant. You must walk on the whirlwind—on the air."

Lew McManus felt the hair stand up on the back of his neck; he took off his hat and bowed his head; for he realized Red Water was speaking to the deceased soldier's spirit. The cavalrymen also removed their hats.

"Do not reach for even a hair of our heads," the Mescalero prayed, "But help us find what we are seeking. Chamahua will find you. You have done God's will, but now you must go. For now you are free of this world."

Rodrigo lowered his arms and the cavalrymen all whispered, "Amen." Juan Villareal, who had walked up as Rodrigo was speaking, made the sign of the cross.

"That was as Christian a burial as I've ever seen," said Jack Burton. He held Mikowski's hat in his other hand. Another soldier, one of the men from Colorado City, had tied a stick to a picket stake, to make a crude wooden cross. He stuck it into the earth, then Burton placed the sergeant's hat on top of it.

"Alright, that's enough ceremony," said Lew McManus. "I'm gonna build a fire and make some dang coffee. Then we have to determine where those desperado bastards have gone."

Later that same morning, Dirt Bradshaw and WaShana Nicole were also disheartened when they found the grave at McNee's crossing. "What a dirty shame," said Bradshaw, seeing the officer's hat; he knew it belonged to Mikowski. "They killed Sergeant Mike."

WaShana bowed her head, then she noticed familiar tracks. "Rodrigo was here!" she exclaimed, pointing to the imprints of Red Water's Mexican sandals.

"That's good, at least," said Dirt. "Big Lew and our boy Juan were here too, I reckon. Let's look around to see which direction they took."

Finding the recent remains of a campfire and a small pile of coffee grounds, Bradshaw determined that McManus had indeed joined back up with his fellow searchers. "See those cigarette stubs? The big lug was here, for sure. They're still half a day ahead of us, I reckon. Maybe they'll make camp at the next stop on the Trail. At Rabbit Ear Creek, there's good water, wood and plenty of game."

"We must hurry then," said WaShana. "All their tracks are staying on the main path. For now."

Dirt was impressed with WaShana's tracking ability. Having lived with the Comanche people, she could tell the difference between the hoof prints of Rodrigo's Apache pony, a cavalryman's horse, the mules, and the large shoeprints of Lew's tall gelding. Fairly fresh wagon tracks also indicated that the searchers were still on the trail of Sergio Oritz and his men.

As they hurried down the Trail, Dirt let WaShana ride his horse, Waukesha, in order to rest the girl's horse. Bradshaw now rode the pack mule, which gave him some difficulty, but it was important to spare each animal from constant burden.

Dirt felt cautiously optimistic; they were well ahead of the Confederate Indian soldiers, who probably camped overnight at the deserted Cold Springs station. Bradshaw had refrained from drinking whiskey for nine days now. His mind was clear, as it had been when he was riding with the Ute Indians back in Colorado. He began humming a song.

"You seem happy," WaShana observed, smiling at him. "Why are you, when we may face danger?"

"Mornings always give me hope," said Dirt. "Even in times of trouble, when things look dire, I take comfort when a new day is given me." He chuckled. "That's something us old people do."

"You are not that old. You are only a little older than Rodrigo."

"Ha, maybe so. But I think Red Water discovered the fountain of youth, when he found you."

WaShana's expression turned serious. "Will I ever see Rodrigo again? What if we never catch up? What if he gets killed?"

"I think your Apache and the Tennessee man know what they're doing." Dirt wanted to reassure her, for he felt like an uncle or an older brother to the former captive. She had been dealt a poor hand in her early youth. Dirt had also heard Rodrigo's life story. "You know, WaShana, both you and Rodrigo have been caught between two diffirent worlds. White, so-called 'civilization' and the natural world of the Indians. I had got just an inkling of the latter, when I lived with the Ute Indians earlier this spring. Like that wild filly you're riding, you have a vitality that your corset-bound sisters back East don't get to express. I don't think you should go back to Kansas."

WaShana Nicole pondered these things. She did indeed have more memories of life with the Comanches, more than her earlier childhood in east Kansas. She did remember meals cooked on a stove, sugared desserts, warm beds, church, petticoats and dresses. "There are good things in both worlds," she said. "How will I know which one to choose, unless you take me back to the place I once lived at—as Nicole?"

Dirt Bradshaw did not know how to answer. On the American frontier, it was common for mountain men, French traders and loners to intermarry with Indian women. On the other hand, a White girl or woman who was taken or made to be the wife of a warrior would be considered a tragedy by most White Americans. People thought the woman was dishonored; any such female would be considered ruined. Dirt knew that if Nicole did indeed find any relatives, they would strongly forbid her from marrying an Apache.

"Um, where is it YOU want to go, Girl?" Bradshaw asked, dodging the question.

"I want to go to Kansas—with you, when you take the gold. And Rodrigo must come too!"

Oh, my God. How naïve, thought Dirt. *How do I explain?* "I tell you what, when we get to the first settlement we find, I will protect you, but I want you to learn some things," said Dirt.

"What?" the girl asked.

"Not all White men will treat you like those bad stagecoach yahoos, back at the Arkansas. But you want to talk to a woman. Whether she's Anglo, Mexicano, or even Chinese, you should converse with a female."

"Who are the women you know? What are they like?" asked WaShana.

Dirt felt stymied once again; he blushed. "Well, let me just say—you need to speak with a lady."

CHAPTER 24

Travelers on the Santa Fe Trail frequently used Rabbit Ears Creek as a resting spot and Lew McManus felt encouraged when his group encountered a wagon train camped at the site. However, the group's scout, Red Water, did not share Lew's enthusiasm. The caravan, mostly composed of traders from Santa Fe and Taos, had been there two days, leaving many tracks. This confounded Rodrigo's ability to search for signs of the gold raiders.

"Cheer up, Rodrigo," McManus told the Mescalero. "This means we'll just ask for information. I'll ask these men if they saw a wagon coming from Cold Spring. And maybe we can send a message back to Dirt."

McManus and the cavalrymen questioned people in the camp and learned that a supply wagon, escorted by a half dozen men on horseback, had indeed passed through the previous evening. "They were a strange group," an old turquoise dealer from Taos told McManus, "because they only stopped long enough to water their animals and do some bartering." The elderly trader seemed to be an odd fellow himself. His long, white hair was braided down both sides of his head, like an Indian; he wore a multi-colored, Mexican serape', a wide-brimmed Stetson, and he spoke with a Texas accent.

"What did they look like?" Lew McManus asked.

"There were two Mexicanos and the rest of them were Anglo. Eight men in all. The older Mexican bought some turquoise bracelets from me—he seemed to be in charge. I thought that was peculiar in and of itself. Usually, an American is in charge."

Rodrigo and one of the cavalrymen, Corporal Burton, walked up while Lew was speaking with the old man. "Was one of the Americans around my age, with brown, wavy hair and a round head?" Burton asked. "He would have a southern accent, and wear boots, like mine here."

"He came along later, with another group. Four men, with three pack mules, who came through just this morning. They were in a hurry, too. And the man you just described, he also asked about the Mexican and the wagon. What's going on?" the trader asked. "Are you chasing them?"

McManus, Corporal Burton and Red Water all exchanged glances. "Should we tell him?" McManus asked.

"Oh, one more thing," the old man added. "After they asked about the first group, those four men did not follow them down the Trail. They took off to the north, like they were going toward the Colorado Territory."

"Aye, that would be Alvin Reynolds!" Corporal Jack Burton exclaimed. "The blackard who betrayed us to the gold raiders is headed back to Colorado."

The trader's eyes grew wide. "Gold, you say?" he whispered. "That explains why neither group would say what they were carrying."

Lew McManus grabbed the old man by the elbow and took him aside, "Breath not a word of this to anyone, Old Feller. We're after a

Federal shipment of gold that was stolen by the Confederacy. Who are you, by the way?"

"My name's Wilson. Buddy Wilson. I came up from Texas years ago, to trap in the Rockies. If you need a guide, I know Colorado and New Mexico pretty well."

Lew McManus took a deep breath, then exhaled. "No, we've got a scout. But we need a favor. Since you're going east, I need you to deliver a message to some friends of mine, at the Cold Spring stage station."

As Dirt and WaShana approached an unknown creek, their horses seemed on the verge of giving out. They had brought along an army bivouac tent from the stage station, so Bradshaw set it up, in order to give WaShana Nicole some degree of privacy. "I see why they call it a 'dog tent'. You could shelter two dogs in it, but two men would have to be pretty tight with one another to share this shelter," Dirt commented.

"Are you sure, Mr. Dirt? We can take turns, if you want," said WaShana.

"You go ahead, Missy. I'll keep an eye on the horses for a bit," Bradshaw remarked. "After I'm double-sure nobody else is coming down the Trail tonight, I'll bed down outside."

After the girl settled in, Dirt spread out his bedroll by a circle of small rocks, where some previous travelers had built a fire. It was just after sunset. Gazing off to the south, Dirt saw the Rabbit Ears, the mountain and butte which served as a distinctive landmark for travelers on the Cimarron Cutoff.

Bradshaw stacked some kindling inside the circle of rocks. He sat down, resting back upon his saddle and the saddlebags containing the gold bullion. *Nicole has no business being out here in this god-forsaken wilderness,* Dirt thought. *Why on earth didn't she go on to Lawrence with Davey and the Federal escort?*

Dirt Bradshaw was familiar with feeling out of place. Although he had experienced a rowdy existence since coming out West, the Colorado gold prospector felt haunted by the twin spirits of desire and loneliness. He often covered his disappointments with humor and acting gregarious; yet in the final analysis, Dirt Bradshaw was a misfit.

"Dammit, I need a drink," he told himself. "No, I only brought that along for medicinal purposes."

Bradshaw had used this excuse, back at the Cold Spring station, when he filled up an extra canteen with Lew's 'wildcat whiskey'. The almost pure grain alcohol, slightly tinged from the oak cask, could be used as either an antiseptic, a pallative for scorpion or snake bites, or even as a way to remove some paints, Dirt reasoned. "And a cure, for lonely nights on the open prairie," Dirt muttered, unscrewing the cap on the canteen.

Inside the army tent, WaShana awoke to the sounds of Bradshaw singing a bawdy chorus:

> Hey, I won't go huntin' with you Jake,
> but I'll go chasin' women.
> So put your hounds back in the pens,
> and quit your silly grinnin'.
> The moon is right and I'm half-tight,
> My life is just beginnin'
> I won't go huntin' with you Jake,
> but I'll go chasin' women!

WaShana stifled a laugh. For some reason, even though Dirt was drinking, she felt safe around this man. Although he was full of bluster, she believed a woman could boss him around. His humor was entertaining, even attractive; but she did not want a man who just made her laugh. She wanted Rodrigo Red Water; she liked it when she herself could make the often-serious medicine man laugh and be playful.

Dirt took to humming the rest of the song, for he'd forgotten the rest of the words. WaShana Nicole's heart now ached within her; she feared some nameless dread.

The Chickasaw scout and Sam Burningtree found a dead bushwhacker in a pile of debris on the North Canadian. Coming up on the same tracks Rodrigo Red Water had seen two days earlier, Will

Dare had traveled downstream to find the corpse. The boy, Burningtree, watched, as Dare waded over to the dead Confederate.

"Yep, he's one of ours. He was with the other bushwhackers," Will Dare said. "They shot him, then roped him to this log."

The young Cherokee teamster sat atop his horse and looked west. "So we go upriver now?" Burningtree asked.

The scout nodded. He held his long rifle under his armpit and pulled himself up onto his horse in one quick motion. "Yes, back to where we first saw signs of the skirmish. The other men, the ones following our raiders—they must be dealt with."

Riding beside the south bank of the river, Dare and Burningtree returned to the area of low sandhills, then they followed a single set of horseshoe tracks south, away from the river. This time, Dare let his novice, Sam Burningtree, interpret the signs.

"The horse is dragging one leg," said Sam, "is he wounded?"

"The man is wounded as well. Or else, he would have put the poor animal down and gone walking."

At one point, it was obvious that the man had dismounted. Burningtree found boot tracks and what appeared to be part of an ammunition belt. "It's another one of the Mexicanos, the one named Rodriguez," said Dare, placing a percussion cap on his rifle. "He cut the belt, to make a tourniquet. Come, we must hurry."

Dare raced forward on his better horse and Sam Burningtree followed. Minutes later, they found the wounded Mexican, sitting up against a boulder. A dead horse lay nearby. Rodriguez had been shot in his leg and his upper abdomen. Sam kept away as Will Dare tried to give the man water. The man drank, then he coughed up blood and bile, mixed with water, as he spoke softly in Spanish.

Sam Burningtree looked away, not wishing to see this man die. Sam imagined how terrible it would be to die slowly like this, alone, out here in the glaring desert.

With ever diminishing gasps, the man died. Will Dare walked over and gave the boy one of the dead man's revolvers. It was a shiny, new CSA Whitney Navy .36 caliber weapon, made from brass and iron, rather than steel.

They rode together in silence after burying the Mexicano. Finally, Sam felt he must ask about the man. "What did the man say?"

"The traitor Reynolds is also a traitor to our Cause," said Dare. "He and some other men are taking off with their part of the gold."

"We should find Mr. Wells," the boy said. Sam wanted to be back with more people, out here on the High Plains. There was safety in numbers.

"HE should try to find us," said the Chickasaw. "Or else, he is not fit to be a commander."

Miles Wells was dealing with desertions. The only other Anglo in the group, Clay Allison, had left for Texas the previous morning and now, three other Confederate rangers were missing. Sergeant Ned Mole, Private Drunk, and Private Peacheater all rode back toward the Cherokee Nation. This division of the Confederate rangers began back at the Cold Spring station, when the hothead Allison picked a fight with Drunk. After pummeling the poor Cherokee, Clay Allison said he was going to Fort Worth.

Wells now had only nine men to command, two of whom were off tracking the gold raiders who had gone south. He and his rangers rode slightly parallel to the Santa Fe Trail, for Miles did not want to encounter any Federal patrols.

Since Sam Burningtree had gone with Will Dare, Lee Sixkiller was driving the platoon's supply wagon. Sixkiller was proving to be a real pest; he kept telling the Confederate agent that they should go south, toward the Rita Blanca.

"Not until we see that Ortiz himself is heading that way," Wells insisted.

Coming up to the McNee's Creek crossing, the platoon had arrived in the New Mexico Territory. Wells noticed a gravesite, so he dismounted and inspected it. He saw Sergeant Mikowski's hat and he squatted down to examine the dirt. "This grave is fairly fresh," said Wells.

"That is not all," Lee Sixkiller interrupted. "There are tracks coming from the south. The other raiders have either joined back up with Ortiz, or they are protecting his rear flank."

"Get your own rear flank back up on that wagon," said Miles. He looked up; all of the Indian rangers stood around the gravesite and they appeared solemn. "Don't worry, fellows. I know this section of the Trail quite well, better than Will Dare. So we go onward."

All the Cherokees stood around and hesitated. "What is it?" Wells asked.

"Are we not in Union Territory now?" one of the rangers questioned. He was a Private named Deerfinder. "And that hat belongs to a Yankee cavalryman, Sir."

"Yes-what of it?" Miles asked.

Another soldier spoke up: "We all agreed to go with you, because we were told we'd be going to Texas. Not Federal Territory."

"This is Mutiny!" Wells shouted.

"I agree, Mr. Wells," said Sixkiller. "I am with you, Sir."

The rangers muttered among themselves. Although he stood beside the Confederate agent, Lee Sixkiller had not yet been allowed a weapon. Miles Wells wondered what he should do now. He gazed over at the grave; now that a Union soldier had been killed, the stakes were higher. It was dangerous to remain here on the Santa Fe Trail, where the U.S. Army would be looking for anyone who might be the killer. "Look, there are riders coming this way," Sixkiller remarked.

Two riders approached from the south. The Indian rangers drew out their rifles and revolvers; however, they were relieved when they recognized Will Dare and Sam Burningtree. "Why do you tarry here?" asked Dare, when he rode up to the crossing.

"You said there would be tracks heading south, but we have not seen any," Miles Wells replied. "What did you discover?"

"Sergio Ortiz is not with the group that went south back at the Upper Spring," Will Dare said, "but we found two of his men down on the North Canadian. One was dead and we found the other one as he lay dying. They were both shot by two traitors." Dare glanced around at the ranger platoon; his eyes narrowed. "You have lost several men, haven't you, Lieutenant?"

Miles Wells nodded. "Who are the traitors?" he asked.

"A Union deserter. One of the men you recruited. You are being careless, Mr. Wells. And the other man is Jack Jernigan." The Chickasaw now noticed Lee Sixkiller. "Who is this?" Dare asked.

Miles Wells felt defensive. "My new wagon driver. He has information about the Federals who are chasing Ortiz. It's good to see YOU, Sam," Miles told Burningtree, who so far had not said a word.

"Mr. Will says an Indian is guiding the Yankees," said Sam.

"He is a half-breed Apache," Sixkiller interrupted. "I know who they are. And they are not all Yankees. They have a young girl with them and a big sonuvabitch from Tennessee."

Miles Wells seemed annoyed. "Tell me something I don't know already. We only want the men who now have the gold."

Lee Sixkiller grew even more animated. "Yes, Sir. Yes! The big man, the one named McManus, took four bars of the gold for himself when he attacked us. Just give me a gun and I will kill him for you."

Miles broke into laughter; he knew the Tennessean. "I would like to see you try! Lew would chew you up and spit you out, like a plug of tobacco."

Will Dare pointed his long rifle at the Cherokee. "How do we know that you are not a spy?" he asked Sixkiller. "You seem to know much about the Federal men." The Chickasaw scout turned to the Indian rangers. "Put this man under guard. And why are you not on your horses?"

Although Will Dare was only one man and not an officer, all the Cherokees feared him. The Chickasaw scout was basically second-in-command to Lieutenant Wells. As Sam Burningtree lashed a rope around Lee Sixkiller, all of the rangers mounted up. One-by-one, they crossed the creek.

CHAPTER 25

Dirt Bradshaw awakened at sunrise and immediately built a fire. He needed coffee to ease a throbbing headache this morning. Spooning ground coffee into the pot while the water heated, he roused WaShana from her slumber. "We need to break camp quickly, Girl. If you take down the tent, I'll saddle the horses, okay?"

WaShana Nicole crawled out, yawned and stretched. Her face was sunburned and her hair had lightened to a golden blonde from days of riding under open skies, "How did you sleep, Miss?" Dirt asked. "I hope my barking at the moon didn't keep you awake all night."

The young woman smiled. "I slept very well, because I was so tired. How much more must we ride before we meet Rodrigo?"

"Who knows? Thanks to you, we know they're heading west on the Trail." Dirt hefted up the heavy mailsack containing the four bricks of gold and headed off to load the pack mule.

The coffee pot was perking when the miner returned. A short while later, as he poured the brew, Dirt heard a horse coming up the Trail. Bradshaw grabbed his carbine and WaShana reached for her 12 Gauge.

Approaching from the west, an elderly man, leading a pack mule of his own, held out the palm of his hand as a sign that he meant no harm. He was white-headed, with a white beard and he grinned when he noticed the young woman. "Be you Dirt Bradshaw?" the old man inquired.

"Yep, I am. How did you know, old feller?'

"I have a message from one of your associates. Hello, Miss." Bud Wilson tipped his hat and introduced himself. "Mr. McManus said you two would be at the Cold Spring station, yet you've just made my quest a lot easier."

Dirt noted the old man's features and tried to imagine what he looked like years earlier, without the braided, silver locks and the strange Mexicano attire. Wilson handed him a folded note.

"Have you read this?" Dirt questioned. Lew McManus had written about a possible rendezvous and stated that he, Juan and Red Water were following some of the gold robbers north. The four Union cavalry soldiers would be waiting for Dirt and WaShana at the Rabbit Ears Creek trail stop.

"No sir, but I've been told your purpose—and the fact that they want you and your lady friend to meet them in Cimarron."

Bradshaw handed the message to WaShana. She only recognized Rodrigo's name and her own; this frustrated her. "Where is Cim-Cimarron?" WaShana asked.

"It's on the Mountain Branch of the Santa Fe Trail," said Dirt. "I reckon the troopers want to eventually head to either Fort Union, or Fort Lyon and take the—well, the recovered items—there." Dirt did not want to reveal everything to Wilson.

"I know about the gold," Bud Wilson said, "and I'm offering to help you people. So, you've got coffee?"

As WaShana Nicole saddled her horse, Dirt and Bud Wilson drank coffee and conferred beside the fire. WaShana felt misgivings about this strange man.

"You're not 'Wolverine Wilson', are you?" Dirt asked. "Have you ever trapped fur up in the Front Range of the Rockies?"

"I've been all over the Rockies. From Taos, all the way up past Fort Bridger. But no, I don't recall that moniker," said Wilson. "When the price of beaver dropped, I took to dealing in silver and turquoise, around Taos and Santa Fe. I can guide you to Cimarron."

WaShana walked back over to the campfire. "We must go." she said. "Dirt, did you forget the Indian soldiers?"

Bradshaw's jaw dropped. "By Jove, You're right! We left Cold Springs, because some Confederate irregulars are after us," Dirt grabbed the coffeepot and doused the dwindling coals of the campfire with the last of its contents.

As WaShana and Dirt hastened to leave, Bud Wilson remained calm. "There's a wagon train coming up behind me." he said "Surely, they will dissuade any Rebels from staying on the chase,"

"WaShana and I cannot take any chances," said Dirt. "If they are after the gold, they won't be giving up just yet. It'll take us three or four days of hard riding to reach Cimarron."

An hour later, Will Dare sniffed the warm ashes in the abandoned campfire. "Coffee," he said.

"I could have told you that. There's a pile of grounds right there," said Miles Wells, standing beside the Chickasaw. The Confederate rangers had changed their appearance, exchanging their gray jackets for clothing from the supply wagon, in order to look like ordinary travelers on the Trail. Miles Wells felt he was back in his element, for he loved to concoct a storyline. For now, he was a medicine salesman once again. Miles told his men they were posing as Pueblos, or as mestizos, hired laborers on their way to Santa Fe.

The Chickasaw scout remained true to form; however, for he wore the same buckskins and carried the same swagger. "We are after Sergio Ortiz, not this Yankee and the girl," Dare insisted. "Ortiz may be going to the deep canyons of the Canadian. Maybe to a place called the Canon Encinoso, where his Comancheros have a hide out."

Once again, Lee Sixkiller spoke out: "But the big man, the one called McManus, is carrying four bars of gold." Sixkiller remained tied up in the freight wagon, next to barrels of pickles, molasses, coils of rope, sacks of flour and cornmeal and two casks of Texas whiskey. "Set me free and I will track him down for you."

"I say we shoot him," Will Dare suggested to Wells. "He can only compromise this mission."

Miles turned and told Sixkiller to be silent. "If you keep talking, I'll have you hung as a horse thief."

Looking around the fire, Dare remarked that another man had joined the man and girl. "All three are now going west," he added.

Rodrigo, Lew McManus and Juan rode northwest at a brisk pace into an area of rocks and mesas. They had left their pack mules back with the Union cavalrymen at the Rabbit Ears encampment, for Lew complained that the extra animals only slowed him down. Lew McManus wanted to get this job done. "We have fiddled around too long already, letting those honchos stay ahead of us," he said.

Although his heart was not in this chase, Red Water led the way, keeping his eye on the tracks of the outlaws. Eventually, the searchers lost sight of the Rabbit Ear Mountain, but now two other prominent peaks appeared on the horizon. Sierra Grande and further north, the Capulin cinder cone, were actually extinct volcanoes, rising steeply from the grassland plains below the Colorado border.

"They are definitely heading for the Colorado Territory," said McManus. "Hope they make camp soon."

They were tracking six men on horseback, along with two mules. At one point, the outlaws had dismounted to water their animals at a shallow creek. From their bootprints, Rodrigo determined that the two men who had shot Sergeant Mikowski were in this group. Rodrigo also noticed one other detail. "One of their horses has grown lame," he remarked.

"So we keep after them. Sunset's only an hour away and I bet they pack it in for the evening.," said McManus. "What do you say, young 'un? Are you ready for a fight?" he asked Juan Villareal.

"Si, I am ready to shoot these banditos," said Juan.

After letting their own horses drink, the three trackers set out once again, this time with McManus taking the lead. Riding due west, into the sunset, they planned to stay on the hunt into the night. The trail led them between the two mountains, then it turned toward the northern peak.

They were now on the edge of a grassy slope. It was well after dark, yet the moon had risen in the east. "Look, there's a light halfway up the hill," McManus whispered. Get down, don't let 'em see us." Quietly as possible, the three riders dismounted. "Stay here with the horses, Juan," said Lew.

"No. No, Señor Lew, I want to fight," the boy replied.

Lew McManus looked at Rodrigo and wanted his opinion. "They have camped on high ground, so they can see anyone approaching from below," Red Water said softly.

"Yeah, but I don't think they know they're being followed," Lew whispered, "or else they wouldn't have built a fire."

Rodrigo Red Water had an idea; he would steal all the men's horses. "The grass on this hill is high. I can sneak up there quickly, before the moon is overhead."

McManus nodded. "If you're goin', go now then. We'll hobble our horses and be right behind you,"

Carrying his Springfield carbine, Red Water eased stealthily up the grassy slope. The five outlaws had camped two-thirds of the way up on the cone-shaped mountain. Their horses were picketed off in a nearby draw. Suddenly the grass ended and the ground turned to black rock and cinders. Rodrigo could get no closer without crawling.

Hiding at the edge of the grass, the Mescalero heard the men talking. Five of them sat around the campfire, eating, their faces and profiles illuminated by the blaze. A sixth man, standing off in the shadows, held a rifle and seemed to be keeping an eye on the horses and mules.

"Come on, Jack, have some of this wild turkey and these beans," one outlaw offered.

"It ain't done yet, I ain't dying of dysentery up in the high plains," said the man standing. "Why did you all leave the Trail? We were all going to meet back up at the Rock Crossing."

"All you've done is complain since you got here, Jernigan," the first man remarked.

"Well, you should have killed Rodriquez outright, instead of wounding the poor Mexicano. You're leaving a trail even a fool could follow."

"What the hell, Jernigan? If you don't like the way I'm doing things, go back to Ortiz down in the desert. Me and my boys are taking our share to Colorado." This outlaw was sharpening a large hunting knife on a whetstone. Rodrigo noticed he was wearing a Union soldier's jacket; it was Corporal Alvin Reynolds, the traitor.

"Just might do that," scoffed the man named Jernigan. He stepped closer to the firelight. Jernigan had sharp features: a prominent brow, long jaw line, and his mouth was clenched in a tight snarl. Rodrigo heard the scrape and jingle of spurs on the rocky ground. This was the man who had shot Sergeant Mikowski.

"Any of you fellahs with me?" asked Jernigan. "Or do you want to stay sitting ducks, fartin' around this damned bonfire?" Some of the outlaws laughed and one of them threw a log on the fire. This was enough noise to cover the sound of Rodrigo crawling off sideways, toward the horses.

Red Water made a split-second decision. He might not be able to steal the men's horses, but he could yank up the picket stakes and scare the animals off. Turning over on his side, he saw a black shape in the grass behind him; Lew McManus grinned back and nodded.

Everything happened in an instant. The horses over in the draw reared up and blew through their nostrils; an outlaw shouted; the horses bolted. Lew McManus quick-fired with both of his big revolvers; the outlaw named Jernigan shot back with his rifle into the darkness. Rodrigo took aim and shot one outlaw in the hand, making him drop his tin plate of beans. Jernigan ran off and grabbed the nearest horse.

The outlaws jumbled about in hasty confusion. Before he could fire another shot, Rodrigo saw Jernigan riding away. He also spotted the Union Corporal; Reynolds was making a break for it, chasing after two mules, which were heading up the mountain.

Juan Villareal now appeared and fired his pistol at Reynolds, but he missed. One of the other outlaws also escaped; two were dead, and the wounded man raised his hands to surrender. "Damn, I'm out of breath," Lew McManus wheezed. He looked winded from hastily crawling up the slope.

"Should I go back for our horses?" asked Juan. He pointed his pistol at the outlaw who had surrendered.

"Go ahead," said Red Water. "We cannot catch the traitor on foot, but he has to come down the mountain somehow," Rodrigo pointed his carbine at their prisoner.

Lew McManus leaned back against a large rock and looked over the outlaw's campsite. Two of the six thieves lay stone dead. Half of a turkey hung suspended on a spit over the fire and a pot of beans had spilled out onto the coals. Lew saw no sign of the stolen gold. "Damn! The gold is packed on those mules," he said. "That's why that feller took off after them."

"You sound like you're from the South," said the prisoner, sitting down on the ground. "Which side are you on?"

"Mine," said McManus, lighting a cigarette.

Up on the summit of the extinct volcano, Corporal Alvin Reynolds finally caught the second mule. The light of the nearly full moon lit up a panorama view of a long mesa, the Sierra Grande Mountain and the snow-capped mountains of Colorado in the far distance. Reynolds could see Kansas, Colorado, New Mexico and the Indian Territories from this height. He felt wonderfully exhilarated. All this gold was his now. Reynolds reached into the pack on the mule and stared at a gold ingot, shimmering in the moonlight. "Hot damn, this is what I came West for!" he exclaimed, standing at the edge of the ancient crater's rim.

The crack of a rifle rang out across the mountaintop; Corporal Reynolds was thrown against the mule. Spinning around, he saw the far-off vista once more; then he fell like a stone, down into the 400-foot, deep crater.

CHAPTER 26

Thirty miles south of the other searchers, Dirt Bradshaw and WaShana joined back up with the four U.S. cavalrymen. With the Rabbit Ears Mountain at their backs, they continued on to Round Mound, another stopping point on the Cimarron Cutoff. The old man, Bud Wilson, asked to join their group, as he intended on going to Cimarron now.

The next day, the group kept following the old trail ruts westward, until they viewed an outcropping of rocks and a mesa. "There's the Point of Rocks," said Bud Wilson. "It has a good spring, so I suggest we stop for the night." The old trapper pointed off to the west, where dappled clouds of a mackerel sky glowed in pink and lavender hues. "There's going to be some storms coming in the morning ."

"Let's look around when we get there. Maybe there's some tracks and other signs that the gold raiders have passed through recently," Dirt suggested.

"Oh yeah, we've been following them all this time," the old trapper agreed. "I've seen fresh horseshoe prints here and there."

WaShana Nicole was saying little. She'd been disappointed since the previous day, when the men decided to keep tracking Sergio Ortiz, rather than heading north—where Rodrigo had gone. There was no guarantee that he would make it to Cimarron.

Arriving at the spring, where cottonwoods and willow trees provided some late afternoon shade, Dirt pitched the dog tent, while WaShana gathered wood. The cavalrymen tended to the group's horses and mules. "It's nice of you to guide us, Old Timer," Dirt told Wilson, "but I thought you were heading east, with that wagon train."

Bud Wilson stacked a small pyramid of sagegrass and sticks to build a campfire. "When you-all said there were Indians on up the Trail, I decided I could just as well sell my turquoise in Cimarron. One good thing about growing old—you learn how to avoid a ruckus."

"Hah, I reckon so," Dirt laughed, "yet that's hard to do in war time. Have you ever been a soldier, Bud?"

"I fought with Sam Houston at the Battle of San Jacinto, then missed the Mexican-American War, by going to trap beaver in the Rockies," said Wilson. "What about you, Dirt? What made you decide to not wear a uniform?"

Bradshaw was caught off balance by the question. "Well, I am working as a scout of sorts, for the Colorado cavalry, you know. I'm more of an independent thinker, going my own way. Like you."

Bud Wilson struck his flint and lit the tinder. "It's a shame we could only trade for beans, flour and sourdough starter back at the wagon train," he said, blowing on the tiny flames. "I sure could use some fresh meat."

Dirt took the hint. "I'm powerful hungry myself. Say, WaShana said she saw what looked like javelina tracks, going back down into that yonder draw." Bradshaw walked over to the tent and retrieved his shotgun, just as WaShana Nicole returned with an armload of firewood. "I'm thinking of hunting down some pork chops for us, Girl," Dirt told her.

"Let me show you where they might be," said WaShana.

Bradshaw and the girl headed off towards a rocky draw, covered with rabbit bush, mesquite and short cedars. Following the wild pig tracks, WaShana kept off to Dirt's right. She held a pistol for protection and worked the cedar thickets, hoping to flush one of the animals. Dirt sat up on his horse and kept his 12-gauge ready.

It was growing dark now. Dirt squinted, trying to see movement in the brush. He heard the javelinas grunting and shuffling about. "Come out where I can see you, Nicole," said Dirt.

"They're in here!" the girl shouted. "Aho, Yo!"

A loud rustling and the thud of a thrown rock made the animals bolt. The javelinas squealed and burst out of the thicket in several directions. Two of them rushed toward the prospector; Dirt fired a load of buckshot and downed one of the wild pigs.

WaShana shouted again, yet this time it was a cry of pain. Dirt jumped off his horse, then he saw a diamondback rattlesnake slither out of the rabbit bush. "A snake bit me!" WaShana cried.

When he got to the young woman, Dirt saw two marks above her ankle. WaShana Nicole sat down, as her lower leg reddened and began to swell. "Do something, please," she pleaded. Dirt picked her up, placed her on his filly and ran beside Waukesha, as they headed back to the campsite. WaShana was experiencing great pain now from the snake toxin. Bradshaw hailed the camp. "What do we have for snakebite?" he yelled to the cavalrymen. "A diamondback got her!"

Jack Burton, the corporal, grabbed a medical kit. As Dirt eased WaShana out of the saddle and laid her down by the tent, he saw the woman's eyes grow glassy. "Take slow breaths Nicole," said Dirt, trying to keep her calm. "We've all got you, Sweetheart."

The men went to work. Bud Wilson heated a sharp knife in the campfire; Dirt ripped the lower seam of the girl's trouser leg, giving him room to make an incision. "Here's the canteen with the whiskey," Private Abramsen said, offering it to Bradshaw.

"I don't know if that will help just now," said Dirt. "Maybe after she pulls through." Dirt wanted to project some confidence. WaShana's leg was still swelling; her eyelids began to droop.

Bud Wilson handed Dirt the sterilized knife. Dirt doused the ankle with alcohol, then made his incision. Black blood oozed out and his heart sank. WaShana seemed to be going into shock. "We need a blanket over her upper torso, "Bradshaw suggested. "Stay with me, WaShana."

Abramson and another cavalryman paced about, not knowing what they should do. Bradshaw sent them off to fetch the dead javelina.

"Dress it out and get me the wild hog's liver. That might suck up some of the poison," Dirt said, glancing at Bud Wilson for confirmation.

Wilson only shrugged. "Best thing is to keep her warm and calm, like you're doing," the old trapper replied.

Dirt took a drink of the wildcat whiskey, spit it out then placed his mouth on the wound. Bradshaw spat out the vile toxins, took another slug and repeated the procedure. Soon as he was handed the hog liver and placed it hard against WaShana Nicole's ankle, using it like a sponge. "Ow, Dirt, that hurts," said WaShana, regaining her consciousness.

"Did Rodrigo leave you anything in that medicine pouch for snakebites?" Dirt asked the young woman. He wanted her to talk.

WaShana thought for a moment. "Bitter snakeroot, maybe. I forget," she said "Maybe some creosote bush?"

Bud Wilson looked in the medicine bag. "I don't know which is which," he said.

"There is willow bark," said WaShana. "It will help, after a while—when my head aches."

"You've been bit before?" Dirt asked her.

"Yes. When I lost my baby," WaShana sniffed. She began to cry from this memory.

Dirt told Wilson to give him the bag. "Creosote has a definite smell," he said. "If it's not there, I have an idea."

Bradshaw threw the bloodied liver away, deciding it was not really helping. He inspected the wound. "Damn, I guess I will use the whiskey. Just to keep this clean." He took the canteen of Taos Lightning and sprinkled the alcohol on the girl's ankle, then he took a deep pull and swallowed the burning liquid. WaShana yelped.

"Can you pray for me?" she asked. "That's what Rodrigo would do."

The prospector hesitated; he had never been asked such a thing before, but reasoned this might keep WaShana calm. Bradshaw tried to remember his mother's prayers. He didn't want to pontificate, like a circuit-riding preacher or church deacon. He knelt down beside WaShana Nicole and took her hand.

"Good Lord help us. Help Nicole just now. Lord, help her get better—help me figure out what to do," said Dirt. He gently pressed his palm on WaShana Nicole's forehead. "Give this young woman peace in her heart. Don't let her die. okay? You have delivered her from bad luck before—stuff far worse than this. We know you can do it."

WaShana opened her eyes and looked relieved. Dirt told her everything would be alright. "If I die, plant flowers on my grave—or bury me in that field of flowers," said the girl. "So that I will grow many colors."

Dirt Bradshaw stayed up with the young woman all night long. He placed WaShana in the tent, where she could stay dry when the rains came. The soldiers and Bud Wilson pan-fried the wild hog's tenderloin, ate their fill, then caught some sleep, while Dirt kept watch. Dirt did not eat; he felt he had brought bad luck on the camp by killing the javelina. Sometime after midnight, he heard thunder and saw streaks of lightning off to the west; the wind picked up and it began to rain. As the storm grew worse, Dirt spoke with WaShana whenever she awoke. He readjusted the tent poles to prevent the shelter from collapsing in the wind. Several times during the night, Dirt leaned into the tent opening to make sure the girl was still breathing. An hour or so before dawn, the rain lessened. WaShana awoke and wanted to talk.

"I was bitten by a rattlesnake before," said WaShana. She forgot she had told Dirt this information earlier. "When I was a Comanche wife. It made me lose my baby. That's why the people thought I was cursed—why they sold me to the Comancheros."

"Well, you aren't cursed, WaShana," said Dirt. His clothes were completely soaked and his wide-brimmed hat had flopped down over his ears. "We aren't so much cursed by things that happen to us. We bring curses down on ourselves, by repeating bad habits that hurt us—and the people around us. Hah, listen to me, boring you with philosophy."

"Thank you, Dirt Bradshaw. You are a good man."

"Hah, last night anyway. We are gonna help you keep that leg, Girl." he encouraged her. "So you can teach that wandering rascal, Rodrigo, how to dance."

Sitting by his campfire at the Rabbit Ears Creek camp, Miles Wells came to a decision; he would divide his force, sending Will Dare and most of the Cherokees north, to track down Union Corporal Reynolds and the gold raiders who were making a break for the Colorado border. Wells explained his rationale to his two scouts, the Chickasaw Dare and Sam Burningtree. "Our group is too small to be an army. And if we stick together, there are too many of us to be effective as spies. I work best alone, or with a select few."

The Confederate agent had taken his two scouts aside after speaking with members of the wagon train heading east on the Santa Fe Trail. Wells had learned a lone wagon was going west, toward the Rock Crossing of the Canadian River. Will Dare also surmised that Alvin Reynolds had split off from the Trail and was heading north. "Sam, you will come with me," Miles Wells added, as he poked at the coals of his campfire with a bayonet. "I need someone to drive the wagon."

"What about our prisoner? Sixkiller?" Will Dare asked. "Captain Yeager said we should kill any man that takes the gold for themselves. It is the way of the Circle," he said.

Sitting on a block of pinewood close to the fire, Wells leaned in and whispered, "I'm in no mood for a drumhead court martial—nor a firing squad. Sixkiller may yet prove useful. He wants revenge on the Federals that are following Ortiz. And he wants that girl."

Will Dare frowned, then he showed the trace of a grin. "You are not cold-blooded enough to be a military leader, Mr. Wells—but you do know how to use men's weaknesses. What is it we must do?"

"We cannot use the Indian partisans much longer. They look too suspicious here on the Trail. While you track Reynolds, I will find Ortiz and his group." Wells thrust the bayonet into the ground and stood up. "I will follow Ortiz all the way to Old Mexico, if need be. And I know how sudden wealth affects thieves, gold miners and any poor gink who strikes it rich. The fools have to spend it! On wine, women, or the thrill of a gambling hall. I'll search every saloon, cantina, and cathouse in the Territory, if I have to—starting with Loma Parda and Las Vegas Grandes."

"Are you okay, Mr. Dirt?" Bud Wilson asked, touching the prospector's shoulder.

Dirt awoke with a snort and realized he had nodded off. "Oh, yeah," he muttered, coming to his senses. It was growing light and the birds were chirping.

"I checked on the girl in the tent," said Wilson. You need to get out of those wet clothes and maybe wrap yourself up in this wool blanket," he suggested. The campsite smelled of wet ashes, hog grease and mesquite; a damp fog enveloped the area this morning. Dirt had fallen asleep while leaning back on his saddle. He sat up and felt pain in his back and a stiffness in his joints from reclining on the cold hard ground. Corporal Burton and another soldier were rebuilding the fire.

"I just need a half hour," said Dirt, taking off his coat and wet shirt and shivering. Unrolling his camp blanket, he kicked off his boots and slid closer to the crackling campfire. When he awoke the second time, Dirt was surprised to see WaShana Nicole sitting beside him. All the horses and mules were saddled and packed and the soldiers were getting ready to leave."Here you go," said WaShana, handing Bradshaw a tin cup of warm coffee. The fog was gone and the girl's blue eyes appeared clear and bright—a welcome change.

"How are you, Missy?" Dirt asked.

"My leg is still a little swollen and I have a headache. But I can ride. Mr. Wilson says the Canadian River is only a few hours away from here."

Bud Wilson walked over. "You're a miracle worker, Dirt. I've never seen someone bounce back from a rattler's bite like this young girl, here," he said.

"That's due to this lass more than me," Bradshaw replied. "I was hoping we'd gotten most of the poison out before her leg started swelling. Maybe we can make up a poultice or something and keep the leg from getting worse. I remember a patch of Black-eyed Susan's down by the spring, Some Indians often mash up the roots and make a poultice,"

Leaving the Point of Rocks, the search party rode southwest on the Trail. Dirt kept an eye on WaShana all morning, to make sure she did not relapse from the reptile bite. They came to the Rock Crossing of the Canadian River early in the afternoon. The river had risen from the overnight rains, but the crossing had a stone floor, which made it the one favorable place to ford the river. Upriver, the streambed was too sandy for a wagon to cross safely. Downstream, a deep rocky canyon made it impossible to cross. "This is bad," said Bud Wilson, who led the way. "There's no fresh wagon tracks anymore."

Dirt Bradshaw urged his horse across the stream; he dismounted and looked around. "Sure enough. The rains wiped out the horse tracks, and the wagon tracks. Maybe they may have crossed before the stream flooded?" he wondered.

WaShana searched around the near side upstream and found tracks where men's boots had sunk deep into some mud, along with an old canvas tarp, tied to a tree. "Dirt, come here and look," she called to the prospector.

Dirt waded back across; he bent down and scratched the stubble of his chin. "They had men waiting. With a boat," he remarked. "Actually, two of them."

Corporal Burton agreed. "Perhaps they unloaded the gold and floated downstream," he said. He and the other three cavalrymen gazed at the high canyon walls, looking for any possible trail they could follow.

"We have no boat and no immediate way to follow," said Bradshaw, confirming their observations.

"I see the wagon," declared WaShana, pointing downstream. Dirt shaded his eyes and squinted. About a hundred yards off, the upended back wheels of the wagon spun about in a deep bend of the river. "Where are they going? What's downriver?" Private Abramson asked Bradshaw.

"Texas, eventually," Dirt replied glumly.

"There are a lot of side canyons before then," said Bud Wilson. "Any number of places they can hide the gold—and themselves." The old man knew the territory better than anyone else in the group. "There's also the Mora and the Concha rivers that flow into the Canadian. They could get out there, as well."

Dirt noticed WaShana Nicole was sitting down by the water's edge and she appeared sick once again. Bradshaw knelt down and felt her forehead. She was feverish! "This is it, fellahs," Dirt announced. "I'm taking our gal on to Cimarron. You can keep tracking, or come with us. But we're abandoning the chase for now."

END OF PART ONE

Part Two

THE REASON OF A
HIGHER PURPOSE

CHAPTER 27

The clomping of horse hooves on the hard-packed main road in Cimarron always drew the attention of the locals, especially when strangers or soldiers rode in from the Mountain Route. Two old men, an ex-miner and a veteran of the Mexican-American War, whittled away on cedar sticks, while chewing tobacco on the front porch of the Maxwell Hotel. When six men on horseback and a group of mules entered the town plaza, the old men paused in their work.

"Old Bud Wilson's got a cavalry escort," said the old veteran. He spat tobacco juice onto the dusty street. "Reckon the Federal guv'ment finally arrested the old fart?"

"What are they draggin'?" asked the miner, whose eyes were beginning to fail.

Four Union cavalrymen, leading four mules, rode alongside Wilson. At the back of the group, a younger man rode a horse, with a make-shift travois trailing behind it. The travois was constructed of willow saplings and an army blanket; a young woman, who appeared to be wounded or sick, was strapped to the stretcher.

"It's some white kid," said the veteran. "I'll go get Mr. Maxwell." He stepped over to the swinging entrance door of the hotel.

The old miner, his back bent crooked from years in a silver mine, rose from his bench and greeted Wilson. "Who you got there, Buddy? What's wrong with the girl?"

"She was snake bit, Earl," said the old trapper. "Where's Lucien?" Bud Wilson knew Lucien Maxwell, the hotel's owner, back when the land baron was only a bachelor mountain man.

"Bob went to fetch him," said the miner.

Several people stepped out on the porch. Lucien Bonaparte Maxwell, a middle-aged man with a prominent black mustache, scowled and squinted as his eyes adjusted to the bright afternoon sun. "What happened?" the hotel proprietor asked the soldiers.

Dirt Bradshaw stepped up on the porch. "This young lady was snake bitten two days ago. And I think she's got an infection." Bradshaw jumped back down to tend to WaShana Nicole.

Lucien Maxwell stepped down to look. The girl was doing poorly; her face and clothes were covered in alkaline dust, making her look like a pale ghost. Dirt Bradshaw produced a wet bandana and wiped the young woman's forehead. "I gave her some tea, with willow-bark for the fever," he said.

Maxwell scowled again. "That damned Indian medicine won't help her," he said. Turning to the people on the porch, he told Bud Wilson to go get the town doctor. "We'll bring her inside the saloon for now," Maxwell added.

Lew McManus stepped out onto the porch. Seeing WaShana and Dirt, the big Tennessean shoved the onlookers aside and helped his friends. McManus cut the travois free with two swipes of his hunting knife, then he lifted one end of the stretcher, while Dirt took the other end.

"Mr. Maxwell, Sir," said the lead cavalryman, "Corporal Jack Burton, "We need to send a telegraph message to the commander at Fort Union." The Cornishman spoke with a new authority, for Sergeant Mikowski was dead and Burton had taken possession of Dirt's four ingots of gold.

"Certainly, Corporal, What sort of message?" Maxwell asked.

"There was a federal escort robbed up in Kansas. We have recovered some of the stolen cargo, Sir."

Maxwell drew the corporal aside. "You're talking about the gold, I presume?" he whispered. "That big fellow brought in eight bars just yesterday and I have it in the hotel safe. How much more have you got? Is there more?"

"It's only part of what was stolen," Burton replied. He glanced around, making sure nobody else was hearing this conversation. "Bushwhackers and Indians killed a U.S. Treasury agent up on the Trail in Kansas. We've been chasing them ever since."

Inside the hotel, Dirt Bradshaw and Lew McManus carried WaShana Nicole over to a small couch in the lobby. "Are you still with us, Girl?" Dirt asked, checking her eyes.

Washana blinked and moaned. "Yes. Where are we?" she asked. The piece of furniture was actually a "fainting couch;" that sat between the hotel lobby and the Maxwell House Saloon and dance hall. Somewhere in the building, someone was playing an unknown tune on a piano.

"You are safe here. No snakes, No Comancheros or Confederates," said Dirt. Turning to Lew McManus, he asked, "Where is Rodrigo? And Juan?"

"Camped out along the creek outside of town," said McManus. "They don't let Indians or Mexicanos into the hotel or saloon. We killed that Union traitor, and a couple of bushwhackers. Took one prisoner, but another outlaw got away." Lew's breath smelled of whiskey.

Bud Wilson arrived with the town doctor. "You are going to be okay now, Miss," said the old man. "Before I leave, I want to give you something." Wilson pressed a cloth-wrapped object onto WaShana's palm.

The young woman looked; Wilson had given her a silver bracelet, studded with turquoise and two turquoise and silver hoop earrings.

"What a splendid gift," said Dirt Bradshaw. "Ain't it, Lew?"

"Yep," McManus agreed. "After the Doc gets you well, I'm buying you a fine dress to match this jewelry, Nicole." Turning to the doctor, McManus told him to take WaShana up to his own hotel room.

WaShana Nicole sat up. "Not yet! Why is Rodrigo not here? I must see him first!" she cried.

"You will, you will. I'll bring him in the morning," Dirt promised. He did not tell WaShana why Red Water was not at the hotel.

The doctor and Wilson helped WaShana Nicole to her feet, then they and McManus escorted her away, up to Lew's hotel room. Three of the cavalry soldiers, minus their corporal, entered the lobby.

"How about a drink, Mr. Dirt? Cousin Jack's gone off to wire Fort Union," said Private Abramsen. "I think you deserve it, as much as we do."

Dirt thought about it for a moment, then the urge felt overpowering. "Why, yes. That would be excellent," he replied.

Clutching a glass of Tennessee whiskey, Bradshaw observed the ornate interior of the Maxwell House saloon. Decorated with deep pile carpet, velvet drapes, a high molded ceiling and paintings in gold frames, it reminded Dirt of Billy Martin's dance hall emporium back in Denver. With his dusty clothes, dirt-caked boots and crumpled hat, Dirt felt out of place. He glanced over at Lew McManus, who was in animated conversation with the hotel's owner.

Lew McManus reclined back against the brass-edged bar counter and swirled a tumbler of Kentucky bourbon in his big right hand. His left hand tapped the ashes of Maxwell's finest cigar. "I am partners with a feller you met last year," said McManus. "Jimmy Carl Gray. We own a ranch up on the Rio Tecolote, raising some beeves and such. Been wonderin' if we could trade some good Texas longhorns to you, in exchange for one or two of your young bulls."

Lucien Maxwell took off his wide-brimmed cattleman's hat and scratched his balding scalp. He was a shrewd businessman, who had married into extreme wealth and the vast acreage of an old Spanish land grant. "Yes, I know Jimmy Gray. He sold me some of your sorry-assed cows a few weeks ago. I don't need any more heifers bringing disease and nose-bloats into my stock." Maxwell was offered business propositions constantly—from other cattlemen and the many traders, gamblers and speculators that passed through Cimarron. He knew how to stifle such solicitations.

Although he was just a rawhide rancher, Lew McManus was undeterred. He decided he would not be easily dismissed, like some low-rent cowhand. "Hey, I know there is more of that stolen gold still out there," Lew whispered. "Maybe we can talk business, when I can just purchase some of your high and mighty bulls outright—along with a fine stud stallion."

The land baron's thick eyebrows arched, like a pair of wooly black caterpillars, at this mention of gold. "I doubt you can afford my stud Arabian," Maxwell replied.

Lew took a long drag on his cigar and exhaled casually. "Maybe with my government reward, after I find that Comanchero and dispatch him, you'll come calling on me," he said.

"I don't need no government gold. I control the egress and the ingress on almost two million acres, boy." Maxwell poured more bourbon for both of them. "There is bound to be free gold on my Land Grant somewhere. We get prospectors, like your friend there, coming in every day." Maxwell puffed on his own cigar and the wooly worms arched high on his brow as he grinned. "No. What I need is a man like you—young, hung and high-strung. Who can knock two heads together, while drawing a pistol on a third. Someone to patrol my property. And collect my overdue rents."

"I ain't no man's employee," said Lew McManus. "Me and Jimmy Carl can take our beef to Fort Union and Fort Sumner and undersell you. We don't have to pay for all these frills and frou-frous." Lew hesitated for a moment, listening to the sound of the piano in another room. "Or pay for any piano-playing harlots," he added.

Lucien Maxwell laughed at the Tennessean's pluck. It reminded him of his own gameness and tenacity, during his years as a mountain man and fur trapper. "Hah! Go ahead, and try, Big 'Un! Most of your cattle were stolen from Fort Sumner in the first place. General Carlton and I could have you arrested, for not returning them all. He could confiscate your petit ranchera like that," Maxwell said, snapping his fingers. "No, what I propose is that you become my range detective. You can even homestead on my Grant. Tell Mr. Gray he is welcome to come here, as well. I'll build more settlements and make you both town Marshalls."

Dirt Bradshaw heard this offer. He eased over and asked, "what about our young lady friend? Could you find work for her?"

Maxwell shook his head. He had heard about Nicole Klausmann's former captivity. "There's only two lines of work for females in this town. Either be one man's wife—or every man's gal friend for the evening. Considering that girl's past, her only future is the latter."

Bradshaw resented this insult, yet he did not reply. The piano music in the other room had stopped, so he turned over his empty glass and walked away. Dirt went to find the cavalrymen, who had already left the saloon.

Cimarron was a stage stop on the Mountain Route of the Santa Fe Trail and Dirt was not surprised to see two stagecoaches now parked on the town plaza. Hearing the sounds of horses on the south edge of town, he turned to look. The Colorado First Cavalry thundered into the settlement.

Dirt recognized Silas Soule, the lieutenant he'd met back at Conejos. Soule was perched atop a bay horse, reddish-brown, with a black mane and tail. The young officer did not acknowledge Bradshaw's wave, but he greeted the four cavalrymen as they came running across the plaza.

The Colorado prospector slinked away, passing by the stagecoaches. He halted, when a young female stepped out of the second coach. She was dressed for travel, in a light gray and black, houndstooth English riding outfit. Dirt's eyes widened, then he flashed his best, "killer grin".

"Hello, Miss Jane!" said Dirt, removing his hat.

"Why, hello, Mr. Bradshaw! We meet again," said Jane Edgarton. "Are you staying here at the Maxwell House?"

"I'm here with some friends," Dirt replied, feeling self-conscious about his rough attire and four-day-old beard. Jane did not act like she noticed; she hugged Bradshaw. "It's great to see you, Missy," said Dirt.

"I'm glad to see you, too, Richard," Jane said, remembering his Christian first name.

Dirt pondered if he should tell Jane all about his recent exploits, then he decided it would seem like bragging. As a stagehand unloaded Miss Edgarton's luggage, Bradshaw offered to carry it inside for her.

As Dirt accompanied the lady musician into the hotel lobby, Jane told him she was still touring the Southwest. "My brother is coming to meet me here in Cimarron," she added.

"Are you going on to Kansas, Jane?" Dirt asked. He had the germ of an idea.

"Yes, we are. With Lieutenant Soule. Are You?"

Bradshaw explained WaShana's ordeal. "There's a girl with us, who needed a doctor. She was once a captive of the Comanches. Her name is—or was—Nicole Klausmann, before she was abducted. She needs some help, Jane."

Jane Edgarton absorbed all this; she sat down on the same couch that WaShana had reposed on only an hour earlier. "How may I be of assistance?" Jane asked.

Dirt told her about Nicole having family in Lawrence, Kansas. He appealed to the lady abolitionist's mission of assisting slaves and former captives. "She needs a refined woman, like you, Jane," Dirt said, "who can help in some other matters. Someone to teach her how to act like a young lady again—how to be civilized."

"This is quite overwhelming," said Jane. She looked at Bradshaw, as if wondering what his own intentions toward the girl might be. Dirt's expression showed real concern. "Silas and I will surely take her," Jane consented. "The poor thing! I can't imagine what horrors she has seen. Let us go speak with Lieutenant Soule."

As Dirt and Jane walked outside, a tall woman stepped into the lobby, paused, then she peered around a corner to gaze at the men in the saloon. The big Tennessean was still drinking and speaking with Maxwell. He had arrived the previous day at Maxwell's and ever since then, Jessica Piedmont avoided the man. She knew he was Lew McManus—Jimmy Gray's partner. Mrs. Piedmont wondered what he was doing in Cimarron and she didn't want to be recognized.

Standing out on the Maxwell House porch, Jane Edgarton called out to Lieutenant Soule. The cavalry officer rode over and he acknowledged Dirt Bradshaw. "Good to meet you again, Mr. Bradshaw," said Soule. "I've been talking with Corporal Burton. Do I understand correctly that you've been hired as a scout by your brother?"

Dirt nodded. "Yes, Sir, Lieutenant. Thirteen dollars a month worth."

The Lieutenant stayed on his bay and studied the Colorado miner. "Do you know much about Kansas?" he asked, being skeptical about Bradshaw's qualifications. "Have you dealt with the Missouri guerrillas?"

"Up on the Cimarron Cutoff—yes I have. And I'll part their hair with my twelve-gauge, if I see 'em again." Dirt was prepared to meet this young officer's challenge; he also wanted to impress Miss Edgarton.

Silas Soule climbed out of the saddle and tied his horse to the porch railing. "I heard about the gold you and Mr. McManus recovered. We received his message just yesterday, by telegraph, at Fort Union." The lieutenant's tone lightened up around Jane and he quickly glanced around to make sure no one else was listening. "My unit is taking the recovered items on to Fort Leavenworth. I already have a scout, but you are welcome to travel with us. If you want to rejoin Lieutenant Bradshaw's platoon. Or do you need to stay in New Mexico—and recover the rest of the government's property?" Soule emphasized this latter option; he was a direct, conscientious officer, who thoroughly supported the Union cause.

Jane Edgarton explained Dirt's request, regarding Nicole Klausmann and her plight. "She has family connections in Lawrence, Silas. Just like you," said Jane. "May we take her with us?"

Soule leaned forward and embraced Miss Edgarton. "Why, certainly, Jane," he said, "I'd be glad to do that for you. There are still Klausmanns in Lawrence. I remember hearing about her family's ambush by the Comanches years ago. Thank God, she survived the ordeal with those savages."

Dirt took note of how close Jane and the lieutenant stood together. When Jane let Soule kiss her on the cheek, Dirt's heart sank.

She can ride in my coach," said Jane, turning to face Bradshaw. "And I have extra clothes she can wear. If they fit. Come, let us go upstairs and see her."

Dirt Bradshaw composed himself. "First, let me ask about something," he said. "Lieutenant, we have a scout of our own, whom the girl trusts more than any other man. I fear she won't go back without him."

"We'll talk about it later," Soule replied. The Union Lieutenant did not want to be seen taking suggestions from a ragged prospector. "We'll need my captain's approval."

"This scout comes with me, or I ain't going," said Dirt. At this moment, Dirt Bradshaw realized how much heartbreak WaShana and Rodrigo would experience if they were separated forever.

"Suit yourself," Soule replied stiffly, then he stepped off the porch and untied his horse. "Jane Dear, let me see to my men, and I'll join you directly."

Dirt looked at Jane and tried to hide his sad confusion. "I'll let you get settled in, Miss Jane, while I go check on my friends. We can check on Nicole later this evening."

CHAPTER 28

In the dry heat of the early afternoon. Dirt Bradshaw, Rodrigo and Juan all sat on the boardwalk outside the Cimarron trading post. The searchers' three horses, their tails switching at flies, were tied up at the hitching rail while their owners waited for Lew McManus.

Dirt carved on a piece of cedar and pondered his next move. He could either go with Lieutenant Soule and Miss Edgarton to Kansas, or he could continue the hunt for Sergio Ortiz and the remainder of the gold. "At least we recovered some of the stolen cargo," said Dirt. "That would justify me staying with WaShana I reckon. But my brother would be pissed as hell, if I show up with only a portion of the gold."

"We never got paid," Juan Villareal complained. "If I go back, will they pay me? We must go back." The Mexican boy was scratching circles in the dirt with the heel of his boot. Restless and impatient about not moving on, Juan was tired of camping out on Ponil Creek outside the settlement.

"Go back where?" Dirt wondered aloud. "To Fort Lyon, or Leavenworth? No telling where my brother is by now." He noticed Rodrigo, staring down at the road. Red Water had not said three words over the last half hour. "Why so taciturn, Amigo?" Dirt asked. "You seem glum, chum."

"I cannot go in to see her. No Apaches allowed, they tell me," said Red Water. Rodrigo was seeing his chances with WaShana slipping away. He also hated White men's towns—especially this town called Cimarron. "She is learning to be a White man's woman," the Mescalero added. "When I saw her from far away this morning, I did not... reckon—what is the word?"

"Recognize. You didn't recognize her," Dirt replied. "I surely sympathize with you on that, my friend. Miss Jane's acting different, too. We all feel out of place here."

"And I cannot read. They all think I am a dumb savage for this," said Rodrigo.

"Heck, Amigo. I can both read and write, but folks think I'm just as much a dumb cluck as any drunk gravedigger." Dirt poked at Juan

Villareal with the cedar stick. "Speaking of ignorance, here's our fearless leader," Dirt added. Lew McManus was walking their way. "Where do we go now, Lew?" Bradshaw asked.

"What do you mean, we?" Maxwell has offered me a job," said McManus. Lew wore a clean white-starched shirt, new trousers and his black hair and beard were neatly trimmed. "I am gonna be a Range Detective," he announced.

"Range Detective? What in Hell is that?" Dirt stood up and threw away the cedar stick.

McManus explained that he would be in charge of enforcing Lucien Maxwell's reign over half of his Land Grant. He was obviously proud to be taking this employment. "That's right—a Range Detective. I'll hunt down rustlers and chase out squatters who don't pay a homestead fee. Or miners who don't pay rent on their claim. I want to do it."

"Yeah, and people in Hell want a cold beer," scoffed Bradshaw. "You ain't going to be nothing but a hired gun. What about us going after that last gold bandit?"

"You all can do what you want. This here job means I can roam over half a million acres—hunt all I want, and maybe even find my own gold," said Lew. "Lucien will fill me in on the details tonight. He invited me to the big dinner party he's giving."

Dirt Bradshaw felt angry; he had not been invited to the event. "Well, don't wear that crumpled hat of yours. And put in a good word for us, while you're at his little venison and duck soiree."

"I will. Maybe I can sneak you all a bunch of biscuits. Before you leave town." Lew McManus checked himself; he realized he shouldn't be mean, for he and the other searchers would soon be parting ways. Lew smiled sadly. "Maybe you can join us for some drinks in the saloon, afterwards, Dirt. Are you all going back to Kansas? Or staying in the Territory?"

Rodrigo Red Water stood up to leave. "I go west. I have enough of being in strange country."

"Si, I am going back," said Juan Villareal, answering Lew's first question. "You going too, Senor Dirt?"

Bradshaw did not answer. He tilted his head toward Rodrigo, who was now adjusting the blanket on his Apache pony. Dirt gave McManus a hard look. "Hold on, Amigo," Lew said to Rodrigo. "Maybe I'll go back with you, to the Rim Rock, before I take the job. I need to settle my affairs with Jimmy Gray anyway. We can ride together," the Tennessean offered. "All of you, stay at your camp one more night, okay? Who knows? Once I have my own place, up along the Vermijo River, I'll have a spot for all of us."

"No, thanks," Dirt declared, reaching for his own horse. It seemed every man was now going in his own direction. Bud Wilson had left town the previous day and now both McManus and Rodrigo were abandoning the chase. "I am going to find my brother—and scout for the Union Army. There is a war going on, remember?"

"Suit yourself, Yank. We'll have us a whiskey at the saloon later. Or maybe that beer you'll want—before you wind up in Hell." McManus turned to Rodrigo. "What about you, compadre? Can you wait and leave with me tomorrow?"

"I will. But I must speak with WaShana," said Red Water. His spirit seemed to return, with one last hope. "Can you tell her I must talk with her? Tonight?"

"I will, Amigo," McManus said. "Dirt and I will carry her out, like a sweet sack of honeyed oats, if we have to. We'll meet you at the camp."

Red Water agreed. He mounted up on his horse, then he looked at both Dirt and Juan. "Do what you must do," said the Mescalero, grinning now.

"Yep, we will,": said Bradshaw. "Yeah, we will all have one last rave-up, before we leave." The prospector and the Mexicano youth unhitched their horses and saddled up.

WaShana Nicole felt she had awakened from a fevered dream—into another world. This place seemed completely different from the elemental life of the Comanches, and even a great change from her day-to-day travels with frontiersmen and soldiers. The former beloved captive now sat within the four walls of an ornate parlor room, in a taffeta chair, next to Miss Jane Edgarton. The Canadian lady served WaShana tea in a white china cup. Jane was instructing Nicole on the proper etiquette of a young woman.

WaShana, the Indian captive, was gone—scrubbed away by scented soap and hot water. Her sunburned neck was lightly-powdered, to match her bare shoulders. She was now Miss Nicole Klausmann, a young, White girl, with ringlets in her golden hair, and petticoats rustling under her gown whenever she twitched. A whalebone corset pinched her torso, constricting her breath in a manner she'd never experienced before; while the low-cut neckline of her dress made her breasts swell every time she inhaled. WaShana felt embarrassed; was this what being Nicole Klausmann would entail from now on?

She was amazed by her dress: pearl-white, with a blue and white, flowered pattern. A sash of pink satin cinched her waist. Nicole was being introduced this evening to the privileged world of civilized men and women. The dress, of course, belonged to the Canadian woman, yet it almost fit Nicole perfectly.

"Sit up straight now. And always keep your chin level. Do not slouch," Miss Jane instructed. The teacup and saucer clattered on WaShana Nicole's lap. "Don't be nervous, Dear. And keep your legs together, like a lady, even if no one can see them. And don't immediately stand, when the men stand up. Wait for my brother to take your hand."

"Why do we do this?" WaShana Nicole asked.

Miss Edgarton laughed. "To maintain enchantment, my dear. We shall make speed for Kansas tomorrow. Yet tonight, Mr. and Mrs. Maxwell want me to show you off to the gentlemen of the Territory. We have made quite a wonderful transformation of you in the last two days."

"Where is Rodrigo? Will Mr. Dirt be there?" WaShana asked.

"No," Jane said emphatically. "Lieutenant Silas and I will chaperone you. And my brother, Trey, is here. He will be your escort this evening. Now remember—you do not have to give details about your life among the Indians. Some of the gentlemen—and certainly the women—will ask you a bunch of questions about those matters. Understand?"

"Are you the woman of that soldier chief?" WaShana asked.

"Mr. Soule is a Lieutenant. He is what we call my fiancé." Miss Edgarton realized this girl, who was only two or three years younger than her, was very perceptive, despite her social deprivation.

"Fee—feeantsay? What is that?"

"It means that we are to be married," said Jane.

"Does Dirt know?" Nicole had seen the way Bradshaw acted around this refined stranger. Dirt and Jane had come up and visited her bedside at the hotel two days earlier.

Jane looked downward and traced the rim of her teacup with her finger. "Well, we have not formally announced it yet, and I will tell him. Now let's get back on the subject. It is not proper for you to eat a great deal tonight. And try to look interested in what men have to say. Do not frown—smile a great deal, but not too much. Some of the ladies might try to hurt or confuse you."

"If they try to hurt me, should I bring my knife?"

"No, no!" said Jane. "I mean they might hurt your feelings. Do you understand?"

"I comprende. Smile a great deal. Like when Mr. Lew sells his whiskey and says 'Great Deal'. Yes?"

Jane grew frustrated. "Not exactly. It just means do it a lot. Not grinning, you don't want to look foolish. Just a slight smile. Oh, and one more thing. Do not go off alone with any man—outside or anywhere."

"I already did that with Rodrigo. He is my fee-antsay."

Jane shook her head. She wondered about this girl's actions of late. "Did you and Mr. Bradshaw spend some time ..like that? Alone together out on the prairie?"

"We were with the soldiers and the others," said WaShana Nicole, practicing her smile. She realized that the idea made Jane jealous. "Why do you ask?" She smiled again.

Miss Edgarton put her teacup aside. "That is much better. I wish I had your dimples. I'm just concerned, my dear. Now, let me show you how to walk and act, when my brother and you make your entrance."

Arriving at the Rock Crossing of the upper Canadian River, Miles Wells also discovered Sergio Ortiz had abandoned the freight wagon. Wells only led a party of three now—himself, Same Burningtree and Lee Sixkiller. After sending Will Dare north and the other Cherokees home, the Confederate agent continued the search on his own.

"We've lost the trail. We can only track the Union group from here," said Wells, standing next to his own wagon. "Maybe they continued the chase. Maybe not." He turned to Lee Sixkiller, who was driving the supply wagon. "You are free to go, Mr. Sixkiller. I release you from further service. Sam and I will sell the wagon and supplies in Las Vegas Grandes."

"I will go that far," said the Cherokee. "The Yankee prospector and the girl have continued down the Trail. There is at least that gold."

Miles Wells drew a long sigh. He could not rid himself of this pesky Indian. "Very well, but you must keep our task secret," he insisted.

"What task is that?" said a voice from the woods upstream.

Wells and Burningtree clutched their rifles. An old man appeared, raising both hands to show he was unarmed. "Come forward, Sir," said Miles, "and don't try anything stupid."

"Oh, I won't," Bud Wilson said. He introduced himself. "I take it you are seeking some lost treasure, just like those soldiers, who passed through here a few days ago."

Lee Sixkiller's face lit up. "Was there a girl with them? And another man?" he asked.

"Why yes. I'm camped up yonder a ways. I've got stuff to trade with ye, if you want. And breakfast."

Sam Burningtree was eager to eat. "I thought I smelled bacon. Can we, Mr. Miles?"

Miles Wells was skeptical, but also curious. "We've got food of our own, Old Timer. What else are you willing to trade?"

"Besides biscuits, hog back and turquoise...well, information, I reckon," Wilson drawled. "Something that might help you-all."

Wells and his two Cherokees followed the old trader along the riverbank to his campsite. Wilson offered to fry up some more bacon; he had also made biscuits in a dutch oven, and there was coffee. "Go ahead, boys," Bud Wilson told Sam and Lee. "Eat up."

While his men ate, Miles Wells drank coffee and spoke with the old trader away from the campfire. "I'm a Texas man myself," said Wilson. "And I know practically every stretch and side canyon between here and the Comanche Nation."

Wells was intrigued. "You look like an old Comanche yourself, with those silver braids. What's with your horse? He's only got one eye?"

"He's blind on his right. And I've got cataracts in my left, so I've kept him. Together, we can see half-decently. That girl your wagon driver mentioned got herself snakebit. The soldiers and the other man took her to Cimarron."

"You don't say," said Miles, sipping his coffee.

"Yessir. So there's little use in following them, I reckon. Who are the men you've been hunting?"

Miles was still reluctant to divulge much information. He had agreed to rendezvous back with Will Dare outside Las Vegas later on, so he didn't need a new scout for now. Still, this old man might prove useful. "The man's name is Sergio Ortiz. You know him?" Miles asked.

"The Comanchero? Hell yes, he killed a close cousin of mine several years ago." This was a lie, the old man had heard about Ortiz from Dirt Bradshaw.

"Well, that proves you've got a motive to help us," said Wells, taking the bait.

CHAPTER 29

"Why are you so late?" Jane Edgarton asked her fiancé. Lieutenant Soule had kept the ladies and Jane's brother waiting at the Maxwell House.

"I told you I had orders to carry out," said Soule. A wavy-haired officer in his mid-twenties, Silas Soule had changed from his flannel fatigue coat into a dark blue dress jacket with a standing collar and burnished brass buttons. "It was quite important, Dear. We can talk about it later. Hello, Trey."

Trey Edgarton shook the Lieutenant's hand. Edgarton stood by a young lady that Soule did not immediately recognize, so Trey took it on himself to introduce Nicole Klausmann. "Oh, hello!" said Soule, startled out of his leering at this young woman. "Oh gosh, my Jane has made you a vision of loveliness, Miss Nicole."

The blonde-haired girl forced a smile; she felt terribly nervous. She wore a pink and white Victorian gown, with short, cap sleeves, a bow accent at her neckline, ruffles along the side and hem, which made the evening gown very elegant. Jane Edgarton was similarly dressed in green and gold.

Jane noticed Soule's distraction, took his arm and the two couples stepped into the vestibule outside Maxwell's dining hall. "We were supposed to keep YOU waiting," Jane whispered to Soule.

"Just be glad I'm here," the lieutenant replied curtly.

All the strangers took notice as WaShana Nicole entered the room on Trey Edgarton's arm. Nicole hated their gaping and the swooshing sound of her gown and petticoats only added to her discomfiture. "Don't worry, I'm here to keep them at bay," Trey Edgarton whispered into her ear. This handsome Canadian's kindness, and his consideration, made Nicole wish she could be alone–with him. *Anywhere but here!* she thought.

For the first few minutes, all the guests mingled about the decorated dance hall that had been converted into a dining area. A long table, or series of tables, had been covered in linen. Candelabras, settings of flowers, delicate glassware and china all added to the evening's mood, yet WaShana felt too out-of-place to enjoy this.

Trey Edgarton was very effective at protecting her, never leaving Nicole's side and diverting conversation away from inquiries as to WaShana's previous life. As a journalist for *The Rocky Mountain News*, Trey was adept at answering questions, then getting the other guests to talk about themselves. His magnanimous nature, along with his bright, brown eyes and warm smile put WaShana Nicole somewhat at ease. She decided that if she focused all her attention on her new friend, the other people would fade into the background.

"There are so many amazing stories in these western territories," said Trey Edgarton, "and yours is the most intriguing of all." He and WaShana Nicole now stood apart from the crowd, as the other guests began to take their seats at the long table. "May I just call you Nicole? I am so glad you are riding with us to Kansas."

"I am happy to be with you, Mister Trey. Yes, call me Nicole. What things do you write about?"

The Canadian's eyes lit up at her question and he spoke about the great fire in Denver, panning for gold in the Rockies and his hopes for covering major events of the war. Trey's sister had instructed Nicole that if she asked any man about himself and showed herself interested in what he had to say, Nicole would be considered a brilliant conversationalist. As young Edgarton spoke, Nicole kept smiling, nodding her head often and replied with phrases like: 'that is wonderful,' 'oh, yes,' and 'tell me more.'

This fawning and WaShana's fresh charm worked almost too well. Jane's older brother seemed amazed by this young, open-hearted woman. He hardly noticed when Jane and Lieutenant Soule beckoned the couple to join them at the dining room table.

WaShana Nicole remembered to sit up straight and her smile was now more natural. "What other things do you write about?" she asked Trey.

"So many things!" Edgarton replied eagerly. "But enough about me. The story about you and Mr. Bradshaw recovering that Federal gold will make a marvelous article. You must tell me of your involvement."

Lew McManus arrived late at the banquet; all the guests noticed when the tall Tennessean entered the dining hall. Lew strode over and first spoke with Mr. Maxwell, the host, over at the head of the table. The hotel's owner nodded and pointed to a vacant seat across from Lieutenant Soule and Miss Edgarton. As McManus passed by WaShana, he grinned and gave her a knowing wink, then he sat down at the table.

WaShana wanted to ask Lew about Rodrigo and Dirt Bradshaw; but she would have to talk across Trey Edgarton and another male guest to do this. Neither the Mescalero, or the rowdy prospector, were invited, of course. Thinking of them, WaShana felt a pang in her heart. *What am I doing here without them?* she asked herself.

A waiter reached between WaShana and Trey and poured red wine into their glasses. "I can tell you more about my life later," WaShana whispered in Trey Edgarton's ear.

The young woman whispering softly in his ear made the young man's head tingle. Trey turned, looked intently into WaShana's blue eyes and he smiled. "You deserve all my utmost attention tonight, Nicole," he whispered back.

The meal progressed as planned. The Maxwells had set out a well-padded feast of wild game, beef and turkey, along with more epicurean dishes. WaShana had never seen food like this—not even in her childhood, before her captivity. She drank wine for the first time; it went well with the roast beef and elk venison. Lew McManus told her this was merlot. WaShana Nicole liked it; the drink made everything seem warm and fuzzy in her head. "I love this Merrr—low," she whispered again to her male escort's ear; then she laughed.

Other guests, mostly the women, noticed WaShana's open gaiety; one by one, they whispered to each other, going down the line to Mrs. Maxwell at the other end of the table. The middle-aged hostess frowned, yet she said nothing. She did not need to speak, for her fixed, fierce stare caught WaShana's attention.

Trey Edgarton noticed as well; in order to reassure WaShana, he reached for her hand under the table. WaShana Nicole turned her palm up and grasped the young man's hand tightly. "We will have much more time later," Trey said softly to Nicole. "More time later, to tell each other our stories. On the way to Kansas."

WaShana squeezed Trey's hand again. "I really hope so," she said, then she fell silent and concentrated on her meal. When the waiter offered to refill her wine glass, WaShana shook her head. The back of her neck began to tingle. She worried she had drunk too much wine, yet then she realized the cause.

Trey was gently tracing his finger, around in circles on the inside of the young woman's wrist, under the table. WaShana Nicole did not pull away. For some reason, the girl remembered a childhood nursery rhyme-'the little dog laughed to see such a sight, and the cow jumped over the moon.' Feeling over the moon herself, WaShana Nicole turned and smiled fondly at Trey.

"I am not WaShana anymore. Yes, just call me Nicole," she said. Nicole glanced over at Jane Edgarton, who nodded and smiled back.

Although the former captive may have thought Jane was approving Nicole's new attraction to Trey, Miss Edgarton was only glad to see the girl refrain from more wine. Jane had her own unfulfilled wishes. She wanted to ask Lew McManus about Dirt Bradshaw, but she decided against it. She was now engaged to Silas Soule. Jane's lieutenant and Lew McManus sat slightly across from each other, but for some reason, they both pretended to ignore one another. McManus seemed thoroughly engrossed in eating; Lieutenant Soule only spoke with Jane and another guest on his left.

After the last course, some guests had dessert, while others excused themselves. The younger men now scurried off to the adjoining saloon, to smoke and drink something stronger than wine. Some of the ladies went over to thank the Maxwells for their excellent supper. Trey Edgarton stayed with Nicole, but Silas Soule got up and left Trey's sister. He dashed off to the tavern.

Lucien Maxwell, the host, walked over and asked Jane if she would mind playing some of her music over on the dining hall's grand piano. "I know we have not discussed this, but my wife would really love to hear you again, before you leave tomorrow," said Maxwell.

Miss Edgarton agreed to play. Since Lieutenant Soule had abandoned her so hastily, Jane felt performing would diminish the awkwardness of this situation.

Lew McManus came over to speak with WaShana. Rather than make her stand up, Lew knelt down on one knee and said, "Dang, girl, you spiffed up real good—in no time! Are you doing okay?"

WaShana Nicole nodded and said, "yes". She introduced Trey Edgarton, who said he was glad to meet the Tennessean. "I'm sorry, I got here late," said Lew, "because I was sending a telegraph message to Nashville—to my cousin. Had to ask her how my folks are doing."

"So you are from Tennessee?" Trey Edgarton asked.

"Yessir. Well, I used to be," said McManus. Lew was reluctant to discuss his home state and the war; he felt helping to recover the Federal gold was proof enough of his loyalties.

"I may write an article about the caravan robbery," said Trey. "Miss Nicole says you fought two groups of Confederates to get the gold back."

"I don't know if they were true Rebs. Just thieves, I figure. Ask Dirt Bradshaw about all this," Lew suggested.

Jane Edgarton started playing the piano and McManus excused himself to go drink at the bar. As Jane's brother and Nicole walked over to listen to her, Miss Edgarton's music was interrupted by loud voices clamoring in the barroom. Mr. Maxwell and his wife came over by the piano and Jane asked the hotel's owner if the noise was this boisterous every night. "I will check and demand that the rowdies must leave," Lucien Maxwell declared.

WaShana Nicole recognized one man's voice amongst the uproar. "I think that's Mr. Dirt shouting," she told Jane. "Mr. Maxwell, please let us go talk to him."

Over in the tavern, Dirt Bradshaw confronted the Union lieutenant. "Mr. Soule, why the Hell have you done this?" yelled Bradshaw. Dirt's face was red with anger and the big Tennessean held the miner back, away from the bar, so that Bradshaw could not strike the Union officer.

"What's eating you, Yank?" McManus asked, standing between the two men.

"Soldiers came to our camp. They arrested Rodrigo!" When Dirt saw Jane and WaShana enter the saloon with Trey Edgarton, he relaxed his fists and explained the matter. "After all Red Water did to help us retrieve their gold, the damned Federals took him away."

"Watch your language, Sir. I had my orders," Soule declared simply, sipping a whiskey and turning his back to the prospector. "And they weren't my men. It was the New Mexico Militia."

"Yeah, but it was you who told them about the Mescalero," said Dirt.

Jane Edgarton stepped up beside the lieutenant. "What's this about, Richard?" she asked Bradshaw.

"Our Indian friend," Dirt said, gazing at WaShana, who stood wide-eyed with disbelief beside Jane's brother. "They took him away—I don't even know where they're taking him," Dirt said sadly.

"Dammit," Lew McManus cursed, releasing his arm hold on Dirt when he saw Bradshaw calm down in Miss Edgarton's presence. "Maybe if I'd been there, we could have reasoned with them. Or put up a fight."

"He was a fugitive from Justice. Take it up with General Carleton," Silas Soule remarked.

WaShana kept her hand over her mouth, to keep from shrieking. Dirt looked at her. "Rodrigo went peacefully. Almost like he was waiting for something like this to happen," Dirt told her. Turning to

Jane Edgarton, he said, "They tell me you aim to marry this Jayhawker. Is this true?"

"I was going to tell you." said Jane. "When it was the right time."

Dirt seemed to shake himself; he stepped back from the bar counter. "The right time was yesterday, Jane. When we would have had time to leave this place with Rodrigo." Bradshaw reached down to pick up his hat.

Lieutenant Soule took his foot off the lower brass rail of the bar and looked coldly at Bradshaw and McManus. "Then I would have tracked you down and shot you as outlaws." Soule was actually embarrassed that Jane had interceded to calm the situation. He was not afraid to fight; other soldiers stood nearby. "And I expect to receive orders to take Mr. McManus into custody, for charges down at El Paso. The only reason I don't is that I respect Mr. Maxwell—and you are basically under his protection." he told McManus.

"Meet me outside, Sir!" said Lew. "And I'll show you what protects me!" Now it was Dirt's turn, to hold McManus back from punching the lieutenant.

"Don't do it, Lew. Let's go talk," Dirt suggested. He released his hold. "We best be going—and let these good folks have their party." Dirt Bradshaw smiled sadly, tipped back his hat and spoke to Jane and WaShana: "Fare thee well, Ladies. It's all bittersweet—and best forgotten."

"No, no!" WaShana cried, grabbing Dirt's shoulder. "Don't leave me now."

Dirt hugged her side with one arm. "Now, Girl, you are better off with Miss Jane and Mr. Trace. They promised to take you back to your people, okay? You are safe now, okay?"

"Goodbye, WaShana," said Lew, embracing her in a strong bear hug. "If things don't work out in Kansas, come find me here—or at the Rim Rock."

"Where will they take Red Water?" Dirt asked Soule.

Lieutenant Soule did not reply at first; Jane tugged on his sleeve. Soule did not know if it was wise to give out such information, but Silas Soule was not a cruel man. Like Miss Edgarton, he and his family had rescued slaves and assisted freedom seekers. "I am not taking him," he said. "The militia will take him to either Fort Union or Fort Sumner."

"Well, John Brown it, maybe we can tell the militia commander how Rodrigo helped us. He would continue to help us, too—if you Federal boys hadn't stuck your nose in." McManus reached over on the bar counter, grabbed his whiskey glass and downed the drink in one gulp. "Come on, Dirt. This party's done soured on us."

Lew and Dirt marched out onto the porch; it was now dark outside. Nicole followed behind them, along with the Edgartons. "Please, go find Rodrigo," Nicole pleaded.

"Remember me in your prayers, ladies," Dirt Bradshaw asked, hugging WaShana Nicole again. Dirt placed his hand on Trey Edgarton's shoulder. "And please, watch over Nicole, okay?"

"Mr. Bradshaw, you have a duty to the U.S. Army," Silas Soule declared, stepping out onto the porch. "You must accompany my unit, as we take the gold on to Fort Leavenworth."

Dirt frowned. This was a chess move, pure and simple. Dirt did not want to be under this Lieutenant's authority; he thought of a way to dodge the issue, without losing face. "I am still assigned to my brother's platoon—and obligated to Davey," he said. "Corporal Burton and the rest of Sergeant Mike's men can guard what we recovered. And take the Mexican boy, Juan, okay? As for me, I am going to recover the rest of the stolen cargo—as Lieutenant Dave Bradshw instructed."

Lieutenant Soule balked; he almost shouted for his men to come arrest the miner, yet now Soule noticed what Lew McManus was doing. Lew had stepped off the porch, gone to his horse and he now held a black steel revolver.

"You go on to the camp, Dirt," said McManus. Leaning across his horses' saddle, the Tennessean casually dangled his Smith and Wesson, to keep Soule at bay. "After I get my stuff and check out, I'll join you in the morning."

CHAPTER 30

Lew McManus roused Juan Villareal just before first light at the Ponil Creek campsite. "I'm taking one of your mules," Lew told the Mexican boy. "Don't fret, I'm paying you for it."

"Those are the Army's mules," said Juan. He looked over at the campfire. Dirt was already up and was waiting for the coffee pot to heat up.

"Well, I paid them, too," said Lew, casting Bradshaw a furtive glance. McManus swung a heavy-laden sack onto the biggest of the pack animals.

"So, where are we heading first, Lew? Off to Fort Union, I reckon? I promised WaShana we'd try to free Red Water," Dirt reminded him.

"Suit yourself, if you think you can. I'm heading straight for the Rim Rock ranch, first. Me and Jimmy Gray's got some settlin' up to do," said McManus.

Bradshaw scowled at the Tennessean's apparent disloyalty, but he kept his resentment to himself. "So, Juan, you ARE going on to Kansas with the cavalrymen, correct? Like we discussed, okay?"

"Si, Señor. To keep my eye on Señorita Nicole," Juan Villareal replied. His face brightened at the thought, for Juan had seen WaShana Nicole in her new attire. She was only two or three years older than the boy.

"Yes. And make sure they pay you, when you get to Fort Lyon. If they don't, you tell Lieutenant Dave I said to give you my pay. My brother owes us that, at least," said Dirt. "And I'm giving you my shotgun."

"Go on back to sleep, Boy," Lew McManus suggested. "And hurry up with that coffee, Yank. We gotta get going."

As he and McManus passed back through town, Dirt Bradshaw gazed at a faint light in an upstairs window of the Maxwell House. Feeling a mixture of imagination and unrequited desire, Dirt wished he was the one traveling with Miss Edgarton, back to Colorado, but Bradshaw had made some promises. He needed to find Rodrigo; in addition, there was still the matter of the stolen gold.

Once they left the settlement, the two men urged their horses into a working trot, for they had a long day ahead, and it was best to cover as many miles as possible before the cool morning became a hot afternoon.

Outside Rayado, a settlement ten miles south of Cimerron. Dirt and Lew rested their horses in the shade of some pines. "Why didn't you go on to Colorado with that Canadian Lady and WaShana, Yank?" Lew asked his friend.

Dirt was filling his canteen from a small brook. He drew a deep sigh. "There's something I haven't told you, Lewis. I may be a wanted man in Colorado. Not that long ago, I sold some bogus stock in Denver, to a few British speculators."

"Huh, well you shouldn't let a few limey winks stop you from going back. It's a big Territory, you know. If she's smart, Miss Jane might not marry that wormy whelp of a Lieutenant. You should marry her. Y'all could raise up a buncha little abolitionists."

Dirt laughed. "Right now, I've got other business, if you haven't noticed. No, sir, the New Mexico Territory is where I need to be. So, tell me, why haven't you gone back to Tennessee?" he asked.

"Just might do it. I ain't heard back about my family yet," said Lew. "I'll ask my cousin to wire me back when I get to Las Vegas Grandes."

"Our Lady of Sorrows of the Great Meadows, is that right? How come they've never named a town after some sorrowful gentleman?" Dirt wondered aloud. He was feeling philosophical again.

"San Francisco," said McManus. "If that ain't good enough, when you strike it rich, you can name the place "Dirt-town. Or Dirthole City! But I understand you wanting to avoid Denver. It's like me, with El Paso. I killed a man, down in Texas. Around last Easter Time."

Bradshaw asked how this happened and McManus explained that the old man was dealing out prostitutes. "He was beating this girl I rescued, down at San Elizario. I did not mean to kill the old buzzard, but when I put him in a choke-hold, his neck snapped—like a chicken for Sunday dinner."

Dirt grimaced, imagining the sound that would go along with such an incident. "Well, maybe confession is good for the soul—but I'll never get over the worst thing I've ever done like that. Back when I was prospecting up on the Front Range—back in the winter of fifty-nine, I shot two Arapahoes. I hated to do it, but I had to. It was either them or me. Maybe that's why I'm not fighting in the war. I don't like killing."

In the spirit of the moment, Lew McManus looked around, then he stepped over to his mule. Reaching into the bag on its back, Lew pulled out a gleaming ingot of refined gold. "This is why I can't go to Fort Union, just yet." the Tennessean confessed.

"What the Hell? How did you?" Dirt seemed very perplexed, then he grew angry. "I thought you gave all the gold back to the government," said Dirt, hardly believing his own eyes.

McManus grinned. "I took out my finder's fee. After all, back at the Middle Spring, we both risked our dang lives for four bars—but you gave it back. Then me and Roderigo risked ours—for twelve of these babies. That's sixteen all total. And I've got four again. That's 25 percent. Split between us, we're only taking twelve percent each."

"I don't want it!" Dirt shouted. "Sergeant Mike gave his life for that. Why are you showing me this now? After all this time?"

Lew put the gold ingot back into the sack. "I've been having trouble sleeping," he admitted, then he grew defensive, "After all we did for the Federal government, look what they did! They arrested Rodrigo."

"Oh no, that don't cut it, Lew," said Dirt. "You decided to keep that way before they took Red Water away. So this is why you are suddenly not so eager to go after the rest of the gold, ain't it?"

"Think about it, Dirt. You and me, we could go to either California, the northern Rockies, maybe even Europe on several hundred ounces of gold. You ever had a French lady?"

"No, Lew, I haven't," said Dirt, looking off into the distance. He stepped over to Waukesha, his horse. "What would I do with..." With his back facing McManus, Dirt reached out and grabbed his Spencer Carbine from the gun boot near the saddle. He turned around with the weapon.

"This?" said Lew McManus. The Tennessean held both of his Smith and Wesson revolvers, aiming them at Bradshaw. "Drop it, Dirt. I don't want to shoot you."

Bradshaw exhaled. "Dammit, Lew. Damn, damn, dammit," he muttered. "Go ahead! What in the hell do I have to live for, anyway?" He let the rifle fall.

"I'll give you time to figure it out," said McManus, grabbing a lasso from off his own horse.

A few minutes later, Dirt Bradshaw was leaning back against a ponderosa pine, hobbled at the feet by Lew's rope. Another length of rope loosely strapped the prospector to the tree, and a leather boot lace bound his wrists.

McManus sat atop his own horse and held the lead tether to the pack mule. Yards away, Dirt's horse was also hobbled. "I'm leaving you your guns, gear and a few biscuits from the hotel, Dirt," said Lew... "It might take a few hours, but you'll eventually be able to wriggle free from that tree rope. All I need is a head start, okay? If you're smart, don't come callin' on me."

Riding in an Overland Mail Coach over rocks and ruts, United States Deputy Marshall Eduard Fazari was on his way to Fort Union to take custody of two Federal prisoners and conduct an investigation. Fazari studied the directive he had received from General Carleton. A valuable cargo of gold had been stolen from a Federal caravan in Kansas and the thieves responsible for the theft were reportedly in New Mexico.

At the time of this assignment, Fazari was thinking about resigning his position. He was tired of Carleton's petty remonstrations and nipicking. In addition, Eduard's law enforcement duties often took him away from managing his own affairs at his Bernalillo ranch. It was time to sell sheep and harvest corn now, but Carelton's directive required immediate action.

Some of the gold had been recovered by the Colorado cavalry, according to reports, but most of the thieves were still at large. They were reputed to be Confederate bushwhackers from Missouri, strangely allied with a group of Comancheros.

Fazari was riding with another Federal Marshall, Jefferson Long, of the Kansas district. The two lawmen had boarded the stagecoach in Santa Fe. Long was a middle-aged, average man with trimmed brown hair and spectacles. Eduard thought he looked more like a desk clerk or lawyer than a law enforcement official, yet Long was far easier on his subordinates than Carleton, the military governor. U.S. Marshall Long let his deputies use their own judgment on cases and, unlike Carleton, Long possessed a sense of humor. "So you and the Department of New

Mexico were having problems, eh?" Long asked. "Why did Carleton have you rounding up lost cows?"

"The General's been tearing his hair out over our Indian troubles. After his troops murdered Chief Mangus Colorado back in January, all the Apaches went on the warpath," said Fazari. "To make matters worse, now the Comanches have been raiding and stealing cattle from area ranches. The General put me in charge of getting some of them back."

"James Carleton has no patience," said Marshall Long. "It's best we leave Indian matters to the Indian agents. Right now, we in the Marshall's service need to concentrate on Confederate espionage and the bushwhackers from Missouri."

Eduard Fazari agreed with this assessment. "I understand you already did some investigating in Denver and Central City, right?" he asked.

"Oh, yes. We were hoping to arrest a Rebel spy master, a saloon owner named Billy Martin. Martin had recruited a host of southern sympathizers here out west, including that Union traitor, Corporal Reynolds. It's all in that report we gave you," Long added.

"Yes, I read it," said Fazari. "Reynolds was killed by one of the same men I had previously recruited to retrieve the General's stolen cattle."

"Well, that should put you back in the General's good graces," the Marshall replied. "Who are the prisoners you're taking back to Santa Fe?"

"One of them is an Arizona Ranger, a Confederate who was captured before he and Reynolds could escape to Colorado," said Fazari. Eduard hesitated to discuss Fort Union's other detainee.

"Send me a report on what you find out from him," said Long. He pushed his glasses up the bridge of his nose and grinned. "We captured a bunch of rebel irregulars up near Mace's Hole in Colorado last year. It provided the leads we needed to identify Martin, Corporal Reynolds and some other Confederate agents. Now, what about the other prisoner?"

Fazari tried to hide his embarrassment. He had recruited Rodrigo Red Water to assist in the recovery of the U.S. Army cattle earlier that year. "Well, he's just an Indian. A Mescalero, who has to be taken to the Bosque Redondo."

"You mean Red Water? The medicine chief who killed Captain Dunhill at La Placita last year?"

"I thought he was cleared of that crime," said Fazari. "There's a credible witness, who testified another Apache did the deed."

Long pushed his glasses up again and frowned. "Well, whatever you find out from him, put that in the report as well." Marshall Long was going on to Fort Lyon with the Overland Stage, while his deputy would be returning to Santa Fe.

Fazari agreed and went back to reading the General's directive. It said a Comanchero, named Sergio Ortiz, still had some of the gold in his possession, and he had gone into hiding somewhere in the canyons of the upper Canadian River.

The Overland coach rumbled on, through the dry, flat country. As it crossed the shallows of the Mora River, a lone rider with a horse and a mule watched from atop a nearby mesa. Lew McManus had avoided going to Fort Union and he was now keeping his distance from this more frequently-traveled section of the Santa Fe Trail.

Fort Union, the largest U.S. military post in the Southwest, was undergoing new construction when the mail coach crossed Coyote Creek and stopped behind the massive earthworks of the Fort. Fazari noticed cannons atop the parapets and new adobe structures. Across the creek, New Mexico Volunteers were building a new arsenal on the site of the first Fort Union.

Along with protecting travel and transport on the Mountain Branch of the Santa Fe Trail, the fort was the major Army supply depot for other military posts in the Southwest. Civilian freight wagons, Union soldiers and construction workers crowded the grounds and Fazari was surprised by all the activity. He hadn't been here in over a year; the last time was when he had been part of a caravan going to Independence, Missouri.

"So, where are the prisoners being held now?" Fazari asked a young lieutenant when he and Long arrived at the commander's office.

"White, Red, or brown?" the officer inquired. Fazari and Marshall Long looked at each other. Seeing their consternation, the lieutenant added, "Indians are housed in the old section. Anglos and Mexicanos in the new jailhouse."

"Tell you what, Eduard. I'll interrogate Graham, the Confederate ranger, while you talk with Red Water," Long suggested. "We'll compare notes later."

One of the prison guards, a corporal, was summoned. As he led Eduard Fazari over to an old, but solid stone structure, the corporal stated that Rodrigo Red Water, also known as Rodrigo Rojas, already had a visitor with him.

This worried Fazari. "Who is with him?" he asked.

"He's an Army scout from Colorado. He has a letter, saying that Red Water is also a scout, on a mission to recover important cargo of the U.S. Treasury Department. He's demanding we release him."

"I mean, what's the visitor's name?" asked Fazari.

"Hah, 'Dirt' Bradshaw. The jail commander has the letter. You still want to see the Indian?"

Fazari remembered the name, but did not immediately recall if he had once met the man. Eduard did remember there was some sort of connection to Lew McManus the previous year. "Oh, yes. I need to see both men," he told the corporal.

The corporal ushered Fazari down a concrete hallway, unlocked a metal door and led him to a series of cells that looked more like a medieval dungeon than a jailhouse. Over in one darkened section, chained to the wall, a dark-haired prisoner sat up on a bale of straw.

"Are you here to release him?" said a man, appearing out of the shadows beside Fazari.

Eduard was startled, yet then he recognized this Colorado prospector. "You? Lew said you were dead," Fazari remarked.

"People keep telling me that," said Dirt Bradshaw. "I'd better check my pulse."

"I am here to talk with Red Water, if you're through with him. In private, if you'll excuse us," Fazari explained, feeling somewhat irritated.

"Well, I'm like his lawyer. And we have a right to know why he's being detained. Habeas corpus. E-pluribus unum, and everything like that, okay?" Dirt snickered and grinned. "I'm speaking on his behalf."

The Union corporal, seeing that the two men knew each other, left the cell. Fazari remembered this man, Dirt Bradshaw, being somewhat of a jester. "I am a U.S. Deputy Marshall, Sir. If you will kindly remove your happy arse, I can do the government's business."

"Oh, like the time you and Big Lew hauled them whores down to Albuquerque?" Dirt questioned.

At this jibe, even Rodrigo Red Water laughed. Bradshaw referred to the time when Fazari and McManus had taken prostitutes from Santa Fe, at the Army's behest, in order to keep them away from Union troops occupying the Territorial capital. "That was official business, mister," said Fazari.

"Yeah, like when you had McManus sell untaxed Taos Lightening up in Trinidad, right? Does that head Marshall you came with know about that?"

"It's illegal to extort a law enforcement officer, Bradshaw," Fazari warned, although this was true. Eduard had sometimes used his position for his own benefit.

"Huh, I'd think you would know the difference between extortion and a little friendly persuasion, Mr. Fazari," said Dirt. "You want to ask Rodrigo about the gold we recovered, right? And what's still out there?"

The Deputy Marshall drew a deep sigh. "What is it you all want?" he asked.

Dirt demanded that Rodrigo should be released to his supervision. He told Fazari that he had given the commanding captain of the prison a letter—signed by Lieutenant David Bradshaw—which authorized Dirt to recover stolen cargo for the U.S. Treasury, and asked for anyone receiving the document to allow safe passage for Dirt Bradshaw, Rodrigo Red Water and one Lewis McManus. However, Dirt did not reveal how he had forged the letter, along with his brother's signature, on some stationary from the Maxwell House in Cimarron.

The Deputy Marshall realized he had little room to negotiate and resigning his commission now would be seen as a major failure. "I'll agree to have him released," said Fazari, "but I have to go along with you both—to find the gold. That's the deal."

Dirt gazed over at Rodrigo and the Mescalero nodded. "Fair enough, what is it you Cajuns say? The more the merrier?"

CHAPTER 31

Jane Edgarton was teaching Nicole Klausmann how to read again. As the U.S. cavalry escorted their stagecoaches north, to Trinidad and then on to Fort Lyon, Miss Edgarton and her brother took turns teaching from both the Bible and the McGuffey Reader. Jane attempted to give 'WaShana' Nicole more of a Christian education with her instruction; however, Nicole enjoyed Trey Edgarton's instruction much better.

This was not because Miss Jane was a less effective teacher; Nicole found Trey to have a more playful sense of humor and he took more breaks in between the individual lessons. This quality and the young Canadian's bright-eyed interest in Nicole endeared him to her.

The Edgartons spent the first night in Trinidad, where Jane gave both a violin performance and a brief lecture on the need for a constitutional amendment to ban all slavery in the United States and its Territories. Nicole only half-listened. With a crowd of strangers around them in the audience, she focused more on holding Trey's hand than Miss Jane's lecture.

The next evening, as darkness fell and the stagecoaches neared Fort Lyon, Trey and Nicole kissed for the first time. They were enthralled with each other; he summoned up wild and irrepressible feelings in the young woman. Nicole felt she had never been happier; she told Jane the next day that she was learning better from the McGuffey Reader than Jane's King James version of the Bible.

"I understand. The McGuffey is more plain English than the Elizabethan prose, with its 'thees' and 'thou', so it's more practical," said Jane. Miss Edgarton gave Nicole a quizzical look, for she had noticed her older brother's intense interest in the former captive. "Well, alright then," said Jane. She and Nicole were preparing to board their stagecoach. "I suppose you should ride with Trey again today. This will allow me more time to concentrate on my National Loyal League speech."

"Yes, Ma'am," Nicole said, as she lifted her new carrying bag, with the clothes and items Jane had given her.

"Just a moment. Trey tells me he is working on an article about you, for the *Rocky Mountain News,* but I have yet to see his drafts," said Jane. "He is indeed doing his research, is he not?"

"Indeed...he is," Nicole replied. "We are both learning," she added. Nicole did not reveal that the main thing Trey was trying to 'research' was some way to get within her petticoats. Her honeyed kisses and his constant embraces on this journey were distracting Trey from his writing and Nicole from her reading.

Juian Villareal, who had been riding along with the cavalry escort, came up and took Nicole's carrying bag. As he and Nicole walked back to the other stagecoach, Juan informed her that he would be returning to New Mexico.

"Why? Why aren't you going on with us, Juan?" Nicole asked. The Mexicano boy was the last person of the gold search party to stay on with her.

"I have been paid, WaShana," said Juan. "That officer, he does not like me. And Señor Dirt needs an amigo to help him find more of the gold."

WaShana Nicole gently touched Juan's shoulder. She sensed he was upset to leave her, yet he had doubtlessly seen how close she and Trey had become. "How will you find Dirt Bradshaw?"

"He goes with Señor Lewis, to get Rodrigo—and take them to the ranch. At San Geronimo," said Juan. "I will go to the ranch, Señorita," he added.

Hearing all the names of her friends, WaShana grew emotional. "Tell them I will miss them. And you, Juan," she said, embracing the boy. "I will ask Miss Jane to help me write to Mr. Dirt. He gave me the address of the Rim Rock—before he left Cimarron." WaShana smiled. "Yes, they are teaching me to write." she added.

Juan Villareal nodded. He climbed up on the stagecoach, secured the carrying bag and hurried away, for he did not want to see or talk with Trey Edgarton. Juan had fallen lovesick for the once-wild girl, yet he knew his adoration was pointless.

Jessica Piedmont recognized the man coming out of the Western Union office in Las Vegas Grandes. She quickly darted behind a freight wagon, parked on the central plaza, then she observed McManus as the Tennessean made his way down the street. This was the same man she had seen days earlier in Cimarron, except now he had cleaned up his appearance and he now carried an army rucksack on his back.

Lew McManus entered a livery stable, next to a blacksmith's shop. He emerged quite a few minutes later, with his horse and leading a pack mule. When he headed northwest on the road to San Geronimo, Jessica surmised that the big man was going back to the Rim Rock ranch, to seek his creole courtesan, Rosa Amarillo Del Rio. Miss Del Rio still lived at the Rim Rock, with Jimmy Gray. Jessica laughed to herself; she imagined Lew's surprise when he discovered the young Señorita was three months pregnant.

"It serves him right, the brute," Mrs. Piedmont remarked. She headed down Gonzales Street, to the south side of the town. Jessica hoped to meet Billy Martin and Miles Wells and tell them about her discovery.

Jessica didn't like walking unescorted through this older, more Hispanic section of Las Vegas Grandes, yet it was full daylight and the traders and workmen she met all nodded politely as she passed. They were actually less of a threat than the drunken, derelict Anglos she might meet after dark. Just to be sure, Jessica had kept a Colt derringer in her purse.

On this sleepy Friday afternoon, inside the adobe-walled cantina, Wells was drinking beer with the head of the spy network, Billy Martin. Another man, a white-haired gentleman, also sat at the table. Jessica was unsure about him. The old man was strange; his long hair was tied back in a ponytail and he wore a big turquoise ring. "Jessica, this is Bud Wilson," said Miles. "Billy sent him down here to check on us last week."

Billy Martin pulled out a chair for Jessica and offered to get her a glass of wine. "Thank you, yes," said Jessica, "you have better manners than Mr. Porter here."

Miles was still using the alias of Miles Porter, pretending to be an expatriate from Texas, a merchant who sold patent medicines. "I am sorry, I was preoccupied with something," said Miles. "Wilson here told us about seeing a wrecked wagon at a river crossing north of here. He thinks there may be something we need to investigate. Have you heard anything from our friend, Jimmy Gray?"

Jessica could tell Miles had been drinking all afternoon. "Yes, I have," She replied. Accepting a glass of sangria from Martin, Jessica set it down on the table without taking a sip. "And I have seen Mr. McManus again. He is here, in Las Vegas," she said.

Miles sat up straight. "Was anyone with him?" he asked.

"No. But he will head for the Gray ranch."

Miles Wells leaned over to Martin and whispered something that Jessica could not hear. Martin nodded, then he conferred with Bud Wilson. Jessica felt she was being left out of the conversation, so she spoke up: "Lew McManus was in Cimarron, and he had put a Confederate soldier in jail. The soldier was one of the men who was keeping the gold for themselves. But that was not all of the gold. I think McManus kept some of it for himself."

All three men looked around the cantina; they seemed worried other people may have heard Mrs. Piedmont. Martin leaned over to her and told her to verify this information somehow. "We need to confront McManus at Gray's ranch. Or, at least you should go, to check that out," he advised.

Heading to the Canadian River from the Coronado Hills, Dirt Bradshaw and Rodrigo led Deputy Marshall Fazari eastward, through flat grasslands and into an area of desert, where the river cut a canyon, with sandstone cliffs. Down below, boulder slides produced a series of whitewater rapids and steep drops in a section several miles downstream from the Rock Crossing.

"There's no way a boat could have navigated that water after that rainstorm," said Bradshaw, pointing down from the edge of a sandstone cliff. "They had to either portage around here, or leave the river, or perish with the gold."

"I hope you're right," Fazari replied, as both men studied the opposite rim and the striking rock formations in the gorge. "But we didn't come here to go sightseeing." The Deputy Marshall shouted, "Hello!" His voice echoed down the canyon. "You haven't a clue where they've gone, however,"

"Yeah, but they had to have left some sign of being here, if they wrecked," said Dirt. "Rodrigo, can you find us a way down into the canyon?" he asked.

"We will have to look around somewhere else," Red Water remarked. He also wondered about Bradshaw's theory.

"Well, it's getting kind of late for now," said Dirt, slapping his hat on his pants to shake off the dust. "What do we say we make camp for the evening over in that oak grove? Where the wind won't be so bad and we'll have plenty of good firewood."

"That will work," Fazari agreed. "I'm ready to roast up some backstrap." Eduard Fazari had shot a pronghorn antelope earlier in the day and he looked forward to the delicacy. Unlike Dirt and Rodrigo, who had spent a whole month in the wilderness, Fazari was enjoying the prospect of hunting, camping and sleeping out under the stars. It was good to get away from the dictates of General Carleton and Eduard's wife.

Bradshaw had a blazing fire and coffee going in no time, while Fazari prepared the dinner. Eduard had spent a good deal of his Marshall's allowance on a horse, pack mule and supplies back at Fort Union and Loma Parda. They had packed enough water, coffee, wine and whiskey for a week-long journey into the canyonlands of the upper Canadian.

Fazari allowed Red Water to go find more firewood and forage for medicinal plants. In case Rodrigo decided to escape, his horse had been hobbled at the campsite; which meant Rodrigo would not go far before being recaptured.

Resting by the campfire, Dirt and Fazari discussed their options. The Colorado miner was taking his ease, reclining back against his saddle and drinking coffee. Fazari uncorked a bottle of Madeira wine. "Do you want some of this, as an aperitif, before the meal?" he asked.

"No thanks. I've got my coffee," said Dirt, raising his tin cup in a mild salute. "But I've got a question. If you were a Comanchero, would you stay on the Cimarron Cutoff and risk being seen by travelers going to or from La Junta?"

"I reckon not. Yet the boats might have been a diversionary tactic. And La Junta is the closest real settlement," Fazari replied.

"Yeah, but it's busy nowadays, with more Anglos than Hispanos," Dirt said. "You know, I've been thinking. A man can't do commerce with bars of refined gold. But what if Ortiz were to visit a blacksmith's shop? Someone he could trust?"

"I ain't following," said Fazari, sipping his wine.

"If a smithy could heat those ingots up enough, he could shape the gold into looking like free gold. You know, into gold nuggets, like us prospectors sometimes found at the beginning of a gold rush."

Eduard Fazari's mouth dropped open. "By gosh, you're right! I haven't thought about that," he admitted.

"And where did we buy that Spanish wine, Amigo?"

"It's not Spanish. It's Portuguese. And yes sir, we bought it at Loma Parda—also known as 'Sodom on the Mora.' But that's right next to Fort Union. It's crawling with Federal soldiers on weekend nights. They wouldn't go there."

"Why not?" Dirt asked. "The best place to hide something from the Government may be right under the Government's nose." He grinned slyly. "You speak Spanish, don't you?"

Red Water returned, dragging a downed oak branch and carrying an armload of dry wood. "That's right," said Fazari. "And Rodrigo does too."

"Si hablo Espanol," the Mescalero assented.

"Si. So we'll go talk to the Mexicanos in Loma Parda, to ask them if they saw this Sergio Ortiz hombre," said Fazari.

"There is something I found, down by the river." Rodrigo remarked.

"There is a trail. Down at the bottom, there is a boat that is broken, hidden in the bushes. And tracks of men and horses.'

Dirt sat up straight. "That means they did indeed wreck—against those rocks! I was right, Eduardo. They tried to float the river, but couldn't do it."

"Even some of the smartest outlaws will always make some mistakes," said Fazari. He jammed the cork back in the wine bottle. "Can you swim, Amigo?" he asked Rodrigo. Red Water shook his head.

Dirt stood up. "You're thinking they may have lost their cargo, right?
"Yeah, I know how to swim. We had plenty of lakes up in Wisconsin."

"Me too. Like a swamp rat in the bayou," said Fazari. "It's too dark
now, but if you think we can manage the current, we'll dive in and
look in the morning."

CHAPTER 32

Nicole Klausmann now lived in an actual home, with a roof over her
head and a bed of her own. Her old relatives, an aunt and uncle she had
barely known before, took her into their house on Adams Street and
welcomed her back to the family fold.

This former captive of the Comanches, now being called only by her
original name, had become fast friends with both of the Edgartons. Trey
Edgarton had persuaded his sister to remain in Lawrence for a while,
in order to insure Nicole's adjustment to the town. Jane introduced
her to Silas Soule's two sisters, who said they would take Nicole under
their wings.

The most important person in Nicole's new life; however, was the
Canadian journalist, Trey Edgarton. Miss Klausmann's bright-eyed
suitor called on her almost every evening. They went on long walks
through town; staying out after the lamplighter made his rounds to
light the gas lanterns, and then they sat together on a porch swing at
Nicole's new home.

Three nights after their arrival in Lawrence, Jane Edgarton spoke
before a gathering of women at a National Loyal League rally. She
brought Nicole with her. A town of two thousand people in east Kansas,
Lawrence was famous for being a center of the abolitionist movement
in the western United States. The anti-slavery martyr, John Brown,
first made his mark here and was considered the town's hero. During

the time called "Bloody Kansas", the free-state and slave-state factions battled each other over statehood.

Nicole was happy to attend the rally, until Miss Jane singled her out, as a shining example of someone gaining freedom from servitude. Jane described how Nicole was taken captive by Indians: "forced to do incredibly hard toil, and even forced to submit to being the wife of a warrior."

As Jane Edgarton spoke, Nicole noticed how the ladies assembled in the hall changed their countenances. Some began to look at Nicole with disapproval and she could feel her face flushing. She wished Trey had come with her, but this rally was only for the women of the town.

The women at the rally circulated a petition after Jane's speech, while Miss Edgarton played two Union songs on her violin. The petition urged the Federal government to pass a constitutional amendment, banning all slavery in all the United States and its territories. None of the women handed the petition to Nicole; she could sense their disdain at the end of the rally. As they filed out without speaking to her, Nicole walked up to the podium to speak with Jane.

As the hall emptied, Jane Edgarton urged Nicole to sign the petition. "Your signature is just as important as anyone else's," said Jane. "Please, sign it, like I showed you."

"What does it say?" Nicole asked.

"Lincoln didn't do enough to just free slaves in the Confederacy. We must free all captives, both black and Indian. I will take it all the way to Washington City—if need be—and present it to Abe Lincoln himself!"

Nicole took the pen Jane offered, and at the bottom of the list, she wrote: WaShana N. Klausmann. Studying her writing, Jane asked, "Why did you sign it that way, Girl?"

"You made me a Comanche again, in front of those ladies. I signed it "WaShana", to show I am not ashamed to be who I am," said the girl.

Over on the upper Canadian River, Dirt Bradshaw and Marshall Fazari climbed down into the gorge to search the area where Rodrigo had found the wrecked boat. Turning the vessel over, they saw where the wooden hull had sustained a foot-long gash. Stripping down to their trousers, the two men stashed their guns and gears under the boat, then they searched first around the boulders below the stretch of rapids. This proved difficult, for the river's current was still too fast for them to scan the bottom adequately.

"Whew! I couldn't do it," Dirt huffed, when he emerged from the water. It's still too swift."

"Maybe if we roped a rock around your feet or waist, that would hold you down," said Fazari, sitting on a rock ledge, his wet hair dripping down around his eyes.

"Be my guest, I ain't aiming to be turtle food," said Dirt, pulling himself out of the stream.

Rodrigo Red Water stood along the footpath above the river bottom. "There is a deep pool, a little downstream there," he said, after walking back from a short hike.

"We'll try it," said Dirt. "After they got that big gash in the boat, they might have gone a little ways before sinking, then they dragged it out onto that sandbar."

"Too bad their tracks were wiped out by that rainstorm," Fazari added.

Bradshaw and Fazari slogged downstream, until they reached a deep blue-watered pool. "It's real clear, at least," said Dirt. He waded over to the sandbar. "And about eight to ten feet deep or more. Let me rest a minute." Despite it being a hot August morning, Bradshaw shivered from the cold water. His face, neck and forearms were tan from the sun, yet the rest of his torso was white and pink.

Eduard Fazari stayed in the river, standing at the edge of the dropoff, in four feet of water. "What's the matter, Yank? I thought you'd be used to cold water, up in them Great Lakes. Or up in Colorado."

Dirt squatted down, squooshing water out of his rolled-up trousers. "I ain't used to diving for oysters, like you, you dang pelican. Here I go! Eeeaayah!" Dirt leapt up, ran off the sandbar and dove into the water.

Rodrigo and Fazari looked at each other and laughed, then Eduard plunged in after the miner.

Red Water watched, seeing the blurred forms of the two men disappear in the shimmering blue water. Bubbles rippled up to the surface. Rodrigo counted; ten seconds...fifteen...twenty. After half a minute, Dirt Bradshaw burst out of the water, gasping for air. Fazari was still at the bottom of the pool. "Did you see anything?" Rodrigo asked.

"Maybe," said Dirt. He took two deep breaths and went back under.

Seconds later, both men emerged and Fazari held a fat brick of refined gold in his hand. He and Dirt whooped with joy; they had found part of the lost cargo.

Over the next hour and a half, Bradshaw and Fazari took turns retrieving the gold scattered around the bottom of the river. Soon the two men were exhausted; however, nine gold ingots lay stacked beside them on the sandbar. "I reckon it's only part of the cargo," said Dirt, "or they wouldn't have left it. How much ya reckon this is worth?"

"I don't know. Maybe ten thousand dollars or more," said the Deputy Marshall.

"And the lives of at least nine men," Rodrigo Red Water declared.

"Want to make it twelve?" a voice questioned, followed by the cold clicks of two revolvers and footsteps crunching the edge of the sandbar.

Lee Sixkiller stood at the river's edge with a six-gun in each hand.

More gun hammers clicked and two men, with rifles, appeared on the bluff above the river. A man Eduard Fazari recognized stepped out of the brush behind Sixkiller. He held a Navy revolver in his right hand and a lasso in the other.

"Miles Wells," said Fazari. "Do you want killing a U.S. Deputy Marshall on your hands?" he sneered.

"No need for that mess," the Confederate agent replied. He waved to the riflemen, telling them to come on down. "We'll tie you and your assistant up, relieve you of your day's work and get out of here. 'Contraband of war', as your President would say."

Rodrigo Red Water stole a quick glance at Dirt Bradshaw, closed one eye, then he said, "I am the Marshall's prisoner—take me with you."

"I have to doubt that, seeing as you're not handcuffed or shackled," Miles Wells remarked. "But since you are an old friend, I'd be glad to free you. See that, Fazari? I can do a little emancipating too."

Speechless, Dirt Bradshaw hung his head, as Lee Sixkiller began tying his ankles together. He had failed his brother one again; in addition, here he was, being hobbled for the second time in just a week.

Insult was added to injury, when the two riflemen appeared at the river bottom. One was just a boy, a Native American. Dirt instantly recognized Bud Wilson, the other gunman. "Thought you only dealt in turquoise, Bud," said Dirt. "What made you change sides, you sonuvabitch?"

Wilson ignored Bradshaw's cussing and took the lasso from Miles Wells. "I did talk Mr. Wells into sparing your life," he whispered. Then he roped Dirt's wrists. Dirt noticed something, yet he did not comment.

"Where is the girl?" Lee Sixkiller asked, as he went to work tying up the Deputy Marshall.

"Long gone, Mister—long gone," said Dirt. He looked over at Rodrigo and mouthed: *go find Lewis.*

"Where is the big man?" Sixkiller persisted, "the one called McManus? He took some of the gold too, didn't he?"

With a furtive glance at Fazari and then Red Water, Dirt smiled slightly and said, "I won't contradict you on that matter. He totally betrayed us. Maybe he was working for the Confederacy all this time. But where he went—your guess is as good as mine."

Miles Wells, who was rolling a cigarette, seemed to take note of this statement. "You all were quite entertaining to watch just now, while you were diving for this treasure," said Wells. You reminded me of pearl divers in the Bay of Bengal. Since you did us a favor by retrieving this gold, we'll do you one in return. We'll leave you one horse, so you can ride in tandem—if you eventually find a way to break free. That should give us at least a days' head start, I figure."

"Leave me the brown filly," said Dirt. "Rodrigo knows which one. So, are you with the bushwhackers or the Comanchero?" he asked Wells, as the Cherokee boy and Wison loaded up the gold bricks into sacks.

Wells sat down on a flat rock, struck a match against it and lit his cigarette. "Neither. Regular Confederacy. Unlike all those traitors and thugs, I am not keeping this gold for myself."

"Hah, I bet. Have you been working with a woman named Jessica Piedmont?" Eduard Fazari asked. This was odd, for the Deputy Marshal was now bound back-to-back with the Colorado miner. He was in no position to interrogate anyone.

Miles Wells leaned down, blew smoke in Fazari's face and murmured, "I don't believe I've ever heard of the woman." Wells laughed. "Alright, Sam. You and Lee go ahead and drag these two over to those trees, so they can rest yonder."

Lew McManus found himself in an uncomfortable situation. Days earlier, when Rosa Amarilla walked out of Jimmy Gray's kitchen, and she was showing a 'pumpkin belly', Lew felt both speechless and guilty. Lew had also awakened his partner from a mid-afternoon nap and Jimmy Carl seemed grumpy, ever since that moment, speaking in oaths and curses. Even though this behavior was customary with the thin Tennessean, this time he and McManus had something substantial to argue about.

"You need to marry that gal!" Jimmy Gray declared, for the seventh time in four days. "It ain't me that's the daddy, dogdammit!" He and McManus sat out on the ranch house's front porch, drinking rye whiskey in the late afternoon shade. Jimmy sat in a rocking chair; while Lew had taken a hardback one from the kitchen.

"You marry her," said Lew. "You and the Yeller Rose have eased into a peaceful co-existence."

"That's only since Joe Piedmont's momma left two weeks ago," said Gray. Ned Piedmont, Jessica's younger son, was now working at the Rim Rock.

"You never told me where she was going," said McManus.

"Cimarron," said Jimmy.

McManus gulped. He'd thought he had seen a woman who looked familiar back at the Maxwell House. Lew wondered if SHE had noticed him, while he was spending money extravagantly. Lew McManus had told Jimmy about helping the U.S. Cavalry recover the stolen gold; he did not inform his partner about the chunks of gold now buried on the back reaches of their ranch.

That's a shame, what happened to Rodrigo," said Jimmy. "He should have stayed out of any towns here in New Mexico. I had to testify about him in Santa Fe last month. I told the Territorial Court that Red Water had nothing to do with that Yankee captain getting killed. I guess they didn't believe me."

A red rooster strutted up to the porch. "Watch this," said Gray. Jimmy leaned forward in his rocker and set his glass down beside it. He poured a little of the rye whiskey into the glass. "This is the only ranch with a whiskey-drinking chicken," said Jimmy.

The rooster leapt up on the porch. It looked sideways at the glass, then it pecked at the alcohol. "So, you think that German girl will be happy in Kansas? Is she back to being Nicole?" Gray asked.

"Far as I know. You shoulda seen her before she left," said Lew. "That girl has become a pretty young woman. There's a lady Dirt Bradshaw knows, who is going to teach her how to read and write. So I gave Nicole our address here. Maybe she'll send us a letter."

Jimmy nodded. The rooster was back at the whiskey glass, wetting his beak in the rye. Both men laughed.

"So where did Miguel go? Maybe he is the daddy," said Lew.

Jimmy explained that Rosa Amarillo and the vaquero were no longer together. Miguel LaHoya was now chief foreman at the Fazari-Martinez ranch in Bernalillo. "I saw him last week, when I bought a young bull from Senor Martinez."

"Well, it's a shame Miguel didn't marry Rosa," Lew said. "Maybe we can talk him into it."

"You're just saying that 'cause you want to get off the hook," Gray replied.

The rooster suddenly crowed, flapped his wings, then it flopped off the porch. "Let's go look at that bull," Jimmy Gray suggested. Springing to his feet, he shouted into the house; "Hey, Rosa! Have supper ready for us in an hour!"

"You already sound like you two are married," Lew remarked, as the two ranchers walked out to the corral.

Inside the ranch house, Rosa Amarilla Del Rio was still washing the dishes from lunch. She angrily clattered plates and rattled pans. Lew McManus was scarcely acknowledging her these days; she also felt Jimmy Gray was taking her for granted. The young criolla woman thought she had been freed only to become a household servant to these Tennesseans.

Rosa threw her washcloth in the sink and stormed into the main room of the ranch house. She sat down in Jimmy Gray's easy chair, looked for the bottle of rye he kept under it, but it was gone. The men were already drinking; she knew it would be a difficult night.

Roas Amarilla thought about going upstairs to pout. Jimmy had converted the attic into a small bedroom for her. She could let the men make their own supper, yet that might get her evicted from the Rim Rock. Rosa reasoned with herself. She had few options; being pregnant, she could not return to the Hot Springs hotel at Montezuma.

The clatter of horses approaching roused Rosa Amarilla from her musings. She gazed out the parlor window and cursed in French. The Texas woman had returned.

CHAPTER 33

"I think I can get my hands free," said Dirt, gnawing and twisting at the rope that bound his wrists. "Bud Wilson didn't tie them that tightly."

"And you know these people how?" asked Fazari. The Deputy Marshall's back was turned to Bradshaw.

"He was some old turquoise trader, whom we met on the Trail. I thought he was my friend," Dirt said.

"Heh, friends like that can kill you," Fazari muttered. "Say, maybe if we stand up we can shuffle over and find something to tear at this main rope." Bracing themselves against each other, back-to-back, the two men struggled to their feet. "Over there to that jagged rock," Fazari suggested. Awkwardly, like a wounded crab, the pair hobbled over to a boulder.

"We're like Siamese twins at a barn dance," said Dirt, laughing. "And neither one knows how to lead." Both of them were barefoot, after diving for the stolen gold hours earlier.

"Try and turn around, to face me," said Fazari. "That way we can see what the other is doing."

"The rope around their waists was just slack enough for Bradshaw to do this, yet they were still tightly lashed together. "Yecch," said Dirt. "Bad idea. You put too many onions and garlic in the food last night. Your breath would knock a grizzly out."

"Hush. Do like me, now," Fazari said, rubbing the rope at his waist against the sharp edge of the granite boulder. "Bend your knees, up and down, so we can fray this knotted part."

"I'm afraid not," said Dirt. "Let me keep trying to get my hands free."

Fazari ignored him and continued to work the rope back and forth. After about ten minutes, the first strand broke. There were about five strands left in the rope. They continued working on them. Eventually, Bradshaw slipped his left hand free from the rope at his wrists, so now he was unbound. "Hey, I can either untie you now—or maybe we can even slide this main lash down over our legs, if we suck in our gut," he suggested.

A few minutes later, both men were free. They hurried up the footpath, to get their shirts, the guns and their boots. "So what do we do now?" Bradshaw asked, as they hiked back to their campsite.

"Let me think. There's four of them—five, if your Indian friend switches sides—against us two. We need reinforcements," said Fazari.

"Rodrigo is not going to switch sides," said Dirt. "And I had an idea back there when they were tying us up. They will head south, right? After all, they are Confederates. Lew McManus has a ranch with his friend Jimmy Gray, down near Las Vegas Grandes. You know where it is, right?"

"Yeah." said the Deputy Marshall, hesitating. "Still more friends of a dubious nature."

As they expected, Bradshaw and Fazari's campsite had been pillaged. Miles Wells and his party had taken almost everything; their food, supplies, Fazari's horse and the pack mule. They only left Dirt's dented coffee pot, his tent and his horse picketed nearby, plus a few chunks of charred meat in the ashes of the campfire. "Well, I can gnaw on that, to get the taste of hemp outa my mouth," said Dirt.

"Is your horse going to hold up, carrying both of us together?" Fazari questioned. "Maybe one of us should ride and the other one walk."

Dirt took one look at the Marshall and one at Waukesha. "She's my horse, and you could afford to lose a few pounds," he said.

"Yeah, but I'm a United States Marshall. And my knee has been acting up. I hereby requisition this horse for the purposes of the U.S. government."

"Government, my arse. Out here in the hinterlands, you ain't got no more authority than me. I've got a better idea," Bradshaw looked in the tent and was surprised to see that Rodrigo had left a saddle and a hunting knife inside. He took the bivouac tent down and reconstructed it, to make a crude Indian travois, much like the one he had used to carry WaShana over to Cimarron. He added some limbs from a tree to sturdy the device. "Since your knee is bad, you can ride in here first—unless Waukesha protests," said Dirt, after finishing the project.

"We'll take turns," said Fazari, climbing onto the saddle.

Nicole did not want Trey Edgarton to go. He and Miss Jane were leaving for St. Louis in the morning, to continue Jane's lecture and concert tour for the Women's Abolitionist movement. Trey and Nicole stayed out late this evening well past nightfall. She had hoped that the young man might finally ask her to marry him this time, but as the couple strolled back to her uncle's home on Adams Street, it seemed like the evening would end only in a fond farewell.

Holding hands, they came to the gate of a white picket fence, then Trey halted before they stepped into Klausmann's front yard. He kissed Nicole's cheek. "I wish I was not going away, my Dearest," said Edgarton, "but my sister needs me—and the cause demands my writing efforts. I have put off a lot of work in the last two weeks, you know."

"Please stay. I will try to not distract you so much," Nicole promised. She embraced him tightly and did not want to let go.

"Ha, I don't see how you cannot," said Trey, gazing into her eyes, then kissing Nicole on the lips. Nicole responded, kissing him passionately, then opening her eyes in hopes of enthralling her lover into an impulsive declaration of marital intent. "Once victory is accomplished, I shall return to you, Nicole," said Trey.

"And?" Nicole's expression flushed with anxious hope and expectation.

"And it is best if you stay here, where you will be safe. You just found your family again, and we may be going through a dangerous region."

Nicole looked downward and bit her lip. She had just gone through a much more perilous journey the previous month; before that, she had lived as WaShana of the Comanches. In this new world; however, she reasoned she must return to being a proper young woman, adhering to the constraints of being female in a society that required a softer path of persuasion. "Why can I not go with you? I want to go with you," Nicole pleaded.

"You will be in my heart and mind the whole time," said Trey. "My, you are growing more beautiful every day." He hugged her, feeling the fullness of her bosom, taking in the fragrance of her scent, as if he could capture it and keep it throughout their separation. "We will write to you. Missouri is torn apart by the War, but this war will never tear you and I apart."

Trey Edgarton's honeyed words scarcely reassured Nicole. She held back from crying, but it seemed every person she befriended, everything she hoped to possess would always leave, would always dwindle down to nothing. She took a blue ribbon from her hair, quickly lashed its satin length around Trey's wrist and kissed his cheek. "I am binding you to this promise," said Nicole, "and I will pray for you every day, until you come back."

They kissed once more, then Nicole ran into the white, wood-frame house of her uncle. Trey Edgarton stood by the fence gate, stunned. His sister was waiting back at the hotel and they needed to pack; yet, for a moment, the young woman's last words held him at the gate.

As the young woman watched from the parlor window, Trey Edgarton hesitated in the moonlight, but then he simply walked away.

Nicole stifled her cry; she did not want to awaken her new-found relatives. She went to bed after undressing. The bedroom itself, which had since grown familiar, now felt strange and disconcerting. Nicole had the wild thought of running away to the Edgarton's hotel and waiting for Trey to see her standing outside, keeping a lover's vigil.

It was a clear, hot August night. Cicadas buzzed in the darkened trees and a barn owl let out an eerie, drawn-out screech. WaShana Nicole could not sleep; she opened a window, hoping the familiar sounds of the outside world would give her peace.

Perhaps, if she hardened her heart, she would no longer have to trust her feelings to another man. But this idea did not bring her sleep. Maybe she could go seek Trey again, in the morning, before he and Jane boarded their stagecoach. Maybe Trey was not sleeping as well; maybe he was staring at the same yellow moon on the horizon, and maybe Nicole could convince her young man to take her with him.

In the predawn darkness, as the night birds began to chirp, Nicole Klausmann finally fell asleep. The town of Lawrence also slept, unsuspecting in darkness, after the moon had set.

Miles southeast of the town, William Quantrill's Confederate raiders joined up with other forces on a mission of bloody vengeance. Four hundred horsemen, including Quantrill, Bill and Jim Anderson, George Todd and Captain Dick Yeager, rode in groups of forty to fifty men. Young Joe Piedmont now rode with Lieutenant George Todd's platoon, but he had no idea about what would transpire.

Todd was a determined killer, a blond, round-headed Scottish-American, who was older than the Missouri farm boys he commanded. Stopping briefly at farms along the state border, his platoon garnered both provisions and new recruits. Joe Piedmont and his new friends, Coleman Younger and Frank James rode at the back of the platoon.

The group halted at a farm Cole Younger recognized. "Why are we stopping here?" he asked Frank James.

"I don't know. Joe Stone's a free-stater," James replied. Younger, James and Joe Piedmont watched as Lieutenant Todd and two of his bushwhackers walked up to the farmhouse.

Todd knocked on the door. The farmer opened it. Joe Piedmont watched as the bushwhackers pulled the man outside; then George Todd beat the man with a musket—relentlessly, until farmer Stone was dead.

Then the lieutenant ordered his men to strike a torch and burn down the dead man's barn.

Joe shook his head. In the first weeks of his enlistment with the Missouri raiders, he had enjoyed robbing a mail coach and a Union bank, where the bushwhackers did not randomly take human life. He had joined these Missouri irregulars in hopes of fighting Yankee soldiers face-to-face, on a field of battle. "This ain't fighting, this is murder," Joe whispered to the Missouri boys. "I didn't sign up to murder civilians."

"None of us signed anything," Frank James replied. "We would be fools, to let the Jayhawkers and the Federals know our names."

"Keep quiet and stick with us, Joe," Cole Younger urged, "Lest Todd stove your head in, for being a deserter."

The column began moving again. Reaching a hill above Lawrence as the clear day dawned, the Missouri rebels checked their weapons, formed a line and prepared to attack. Joe spotted the guerilla commander, William Quantrill, riding down the lines and giving each officer their allotted task. Quantrill wore a black slouch hat, a decorated hunting shirt and four revolvers. "Kill every man—and boy big enough to carry a gun," he ordered.

Joe Piedmont surveyed the town; people were still sleeping in their houses on this Friday, August 21, 1863. He saw no signs of an army. Gazing down the line, Joe noted only a few gray Confederate uniforms among these men. The bushwhackers would lead the advance.

Quantrill raised his hand, then swung it downward.

The rebels slapped and kicked their horses upon his signal. Soon the low rumble of a thousand hoofbeats turned to a rolling thunder. Men whooped and gave the rebel yell. Charging ahead of the regular Confederate troops, the bushwhackers roared into town.

Rifles and shotguns cracked and boomed; revolvers fired at every human target. Joe saw someone shoot a man who was milking a cow in his backyard. An old, white-bearded grandfather, taking a morning walk, was gunned down.

"Kill all the Nigras and Germans you see!" Lieutenant Todd shouted, as his group split off from the main advance. They came upon the bivouac camp of the Second Kansas Colored Regiment and some of the Fourteenth Cavalry. Todd's group and another company quickly slaughtered about twenty new Black recruits before any of them could fire their first weapon.

A boy, dressed in pajamas and appearing no older than Joe's younger brother, stepped out on his front porch; Joe watched in horror, as two bushwhackers shot him four or five times. Joe Piedmont's heart ached. Women and children were screaming and shrieking inside the houses, for now the bushwhackers were sticking torches to hay sheds and throwing the torches upon the wood-shingled rooftops.

The Confederate raiders streamed out in several directions from the center of town, setting buildings and houses on fire, shooting every man in sight and terrorizing women and children. Joe Piedmont spotted Cole Younger, now dismounted, helping some women carry furniture out of a burning house. Deciding to pitch in and help, Joe climbed off his horse and grabbed one side of a dresser.

"I lost my horse," said Younger. "This is madness. Madness! After we get this stuff out, ride over and find Colonel Holt. Get him to stop this!" Younger referred to Colonel John Holt, Commander of the regular Confederate troops. "Maybe he can stop this mayhem."

Lieutenant George Todd rode into the yard where Cole Younger and Joe were assisting a family. "What are you farm boys doing?" he shouted, anger burning in his eyes. "Get back on your horses and fight! I have a list of free-state settlers, who are to be executed—whose houses we must burn. Mount up and follow me."

Cole Younger looked at Joe. "Go get the Colonel," he whispered. "I'm coming, Lieutenant! Have to find a horse first, Sir," Younger told Todd.

Riding through the streets of Lawrence, Joe noticed more houses on fire and the bloodied bodies of men strewn out in their yards. Women were screaming and shouting for help. William Quantrill's men now attacked the business center of town. The rampaging guerillas broke into the saloons and stores along the main avenue, breaking glass and pillaging liquor and merchandise. One raider had torn down an American flag and set it on fire, trailing it behind him as he rode down the street. Another group was ransacking the town's hotel, shooting out the windows and looting its tavern. Joe heard shots inside; the bushwhackers were killing male guests in the hotel.

The relentless slaughter raged on. Men were pulled from their homes and shot to death, right in front of their wives and children. Joe kept riding, with his revolver drawn, to show he was still a Confederate, yet he did not shoot anyone.

The young Texan finally found Colonel Holt's troops in another section of the town. They also were not taking part in the massacre. Being more disciplined than the Missouri bushwhackers, the soldiers were putting out fires and protecting huddled groups of women and children from the terrorists.

"We've cordoned off this section," said Colonel Holt, when Joe told him about the carnage being wrecked on the eastern side of town. "There's more townsfolk, hiding in that cornfield over yonder, and we're protecting them too. You can go tell any women and families to seek shelter there," said Holt. "Hurry, go quickly!"

Over on Adams Street, a young woman stood on the front porch of her uncle's house and stared in utter disbelief at the massacre. Still dressed in her night clothes, WaShana Nicole held her uncle's shotgun, keeping a few raiders at bay. Miss Klausmann's uncle had fled to the cornfield with his wife, but Nicole had insisted on protecting their home. People were running about everywhere now, but WaShana Nicole stood her ground.

Nicole realized now why the Comanches called Americans "White Eyes". The whites of their eyes glared wide when confronted by terror— or when the eyes showed rage, like these southern Americans as they ripped through the neighborhood. WaShana Nicole saw two raiders' eyes turn white, when they approached the house with their torches and she chased away with her shotgun.

When it appeared that more Confederates, these all wearing gray uniforms, were now protecting the area, Nicole knew her house was safe. She felt a new concern and a surge of panic; she must go find Trey and Jane Edgarton! Changing into a housedress and leaving the shotgun, Nicole stepped back outside. She had a hunting knife hidden in the vest pocket of her jacket.

Running to the Edgarton's hotel, Nicole's heart fell when she saw inflamed rooftops and broken windows on some shops and storefronts.

A few wild-eyed Missouri horsemen rushed up to the girl, but then they rode away when she brandished her Bowie knife.

WaShana Nicole found Jane Edgarton weeping outside the torched hotel. Still dressed in a white lace nightgown, kneeling in the street, sadly looking at the flames now licking up along the broken windows, Jane hugged her chest and keened in sorrow, just like a Native American wife or mother. WaShana feared that Trey Edgarton might be dead.

"I must take the blame! I am to blame," said Jane, gazing at the crucifixion of her hopes and her brother's love. "They killed our dear Trey!"

WaShana's heart surged as she embraced Jane upon the broken glass. When bricks began to drop off the burning walls of the hotel, she pulled Jane away from the building. "It's my fault! I should have not brought you here. We should have not stayed so long," Jane sobbed.

WaShana kept silent, hugging her friend; but she felt every conception of her life as Nicole Klausmann was now breaking off or being burned away. Her fears, her shock—even her new grief—now turned to anger.

"This is the world of the White Eyes?" WaShana wondered aloud. "This is what they call 'civilized'? First they attack our People, our nations—now they attack each other?"

A unit of Confederate soldiers, mostly men dressed in gray uniforms, appeared on the street. They were telling onlookers to head for the north edge of town. "We can protect you there," said a young Rebel, who only wore the butternut trousers of the Confederacy.

WaShana realized this young man was speaking to her and Jane. "I don't want your protection!" she shouted, flashing her knife. "Go away!"

Stunned by this young woman's fierce expression, Joe Piedmont felt tremendous guilt. "I am so sorry," he murmured, turning away from the two women and then he walked off to join the other soldiers.

"Trey protected me," said Jane, now rising to her feet. "Trey stood outside our room, protecting me, when those men murdered him. As he lay dying, Trey called out your name, Nicole. I held him in my arms and told him you were safe, but I did not for sure." Miss Edgarton's tear-streaked face, now covered in soot and ashes, appeared the very picture of sorrow. "You are far too innocent to have witnessed this tragedy."

WaShana shook her head. "No, I am not so innocent," she said, a hardened look in her eyes. "Not anymore!" The girl hesitated, then she confessed a secret she had kept from both of the Edgartons. "I am now.... I now carry Mr. Red Water's child."

CHAPTER 34

High up on a rocky ledge, looking down upon meadows and the green pines of the Rim Rock ranch, Dirt Bradshaw wondered if this was the right strategy. He could not wait for Marshall Fazari to arrive with the New Mexico militia. Bradshaw felt that he himself could accomplish more by stealth and persuasion than the Marshall might by force of arms.

Dirt had informed Fazari about Lew McManus appropriating some of the Federal gold for himself. After freeing themselves of their ropes back on the upper Canadian, Bradshaw had tracked Miles Wells and his group to Las Vegas, where Fazari asked around, trying to get men to help apprehend the Confederate agent and his accomplices.

The bluffs where Dirt had chosen to survey the ranch ran in a jagged line, on the southwest section of the property. Nestled among the foothills of the Sangre de Christo mountains, this end of the ranch consisted of woods and small grassy meadows. On the eastern side, beyond the barn and corral, there were fields where Jimmy Gray kept his cattle. Dirt could see a narrow plume of smoke rising above the treetops, where the rancher's house was hidden.

It was mid-morning; Dirt detected the sounds of men working and speaking to one another. He heard metal clanking, the thud of a sledgehammer on wood, someone working with horses—and every now and then, someone cursing.

Earlier, a shift in the wind had brought the scent of woodsmoke, and the aroma of bacon to Bradshaw's nostrils. He wanted to hike down and have breakfast with his friends, but he had seen a group of men coming from the north end of the ranch and then leaving, shortly after dawn. The chance that they might be Miles Wells and his gang made it too risky. Dirt could only watch and listen.

Sneaking over to the next ledge, which was closer to the barnyard, Dirt spotted a cinder block building—what appeared to be a springhouse or maybe a root cellar.

A short time later, a man approached the small blockhouse. Dirt recognized Rodrigo Red Water, who was carrying two empty buckets. No one else was with the Mescalero.

Seizing this opportunity, Bradshaw flung a rock toward the springhouse. It missed, landing in the treetops. Dirt picked up another stone, threw it harder and with a higher arc. The stone pinged on the tin roof of the springhouse. Rodrigo dropped his buckets and drew out a gun.

"Hsst, Rodrigo! It's me—don't shoot," Dirt said, hoping his voice would not carry too far. Bradshaw stood up and waved his arms.

Red Water cocked his head, to look through the trees. Now, he grinned and signaled that Dirt should not approach; he would climb up to meet the prospector.

"Did you bring me a biscuit?" Dirt joked when Rodrigo gained the top of the bluff. "I smelt you fellows making breakfast earlier."

Rodrigo shook his head. "I told Senor Miles that he could hide the gold up in Blue Canyon, north of here. Then they came here to the ranch. This morning, they left with their wagon, but they may return soon," he remarked. "It's good to see you, Amigo."

"I'm glad to see you," said Dirt. "Walk back with me, into the woods. The pines will muffle our voices."

When they reached the cover of the evergreens, Dirt asked how Lew McManus and Jimmy Gray had reacted to Miles Wells' arrival on their ranch. "Did you bring them here?"

Red Water frowned. "No, a woman brought them here. Wells tried to convince our friends to join the Confederados. But Señor Jimmy and Señor Lew would not do it. There is another thing. Now two women are staying at the ranch and they are.... big trouble."

"Who are they?" Dirt asked.

"A lady from Texas. And a brown woman, younger, who is called 'The Yellow Rose'—Rosa Amarillo, who does the cooking."

Dirt nodded his head. "Lew told me about Rosa. Is the other lady named Jessica?" Bradshaw asked.

"Si, and her boy now works at the ranch," said Red Water. "This is why you cannot be seen. He will tell his mother, who will tell Miles Wells."

"You've got to go warn Jimmy and Lew," said Dirt. "They can't be harboring Wells—because the Militia is coming here later! And both you and I must get away before they come, or you'll get arrested all over again, Rodrigo."

Red Water looked away and seemed to consider the matter. His expression grew worried, yet he was concerned not for himself. Rodrigo asked about WaShana.

"She made it back to Lawrence," said Dirt. "Back in Las Vegas, I sent a letter to Jane Edgarton. You know, the lady who is helping Nicole,"

Upon hearing WaShana's Anglo name, Rodrigo's countenance turned grim. Dirt saw that he was still heartsick over the young woman. "You come with me, compadre," Dirt offered. "We can both be scouts for the First Colorado."

Red Water shook his head. "No, after you get the gold, I want you to take me to the Bosque Redondo. I will surrender there. Even if it is bad medicine, I must go and be with my people."

Dirt was disappointed to hear this. He asked why Rodrigo had come to this decision. Red Water explained how he and a Mescalero woman, named Broken Wing, were once very close through the years. He hoped to find her among the captives at the internment camp.

"I'm sorry," said Dirt, "it seems every promise we Americans have made to the Indians, gets broken. And it's often been us gold miners leading the advance into your lands."

"The gold is not far away," Red Water remarked. "I persuaded Senor Wells to hide it up in Blue Canyon. But tell me—why do men seek the gold? To us Apache, the oro has little meaning, other than ornamentation on a puffed-up man."

"Well, men think it's quick money—and part of their dream to get rich," Bradshaw replied.

"White men's dreams are strange then. Better to go seek a vision, to find one's power on one's own. Searching for what others also seek leads to bad medicine—competition and wanting to take away what others have."

Dirt mulled this over. "By God, you're right, Amigo. You seem wiser than the Greek Philosophers, or the Wise Men of the Hindu Kush. But let's deal with the situation at hand. Who all is down at the ranch house now, besides the women?"

"There is a Cherokee boy, working with Senor Jimmy and Big Lew, in the corral. Wells and two men are riding off to San Geronimo, to buy ammunition."

"So that's who I heard riding off earlier," said Dirt. "This seems manageable. Let's go to the house, Amigo—and keep your gun handy. I need to speak with Jimmy and Big Lew."

Following Red Water on a trail through the pine grove, Bradshaw led his filly down to the barnyard. Gray and McManus were in the corral, working with some horses. McManus had fired up a blacksmith's forge at one end of the barn and was hammering away on a bent horseshoe. "What do you say, Yank?" Lew asked, in a surprisingly matter-of-fact way, when he saw Bradshaw approach.

Dirt grinned. "Hope this ain't a bad time, Lew. Hi, Mr. Jimmy, how are you doing?"

Gray was leaning over the corral fence, nonchalantly smoking a cigarette. "Fine, but we've had a lot of damn visitors lately. You missed breakfast."

Dirt noticed two boys—one white and the other one, a little older, who looked Native American. They had saddled a short mustang over in the far corner of the corral. The older boy eyed Bradshaw with great suspicion. Dirt realized he was the Cherokee who had been with Wells and Wilson at the river. Bradshaw pulled the brim of his hat down low and walked away, over to where McManus was working.

Lew McManus pulled a glowing red horseshoe out of the forge and commenced to pound it on an anvil. Dressed in a heavy black apron, his face and mighty forearms blackened by soot to match his beard, McManus looked like the Roman God Vulcan. He appeared intent on not discussing the purloined gold, but kept clanging away.

The noise made talking difficult, but Dirt managed to tell Jimmy Gray about Fazari and the militia coming to visit. The thin rancher's eyes widened; he seemed exasperated. "Let's go inside," said Gray.

While Rodrigo stood guard out on the front porch, Dirt followed Jimmy into the cooler interior of the adobe-walled home. "Why are they coming?" Jimmy asked.

"I don't know what Lew has told you, but there's fixing to be a skirmish. If the Deputy Marshall catches Miles Wells at San Geronimo, you won't have trouble. But if Wells and his Confederate Indians return here first, you will," Bradshaw warned.

"Dogdammit," the rancher swore. "Where's my rifle?"

Dirt glanced around the main living room. Empty whiskey and tequila bottles, dirty plates and glasses lay on the side tables and on the fireplace mantel. The smell of cigarette ash still hovered in the air. There had been some sort of revelry the previous evening. Back in the ranch house kitchen, someone was clattering dishes.

At the top of a small flight of stairs, a woman appeared in a doorway. "I told you—you shoulda left yesterday," Jimmy Gray growled at her.

Jessica Piedmont ignored the rancher's complaint. "Hello, Mr. Bradshaw. We meet again," said Jessica.

"Indeed. But I'm afraid it won't be for long. I just came to—well," Dirt stopped himself. This was awkward; Jessica Piedmont was rumored to be a Confederate spy. "To say howdy-do, and then fare-thee-well, I guess." Bradshaw doffed his hat, then placed it back on his head. "Rodrigo and I must go right now," he told Gray.

"Go ahead and git," said Jimmy. "As for you, Lady, pack your bags. It's check-out time."

"I'm not leaving," the Texas widow replied. "Not until Miles returns." She gazed down at Dirt Bradshaw. "Everyone knows," Jessica said coldly. "I know why you came here."

"None of that matters!" said Gray. Turning to Dirt Bradshaw, he added, "Welcome to the Rim Rock ranch! It ain't much, but it's worth protecting. Come back sometime, after this shitty war is over."

Dirt took the hint. Another, younger woman emerged from the kitchen. Dirt realized she was the Rosa Amarillo that both Lew and

Rodrigo talked about. Once enslaved and forced into prostitution, she now lived at Jimmy Grays' ranch.

"Mon Dieu, are we being invaded?" the dark-haired girl asked, with panic in her voice.

"It's just the damn Federal government," said Jimmy, trying to calm her down. "I expected them to swarm down on us any day. I've had my fill of them. They're like blackflies and gnats, when you're fishing a creek. You know, Dirt. No big trouble, as long as they keep their distance—but when they get in your face, dogdammit, they'll drive you loco."

Dirt liked this New Mexico rancher, who mixed both the profane and the profound in his speech. Jessica Piedmont now headed back into the upstairs bedroom and closed the door. "So, what do you want me to do?" Dirt asked Jimmy.

Jimmy Gray tilted his head toward the creole girl, who was taking off her apron. "You and Rodrigo take Rosa up into the woods, past the bluff behind this house. When Fazari and the damn militia get here, I'll talk sense into them."

"I doubt you can," said Dirt. He noticed Lew McManus stroll in from the porch, where he might have been listening. McManus asked what was going on. Dirt rolled his eyes. "Don't act innocent. They're coming for that stuff you kept. Miles Wells and his Confederado Indians also have nine bricks of gold. I didn't tell the Deputy about you, but that Cherokee, Sixkiller, did. Fazari and the New Mexico Militia are coming to search the place."

Lew's eyes widened. "Let me wash up, first. Then I'm leaving."

"Que Pasa, Lew?" Jimmy questioned. "You've been acting very differently, ever since you came back here."

"For all I risked, I deserve a reward!" McManus bellowed. "You weren't there, so don't judge me."

"Dogdammit! Hell, I shoulda known!" Jimmy Gray replied. As the two Tennesseans cursed and argued, Dirt eased over to the young woman. He advised her to get a jacket and accompany him to hide in the woods.

"There might be a gunfight," said Bradshaw. Not knowing how long they would have to hide, Rosa Amarilla stepped back into the kitchen. Dirt followed her. She was beautifully exotic, slight, dark-haired, with flashing eyes and lithe in her movements. Rosa started packing ham, some bread and a glass jar of pickles into a basket. Inside a small metal icebox, she found a wedge of cheese. "What's this?" asked Dirt as she added three apples to the basket. "Are we having a picnic?"

Rosa Amarilla smiled, "I am French. One must be prepared for adversity," she remarked, grabbing a bottle of wine, then wrapping her hair up with a bandana.

"Oui. That's a good idea," Dirt agreed. "Shall we go?"

Rodrigo appeared at the back screen door. "I have your horse, Dirt," he said. Red water was confused for a moment, seeing Bradshaw holding a basket of food and having the creole girl on his other arm. Before Dirt could explain, rifle shots echoed from the south end of the ranch.

Eduard Fazari and Miguel LaHoya rode in front of the New Mexico Militia as the volunteer detachment streamed out of San Geronimo. They had learned that two Anglos and two Indians had just left the village trading post with a wagonload of supplies only an hour earlier. The military detachment was led by James 'Paddy' Graydon and included twenty-four men—twenty-six with the addition of the Deputy Marshall and the vaquero. Except for a sergeant and one of the corporals, the soldiers were all Mexicanos. They carried muskets and reconstructed Springfield carbines. Eduard Fazari worried about Captain Graydon; he was an Irishman and prone to excessively violent measures. Graydon had fought at both Valverde and Glorieta Pass the previous year. He had a history of dealing treacherously with the Mescalero Apaches, slaughtering some of their chiefs once, while under a flag of truce.

"Look, they are ahead of us," said Miguel LaHoya. The vaquero pointed to a cloud of dust, trailing behind the dark shapes of a wagon and three riders. They were following the line of a narrow creek, heading to Jimmy Gray's ranch below the foothills.

"Come on, we've got to stop them," said Fazari, slapping his horse into a full gallop. The vaquero spurred his horse and followed. Within a minute, they were both far ahead of the volunteer company and gaining on the wagon.

Somehow, with dust swirling on the dry flat plain, neither man saw two of the men they were pursuing halt and take aim with their rifles. Just as Marshall Fazari heard two shots ring out, the young vaquero fell from his saddle.

The Deputy Marshall turned his horse to give aid to Miguel—but then his own horse was hit by another shot. The horse reared back, then collapsed upon its rider. Fazari's left leg was stuck under his dying mount. His leg was not broken, yet he could not pull it free; at least the horse's rear flank shielded Eduard against another series of rifle fire. Then the shooting stopped.

A minute later, the militia unit rode up. Several of the Mexicano soldiers dismounted and aimed their guns, but the wagon and the fleeing outlaws were now out of range. "How is Miguel?" Fazari asked Captain Graydon.

"The vaquero is dying. You were fools to not stay with us," said the Irishman. Several soldiers lifted Fazari's dead horse and pulled him free. Fazari's leg was numb and his knee was sprained.

"Don't go to the ranch without me. Maybe I can negotiate something with Gray and McManus," Fazari advised. "Help me up," he asked the soldiers.

"If they are harboring that group of picaroons, I am ordering my lads to take no prisoners," Paddy Graydon replied.

"But I have a man watching the place," said Fazari. He limped over to Miguel LaHoya's horse. "You might shoot him by accident."

Graydon instructed two soldiers to stay back with Fazari and the fatally wounded vaquero. "The rest of us will ride on. Muskets at the ready!" said the captain.

CHAPTER 35

Jimmy Gray ran out to the corral with his rifle in hand. "Open the gate! Shoo off all the horses, Ned!" he shouted to the Piedmont boy. "You! Get Rosa's milk cows out of the barn," Gray told Sam Burningtree.

Lew McManus shuffled out of the ranch house, armed with his revolvers and chucking rimfire cartridges into his Spencer .52 caliber repeating carbine. "I'll be up in the hay loft," he told Jimmy. "You go back inside."

Gray stood out in the barnyard. Gazing up, he saw Jessica Piedmont open the upstairs window. With loud shouts, Ned Piedmont and the Cherokee boy ran off the ranch's new mustangs. Jimmy unhitched his own horse from the corral fence, then he led it around to the back side of the ranch house. Dirt Bradshaw, Rodrigo and Rosa Amarillo had already escaped into the piney woods.

When Miles Wells and the supply wagon barreled into the yard, rancher Gray stood with his Henry rifle and cursed him. The old man, Wilson, drove the wagon, while Wells and Lee Sixkiller rode in on their horses, with a stranger. The man was lean and tall; dressed in buckskins and armed with a long hunting rifle, he seemed part Indian. "This is Will Dare, my Chickasaw scout," said Miles Wells. "We met back up, in San Geronimo."

Will Dare nodded to Jimmy, yet Gray did not greet him. Instead, Jimmy asked Wells the meaning of the earlier gunshots.

"It seems you will soon have company," said Wells. "About two dozen soldiers, I garner."

"Dogdammit, then why did you come back here? You just blew away any chance for me to talk with Marshall Fazari."

"Fazari, heh? Damn, we should have dispatched him back on the Canadian," Miles remarked, turning to Bud Wilson.

"I may have killed the man for you," Will Dare announced. "There were two civilians riding ahead of the cavalry. Both went down to my rifle."

"Well, who asked you? You only cockamamied all hope of a settlement with that move, Davy Crockett!" said Gray. "This is gonna be like the Alamo now."

"Wilson, you and Sam unload the gunpowder," Miles Wells ordered. "Then Sam, take up a gun position. I need both of you to provide us with a delaying action."

"Like hell—get the hell off our ranch!" Lew McManus shouted from the hay loft window. "I don't want them in here with me!"

Jimmy Gray shook his head. "Just what I need—more generals than foot soldiers." He pointed at Ned Piedmont, "Boy, go join your mother upstairs. I'll be in directly. As for the rest of you dang bastards, I suggest you surrender, or it's every man for hisself!"

Miles Wells reached into the supply wagon, stocked with expedition gear, shovels, black powder and dry food. He pulled his Volcanic, a repeating pistol stolen last year from the Union troops in Santa Fe. "This is my only reminder from our failed Texas campaign," Wells told Gray. "If you do not join us now, the Federals will succeed again."

"Piss on you. I'm just trying to save my ranch," said Jimmy. "At least let me talk to Fazari or the militia commander, before you start shooting. Go hide yourself. I'll tell them you passed by and kept going."

Wells doubted this would work. He told Bud Wilson to hurry up and unload the black powder. "Then you and I will hightail it to the foothills with the wagon, Bud, as we agreed. Quickly, now! The rest of you, hide yourselves, somewhere advantageous. So we can hit them from all sides."

Lew McManus watched as Lee Sixkiller and the younger Cherokee ranger headed to a line of cottonwoods with their rifles. He heard someone unloading the wagon in the barn. Lew could not tell where the tall Chickasaw scout might be. He wondered what Miles Wells was doing, by following Jimmy into the ranch house. "And what are YOU doing?" Lew asked himself.

The column of blue-coated soldiers appeared out on the road and McManus panicked. "There's too damn many of them!" he exclaimed. McManus stepped away from the hay loft window, just as Will Dare climbed up from the lower level of the barn. "You can have my spot," Lew told the Chickasaw. "I'm leaving."

Inside the ranch house, Jimmy Gray looked out the window of the main room. Ned Piedmont had gone upstairs to his mother. When Miles Wells walked in from the front porch, Jimmy cursed under his breath. "Stay down—out of sight," Gray hissed. "Let me talk first."

The militiamen were green troops, riding in too quickly ahead of Captain Graydon. All bunched together, they did not know they were surrounded on three sides. "Spread out, damn you!" Captain Graydon shouted. "Hello, the house! Surrender, or be shot!"

Recognizing 'Paddy' Graydon's voice, Jimmy Gray gave up all hope of reasoning with the Irishman. "The window's all yours," he muttered to Wells. "I'll take the one in the kitchen."

When the back screen door slammed shut, Wells knew Jimmy Gray had taken flight. He considered his own options. The Indian rangers could surrender, but he, being a spy, would surely hang. He needed to leave right now.

But it was too late; the militia rode in with their guns drawn. The massed troops proved too tempting—or maybe someone possessed an itchy trigger—for suddenly the crack of a rifle changed everything. More shots rang out from the cottonwoods. Miles broke a pane out of the front window and fired his Volcanic.

A fusillade of musket fire answered back, exploding shards of glass as Miles ducked down to shield himself. He crouched low and eased over to the stairwell. "Jessie! Ned! We have to get out of here," he shouted.

While the militiamen attempted to reload their guns, Miles heard the sound of his supply wagon rumbling out of the barn. Before the soldiers could stop it, they were caught by enfilade fire—from the barn, the cottonwoods and the upstairs window. Men fell; horses swirled about in a confusion of dust and gun smoke. The soldiers did not know where to shoot.

"Form a line! Captain Graydon shouted. "Corporal Hernandez, have your men torch the house. Sergeant! Take your first squad and charge that grove of trees! Everyone else take cover. There are snipers in the barn!"

Inside the house, Jessica Piedmont and her son hurried downstairs. "This way," said Miles Wells, standing in the hallway to the kitchen.

When the first shots were fired, Dirt Bradshaw, Rosa Amarilla and Rodrigo were safely hidden in the pines above the ranch. Rosa cried out; she looked over at Red Water for reassurance, but the Mescalero seemed stoic about the matter. Bradshaw paced back and forth nervously; he wanted to see what was happening.

In the brief pause before the next round of gunfire, Dirt thought he heard the sound of a wagon being driven up along Tecolote' Creek. "I've gotta see—I'm going back to the ledge," he told his companions. "Stay with Miss Rosa and watch my horse." he asked Rodrigo.

Stepping over fallen pine branches and ducking under low-hanging tree limbs, Bradshaw made his way to the bluff overlooking the meadow by the creek. He reached the open outcropping just in time to see the Confederates' supply wagon rumbling away from the battle. Bud Wilson was in the driver's seat.

Red Water and Rosa joined the prospector at the ledge. "Where does the creek run to?" Dirt asked.

"It joins the Blue Canyon several miles away," said Rodrigo. Red Water had led Dirt's horse up to the overlook. "That man has gone after the gold."

"Stay here with the young lady," said Dirt, taking the reins of the filly. Quickly, he led Waukesha along the top of the bluffs, then into the woods along a game trail.

Smoke began to rise, back where the ranch house and barnyard were hidden from view. Rosa Amarilla put her hand to her mouth; the soldiers were setting fire to the buildings. She bolted and tried to run back to the trail going down to the ranch, but Rodrigo held her back. "We go back to the pines," he suggested.

The gunfire continued. After another series of blasts, the shots became more sporadic. Jimmy Gray looked back once he gained cover in the pines and saw the black smoke. His worst fears were confirmed. "Dammit, the house!" he yelled, when Rodrigo and Rosa appeared on the trail. "They're burning down my house!"

With a loud boom and a burst of flame visible through the treetops, the Rim Rock's barn exploded from the keg of gunpowder stored inside the structure. Men shouted; a few more gunshots echoed; then one could only hear a great whoosh of hay igniting and the crackling of dry wood catching fire.

Gray sat down on a flat rock and exhaled. "They're destroying everything," he muttered. Jimmy gazed at his horse, its reins tied to a pine. "Everything I worked for! I might as well ride back to Tennessee." Jimmy's two dogs, the coonhound and the Airedale, ambled up and sniffed around. They had both fled when the militia fired the first volley.

"The house can be rebuilt—so can the barn," said Rodrigo, attempting to pull the rancher out of his shock and despair. "We will help you."

"*Oui, c'est possible,*" Rosa Amarilla said, kneeling down beside Jimmy. "And I am sure this child is yours. I will stay with you."

This provided small comfort to Gray. "Big Lew was holed up in the barn! There's no way he made it out, I reckon. Dogdammit to Hell, he's gone!"

Minutes later, with a grinding screech of metal, the tin roof of the barn crashed to the ground. Rosa cried out; Jimmy cursed under his breath and Red Water crouched down to get a better view. Someone— several people—were coming up the trail from the house and yard. Rodrigo drew out his pistol.

Miles Wells appeared, leading Jessica Piedmont by the hand. Ned Piedmont followed them, looking back frequently to make sure the soldiers were not giving chase.

Jimmy Gray's shock now burst into anger. "You both are the cause of this!" he declared. Springing to his feet, the rancher stepped over to his horse and reached for his Henry rifle,

Miles Wells seemed ready to run, but Mrs. Piedmont told Gray to stop. "No, this is how the Yankees repay you and Lew McManus for your help? You should be angry at THEM. Will you join us now?" she asked Jimmy.

"Hell Naw!" said Jimmy. He still held the gun aimed at Wells. "Git outa here! Vamoose, you hear?"

"Help us dig out our spoils and we will," Miles said calmly, holding up his arms. "You can see I am unarmed, Sir," he added.

Rodrigo stepped between the two men. "Dirt Bradshaw has gone to catch your man in the wagon. Up in Blue Canyon," said the Mescalero.

Jimmy Gray stepped backwards, toward his horse. Gray kept the rifle pointed at Wells. "Then I'm going to go help him," said Jimmy. He nodded at Rodrigo, who also held a weapon. "Keep my dogs from following me, okay?"

Rosa Amarilla drew out a carving knife from her basket and gestured at Jessica Piedmont. "Stand back, Madame, or I will use this!" she threatened.

Both of the Piedmonts seemed shocked at this. Jessica sneered at the creole girl, yet she did sit down and told Ned to do likewise.

Miles Wells lowered his arms and chuckled. "Hah, I'm sure we can all be reasonable here, Amigo," he said to Rodrigo. Miles leaned back against a ponderosa pine and gradually slid down to a sitting position. "Do you mind if I roll a smoke?"

The Colorado miner rode along the Tecolote, following a logging road. When the road divided at Blue Canyon, Dirt took the left fork, where the trail trended upward onto a wooded ridge. Dirt came upon an open woods of tall aspen and ponderosa pines. He searched for the tracks of the supply wagon, looking for where it either matted down dead pine needles or left mud-filled ruts in puddles. Bradshaw did not find any fresh sign of Bud Wilson's wagon now, but he pressed on, hoping to find and overlook, where he could spot the old man down in the canyon.

The road climbed higher above the hollow on Bradshaw's right. Gradually the wooded ridge grew more narrow, more exposed to the wind and the trees began to thin out, offering a view of the canyon itself. Dirt gained the top of the rim, where he climbed off Waukesha and grabbed his Spencer carbine.

"He must be down there somewhere," Dirt said to his filly. He tied the horse's reins to a fallen ponderosa. Bradshaw then eased down the side of the ridge, stopping every so often to listen. There was a slight breeze whispering through the pine forest, just enough sound to muffle his footsteps. He heard a sound. The prospector recognized it immediately—the chink of a pick striking rock.

Since he was well above whoever was digging, Dirt did not return down the logging road. He crept over to a spot where he could see down into the canyon, The late afternoon sun cast shadows, making it difficult; yet a moment later, Dirt saw movement. A man was swinging the pick, the sound of it striking rock coming a split-second later. Figuring that Wilson was at least four hundred yards away, Dirt knew he had to find a way to get closer. When the wind shifted suddenly, Bradshaw heard voices. He sat down and listened.

"That's enough, Old-Timer, let a young man do it," said a voice Dirt did not recognize. The digging continued. It sounded more vigorous. Carefully watching his footsteps, Bradshaw snuck down the steep side of the ridge, along a narrow game trail.

Now, when the work halted again, Dirt Bradshaw realized there were several men having a discussion.

"It's great that you brought the wagon, Bud," one man remarked. "Once we get it loaded, we can head up to El Porvenir and avoid the militia. Alright, it's your turn, Jack."

Dirt drew a quick breath. He thought he recognized the man's voice. Someone from Denver, he figured, but who?' The digging resumed, yet this time two men were using shovels and someone was rolling back rocks. Dirt crept closer.

"Yee-hah!" one man shouted. "There it is!"

The shoveling halted and the voices grew animated.

"Shouldn't we wait for Mr. Wells to get here, Billy?" Bud Wilson asked. "After all, it was his idea to bury it here."

"From the sounds of things back at that ranch, I really doubt Miles will make it out alive," the man in charge replied. "We're taking it south, as General Pike directed."

Dirt realized who this man was; he was Billy Martin, the owner— or former owner—of the Golden Slipper in Denver! Dirt Bradshaw suspected that Martin might be the mastermind of the Confederate spy ring that had employed Miles Wells and Jessica Piedmont. He figured these men were digging up the same gold he and Eduard Fazari had discovered in the upper Canadian River.

Bradshaw had two options: either he could sneak his way over near the wagon and intercept the men there, or he could crawl out on a ledge and begin shooting.

He chose the former and went back to fetch the filly.

Dirt realized that old fox, Bud Wilson, had doubled-crossed everyone in the Union search party, by befriending both he and Wa Shana, while continuing to work for the Confederacy. Hurrying back to his horse, Bradshaw was up for a fight. Looking out toward the southeast, he saw black and gray plumes of smoke billowing up from the Rim Rock ranch. "Darn the dern militia—and you too, Fazari! You didn't have to do that," Bradshaw murmured.

Arriving back at the mouth of the canyon, Dirt Bradshaw checked his weapons. He spun the chamber on his Navy colt, making sure he'd loaded each one. The Spencer carbine was also ready; he placed it back in the gun boot, then clicked his tongue to urge Waukesha forward to the affray.

"Hey Yankee," someone whispered on the trail behind him. Bradshaw turned and saw Jimmy Gray on his mustang.

"Glad to see you're still kicking," Dirt whispered. "Care to join me?"

"Damned straight. Who's up in the canyon besides that man, Wilson?" Gray held aloft a long-barreled Henry rifle and he had two revolvers stuffed inside his belt.

"Several men. One named Jack Jernigan, who killed a friend of mine—and another man, named Billy Martin, whom I believe is the mastermind of the whole operation. Miles Wells might have been just a pawn in his game, if you ask me," said Dirt.

"The time for asking anything is long gone, dammit," Jimmy Gray swore. "These bastards are the reason why my home went up in smoke. You ready, Dirt? We're riding in hard and fast."

Over in a side draw, Wilson, Jack Jernigan and two other men were stacking gold bars under a canvas tarp. Billy Martin stood beside the wagon with a rifle in his hand. "Hurry up, fellows," said the former saloonkeeper. "The sun's fixing to fall beyond the mountains. It will be hard navigating these hills after dark."

"Stop! What's that sound?" asked Jack Jernigan. All the outlaws paused to listen. Something was splashing down on Tecolote' Creek.

"Probably some otters," mused Wilson, who placed the last bar in the wagon bed and pulled the tarp over the stack.

"Otters, hell!" said Jernigan, leaping from the wagon. Billy Martin raised his rifle to shoot the lead rider coming up along the creek, but before he could fire, a blast from Jimmy Gray's rifle spun Martin sideways.

Two men crouched in the wagon and fired their pistols, yet Bradshaw swerved his horse behind a ponderosa for cover. Dirt slid off Waukesha and saw Jimmy Gray quick-firing both his revolvers at the outlaws. Bradshaw joined in and the two men fell from the wagon.

Coming out from behind the tree, Dirt spotted a third outlaw bolting up the opposite side of the hollow. He tried to get a shot at the outlaw; but Jack Jernigan kept to the cover of some thick juniper bushes. The outlaw fired a shot back at the prospector, but he missed.

"Stay hidden," Jimmy whispered. "He's got the high ground."

Bradshaw and Gray waited, until they heard the outlaw riding off on a horse atop the canyon, then they approached the wagon. "This is strange, there were five men here," Dirt observed. "That one fellow got away, but I only see three bodies."

Jimmy Gray agreed. "I don't see that old man."

Dirt peered into the supply wagon. Lifting up the canvas tarp, he saw Bud Wilson, curled up and cowering. "I—I spared you, Dirt," the turquoise trader stammered, putting his hands up to show he had no weapon. "Please, do the same for me, Dirt."

Dirt Bradshaw exhaled. "You could have spared us a lot of trouble, by being an outright bastard in the first place," he said.

CHAPTER 36

Eduard Fazari believed the frontier militiamen were too undisciplined, charging in on the ranch without considering what they faced. He was also incensed at their commander, Captain Graydon, for setting fire to the RimRock's ranch house. "You should have taken a secure position first, then offered terms of surrender," the Deputy Marshall advised. "It doesn't hurt to try negotiating first."

"Oh? And how many battles have you been in?" Graydon asked. He and Fazari stood between the smoldering ruins of the hay barn and the blackened adobe walls of Jimmy Grays ranch house. "You were late getting here anyway."

"I was tending to Mr. LaHoya. He died of his wounds," said Fazari. Eduard's anger now turned to self-condemnation and remorse. He wished he had not brought Miguel along; LaHoya would have still been alive if he had stayed at the Fazari-Martinez ranch.

The New Mexican volunteers searched through the smoking remains of the ranch, yet they had yet to discover a body in any of the buildings. Every now and then, a stray piece of ammunition exploded in the hot embers of the barn, so the soldiers stopped raking the ashes and backed away.

Other militiamen came out from the distant tree line with two wounded prisoners. The Cherokee youth, Sam Burningtree, had been shot in the forearm; Will Dare, the Chickasaw scout, wore a bandage on his lower leg.

"I imagine we can either hang them later, or shoot them here—and save Fort Union the trouble," Captain Graydon remarked.

"You best treat them as prisoners of war—captured soldiers," said Fazari. "The government cannot afford to alienate the Indian Nations. Dirt Bradshaw told me they are Confederate Cherokees."

"I am a Chickasaw," said Will Dare, as he was brought forward. "The boy is a Cherokee, as is the dead man in the woods." Dave referred to Lee Sixkiller, who had gone down fighting.

Fazari told Graydon he wanted to interrogate the two Confederate rangers. He had them sit down beside the corral. "Where is Miles Wells?" Fazari asked them. "We may go easy on you, if you help us catch him."

"We are soldiers, not spies," said Will Dare. "How the Hell should we know?"

The Deputy Marshal turned to the Cherokee boy, who seemed terrified about being executed. "You were with Wells back on the Canadian," Fazari noted. "Where did you all take that gold?"

"Gold? What gold?" the Chickasaw scout interrupted. "We are soldiers, not thieves. I can prove it." Dare reached into his inner coat pocket. "We were paid with these Confederate banknotes—proof of a soldier's pay." Eduard studied the notes. One was for twenty dollars, payable from the Bank of Montgomery, Alabama. The other was from the Bank of Richmond and had George Washington's portrait on it.

"See? It's good money," said Dare. "Good after two years, from July 25ᵗʰ, 1861. So it's redeemable now—with eight percent interest!"

Fazari laughed. "You didn't read all the fine print, soldier. It says they are legal tender six months after the date of a peace treaty, between the United States and the Confederacy. I hate to tell you, but Mr. Wells duped the both of you! It's worthless. So where did he go?"

"He was in the house, last I'd seen him," said the boy.

Captain Graydon walked over to see how Fazari's interrogation was going. "We didn't find any bodies in the barn," said Graydon.

Eduard Fazari resented the captain's intrusion." You had better get your arse back to Santa Fe then. And tell General Carleton you failed to enlist those ranchers, Captain. Let me do my job—and you do yours."

The Irishman's face turned red. "I'm not leaving without these prisoners," he demanded. His soldiers had retrieved their dead and were mounted up on their horses. "We should hang them right now."

Eduard had an idea. "Here," he said, opening the inside of his jacket and unpinning his U.S. Deputy's badge. "Tell General Carleton I'm forced to resign my commission. And we failed to find the U.S. Treasury's gold shipment. They'll want to talk with you—and so will the Marshall's Service."

"Wha-what?" Graydon sputtered. "Sure-surely, you shouldn't." The thought of explaining his actions to the Federal government seemed to unlodge Graydon from his self-assurance. "Well, then, keep 'em, dammit. Take them to Fort Marcy, Fort Union, or to Hell with ye. I don't care."

"Good day to you, Sir," said Fazari. "Good luck with your future endeavors. You've done quite enough here."

Watching from the woods, Rodrigo waited for the militia troops to leave. He felt little need to guard his prisoners any longer. If Miles Wells wanted to abandon the pines and risk himself getting caught, it did not concern the Mescalero. Rodrigo was more worried about the creole woman. He feared he would have to tell Rosa Amarilla that Lew McManus was dead.

Miles Wells and the Piedmonts were hiding further back in the evergreens. "We must have horses," Miles told Ned Piedmont. "It's our only chance to escape."

"Mr. Jimmy told me to run off all the horses," Ned replied, "or the Yankees would shoot them—like they did at Glorieta." The boy looked over at his mother, to see if this upset her. Jessica Piedmont's husband, Harry Piedmont, had been killed at the battle of Glorieta Pass.

"Those soldiers aren't Yankees. They're mostly Mexicano volunteers," said Wells. The Confederate agent sat on the stump of a black oak, biding his time and considering his next move. "Once they leave, ask Mr. Red Water if he will go with you to fetch our horses."

Several yards away, the two women eyed each other. Rosa Amarillo Del Rio stood behind Red Water's back and she still brandished her kitchen knife. Jessica Piedmont leaned back against a tree, wondering if she would get a chance to draw her derringer out of her left riding boot.

"For God's sake, ladies, you remind me of two cats—circling each other," said Wells, upon observing their behavior. "Open that bottle of wine, Miss, and let's pretend we're on a picnic."

Rodrigo Red Water glanced back and nodded. "If the soldiers hear us fighting, they will come looking for us all," he whispered.

All the shooting had stopped. Red Water eased closer to get a better view. He saw soldiers milling about; others were tending their wounded, and a few had climbed back on their horses. Moments later, Rodrigo spotted Deputy Marshall Fazari, talking with his prisoners, the Chickasaw scout and the Cherokee boy, out in the barnyard. A blue-coated Union officer came over to speak with Fazari. The two men argued.

After the heated discussion, the officer shouted for his men to mount up. Rodrigo went back to inform Wells and the others. "The soldiers are leaving now," he said, "but the law man from the government is still here."

Miles Wells sat next to Jessica Piedmont on a blanket and they were passing a bottle of wine. "We need horses," said Wells, "Can you and the boy go find us some?"

Rodrigo thought this Confederate agent had a lot of nerve to ask such a favor. "Get up and find them yourself. They will be in the south pasture. Señorita Rosa, come with me."

The young woman stood off aways, gazing off to the northwest, toward the foothills, where Dirt Bradshaw and Jimmy Gray had gone. "I thought I heard guns shooting—far away," said Rosa.

Both Rodrigo and Miles Wells looked startled. They listened; only an evening breeze fluttered in the pines. "Are you sure?" asked Wells. "I didn't hear anything."

"Oui, but you and that woman were busy talking," Rosa Amarilla sneered.

"I must go talk to Señor Fazari," said Rodrigo. He turned to Wells and the Piedmonts. "You three must go now. Go find your horses and leave."

Dirt Bradshaw held the reins as the wagon trundled back down the road toward the Rim Rock. His filly was tethered to the back and Jimmy Gray led the way on his own horse. Bud Wilson was tied up, with his back to the prospector. "So, do you know where Ortiz took the rest of the gold—if there is any?" Dirt asked his prisoner.

"I was not privy to that information," said Wilson. "Suffice it to say, each arm of the Rebel octopus operates independently."

"How did you know Billy Martin?"

The old man laughed. "Who didn't know Mr. Billy? Any miner or trader who bought a drink in Central City or spun a roulette wheel in Denver knew Billy Martin! But I did not know he was here in New Mexico, until he came to see Miles Wells at Las Vegas Grandes."

Jimmy Gray slowed his horse and waited for the wagon to catch up. "Why in Hell did you and Wells choose to bury your cache so close to my ranch? In Blue Canyon?" he asked.

Bud Wilson hung his head. "You'd have to ask Mr. Wells. I guess he'd say it seemed like a good idea at the time. He did tell me he was hoping you might come back to work for the Confederacy."

Jimmy Gray cursed under his breath and urged his horse onward. "If he's still around, I'm gonna shoot his ass!" he vowed.

It was now sunset. Gray's two hunting dogs ran up to greet the wagon. They did not improve Jimmy's mood; his home was destroyed. He rode on, stopping only once, to reload the Henry rifle.

In the dim twilight, Jimmy saw his flattened barn. The smell of smoke and spent gunpowder still remained in the air. Only three people stood in its shadows. Gray slowed his horse to a walk and raised his rifle.

Rodrigo Red Water stepped out in the open, his palm raised. Jimmy also saw Rosa Amarilla, bent over and crying. The third person was Eduard Fazari.

"You're late, Fazari," Jimmy told the Deputy Marshal. "Is Lew dead?"

"Most likely. We've been lookin'. And your former ranch hand, Miguel LaHoya, was killed earlier," Fazari replied.

This remark made Rosa Amarilla break down into deep sobbing. Jimmy dismounted and let her cry on his shoulder. "Where is Bradshaw?" Rodrigo asked.

"He's coming on," said Jimmy. Turning to Fazari, he added, "We've got your damn gold, too."

The Deputy Marshall's face brightened. "Really? That makes up for that rascal, Wells, getting away," he said. "I am terribly sorry the militia burnt you out."

Jimmy Gray tightened his mouth. Somehow, cursing seemed inappropriate now, what with Rosa Amarilla deep in mourning.

Fazari announced that he had two prisoners in custody. He pointed over to the corral, where Will Dare and Sam Burningtree were lashed to some fence posts. The rancher's anger now flared up again; perhaps they were the Confederates who had killed Miguel LaHoya. He stomped over toward the corral and drew his gun.

Rodrigo stepped between Jimmy Gray and the two Indians. "They did not burn down your ranch or kill Señor Lewis," said Red Water, "there's been enough death for this day."

With a rumble and a shout, Dirt Bradshaw drove the recovered supply wagon into the yard. "Whoa, whoa!" Bradshaw hollered at the two draft horses. "Hello, ladies and gents."

Dirt's jubilation lessened upon seeing the destruction of the buildings and the creole girl's sorrow. "We got almost all the outlaws—and a prisoner for you, Marshall," he told Fazari.

"I see that. Now let me see the gold," said Fazari, walking over to inspect the wagon.

Dirt lifted the tarp. "Only eight bricks. I suspect Miles Wells appropriated one of them for his own self." Bradshaw now noticed the two Confederate Indians staked over by the corral. "Did Wells get away?" he asked.

Rodrigo shrugged. He did not want to reveal any more bad details with the U.S. Marshall present. "What about that Piedmont lady?" Dirt wondered aloud.

"If she took off with Miles Wells, that's her choice," said Jimmy Gray. "And a piss-poor choice at that." Gray was actually relieved that Jessica had escaped. He motioned for Bradshaw to walk over toward the springhouse. "I need some water," Jimmy remarked.

Once the two men were some distance away, Jimmy told Dirt that Rosa Amarilla had lost both McManus and her previous lover, Miguel LaHoya. "Go talk with the girl. You're better at talkin' with women than me," Jimmy said. "I want to go look around and try to find Lew's body. Don't want her to see that."

Dirt nodded. "Let me wet my whistle first," he said, then he surprised Jimmy by pulling out a metal hip flask rather than continuing on to the springhouse. "I found this on one of the dead men," said Dirt, taking a long swig. "Take a good slug, Jimmy. You've lost far more than me, so here you go. Knock it out."

Jimmy accepted the flask, took one drink, and handed it back.

Once he was sure Bradshaw had returned to comfort Rosa, Jimmy walked around the perimeter of the barn ruins, to see what could be recovered. He kicked around in some ashes, found an empty glass jar, then lifted a sheet of tin from the barn's roof.

Pushing aside more debris, Gray found an old chain, some nine-inch nails and a metal pan, but no bones or body. He trudged over to the place where Lew McManus had set up a blacksmith's forge, but found no sign of McManus.

Jimmy Gray gazed over toward the ruined ranch house. He was now out of sight from everyone. The rancher bent over, hugged his chest and yelped out a deep cry of anguish. "Oh, ohhh...no. Dang you, Lew, why did this have to end this way?" he moaned.

He heard a muffled sound. He saw his coonhound, Johnny Bob, sniffing around the barn's manure pile and studied the putrid mound of cow and horse manure, chicken shit, kitchen garbage and old straw.

A big, grimy hand appeared out of the excrement! A horrific visage emerged, like a ghoul from Hades. This creature's eyes opened and then a mouth formed.

Lew McManus gagged, then spewed out the vile filth. He stood up and took deep breaths. Pulling himself out of the compost heap, Lew coughed, vomited and gasped. "Haw, haw, Jimmy Carl! I fooled 'em, didn't I?" he roared.

"You scared the shit outa me!" said Jimmy. "What the hell you doing?" His shock and amazement switched to laughter. "Hah, you look like crap, Claw!"

Dirt Bradshaw and Rodrigo came running. "Look what sprouted out of our fertilizer," Gray declared.

"That's the ugliest mushroom I've ever seen," said Dirt.

McManus shook compost off his shirt and trousers, then he brushed more filth out of his hair. Eduard Fazari and Rosa Amarilla joined the group; Rosa almost hugged Lew, but backed away when she caught his stench.

"Go wash yourself in the creek," said Jimmy. "There's some horse blankets on the corral fence."

McManus looked around at the destruction—the collapsed metal roof of the barn, the charred adobe walls of the ranch house and the tear-streaked face of Rosa. "Who got killed?" he asked somberly.

"Miguel got shot before we got here," said Fazari. "And one of the Indians that came with Wells. Along with some of the New Mexico militia."

"Dirt and I killed three of the gold robbers—and captured a fourth," Jimmy Gray added. "They were back in Blue Canyon."

"Really?" McManus glanced over at Bradshaw, then he looked away, for Bradshaw knew about his keeping part of the gold heist. Jimmy also knew about it now—yet had they told the Deputy Marshall? For a moment, the Tennessean wondered if everything could remain a secret.

Dirt Bradshaw coughed. Lew tried to avoid his gaze, but then he noticed Red Water staring at him. The Mescalero's eyes, affixed in a hundred-foot stare, seemed to bore right through Lew's deception. McManus recalled Rodrigo saying: "that which we keep secret rules us."

"Aw, shit," said Lew. He back-stepped to the compost heap, reached his huge hands into the pile and pulled out a burlap sack. The others watched, as McManus drew out his two revolvers. He laid them on the ground, then Lew upended the sack. Chunks of refined gold, his gold "nuggets" fell out and everyone except Dirt and Rodrigo were amazed.

"Take it, dogdammit," said McManus, "and leave me be!"

Jimmy Gray, Rodrigo and Dirt exchanged looks, then all three men roared with laughter.

CHAPTER 37

Lieutenant Dave Bradshaw found his brother-in-law, Charles Larsen, digging graves on the edge of town, where the Third Colorado Infantry was assisting the relief effort after the Lawrence Massacre. Dave saw that even though Charles now wore Sergeant's stripes, the Swede worked right alongside his men.

"This is so very grim, ain't it, Charlie?" said Dave, upon seeing all the graves.

"Yah, it is terrible." Charles was chiseling the sides of a grave pit, making sure the sides were even. He and his men had been digging graves all day. "The worst ones are the ones we dig for the children."

"I hope we get the hateful wretches who did this," said Dave. Bradshaw's company was now stationed at Fort Larned, about two hundred miles west of Lawrence. "I wish we were fighting in Missouri with you fellows, instead of guarding the Santa Fe Trail against Indians."

Weeks earlier, Lieutenant Bradshaw had been detained at Fort Leavenworth, after arriving with only half of the Federal gold shipment. David had narrowly escaped a reprimand after a formal inquiry; he was spared when Lieutenant Silas Soule brought back a portion of the stolen gold.

Two mule-drawn hearses arrived, with more of the dead. Dave reached down and grasped Charlie's hand, assisting him out of the pit. The Colorado soldiers began to unload the bodies and Bradshaw was astounded to see that all of the dead men were Black.

"They were in the Second Kansas Regiment," Sergeant Larsen explained. "We fought alongside them in the Indian Territory—at Honey Springs and Cabin Creek."

Dave helped Larsen and his men intern the dead soldiers. Since there were so many men and boys killed at Lawrence, there were not enough caskets; these soldiers were only wrapped in army blankets as they were lowered into the earth.

The afternoon was very hot. Both officers had taken off their jackets and rolled up their shirt sleeves. After all the dead were buried, the Third Colorado men took a break before the hearses returned with more casualties. Larsen and Bradshaw walked away to talk. Charles listened to Dave's story about the Kiowa raid and the gold heist on the Santa Fe Trail.

"And then, guess who showed up? My no-count brother, Dirt, along with that Tennessean who worked our mine last year," said Dave. "I made Dirt a scout and sent him off to recover the wagons."

"Och, you finally convinced your brother to join us, to fight the Rebels?" Larsen asked. "I tried to persuade him several months ago. At Fort Garland. Did he find the gold?"

"Part of it. I don't know if he's still looking," Dave replied. "One never knows, with Dirt."

Charles Larsen asked Dave if he was going to re-enlist after his term of service ended in January. Dave Bradshaw was not sure; because of his perceived failure with the gold shipment, he felt his chances at being promoted to a captain's rank were very slight.

"Well, if you don't, Erica told me in her letter that she needs you, back at Boulder Creek. Och, you should go back," said Charles. "It will be a hard winter for her, if she is alone again."

"I know. She wrote to me, too," said Dave. "I miss her dearly. And my son." Lieutenant Bradshaw stared off toward the town. His wife,

Erica, had given him a boy that spring; David yearned to see his family again, yet he was constrained by duty and honor to the First Colorado. Seeing the new graves of the freed Blacks, who had used their new-found freedom to defend the very country that once allowed slavery, made Dave realize that not getting a promotion was insignificant by comparison.

Seeing the burnt-out homes and other buildings now, and another hearse on the edge of town, Lieutenant Bradshaw felt overwhelmed. "This massacre was awful," he remarked. "How can a just God allow this to happen?"

Sergeant Charles Larsen stood up and grabbed a shovel. "The Lord is not in this destruction," said the Swede. "Men are allowed to choose between the greatest good—or the greatest wrong. God is in the recovery, not in the evil that some men choose."

As summer ended and autumn beckoned, it was a time for action. Crops had to be harvested, food preserved and arrangements made for winter. Up in the foothills and forests of the Sangre de Cristos, the aspens turned to a golden yellow, the acorn mast had fallen, and the bull elk bugled in the alpine meadows.

Lew McManus sat silent under a giant oak, listening to the sounds of hammering down in the ranch yard. Lew heard Dirt Bradshaw and Jimmy talking, yet he was too far away to pick up on their conversations.

Two weeks earlier, the men began rebuilding the Rim Rock's barn and ranch house. The Mexicano boy, Juan Villareal also arrived and pitched in with the others, erecting the barn first. Now they had laid the foundation for a new ranch house and were setting up hewn logs for the exterior of the residence.

Lew's physical contribution to the reconstruction ended when he heard the first elk bugle up in the highlands. McManus told the others he was going to hunt; from now on his job was to put fresh venison on the table, along with other wild game. Lew loved to hunt and these woods and mountains held grouse, turkey, deer, bear and elk in abundance. He and his dogs had already harvested game birds and an elk, feeding all the bachelors down at the ranch.

McManus did not feel guilty about not working on the farmhouse. His heart was just not into being a rancher again. Not all of his hammered-out gold had been stashed in the grain sack on the day of the militia's visit. Lew had buried another part under a fence post on the north end of the ranch. He had contributed some of his wealth to help purchase the lumber and nails for the new barn, but he and Jimmy Gray would have to sell off some cattle and maybe a few mustangs to have enough money to rebuild the Rim Rock the way they wanted.

Rosa Amarilla Del Rio was another matter. Lew did feel guilty about the creole girl. She had elected to return to Las Vegas Grandes, rather than camping out with five men and not getting a marriage proposal. Rosa was also still grieving Miguel LaHoya's death.

This morning was cool, with a bright blue sky and a steady breeze shimmering the yellow aspens. McManus heard some rustling down in the hollow. As the noise grew closer, he determined there were two animals, probably deer, coming up the ridge. Lew clicked the hammer back on his Sharpshooter rifle; he was ready, but then the Tennesseans' two dogs emerged into view. The lean Redbone, Johnny Bob, led the way with his nose to the ground. Bruno, Lew's Airedale, followed close behind, wagging his stubby tail.

McManus was angry at first. He had told Jimmy Gray to keep the dogs penned while he hunted. For a moment, Lew considered using the dogs to hunt some turkeys, but it was late morning now. "Jimmy probably let you all loose in order to make me stop my elk hunt," said Lew to the canines.

Bruno scurried up and licked Lew's boot. He scratched the Airedale behind the ear and stood up. "Alright, Jimmy, I'm coming, dang it," Lew muttered.

Jimmy Gray sat on a stack of hewn pine and smoked a cigarette while taking a break from his labors. There would be six rooms in the large cabin, including two upstairs bedrooms. He also contemplated the addition of an upstairs balcony; Miss Rosa would like that, if she returned.

Gazing around the construction, Gray felt the Rim Rock finally had the beginnings of a real outfit. Rodrigo and Juan Villareal were setting flat rocks from the creek to make a chimney. Dirt Bradshaw, shirtless, was splitting pine logs over near the rebuilt barn. If Lew McManus would pitch in a bit more, the house would be ready before the first snow.

Lew McManus appeared with the two dogs. "No luck today?" Dirt asked him, though it was obvious Lew had returned empty-handed.

"Just saw a bunch of squirrels—and these two sumbitches," said Lew, pointing to the dogs.

Dirt placed an iron wedge in the middle crack of a pine rail, lifted his heavy hammer and brought it down with all his might. The rail split, yet not entirely. Bradshaw repeated the stroke and both pieces fell free. "Whew," Dirty huffed, wiping his brow. "Are you sure Honest Abe got his start this way?"

"Keep it up, Yank. Haw, maybe one day, you can run for President," said Lew, laughing at the idea. "Although, I don't know if I'd vote for 'Dishonest Dirt', right?"

"We need nails," Jimmy Gray interrupted. "A bunch, to frame up the walls inside. And it's your turn to buy food, Claw. The wagons all hitched up. If you'll hurry, you can be back before supper. We need coffee, sugar, flour, and lantern oil. Oh, and get me some Durham tobacco."

"Like hell. I'm going over to Las Vegas," said Lew. "Gotta check at the Western Union and the Montezuma."

"I'm going, too, then," said Dirt. "Juan brought my scout pay last week and I'm itching to spend it."

"That means you won't be back till late tomorrow," Gray complained. "You're goin' to see Rosa, ain't you, Lew?"

McManus grinned. "Maybe if you hadn't run her off, she would be a lot more handy. And no, Yank, you aren't coming along. Don't want you."

Bradshaw turned to Jimmy and said he would ride into the village and get the nails and tobacco. "I need to take Waukesha out for a ride anyway," he stated, "lest she get fat and lazy from just grazing around the last few weeks."

Dirt accompanied Lew as far as San Geronimo, which was on the way to Las Vegas Grandes. "You and Jimmy have to come to some agreement on the girl and other things," Dirt advised. "I'm tired of playing peacemaker."

"Who asked you? It ain't none of your business," said Lew, as he hurriedly drove the supply wagon over bumps and ruts. McManus was in one of his surly moods.

Bradshaw decided to change the subject. "You know, I tried to talk Red Water into staying on the ranch. After we gave the gold to Marshall Fazari, he wasn't as adamant about Red Water going to the reservation. Can you talk to him?"

"Rodrigo can make up his own mind," McManus said. "And don't worry about Jimmy Carl Gray. He can run the ranch okay without any of us. Juan and he know plenty of Mexicanos who can help when needed."

Bradshaw and McManus both stopped at the trader's post when they arrived at the village. Lew bought a quart of whiskey and Jimmy's tobacco, while Dirt purchased two boxes of nails. The store owner, who also served as the village postmaster, told Dirt he had a letter.

Dirt was surprised to see the letter was postmarked from St. Joseph, Missouri. Jane Edgarton had written to him! Bradshaw sat down on the trading post steps. The letter was dated August 27th, 1863 and it read:

Dear Richard:

It is with the deepest, darkest sorrow and heartbreak that I write these words, but I must express my despair to someone. My dear brother is dead! Trey has been murdered in Lawrence, along with so many men and boys! He was murdered by Missouri bushwhackers— cruel animals, criminals, who dare call themselves soldiers of the Confederacy. Many women weep and mourn, as Nicole and I do now. The Missouri newspapers say no women were harmed in the "battle". Would that this was true! Men can bleed, men can die, but their women cry out in anguish and will suffer for years. We are lost—without husbands, sons, brothers and fathers. Would that our suffering could end suddenly, like them. Would that I was a man and could avenge

Trey's death! Alas my gender denies me the chance to strike back at those cruel, heartless hellions!

Nicole is with me. She is stronger than I am. Perhaps it is because she has witnessed savagery among the Native Peoples, but I cannot imagine more cruelty than this!

We are heading to St. Louis, and then Cincinnati with Trey's body. Lieutenant Soule said I should not take Nicole with me on the train, but I am lost without her. I have enclosed my address in Ohio.

Richard, please embolden yourself! Are those men and the innocent boys of Lawrence to die in vain? I know you are a good man, and were a good friend to Trey. He would not want you to join this fight out of cold vengeance—nor I, after some thought. Would you fight for the Reason of a Higher Purpose? For the Cause of Liberty?

Please forgive me if I offend you. Please understand my heart in all this. Nicole and I met your brother at Lawrence—and your friend, Sergeant Charles Larsen. They were with the Colorado soldiers assisting in the town's recovery.

May the Lord keep you safe, Dirt Bradshaw! May He strengthen your heart for His Purpose. If you still have that fast horse, may God speed! If this letter does not reach you, it is still a prayer, my supplication to God, a psalm of hope and gratitude to you.

May God keep you, and I keep you, in my thoughts and prayers,

In Christ's love,
`Jane A. Edgarton

Dirt Bradshaw felt overwhelmed. Gripping the pages with both hands, he read the letter a second time. "What's the news about WaShana?" Lew McManus asked, when he stepped out of the trading post.

Dirt took a deep breath. He felt speechless and handed the letter over to Lew. Stepping away from the store, Dirt felt a surge of emotion and decision.

"Yeah, I heard they killed a lot of men and boys in Lawrence," Lewis remarked. "I'm sorry about that Edgarton fellow—but at least Nicole is safe."

"Safe? Ain't nobody safe!" Dirty replied angrily. He took the letter back. "I'm wasting my time here. Damn the gold—I've gotta do something."

McManus was taken aback by Bradshaw's sudden anger. "What are you going to do, Dirt?" he asked.

"I will take the nails back to Jimmy. But then I'm going to fight those damned bushwhackers," Bradshaw declared.

CHAPTER 38

As the train left St. Louis, WaShana haltingly read aloud from Jane Edgarton's Bible. "Whither...has your...beloved gone, O fairest...among women?" she read.

"Very good. Keep going," said Jane. Both women wore black, to hide the soot from the coal-fired steam locomotive—and to properly mourn Trey Edgarton. Jane and WaShana Nicole sat in a private compartment of the train as it clicked and clacked across the Mississippi River bridge.

"Whither has your beloved turned, that we may seek him with you? My beloved has gone down to his...garden and to gather...lilies," the girl read. "I am my beloved's and my beloved is mine. He...pastures... his flock among the lilies." WaShana stopped again. "Did God write this?" she asked.

"Well, yes, in a way. He had to use several men to write it down," Jane explained. "This is the Song of King Solomon."

"It sounds like a woman wrote it—with all those 'beloveds'-to me," WaShana remarked.

"If you want, we can read something else. This might be a trifle exotic for young readers," said Jane.

"No, I like it," WaShana said. She read on, about the Shulammite daughter of a Middle Eastern prince. There were descriptions of sandaled feet, graceful legs, and "breasts like two fawns, twins of a gazelle."

Jane Edgarton blushed. "This is about two lovers," she told her friend, "about how much they love each other." Gazing sadly out the coach window, Jane sighed, as the train rumbled on through the farmlands of Illinois.

"Why have you not become the wife of Mr. Soule?" WaShana asked, interrupting Jane's thoughts.

"We had a disagreement. Silas said I should have left you at Lawrence—or taken you back to Cimarron."

"Why did he want that?" the girl asked.

Jane frowned. "Silas said you are a 'creature of the High Plains', that you could not be happy in a civilized world. It made me angry."

WaShana Nicole handed the Holy Book to Miss Edgarton. "You read now—and show me the words," she urged.

Jane traced the lines with her finger, as she read aloud. "Place me like a seal over your heart, like a seal on your arm; for love is as strong as death, it's ardor unyielding as the grave."

"What is 'ardor'?" asked the former beloved captive.

"It is the strength of one's love," said Jane. "It is love's depth, its intensity."

"It is '*Puha*', then. It is love's power, yes?"

Jane nodded and read on: "It burns like a blazing fire, like a mighty flame. Many waters cannot quench love. Rivers cannot wash it away. If one were to give all the wealth of his house for love, he would be utterly scorned."

"I loved your brother. I loved Trey," WaShana Nicole declared. "I wish this child within me was his. But it's not," she confessed. Tears welled in her eyes.

"It's okay," said Jane, touching her friend's hand. Miss Edgarton began to cry as well. "Did you...love Mr. Red Water, too?" she asked, her voice breaking.

"Is that wrong?" WaShana asked.

"I cannot judge you on that. Sometimes we choose to love—and maybe sometimes love...chooses us?" Jane wondered.

"I know I would love this child, when he or she is born," said the young woman. "I lost my first baby."

Jane's eyes widened and she saw the sorrow in WaShana's expression. "I am so sorry—I didn't know that," she said. Jane now wondered if Lieutenant Soule had been right. At the same time, she was glad she and Nicole were traveling in a private compartment, where other passengers could not eavesdrop. Nicole Klausmann seemed to grow more admirable to men every day. She was not showing her pregnancy just yet. Although Miss Edgarton hated deception, she began to develop a plan. The young Canadienne had seen expectant women on her lecture tour, which raised funds for the Union Widows Relief fund. If she and Nicole continued to wear black for a year, people would assume Nicole had gotten pregnant before her husband went off to die in the war. This would remove any stigma attached to her pregnancy.

On the other hand, Jane thought, what if the child looks mostly Indian? Jane drew a deep sigh as she pondered this possibility. "What's wrong?" asked WaShana Nicole, seeing Jane's perturbation.

Jane composed herself, smiled and patted the girl's knee. "We'll just have to take things one day at a time, for now," she said, closing the heavy Bible with a thud.

Jimmy Gray felt everyone was abandoning him at Rim Rock. First, Dirt Bradshaw returned full of fury and new-found purpose. "Sorry, but I have to go to Kansas—to Fort Larned," said Dirt, handing Gray his tobacco, nails and a quart of rye whiskey.

"What the Hell?" asked Jimmy, sitting on the completed floor of the new ranch house. The sun was setting behind the reddened peaks of the Sangre de Cristos. Rodrigo Red Water and Juan Villareal were putting the final touches on the new chimney.

"I'm packing up in the morning," said Dirt. The ranchers had built a cooking fire several yards away from the house, so Bradshaw grabbed a tin plate and filled it with leftover venison, beans and a biscuit.

Jimmy Gray uncorked the rye, poured a little of the whiskey into a coffee cup, then handed the bottle back to Bradshaw. Almost immediately, the same red rooster hopped up on the platform. "Of all my damned critters, this ragged bastard had to survive," said Jimmy. He drank from the cup, then placed what was left down by the bird and laughed.

Dirt took a slug from the bottle and handed it back to his friend. While the men and the fowl drank, Bradshaw described Jane Edgarton's letter and the massacre at Lawrence. "So WaShana is a lady now? And heading east?" Jimmy questioned. Of all the events Dirt described, this seemed to draw the most interest from the rancher.

"I reckon so. We didn't know we had a real diamond-in–the rough," said Bradshaw. Dirt glanced over at Red Water, who was washing mortar off his hands. "She broke Rodrigo's heart by going, you know. Maybe Juan's too."

"Hell, it's all for the best," Gray remarked. "She couldn't marry an Indian. And it's better to be a lady in Ohio than a whore in New Mexico."

"You could have married her, rather than let that last thing happen. Speaking of women, what gives with Rosa Del Rio?" Dirt asked.

"Now that Miguel's gone, Lew's got first dibs." said Jimmy, taking the whiskey cup away from the rooster. "That baby is Claw's. I bet on it."

"Maybe so. But you two need a woman on this ranch. Someone put chili pepper in these beans," Dirt said, setting the plate aside. He settled on eating the meat and biscuit. "And they're burnt, too."

That evening, Rodrigo surprised everyone, when he decided to drink with Bradshaw and Gray. Juan Villareal, who was sixteen now, also joined in. "Here I go, corrupting both wisdom and youth, on my last night in New Mexico," Dirt Bradshaw remarked, after his second glass of whiskey. He and Rodrigo walked out by the corral and were gazing up at the vast Milky Way. It was a crystal-clear night and a hint of winter hung in the air.

"You have not done anything wrong, for it is each our own choice," said Red Water. "We will be going in separate directions—walking in the four ways of life soon."

"How is that, Amigo?" Dirt wondered.

"You are seeking a purpose. I am going to find my people. Señor Jimmy seeks to remain—to rebuild what he lost."

"Who's the fourth? Oh, yeah, Big Lewis. What's he seeking?"

"I do not know," Red Water admitted. "More will be revealed. You and he are restless souls. But do not mix your restlessness with revenge, Señor Dirt. It only brings a circle—of death."

"You're describing war, my friend. This country is at war with itself. Something I haven't fully admitted," said Dirt, as the two men walked back to the others.

"As long as you work toward men being free, you will have a purpose bigger than yourself. If you go fight to avenge that massacre, there will only be more massacres. Before now, I sensed a reason why you are not a natural-born killer. Why is that?"

Dirt felt humbled. "Years ago, I shot two young men. Both Arapaho. It's something I still regret. Something I cannot amend."

Red Water halted. "You were a healer, when you saved WaShana. I know, from being a *curandero*, that when we heal, we set up all sorts of possibilities. But when men kill, they end certain...things. Besides just life."

"Yes...yes," Dirt agreed. "One ends...another person's potential. Maybe their destiny. A man cuts short another man's chance at doing good, at learning to love...to grow into their destiny."

Rodrigo gazed off at the campfire, where Jimmy Gray was talking with Juan Villareal; the boy was listening intently. "You see that? Señor Jimmy is being like a father. And you, Bradshaw, may someday be a father."

"You too, Amigo," said Dirt, "and you would be a fine one, I'm sure."

Lew McManus arrived the next morning with the supply wagon— and a passenger, Rosa Amarilla. Jimmy Gray was nowhere in sight, but Juan and Dirt were passed out under wool blankets on the decking of his ranch house. Lew assisted Rosa down from the wagon then he walked over and noticed the empty bottle of rye. "So you didn't leave me any, huh, Yank?" Lew commented, as a bleary-eyed Dirt Bradshaw sat up. "Tied one on last night, didn't you?"

Before Dirt answered, Juan Villareal emerged from under the other blanket. "Aiiee, my head hurts," the boy moaned.

McManus normally would have roared with laughter, yet he seemed in a dark mood this morning. "Where's Jimmy Carl, dammit? I've gotta have words with him."

Dirt scratched the stubble on his chin. "He must have risen early, to go hunting," said Bradshaw, seeing Gray's folded blanket on the floor. "Red Water slept in the barn and may have gone with him."

An ash covered coffee pot sat by the stones of the extinguished campfire. McManus inspected it; he found it half-full and not warm. "He's been gone awhile," Lew muttered. "You're leaving today, Yank?" he asked Bradshaw.

"I reckon. How are you, Miss Rosa?" Dirt asked, remembering his manners. "I am fine," the young woman replied, yet she seemed reluctant about returning to the ranch.

"I got a telegram—and a letter, from Nashville," McManus announced. "My brother was killed!"

Dirt stood up and said he was sorry. "How did it happen?" he asked.

"The Yankees wounded him badly at Chickamauga. He died a few days later," McManus explained. "My family needs me, so I'm going back to Tennessee."

Juan Villareal struggled out of his bedroll, expressed his sympathy, then the boy lurched over to the back edge of the platform and vomited.

While Rosa Amarilla tended to Juan, Dirt rebuilt the cooking fire and spoke with the Tennessean. Lew said he needed to check on his family, who lived some distance south of Union-occupied Nashville. "I thought about going through the Texas panhandle, but that's Comanche country," said Lew. Dirt did not catch what Lew was implying. He was busy reheating the coffee. "Listen up, Dirt. I'm going with you...as far as Fort Larned. Then I'll take the Cherokee Trail to Arkansas."

Bradshaw glanced up at McManus and frowned. "I told you, Lew. I'm going to join the Union Army."

"Fine. You do that. I'll make a deal with you," Lew said, "I'll stay out of Missouri. You just stay the hell away from Tennessee, okay?"

CHAPTER 39

Exiled from their native lands, the Mescalero were now concentrated at a camp on a flat, barren bend of the Rio Pecos. General Carleton had ordered almost all the tall trees of the "Round Forest" cut down, to build Fort Sumner. As a result, the waters of the Pecos had turned black and brackish.

Having forced the Apaches to the 'Bosque Redondo' camp, the Bluecoat soldiers counted their numbers every day. The count fluctuated—decreasing by deaths, or increasing, when new groups arrived. After some younger warriors escaped, the 'Star Chief', Carleton, ordered his Union soldiers to post guards at a forty-mile perimeter around the camp and shoot any Indians found outside the reservation.

Most of these soldiers at Fort Sumner had come with General Carleton from California, where they had experience killing the native peoples. On this raw day in early December, the guards were escorting some Mescalero women out on a work detail. The women were gaunt and wore ragged clothing. They had been brought out to gather mesquite and other brush for their cooking fires.

Broken Wing was now one of the prisoners. Forced to surrender by deprivation and hunger, she had arrived months earlier with her infant girl. Broken Wing found the Nit'ahende People living like prairie dogs, forced to dig burrows in the sandy ground. As winter approached, harsh westerly winds kicked up the sand and swirled it into everything—eyes, food and hair. Every day, the Mescalero mother prayed to her mountain gods that her milk would not dry up, lest she lose her child.

This winter would be difficult for the Deer People, Broken Wing realized, yet she was determined to survive. On this day, she felt glad to be away from the burrows of the concentration camp—even if it meant hard labor.

Hacking away at the hard roots of the mesquite with a small hatchet, Broken Wing wondered how she could fool the soldiers. After each work detail, the women who were doing the cutting had to give up their tools before returning to the camp. They were seven or eight miles away from the compound, because no wood could be found there anymore.

One of the soldiers shouted and Broken Wing turned to look. Off to the north, there was a dust cloud that appeared to be drawing closer. "Everyone, stop working!" a sergeant ordered. If this was a dust storm, it could offer cover for an escape. The Mescalero women stood and watched. Moments later, they heard the rumble of a cattle herd and horses approaching.

This meant food! Several riders were driving the beef herd toward the Fort. For several weeks now, the soldier chiefs had promised better food, blankets and clothing for the Apaches. Fifty to sixty cattle comprised this new herd.

"Go head those drivers off," the sergeant told his men. "Send the more healthy animals to the fort and have them pick out the thinner ones for these squaws."

Broken Wing felt a great bitterness. The Mescaleros were always given the lesser things, the scraps that fell from the White Man's table. She gazed out at the cattlemen who had brought the herd as the soldiers halted them. One of the men on horseback seemed familiar.

"Why is your prisoner not bound?" the sergeant asked the lead Anglo rider. "All Indians have to have their hands tied when they arrive."

"Dog-dammit, how is he gonna help us drive these damned steers like that?" Jimmy Carl Gray demanded. Gray and Rodrigo had hired Juan Villareal and three other young Mexicanos from San Geronimo to drive the herd.

When Broken Wing realized Rodrigo Red Water was among the riders, she dropped her hatchet and ran toward him. "Stop! *Alto!* Halt right there, Woman—or I'll shoot!" a corporal shouted, pointing his carbine at Broken Wing.

Red Water saw the Mescalero woman standing out from the huddled prisoners and his heart went out to her. He nodded and waved slightly, but did not speak. Two soldiers came with ropes and tied up Rodrigo's hands to the horn of his saddle.

"Do you want these damned steers or not?" yelled Jimmy Gray. "I'm taking them and Red Water to your head commander. So let us pass!" It had been a disappointing autumn for the rancher; McManus and Bradshaw had left and the ranch house was not finished. Jimmy was forced to sell off half of the Rim Rock's cattle in order to settle up with Lew, for they had dissolved their partnership.

After herding the cattle into Fort Sumner's stockade, Jimmy and Rodrigo were escorted to the commanding officer. The major was middle-aged, with a harried demeanor. Jimmy was also introduced to the Indian agent in charge of the reservation. "So you are sure there's to be no execution, right?" Gray questioned, when he entered the office.

"If General Carelton wanted your man dead, he would have done it at Fort Union," said the major.

"I asked, because Red Water came here of his own accord. And he helped the U.S. Army recover a bunch of gold stolen from the government." Jimmy gazed out in the hallway, where Rodrigo was being guarded by two soldiers.

"We appreciate that." The major opened a desk drawer and drew out a small stack of "greenback" dollars. "This pays you for both the Apache and the beeves," he said, handing them to the rancher.

"I had to ask," Jimmy Gray remarked, "because if anything happens to Red Water, you all are gonna make me feel like a Judas, understand? Can I have a minute to talk with him?"

The commander agreed. As the soldiers escorted Rodrigo to the Mescalero compound, Gray walked beside his friend. "I guess this is it, Amigo," said Jimmy, "At least the Mescaleros are getting their medicine chief back. I hope you do not have to stay here long."

Red Water's expression seemed fairly serene. "I remember the words of that strange hermit priest. 'This too, shall pass. The soldiers also tell me that the woman, Broken Wing, has a young girl-child. It may be mine."

"Hah, so you got your prophecy all wrong," Gray laughed. "You're the one who will be a 'Father to a People'—not me."

They reached the holding area, enclosed by a high, hog-wire fence. A metal gate served as an entrance to the camp. Red Water turned and grasped his friend's hand with both of his bound hands and they shook. "*Vaya con Dios, compadre*, I follow my own path now. Good luck, as you follow yours," he said.

Gray used part of the money to pay the Mexicanos. Next day, he rode silently behind the group as they returned north. Just before dusk,

Jimmy asked Juan where the nearest town or village was located. They were following the Pecos and were still a full day's ride from the Rim Rock. "Anton Chico. It is not much," the boy answered.

"As long as there's a cantina, it will do," said Gray. "I feel like pitchin' a dog-ass drunk."

CHAPTER 40

Jane Edgarton took it upon herself to finish her late brother's story for the *Rocky Mountain News*. After Trey Edgarton's burial in the Cincinnati cemetery, the young Canadienne sought solace by reading her brother's rough draft and notes about WaShana Nicole Klausmann, "The Beloved Captive of the Comanches." It was a tangible connection with her brother and a way of honoring him.

Miss Edgarton had found it difficult to keep performing as a musician after the trauma of the Lawrence Massacre. Being confined before indoor crowds now caused her to panic. Like Trey, Jane had been tutored as a child; she was educated enough to communicate her thoughts and her observations on paper.

Jane's parents lived in a two-story frame house on the northwestern edge of Cincinnati. The home had a wraparound porch, several projecting gables and a well-tended yard surrounded by a decorative iron fence and low, stone walls. WaShana Nicole loved to sit out on the porch while Jane shut herself in her own room, writing.

Unlike Jane, Nicole no longer dressed in black: it did not seem appropriate to sit out in the autumn sunlight in funeral attire. WaShana Nicole had developed into somewhat of a beauty. Blonde ringlets framed her tanned face; a regular diet had filled out her bosom; and most noticeably, pregnancy gave Nicole a vivacious glow.

WaShana Nicole had drawn the attention of several men, when she was first introduced as a wartime widow at the family's Episcopal church.

She met Union soldiers on leave, for President Lincoln had declared a national Thanksgiving holiday in November. Two of them engaged Nicole in conversation after church one Sunday. They were surprised, when this girl in black spoke boldly and acted quite gregariously for a grieving widow; the young lady laughed openly and even ate chicken with her fingers. This turned one soldier away; yet the other, a young lieutenant, was attracted to Jane's friend.

On this warm, sunny Saturday, Lieutenant Reed Allen called on Nicole. He found her reclining in a porch swing, without a hat, taking in the late morning sun. Allen was tall, with a light brown, trimmed beard, and one could tell he was a soldier, even though he wore a tweed jacket and plainclothes on this day. "I hate to impose on your musings, Mrs. Klausmann," said the lieutenant, "but may I join you?"

"Yeah. Sure," said Nicole, in a matter-of-fact way. This directness was exactly what had attracted Reed Allen at their first encounter. He stepped up on the porch.

"How is Miss Jane?" the young man asked.

"Oh, she's good. Do you want me to fetch her?" WaShana Nicole asked, remembering to act like a lady and sitting up straight.

"If she's busy, or writing, that won't be necessary. I really wanted to speak with you, Ma'am," said Allen.

"You don't have to call me that. 'Nicole' will do fine, okay?" Nicole brushed back a loose ringlet. She felt Jane would chastise her for not wearing a hat, waistcoat—or even a scarf this morning. "What brings you here, then?"

"I found it impertinent to ask you last Sunday, but I was wondering..." the lieutenant began. "How long ago did your husband die?" He sat down in a wicker chair.

"Earlier this year," Nicole answered, not thinking fully at first. Then, a few seconds later, she added, "well, not that long ago." She pointed to her torso. WaShana Nicole was four months along now in her pregnancy.

Reed Allen seemed embarrassed. "I should have figured that out." he said. "Again, I am terribly sorry."

WaShana Nicole realized where this conversation was going. Judging by the earnestness in the young man's blue eyes, and the way he leaned forward in his chair, the lieutenant had not come to merely offer more condolences. "Jane has sent off some articles to some newspapers," she said, changing the conversation.

"Oh, really? About what?" the officer asked.

This was not good. The articles were about WaShana's captivity among the Comanches. "Oh, about abolition, and women's... issues. She is also writing about ...how women can be more free—out West."

"Indeed" That's interesting," said Allen. "Did your husband serve out West?"

"He died in Texas." WaShana now felt uncomfortable.

"What battle? Do you mind my asking?" the soldier persisted.

WaShana Nicole was tired of this game; she hated lying. The truth would soon be out in Denver, so what use was it, to live a lie back East, here in Cincinnati? "The Palo Duro Canyon. He was killed by Texans," said WaShana. Actually, this was true of her late husband, a Comanche warrior.

"I am not aware of that battle. And yet there have been so many battles and skirmishes—and men dying from disease, as well," the lieutenant said, sorrowfully.

WaShana could not keep disguising her past. She did not want to encourage this young man's desires–or her own; she could not endure more heartbreak, so she decided to be blunt. "You may learn soon enough, Sir. My dead husband was a warrior—of the Quahadi People," said WaShana. She looked away, off to the west. "My baby is...partly an Indian." For a moment, she thought about telling this soldier about Rodrigo, yet this was already enough truth for now.

Lieutenant Allen's face dropped in disbelief, yet then he saw the resolute expression in the young woman's face. Reed Allen's face grew red.

"Please understand why I kept this a secret," WaShana Nicole added. "Out of respect for Jane...and Trey. You may read about me one day. After the news gets back East. And after...I have left."

Lieutenant Allen stood up. "I am sorry. Please give my best to Miss Jane," he said.

Dirt Bradshaw looked around everywhere in amazement at the new details of his world. An eye doctor in Kansas City had diagnosed the army scout as near-sighted and Bradshaw now wore spectacles. Standing on a street corner with Sergeant Larsen in Springfield, Missouri, Dirt could now recognize people's faces from a distance and spot fair-looking women from afar. "Dang, I can see the gravel in the street and count the nose-hairs on a bullfrog," Dirt laughed. "And there's 'Shanghai Bill' Hickock, as I live and breathe! Let's go talk with the bastard."

Dressed in a black frock coat, low-brimmed hat and carrying ivory-handled pistols in a red sash across his waist, Hickock looked like a gambler as he stood in the dirty packed snow outside a saloon. Dirt had previously met James Butler Hickock when Hickock worked as a teamster in Colorado. "Hello, Bill, how ya doing?" Dirt asked.

At first, Hickock did not recognize the elder Bradshaw because of his glasses, trimmed hair and lack of a bushy beard. After Dirt identified himself, Hickock shook his hand.

"Bill, this is Charlie Larsen. He was our partner back at our Boulder Canyon mine," said Dirt. "What are you doing in Missouri?"

Hickock replied that he was a police detective, for the Provost Marshall of the Springfield District, and he showed Dirt his badge as proof. "They've got me counting how many beers you Colorado boys are drinking."

Dirt grinned and slapped Hickock on the shoulder. "Then come on in and count with us," said Bradshaw. "I'm working as a scout for the Second Colorado and we're on leave today."

Hickock followed the two cavalrymen into the saloon. They took a table over in a far corner and 'Shanghai Bill' sat down with his back against the wall.

"That's good you've got glasses now, Dirt. Otherwise, you'd be the blind drunk, leading the blind." Hickock signaled the bartender for a pitcher of beer and three mugs.

"Hell, the Army wanted me to become a glorified clerk, after I got these and they found out I could read and write," said Dirt, pushing his glasses up on his nose. "But I signed up to fight those Rebel guerillas"

"If you're literate, they'll eventually make you an officer," Hickock predicted. "The Army needs men who can write reports, read messages and send letters to the families of dead soldiers."

This was a grim comment; yet the mood lightened when the barkeeper brought the beer mugs and glass pitcher of St. Louis beer. "Where's your card-cheatin' brother?" Bill Hickock asked Dirt.

"Back at Fort Weld. His enlistment is expiring next month," said Dirt. "Davey's trying to resurrect our mining operation." Dirt let the foam settle on his glass of brew. "I guess you heard about him escorting a gold shipment from Denver."

Hickock nodded. "Don't talk about it here Dirt," he whispered, glancing around at the civilian customers in the saloon. "Here in Missouri, when you come up on a farmhouse, you don't know if you're gonna be greeted by either a bullet, or a glass of buttermilk. If some folks hear the word 'gold', they might rob you in a dark alley."

After drinking one beer with Dirt and Charlie, Hickock excused himself and left. Both men drank in silence for a moment, then Larsen asked about Jane Edgarton.

"Well, you know I got that letter. That's why I joined up," said Dirt. "And I got a telegram while we were in Kansas City. She and Miss Nicole are going to travel to Chicago and St. Louis, on some lecture tours."

"Is she still going to marry Captain Soule?" asked Charlie. Silas Soule had been promoted.

"I don't know. She didn't say," said Dirt, glumly sipping his beer.

"I am sorry for you Dirt," the Swede remarked. He leaned forward. "May I ask you something? If it...would you be mad, if..."

"It's about Christina Jones, right?" Dirt replied, seeing Charlie's hesitation.

"Ja. She wrote me a letter. Are you angry?"

Dirt Bradshaw grinned. "Charlie, you and I go back a long way. Now you are my brother-in-law. I blew my chance with Mrs. Jones. You should have better luck than me." Christina Jones and Bradshaw had once been engaged to marry, yet the Union widow had run away from the relationship two years earlier.

For a moment, Charlie Larsen again saw the rough and ready prospector he once knew in the mining camps of gold-rush Colorado. Dirt was a fair-minded individual. He believed in giving his close friends equal opportunities at gold strikes and women. "Christina has decided not to homestead after all," Charlie said. "She and her younger sister are moving to Denver City."

"That's good. It's too dangerous for a woman to be out in the wilderness, with the Indians making trouble," said Dirt. Bradshaw lifted his mug up to his mouth, to hide his sadness over Christina Jones. "Has she ever asked about me?"

"*Ja,* and I told her about you going after those gold thieves. I told her we are both fighting the Rebels now."

Dirt took a sip of beer. It surprised him that Charlie Larsen had written back to Christina. Dirt remembered the hopes that he and the Union widow had once shared; he remembered first meeting her in Taos, about their brief time together in Santa Fe—and her running away from their engagement. It all seemed so far away, so distant in time, yet the hurt still lingered. "Her child. The little girl—how is she doing?" Dirt asked.

"*Ja,* she is good. I saw her last Christmas, at Boulder Creek. Loralie is over a year old now," Charlie remarked. "Dirt, is it okay, if I... keep writing to Christina?"

Bradshaw hesitated for only two seconds. "Sure. yah, Charlie. You don't need my permission," he said.

CHAPTER 41

After leaving Cincinnati, Jane Edgarton and Nicole Klausmann rode trains throughout the MidWest, to Columbus, Fort Wayne and then Chicago. WaShana Nicole Klausmann was now causing quite a stir in these cities. People wanted to see this young white woman, who had survived years as a prisoner of the wild Plains Indians and was rescued back into Christian society.

Jane had initially brought on WaShana's fame through news stories about the former "Beloved Captive" in the *Rocky Mountain News* and

Kansas City's *The Daily Journal*. Jane had found a new career as a journalist and lecturer. She wrote stories about WaShana, the Lawrence Massacre and the people she met out West. By the first of 1864, Miss Edgarton's feature articles had appeared in the *Cincinnati Enquirer*, the *Chicago Tribune*, and the *St. Louis Republican*.

Weeks earlier, Miss Klausmann had told Jane that she no longer wanted to impersonate a Union widow. "I am WaShana and I am not ashamed to tell the truth," the young woman declared. "If you want to tell my story, go ahead—but I cannot remain here in Cincinnati."

At first, Jane had been hesitant. Although a lecture tour would provide a good income and bring in funds for the Union Widows Relief Fund, she had doubts about Nicole sharing the podium as WaShana. The catalyst for this tour came about when a famous promoter, P.T. Barnum wanted Nicole to sign a contract and make appearances on the East Coast. Jane told Nicole she did not want "WaShana" to be a museum act, like "General Tom Thumb", the "Feejee Mermaid", giantess Anna Swan, or the "Siamese Twins". As a result, Miss Edgarton's "Surviving War and Savagery" lecture series was born.

On the route to Columbus, Jane let the former captive study the words of her own story. WaShana Nicole learned quickly and by the time they reached Chicago, she felt she could speak for herself. Bravely answering questions from the audience that night, WaShana gave the lecture a whole new meaning and depth.

"I am so proud of you, Nicole. I only wish Trey could see how you have blossomed," said Jane, as the two women boarded the Illinois Central train for Springfield, Illinois.

"He would be proud of you, Jane," said WaShana, collapsing into her seat in the covered passenger car. Union soldiers, either on leave or returning to their posts in the trans-Mississippi region, were also on the train. It was now 1864 and the tide of war was shifting in the Union's favor. A tall, uniformed officer approached Jane and told her he had attended her lecture in Chicago.

"I am sorry about your brother," said the Lieutenant, a sandy-haired young man with a neatly-trimmed mustache. "I'm an Ohio man myself. If it's any consolation, we are on our way to Fort Scott, in Eastern Kansas—and hope to punish those criminal bushwhackers."

Jane thanked the officer and introduced him to Nicole. Overhearing Miss Klausmann's name, the man sitting in front of the ladies turned around and said he was a reporter for the *St. Louis Republican*. "May I talk with you, Miss?' he asked.

"Oh, I wrote a feature for your paper two months ago," said Jane, "so that somewhat makes me a colleague."

The journalist, a paunch-bellied man with bushy, brown sideburns that merged with a sweeping mustache, gave Jane a condescending look. "Not necessarily, Ma'am," he said. "Ahem, I am Herman Stigler, from St. Louis," he said to Nicole. "So you are the maiden who was taken captive by the Comanche Indians?"

Nicole nodded, yet she did not feel like talking with this stranger. His breath smelled of cigars and onions and he reminded Nicole of a groundhog, popping up out of his hole in late winter.

"So, you were forced to live as one of them?" the reporter asked. "You had to become a squaw?"

Jane Edgarton picked up on Nicole's discomfiture. "It was all in my story, Sir," she told Stigler. Miss Jane glanced at the Union Lieutenant, who had taken a seat across the aisle.

"I apologize," said the reporter, yet he did not turn away. "Is it Miss—or Missus Klausman?" he asked. The man seemed to notice that Nicole was pregnant.

Here we go again, thought Nicole. She felt no stranger had the right to question her honor. "My husband is gone," she murmured.

The Union lieutenant coughed into his fist, to get the journalist's attention. "Sir, why don't you attend Miss Edgarton's lecture yourself, when you get to Springfield?" he suggested. "Then she and the young lady can answer your questions in the proper format."

Mr. Stigler turned back around and sank down in his seat. "I might do that," he said, taking out a small notepad and scribbling a few remarks.

Nicole and Jane did not see Stigler in the audience at Springfield. Jane assumed the reporter had gone on to Missouri with the Union soldiers. Springfield, the home of President Lincoln, felt safe, far away from the war. Riding around in a carriage, Jane pointed out Lincoln's home on Eighth Street. "Abraham Lincoln and Stephen Douglas were both lawyers for the Illinois Central Railroad," Jane explained. The two-story house, with its many windows and side porch, reminded Nicole of Lawrence, Kansas and her brief home before the massacre. "I think I want to have my baby at my uncle's house," she told Jane. "Is there any way that you can take me back there?"

"In due time," said Jane. "First, we must go on to St. Louis, Terre Haute and Indianapolis."

On the evening of Miss Edgarton's lecture in St. Louis, Nicole felt extremely on edge. Instead of a modest lecture hall, the event was scheduled in a theater. Jane and WaShana had to stand on a stage, with bright lights in front of a large audience. In keeping with Jane's previous Union Widow's Relief Fund events, women composed a majority of the crowd, yet there were several men.

As Jane was introduced by the St. Louis mayor's wife, Miss Edgarton and Nicole sat in chairs behind the podium. Jane still wore black, but Nicole was modestly attired in a brown skirt, white blouse, reddish-brown vest and a jacket that partially hid her pregnancy. Nicole avoided looking directly at the crowd, until Jane approached the podium.

"Ladies and gentlemen, I thank you for coming here tonight," Jane began. "Tonight, I am speaking about grief, recovery and freedom. As many of you know, the Union was ripped asunder by the forces of slavery, the reckless arrogance, of those who would hold other men—and women—in bondage."

Miss Edgarton first described her own family's participation in the Underground Railroad. Nicole had heard this speech numerous times, so at first, she hardly listened. Scanning the audience, she caught her breath. There, in the second row, she spotted Herman Stigler, the newspaperman.

As Jane continued speaking, her words barely registered to Nicole. Her nervousness, the tightness of her vest and the physical feeling of entrapment felt worse than being roped and bonded to a moving horse.

"My guest here tonight is Miss Nicole Klausmann. She is a young woman, who has experienced both the bondage of being held captive by the Comanche People—and the chaos, cruelty and carnage of the Lawrence Massacre. My friends, her experiences mirror the horror, the hopelessness and the bondage of slavery. But she is now free!"

Nicole's face reddened. Unlike previous performances, Jane left out the name 'WaShana'. Nicole tightly gripped her own written speech, which she would read after Jane introduced her a second time. The paper fluttered in her hands, like a captured bird.

Jane went on, describing the efforts of the Widow's Relief Fund and a plea for donations to help the widows in Lawrence. Nicole felt Miss Jane's speech was rising toward an eventual crescendo, after which, she herself would have to speak. Nicole could feel her own heart beating, her upper shoulders ached and she almost felt like she would faint.

"Kind ladies and gentlemen, please welcome Nicole Klausmann, the former Beloved Captive of the Comanches."

Nicole's feet felt like lead, as people applauded and she took the podium. She coughed, took a deep breath, unfolded her notes, and exhaled. "I am Nicole and I once...had a...family," she stammered. "But they were taken away." Here Nicole paused, as instructed by Jane, to magnify the effect on the audience. For some reason, Nicole felt she was speaking to an iron wall this time. No one gasped, no look of pity seemed to emanate from the first and second row. A woman who sat next to Herman Stigler now whispered to the reporter. Nicole felt he had been gossiping about her.

Steeling herself, Nicole nevertheless persisted. Her fear now turned to anger. She raised her gaze from her written statement, stepped aside from the lectern and spoke:

> "And so I became WaShana. I am what is called a
> 'Beloved Captive'. The Comanche people took me in
> as one of their own. Yes, I became a Comanche."

Many people in the audience began murmuring. To WaShana, they seemed like cicadas or grasshoppers, chirping and buzzing at dusk on a prairie summer's evening. "My blood has always run red, like every human being!" WaShana said proudly. She was now improvising. "Like a Black man. Like a Comanche woman! Like the warrior who was my husband."

The murmurs turned to gasps and angry mutterings. A couple in the back row stood up and left. Sitting behind Nicole with the mayor's wife, Jane glanced at a copy of Nicole's statement; her friend was going totally off script.

"Women have lost husbands, sons, brothers and fathers," Nicole said. Now Jane relaxed; this was part of the written statement. "They were lost in the war and at Lawrence, Kansas." Nicole looked over at Stigler, who was scribbling on his notepad. "And in my nation. When the Tejanos killed my husband," WaShana added.

People in the audience looked at each other. They didn't know that 'Tejanos' meant Texans. Some were confused, for they realized the word was Spanish. Stigler stood up. "So he was killed by Mexicans, you're saying?" he questioned.

"All of these people were killed by White men," WaShana declared. "But not all the widows are white. Not all the orphans are Anglo!"

Several people stood up in protest. "Is your baby not White?" Stigler shouted.

Jane Edgarton now stood by Nicole's side. She gripped her friend's shoulder. "You don't have to answer that," said Jane. "He is Apache!" WaShana exclaimed, glaring at the journalist with a fierce fire in her eyes. A woman shrieked, men cursed in low whispers and people began to walk away, yet WaShana stood her ground.

CHAPTER 42

Rosa Amarilla Del Rio gave birth to a boy in early March of 1864. Shortly thereafter, Jimmy Carl Gray's relationship with the Criolla woman soon soured. The child came out with a big head of thick black hair, a broad nose, and eyes like Lew McManus. He was not Jimmy Gray's or the late Miguel LaHoya's boy.

Although she had not heard from McManus since his departure, Rosa held out hope for his return. She named the boy Mack Del Rio.

"Mack Del Rio, huh?" said Jimmy. "With a name like that he's bound to become some dang outlaw, like his daddy."

With this insult, Rosa Amarilla packed her belongings and persuaded Juan Villareal to take her and the child back to Las Vegas Grandes. Gray was left alone at his half-built ranch house, with only his red coonhound and Lew's Airedale for company.

A week later, Jimmy's Mexicano ranch hand finally returned to the Rim Rock and told Jimmy he was in love with the Señorita. "Why, you're only sixteen!" said Jimmy. "She's just using you, I bet."

"No, she promised, when I turn older, she will marry me next year," said Juan, scowling at the rancher.

"Hah, good luck with that!" laughed Gray. "I hope you and the Whore Angel are happy together, with you bouncin' Big Lew's baby on your knee. When you aren't bouncin' yourself on her belly."

Juan Villareal drew his wages and rode off in a huff back to Montezuma's Castle, the Hot Springs Hotel where Rosa had taken residence. Now it was just Jimmy, the dogs, four horses, some chickens and forty-seven cattle at the ranch. It was the time of year when the cows were beginning to give birth.

"I need help, dammit," Gray finally admitted to himself. The next day, the rancher rode over to Fort Union, where the two captured Confederate Indians were being held. Extracting a promise that they would not again take up arms against the Federal Union, the camp commander paroled Will Dare and the young Cherokee, Sam Burningtree, to Grays' sponsorship. They agreed to work at Jimmy's ranch for at least a year.

Sam Burningtree proved to be a good ranch hand, but the former Chickasaw scout disappeared the night after he first got paid. "It's just as well," said Jimmy. "I never liked the surly beanpole."

As the snow melted and the days hinted of spring, the bushwhacker guerillas returned from Texas. Fears of another massacre like that in Lawrence spread throughout the towns of eastern Kansas. In retaliation to the massacre, Union General Thomas Ewing, Jr. had issued "General order number 11", that called for the forced removal of residents in four western Missouri counties. Ewing believed William Quantrill's Confederate raiders drew their support from the farmers in Bates, Cass, Jackson and Vernon counties. Residents who could prove their loyalty to the Union were permitted to stay, but many farms and homes were burned down and looted by Kansas Jayhawkers and members of the Missouri militia. The region became known as the 'Burnt District'.

The order was repealed when Union General Samuel Curtis took command. Curtis kept the Jayhawkers in Kansas and replaced them with other troops, which included the Second Colorado Cavalry. These Colorado units were less prejudiced and more fair toward the people in the four Missouri counties, yet they had to stay on guard. The Rebels were now using new tactics.

Dirt Bradshaw was no longer just a scout. True to "Wild Bill" Hickock's prediction, Charles Larsen was promoted to Lieutenant, so Dirt Bradshaw enlisted as a sergeant in Larsen's company. Bradshaw's unit often rode back and forth between Kansas City and the Osage River, repairing telegraph lines the bushwhackers had torn down, or carrying messages and supplies. There were some skirmishes with the Confederate irregulars, but the Rebels always seemed to be one step ahead of the Federal Army.

Bradshaw's unit, composed of twelve men, were repairing the lines to Pleasant Hill one morning. Dirt was speaking to Private Marshall Barnes. "Darn, I wound up working the telegraph lines after all. The Army wanted me to be a telegraph operator, you know," Bradshaw told the private. Dirt used his natural camaraderie with his men to instill loyalty, rather than harsh words and strict discipline. After all, these were Colorado men, former prospectors, bar keepers and frontiersmen; Dirt did not order his men to do anything he wouldn't do himself. He and Barnes were unspooling a roll of telegraph wire along a section of damaged lines. "Naw, I didn't want to be an operator. I wanted to be out here, in the spring mud, humping these spools across God's glorious countryside." said Dirt. "Anyway, that's the long and short of it."

"At least the bushwhackers left the poles," said Private Barnes. He and Bradshaw put the spool down.

Dirt handed Barnes a pair of wire cutters. "You know how to splice everything, right?" he asked. "I'm too old and creaky to climb like a ring-tailed racoon up there."

The other cavalrymen now gathered around and some commented that the Confederates were stupid for leaving the telegraph poles. "The Rebs can destroy, but they can't strategize," one soldier commented.

"Yeah, they ain't professional. They can use pistols, but not their brains," Barnes added.

"You men line up!" Bradshaw ordered. "Get in line and stand at attention!"

The Colorado soldiers were confused, but they did as Dirt commanded. Walking down the line, Dirt tried to act gruff. "Okay, soldiers. Now, I want you all to pull out the front of your trousers. Do it—all of you!" The young soldiers complied with the command. "Now, look down at what you've got, okay?"

The men frowned, yet glanced down. "What you see is where your brains are," said Dirt, "Now, look back at me. Raise your hands if you joined the cavalry in order to fight slavery." One soldier, a young man who wore glasses, raised his hand. "Who joined to preserve the Union?" Dirt watched as three more men raised their hands. "Now then, how many of you joined to impress a female? A sweetheart or a gal you were smitten by?" Bradshaw raised his own arm and his soldiers raised theirs. "Yeah, we are all geniuses in that department," said Dirt. "And the Rebels are too. Except they may be quicker on the draw—and shoot their wad faster than us, right boys?"

The cavalrymen all laughed. "But don't we have better reasons to fight, Sergeant Dirt?" Barnes asked.

"Reasons? Old men cite reasons, but it's young men who do the fighting. You cannot reason with these bushwhackers, men. You have to use the driving force of life—what brought you here—to battle and survive. You all are young, hung and fulla piss and vinegar! Now, shimmy up those poles!"

Dirt watched as his men strung up the news telegraph wires. One by one, as they finished their work, the soldiers climbed back down. Only two cavalrymen were still working when one of them shouted back down to the sergeant.

"There's riders approaching, Sergeant Dirt," said the Private, pointing off to the East.

Bradshaw looked down the Warrensburg Pike, but could not see the riders. He took out his spectacles and put them on. "Sure enough, I see them now," said Dirt. "Climb on down, boys. Everyone, grab your rifles."

The Colorado troopers were armed with new Spencer repeating carbines. Up close and without these new rifles, the dismounted cavalry men would have little chance against the revolver-carrying bushwhackers from Missouri. Sergeant Bradshaw climbed up on Waukesha and pulled his carbine out of the gun boot.

About fifteen or sixteen riders, wearing blue jackets, were herding a group of horses up the pike. "Mount up, fellows," said Dirt. He felt suspicious, for the riders did not look like a regular cavalry unit. When they were within a hundred yards, Sergeant Bradshaw raised his rifle and an open palm and commanded them to halt. "Identify yourselves! And state your purpose!" Dirt shouted.

A blonde-haired, bearded second lieutenant trotted a bay horse up closer. He announced that they were the Missouri Militia. "We are taking these horses on to Independence," the officer explained.

Dirt looked these militiamen over. For this week, Bradshaw and his men wore orange bandanas tied around their right sleeves, to show they were not counterfeit Union soldiers. None of these other horsemen were wearing any bandanas, as ordered, and their trousers were not Army issue. "Not good enough, Sir," said Sergeant Bradshaw. "Sir, we need to know your company and regiment." Dirt had to follow protocol.

The militiamen, most of them looking in age from seventeen to their early twenties, shifted nervously in their saddles. Dirt noticed they each had two or more revolvers tucked into their belts.

"Let us pass, Sergeant," the lieutenant demanded. "I outrank you, and that's an order. We are the twenty-second Missouri Volunteers. Now you identify yourself. So I can report you to your commander." The lieutenant's round face grew red with anger.

"Sergeant Bradshaw, Dirt Bradshaw, of the Second Colorado Cavalry. And your name, Lieutenant?"

The metallic click of a revolver hammer was like a spark. Both groups drew their guns; as Bradshaw took sudden aim with his Spencer, the Rebels' lead officer wheeled his bay about and Dirt missed him. Bradshaw's men; however, were more effective, firing their carbines and wounding several of the Missouri men. Gunsmoke and dust swirled about and obstructed Dirt's view as soldiers shouted and shots rang out.

The remuda of horses bolted every which way; when Dirt was knocked off his Ute filly by the onrush, it probably saved his life—for the Rebel lieutenant and the bushwhackers were quick-firing at the Colorado troopers. Still holding his carbine, Dirt rolled off into a ditch, used it as cover and shot the lieutenant off of his mount.

The bushwhackers scrambled back down the road, abandoning their dead and the horses. They had been driven back by the Colorado Cavalry. "By God, that'll teach them outlaws to tangle with mountain men!" Dirt exclaimed. When Bradshaw looked about; however, he stopped cheering. Two of his cavalrymen were sprawled out on the road—dead—and another was wounded in the shoulder. One slain trooper was the young private who said he had enlisted to fight slavery. His glasses lay beside his wounded head, shattered. There was no glory here—only sacrifice.

Dirt and his men found six dead bushwhackers, including the man who had posed as a Union lieutenant. "I think we wounded some more of them, too," said Marshall Barnes. "We whupped 'em, didn't we, Sarge?"

Dirt frowned. "Yeah, but I wonder. Where did they get all those Federal uniforms? Does that mean they killed over a dozen of our soldiers?"

"I think it means they were at Lawrence, Sergeant Dirt," said another cavalryman. "I was with Lieutenant Larsen there, when we had to bury the dead. Some of the Second Kansas men had been stripped of their jackets."

"This is just the start then, men," said Sergeant Bradshaw. "We're going to hunt them down like foxes." The prospector was now at war.

CHAPTER 43

WaShana and Jane Edgarton left St. Louis in separate directions; Miss Edgarton, angry at WaShana's outburst at the lecture hall, wanted to continue her tour on her own. Before leaving, Jane gave Nicole enough money to return to Lawrence, in order to give birth at her uncle's home. Although both women said they would remain friends forever, they were now on different courses in their life—Jane going east and WaShana heading west.

WaShana set off on her own, boarding the Hannibal and St. Joseph train to cross Missouri. Seven months along in her pregnancy, she again donned black and avoided talking with anyone. The young woman did not know what she would do after her child was born; she felt heartbroken over losing another friend and knowing few other friends in Kansas.

Arriving in St. Joseph with only a carpetbag of some clothes and belongings, the young woman took a stagecoach to Weston, Missouri. Weston was a known starting point for travelers on both the Oregon and Santa Fe Trail. Covered wagons, people buying supplies, horse traders and teamsters crowded the town's roads. The first caravans of the season were assembling for their long journeys westward. Men were loading freight and supplies; women oversaw the packing of the ox-drawn wagons, and people were trying to decide which household items should be taken or left behind. As WaShana walked down the line, she saw abandoned bureaus, chests of drawers, a table and even a mirrored hall tree. It reminded her of the time her parents prepared to cross Kansas, when decisions on what to take meant the difference between life and death.

WaShana looked in the hall tree mirror and adjusted her bonnet. She decided to take it off, just as a group of Federal soldiers rode by.

"Miss Klausmann? Is that you, Miss Nicole?" a cavalryman asked. WaShana glanced up and she saw Private Gregory Abramson, turning his horse out of the line of soldiers. Abramson was the Swede who had once served with the late Sergeant Mikowski, who had gone with WaShana and Dirt Bradshaw to recover the stolen gold.

"Yes, yes, it's me! It's so good to see a familiar face here," said WaShana.

"Och, you look so different from when we were on the Cimarron Trail," said Abramson, "with your blonde hair grown out and a dress now. I hardly recognized you."

"Are you part of the troops protecting the border?" WaShana Nicole asked.

"Yah, but now we are going to escort this caravan to the territories, to Colorado and then New Mexico." Gregory Abramson, sandy-haired and now tanned from months in the sun, seemed more mature and handsome than when he had set out with Dirt and Lew McManus' search party. He put two fingers in his mouth and whistled loudly. "Jack, Jack!" he shouted. "*Kommen und* see who is here!"

Corporal Jack Burton appeared out of the crowd. "Well, I must be seeing a mirage. Is this our wild WaShana?" the Cornishman questioned. Burton hugged the girl. He took note of her being pregnant and wearing all black, in the middle of a sunny day. "Oh, Lord, Miss, you were living in Lawrence at the time of the massacre, weren't you? Did someone in your family get killed? I'm sorry."

WaShana drew a deep breath and exhaled. Private Abramson swung down off his horse and embraced her. The three of them stepped away from the wagons and WaShana explained about Trey Edgarton. Having been on a long journey with these men previously, WaShana Nicole felt no need to withhold secrets from them. She confided how she was expecting: "With Rodrigo's child," she confessed.

Both of the cavalrymen were wide-eyed in amazement, yet they did not condemn her. "Whither you go now, Miss?" Jack Burton asked.

The young woman hesitated. The fires at Lawrence, the shootings and Trey Edgarton's death—these images and catastrophes—all came rushing back into her mind. "I do not want to stay in Lawrence anymore," she declared. "I do not belong there, any more than here in Missouri or Cincinnati."

Private Abramson nodded. "Is there any way we can help you, Miss Nicole?" he asked, using her Christian name.

"Are you back with Lieutenant David Bradshaw? Dirt's brother?" she asked. Abramson told her Lieutenant David Bradshaw had not extended his commission, that he was back in Colorado with his wife and family. "But Dirt Bradshaw and his company are hunting down the very men who attacked Lawrence," Corporal Burton added.

WaShana Nicole gazed back at the wagons and the people, the pioneers, who were busy loading their belongings. "I want to go along, on your wagon train," said WaShana. "If there's any chance I can find Rodrigo Red Water—or Big Lew McManus, I must take it. Please, take me with you. I only have this one bag, with some clothes my friend Jane gave me."

★   ★   ★   ★   ★

WaShana rode west in a covered wagon. As the caravan slowly rumbled across the Great Plains, she was riding with a recently married couple from Illinois, who were heading to Denver City. This wagon train moved much slower than WaShana's previous journeys on horseback and by stagecoach. The ox-drawn wagons did well to make sixteen miles a day. The caravan stopped often along the way, for wood, grazing and fresh water.

The Illinois woman's husband was a wounded war veteran, who had lost a hand at the battle of Perryville in Kentucky. He and WaShana took turns driving the oxen. The man's wife was glad at first to have someone assist her with the cooking, but as the days passed, she kept her husband away from being alone with this strange girl.

On the ninth day out, the caravan halted at Council Grove and stocked up on more supplies such as flour, bacon, cornmeal and water. Some of the travelers also swapped out their oxen and horses for new animals. On the tenth night, they camped at Diamond Spring, where a stage station and a small settlement provided another break. WaShana wished she had saved more of the money Jane Edgarton had given her, in order to switch to a stagecoach; instead, she would have to keep enduring this slow pace.

Two days later, there was no wood available, so WaShana had to gather buffalo chips for cooking fuel that night. It was now April and she was well over eight months along. Riding over ruts and rocks began to hurt her now, yet the former captive of the Comanches did not complain. At night, she slept by the remains of the campfire, while the married couple enjoyed each other's company in the bed of their wagon.

Corporal Burton and Gregory Abramson checked regularly on WaShana. They were worried about making it to Fort Larned before her child arrived. Abramson shot an antelope near the Owl Creek crossing and WaShana was happy to have a change from beans and bacon.

The next night, the spring rains arrived in a downpour. It rained all the next day. Wagons became stuck in the mud and WaShana was too sick to do anything other than lie down in the married couple's wagon. She had traveled over two weeks ; the journey was beginning to wear on her.

WaShana was not sure if they had journeyed sixteen or seventeen days by the time the caravan reached a trail station on Walnut Creek. This was a ranch and major stage stop, with a post office and store. A log stockade had been built on the north side of the Trail. Mr. Charles Rath, a dark-haired trader with a lush mustache, owned the ranch. He had a Cheyenne wife, named 'Roadmaker', who insisted that WaShana be given a good bed for the night. Seeing the girl in obvious pain, the Cheyenne woman told WaShana that she was almost ready to give birth.

The ranch also boasted a tavern, so many of the men, including the soldiers escorting the wagon train, began to drink that evening. WaShana was taken to a room at the rear of the station, where there was a bed, a straw mattress and a side table with a wash stand. She was grateful to have a place to rest indoors for a change. In the dim light of an oil lantern, she could see a sod roof overhead. A heavy, canvas tarp, probably from a covered wagon, was used as a rug to cover the dirt floor.

It had been raining all day again and WaShana felt strong pains. As a steady drip began to leak out of the roof, the Cheyenne woman, Mrs. Rath, placed a tin bucket beside the bed. The raindrops seemed to fall in a steady beat, accompanying the din of men carousing out in the tavern.

WaShana's water broke shortly thereafter and her contractions soon grew worse. Corporal Burton and Private Abramson looked in on her, but the Cheyenne woman turned them away.

A Native American midwife soon joined Mrs. Rath. WaShana found out later that small parties of Cheyennes and the Arapaho People camped near the trade station during the winter months. They traded buffalo robes, furs and skinned hides for corn, flour and other supplies.

This Arapaho midwife was older than Mrs. Rath; her face was wrinkled and dark by age and weather, yet when she smiled her eyes lit up and WaShana thought she looked beautiful. She hummed and sang in her native language as she tended to WaShana; her voice was wondrously calming to this young mother-to-be.

WaShana's labor came hard now; she was told it was okay to scream or yell out. "You must take deep, steady breaths now," said the midwife, as the rainwater now plopped in the half-full bucket. "When the next pain comes, you must push!"

In the middle of the night, the child was born. Wringed in sweat, WaShana felt such joy when she took the boy-child in her arms. He was beautiful, with reddish-brown hair and his eyes, brilliant and brown, with the dark intensity that bespoke Native American ancestry, now focused on his mother. WaShana detected a trace of blue glint in the boy's eyes and she instantly knew what she would call him.

"This is Trace. Trace Red Water," said WaShana. "His father is an Apache."

The midwife cut the umbilical cord. "In the Comanche ways, it is hung in a hackberry tree," WaShana remarked. "If it is not disturbed before it is rotted, the child will lead a long life."

"Give him to me and I will sing for him, if you wish," said the midwife. WaShana agreed and let the Arapaho woman take the infant. Wrapping the boy in a soft white cloth, she lifted Trace up, then she sang both to the child and his mother:

> Child of the water, come!
> Let your heart not be troubled.
> Son of the great earth,
> May long-life happiness
> Surround you with its protection.
> (Here the woman turned to WaShana)
> Because of this, he is in your hands,
> Receive him, wash him, feed him.
> For you are the one,
> You know the way,
> He is left in your hands.

May his heart, his life, be good,
Perfect and pure, so he may live,
beautifully, calmly on the earth.
As he flows on the river of life,
May he both receive and give joy.

For this is our lot and our portion.
This, we were once granted—
In the ancient night,
that we wash, that we clean the future,
For this child who comes before you.
May his heart be generous—and yours!

WaShana was overwhelmed. She took Trace back with tears in her eyes and thanked the woman. "Trace, Trace," she whispered, "I will never leave you."

In the middle of the night, Red Water dreamed that he was back in his beloved mountains. He was hunting in the pine forest, where his fathers and grandfathers had hunted. In the dream, there was snow on the ground. It must have been the rutting season, for the Mescalero noticed rubs on the saplings, where a buck or elk had scraped off bark with his antlers. As he moved slowly through the woods, Rodrigo came upon a clear, running brook that shone like diamonds under a full moon.

Somewhere, in the dream, Rodrigo encountered his father, the Chieftain named Black Deer. His father hovered alongside Rodrigo as they moved down the trail; it seemed like Black Deer was riding an invisible horse. His father then spoke in an angry voice, sounding like he did when Red Water was a boy. "You are slow to learn the ways of a warrior," said Black Deer. "Set your feet on higher ground if you must be a Medicine Chief—or our people will die."

CHAPTER 44

Rodrigo awoke. He felt both sad and thirsty after the dream-vision. Instead of the mountain streams of the Sierra Blanca, he was back among the alkaline waters of the Rio Pecos, which always tasted bitter. Still imprisoned at the Bosque Redondo, the reservation the White Eyes had created, Rodrigo looked down at the shackles around his feet. Sitting up in the crude cowhide tent, he pulled back the flap and saw the bluecoat soldiers coming his way.

"You're on a work detail today," said a two-stripe soldier. "So we're taking off your chains." The corporal bent down and unlatched the foot shackles with a key.

Red Water was grateful to be doing something for a change. Other Apaches were with the soldiers, who guarded them with rifles. The corporal and his squadron led the prisoners toward the edge of the camp, where they would be digging an irrigation ditch.

The Apaches had been digging for several hours, when more soldiers appeared, with a large group of new captives. They were escorting the first Navajos to arrive at the Bosque Redondo, in what would later be called "The Long Walk." This was an anguished, forced march from their native country through scorched land, blizzards, hostile settlements and the dry, cracked desert to get here.

Hundreds of the Dine' had died along the way; this first group looked pitiful, sick, starved and ragged. Although the Navajo and the Apache spoke a similar language, the two nations were long-time enemies. Some of the younger Mescaleros working with Rodrigo began to shout angry and derisive taunts at the new prisoners, but Red Water demanded they be quiet. "Would you want what they have had to endure?" he remarked. "Do you not remember how you felt when you were first brought here?"

The other Apaches respected Red Water, so they fell silent as the soldiers and the Navajo prisoners passed. Rodrigo noticed one older captive who looked familiar; he recognized the sharp features of Johnny Calling Rock's face, the beaked nose and piercing eyes of the old warrior. Calling Rock was the only Navajo among the group who had his hands shackled. Red Water called out his name and waved. The Dine' war chieftain nodded, yet did not speak. Rodrigo knew he would probably be put in the same log jailhouse that Rodrigo had been housed in when he first arrived at the internment camp.

When he arose the next morning, Red Water decided he must talk with Calling Rock. He had last seen the Navajo back in 1862, at the Sandia pueblo, back when the Texas Confederates invaded New Mexico. Unlike Rodrigo, Johnny Calling Rock had wanted the different tribes of the territory to unite while the White men fought each other.

By virtue of his steady compliance with the camp's rules, Rodrigo had established some trust with the reservation guards. He was respected as a Medicine Chief as well, as long as he did not cause trouble. On this day, Rodrigo was fortunate. The officer in charge of the escort soldiers was none other than the "Eagle Chief", Colonel 'Kit' Carson. Despite Carson being well-acquainted with the Indian Tribes of the Territory, he and Red Water had never met. The Mescalero asked to meet the commander and he was granted a meeting.

Both men were surprised when they met, for they had heard of each other. Red Water expected to see a burly, strong man, along the lines of a Lew McManus. The famous frontiersman was shorter and more wrinkled than Rodrigo imagined. Kit Carson was now in his mid-fifties; his face looked haggard and he appeared to be experiencing pain as the two men walked back into an office at Fort Sumner.

Colonel Carson had expected to meet a broad-shouldered Apache chief, a fierce-looking Apache like Mangas Coloradas, or the legendary Cochise. Across his desk stood a thin, average sized mestizo Indian, with the high cheekbones of an Apache, yet with some Mexicano features. Red Water wore an oversized, white paisano shirt, that hung down to his knees like a tunic, and Mexican sandals. His long brown hair was set back behind his ears by a red bandana headband and he seemed to possess a serene confidence. Carson thought this man looked more like a beardless Jesus Christ than the warriors he had fought during his career.

"Ye are here, wantin' to see the Injun named Calling Rock, I reckon?" Carson asked. His voice had a Missouri twang.

"Si. Yes, he has been a compadre of mine for several years," said Rodrigo.

"Are you a chief? I was told you are dangerous," said Carson, smiling with amusement.

"Did they tell you that? But I have heard the same about you, Sir," Red Water replied. "But they also say you always speak the truth, even if you burn down orchards." The Mescalero referred to General Carleton's 'scorched earth' campaign that Carson had carried out, by destroying villages, peach orchards and livestock that sustained the Navajo Nation.

Kit Carson frowned, yet he was not angered by the remark. As he shifted in his chair, he winced in pain, "Forgive me, a horse fell on me several years ago," he said. "I don't move as quickly as I used to. So, ye are a medicine chief, not a warrior. Maybe I could use your advice."

"Maybe some willow bark. Or two or three juniper berries," said Rodrigo.

"Callin' Rock is considered a prisoner of war. He and his raiders have attacked settlements and killed people," said Carson.

"He was only trying to free young people, who were taken as captives from his tribe—by the Mexicans and Americanos. They were made slaves and servants," Rodrigo said. "Are you not fighting a war yourselves—to end slavery?"

Kit Carson nodded, acknowledging this inconsistency. This Mescalero seemed intelligent and adept at diplomacy. "Maybe we can barter a deal, compadre. If ye can persuade your people and his people to settle in and not fight with each other, we won't hang Mr. Callin' Rock."

"Johnny has never taken a scalp," said Rodrigo, "and I can reason with him."

The frontiersman and the medicine chief conversed for a while, talking about their expeditions and war stories. Red Water told Carson about the Deer People and his own cooperation with ranchers Gray and McManus, as well as the recent recovery of the stolen gold shipment. Kit Carson recalled the Fremont explorations into California and the old days at the Taos trapper's rendezvous.

The next day, Rodrigo was allowed to speak with Calling Rock. "It is better that I die," the Navajo declared. "I cannot live like a slave, here in this musty prison, chained in darkness."

Rodrigo waited for the jailhouse guard to leave before speaking. The thin streak of sunlight that beamed in from outside highlighted Calling Rock's profile; the Navajo's face reminded Rodrigo of a hawk, now trapped in a cage. "I was kept here for several days. They will let you go outside soon," said Red Water.

"Help me escape. Maybe then we can die, as warriors," said Calling Rock.

"How did they capture you?" Red Water asked.

Calling Rock laughed scornfully. "They got lucky. Most of my warriors were chased down and killed. Carson burned our cornfields, and our fruit trees were hacked down. His men took our horses and sheep from us. They starved the Dine', then the women and children began to turn themselves in. I was betrayed, by some of the same people I had freed earlier. They told the Bluecoats where I was hiding—in exchange for bread!"

Red Water sat down on the straw beside his friend. "I am not surprised what one will do, in order to survive," he said. "You must think about how you can stay alive, to be here for your people, Johnny."

"How did you get captured?" Calling Rock asked.

"I decided to come here," the Mescalero replied. "My friends brought me here."

"Friends? How can 'friends' let you do such a thing?" Johnny Calling Rock questioned. "Who were they?"

Rodrigo explained how he had helped his ranch partners recover stolen cattle and how he had helped cavalry soldiers recover gold stolen by the Confederates—the Greycoats. "Except these thieves did not dress like soldiers," Rodrigo said. "Oh, and we rescued a girl from some Comancheros."

"You are loco," said Calling Rock. "Was the girl an Apache?"

"No, she was a young white woman who was taken by the Comanche years ago. We...we loved each other—after that."

Johnny Calling Rock stared at the Mescalero like he was bewitched. "I don't know if I should congratulate you, or knock you on the head. Is this your way of 'counting coup' on your enemies? You only have to touch them—and not in that way!"

Both men laughed. The guard looked in on them, then he walked away again.

Rodrigo became serious. "Up in the Sangre de Cristos, I met a strange man, from a faraway country. He was once a Padre—a Priest. He told me, 'All things must pass.' But first, they must be endured. When the Anglos find out there is no gold in your lands, they might let you go back. Your people need you here, Johnny. For them, you must endure—for time and another season."

"But if I die here—if I do not die as a warrior—my men will not slay my horse. This is the way of the Dine', understand? I will have no horse in heaven," said Calling Rock.

Rodrigo remembered his dream-vision. "The Nit'ahende do not bury horses. Yet I dreamt I saw my father, and it was like he was on a horse. An invisible horse! It was him, for he spoke as hard-assed as ever!"

Johnny Calling Rock burst out laughing again. "What did he tell you?" he asked.

"I must seek a higher purpose," said Red Water.

"I will remain here, as well. As long as you choose to stay, too," said Calling Rock.

Red Water tilted his head as he looked at the Navajo. "Who said anything about staying? I came to this place to figure out how all us Apaches can get the hell out of here."

CHAPTER 45

Riding around on his property often cleared Jimmy Gray's mind and helped him think about his business options. He still owed the Fazari-Martinez ranch some money for the Durham bull. Gray had only a little cash left from selling the cattle at Fort Sumner, yet it was not enough to pay that debt.

It had rained a few days earlier and the Tennessean found his herd grazing on the new grass up in the foothills, past the outskirts of his property. Jimmy tried to urge his coonhound and Lew's Airedale into forcing the cows and steers back to the ranch; however, the dogs had other interests. The Redbone, Johnny Bob, found some strange new scent and ran off lickety-split, into the pine forest. "Leave go of that trail and help me, dog-dammit," Gray cursed, as the Airedale followed the coonhound.

Jimmy's shout startled his half-wild longhorns and the cattle scattered in three directions. The Tennessean gave up. "Go ahead and open range then, damn you," he muttered. Since Juan Villareal had not returned, Jimmy decided to go and hire some other Mexican boy from the nearby village.

As he rode over to San Geronimo, Gray reproached himself. "I wish I'd never taken Rodrigo to the reservation," he said. "Or had not run off Rosa and Juan." Gazing south at the open valley of San Geronimo, a rush of loneliness lessened his spirits. "God, give me another chance with a woman," he wished aloud. "And I won't be such a hammerhead next time."

Jimmy Gray checked first at the village mercado, to see if there was any letter from his ex-partner, Lew McManus. There was none. For a moment, the rancher thought about riding on to Las Vegas Grandes, to make amends with Rosa Amarilla, but he changed his mind. It was best to leave well enough alone; instead, he purchased a pint of rye.

Two days later, after hiring a local paisano, an old goat farmer, to watch the ranch, Jimmy Gray headed off to Cimarron with two good horses, young mustangs that he had tamed. Jimmy hoped to broker some deal with Lucien Maxwell, the land grant baron.

Cimarron had fallen on hard times after a tough winter. There was little traffic on the Mountain Trail out of Colorado and caravans were not venturing out from Santa Fe, for fear of Cheynne and Comanche raiders. Still, there was some activity in the tavern and the hotel. Trappers visiting from the mountains and new gold seekers from the east had come to town. Jimmy Gray was not the only lean and hungry young man in Maxwell's saloon when he arrived in the early evening.

Although his patched denim jeans and his worn canvas coat were covered in dust from the trail, the rancher from the Rim Rock was known as a paying customer. Pete Maxwell, the owner's son, instantly laid out a shot glass on the bar counter and produced a bottle of red rye.

"Is your Paw home?" Jimmy asked, ignoring the liquor.

"The Old Man has gone to Taos," said the younger Maxwell. "Which is strange, as one-quarter of Taos is here. Are you not drinking?"

Jimmy noticed how Pete resembled his father; his black eyebrows, fierce eyes and direct manner made him look like the trapper and explorer of Lucien's younger days. Gray shook his head, so Maxwell scooped up the filled glass and downed the shot himself in one quick motion.

"What's your business, then?" asked Pete. Two of Maxwell's dance hall girls were now eyeing the lean Tennessean from the end of the bar. "How about a girl? Care for any female companionship?" the bar keeper whispered, leaning across the counter.

"Don't have the money for such frivolities," said Gray, scowling. Then he added, "Not yet, anyway. I want to sell you all some fine horses."

"We don't need none of your wild-ass mustangs," said Pete. "Ain't buying nothing right now. Just selling. Either liquor, beer, overdone beefsteak—or overdone females. if you catch my drift. What'll it be?"

Jimmy Gray pointed to the empty shot glass; Maxwell filled it.

Maxwell's demeanor became more hospitable. He leaned forward again and one black eyebrow arched like a caterpillar. "Well, if you don't like those two, stick around for another day. I'm workin' on a new gal, who's here at the hotel. She's pretty, young and blonde. We'll overcharge her and then offer a way for her to work out the debt. You ain't the only one breakin' in wild critters," Pete Maxwell snickered.

"Look you damn pimpernel. I ain't interested," the rancher snarled. "Tell your Daddy that Jimmy Carl Gray came by. He gave me a proposition two years ago, knows who I am, and what I'm talking about." Jimmy downed the shot.

Pete Maxwell grinned. "Oh, that's what you're here for," he said. "You're good with a gun, right? Yeah, Paw will be back in a day or two. Stick around, Amigo!" Maxwell refilled the shot glass. "The first two are on the house," he added.

Jimmy Gray didn't know what to think. The Maxwells sometimes hired fast 'shootists', to collect rent and prospecting claim fees on the vast acreage the land owner controlled, and to maintain some order in the saloons. Whiskey on credit, and dalliances with the dance hall trollops, often kept such men ensnared—until a faster gun came on the scene. Jimmy took his time with the drink. He decided he could camp outside of town rather than take a room.

After finishing the drink, he told Pete Maxwell he would come back in the morning. Stepping out into the hotel's lobby, Jimmy thought he saw the young woman that the barkeeper had described. He paused; something vaguely familiar in the girl's face caught his attention.

The young lady had reddish-gold ringlets in her hair; she seemed about eighteen or nineteen, wore a blue and white dress, and seemed too homespun and healthy to be a dance hall girl. She caught the rough rancher staring at her, then turned to look at him directly. Her eyes were bright blue.

"Mr. Jimmy?" WaShana Nicole asked.

Jimmy Gray blinked and his jaw dropped. "Dang, Nicole, I hardly recognized you!" He laughed and touched her shoulder, unsure if he should hug her. WaShana stepped up and embraced him.

"I am so happy to find you, Mr. Jimmy," she said, ignoring the looks from other guests in the lobby.

"You sure aren't a Comanche no more," said Gray. He could not believe this was the same captive he had freed the previous spring. "How did you get here? I thought you were in Kansas."

"We came here with the first wagon train of the season two days ago. I thought Lew McManus would be here in Cimarron, but they said he didn't take the job Mr. Maxwell had offered him."

"Lew went back to Tennessee," said Jimmy. "So, who's with you? That Canadian lady? Or Dirt Bradshaw?"

WaShana Nicole glanced over at the people in the saloon, then she answered, "I came alone." Seeing the rancher's perplexed expression, she added, "Well, not entirely. Come up to my room, Mr. Jimmy—I need to show you something."

Caught again by surprise, Jimmy was led upstairs to WaShana Nicole's room. She had taken him by the hand. He felt her warm, soft palm against his rough fingers. WaShana opened the hotel room door.

The light was different in the room—brighter, more suffused. The sunshine from the west-facing window beamed down on a bed, where a wicker basket was positioned to catch its warmth. The room had a scent, a fragrance of washed linen and vitality. Jimmy Gray sensed that WaShana embodied the same fragrance when she had hugged him downstairs.

A newborn baby slept in the basket. The child had reddish-brown hair that matched his complexion. WaShana let go of Gray's hand and picked up the basket, cradling it in her arms. "Yes, this is Red Water's son!" WaShana said proudly.

"Well, I'll be..." Jimmy stopped himself. Cussing seemed inappropriate just now. He gazed at the infant, looked up at the child's mother and he was amazed at the devotion glowing in this young woman's eyes. "Wha-what's his name?" Jimmy stammered.

"Trace," said WaShana, pulling her son out of the basket. He was wrapped in a light blue blanket. "Do you want to hold him?"

Jimmy nodded. When WaShana handed him the baby, the boy opened his eyes. They were brilliant and brown and stared at Gray with a mesmerizing intensity. Trace had some European features; like his mother, his nose was thin and he had dimples, for he smiled at Jimmy. "He is beautiful, WaShana!" he exclaimed. "Aha, you're a mamacita!"

"Is Rodrigo at your ranch?" the girl asked. She saw the rancher's face go sad. "Where is he?"

"The Bosque Redondo. It's what they call an Indian reservation... down on the Pecos," Jimmy said softly. Handing the boy-child back to WaShana, Jimmy explained how the U.S. Government was rounding up the Apaches and the Navajo People. "He had little choice...he decided it was better, if he went peacefully. WaShana, he didn't know..."

WaShana Nicole sat down on the edge of the bed. Absorbed in thought with the shock of this revelation, she rocked her baby back to sleep. She wondered what to do now. There was an awkward silence.

"I'm sure you had a rough journey," said Jimmy Gray. "Especially if you had that boy on the way. Lew told me that you went off with a Canadian lady—one of those abolitionists. And her brother."

Tears formed in WaShana's eyes. Her rocking back and forth grew more frantic. "Those men...from Missouri, they killed Jane's brother." WaShana drew a deep sigh. "His name was Trey. Jane took me back East, across the Big River, but I could not stay. I did not belong in the towns of the East."

"Yes, Ma'am. I bet that took some adjusting. After you had lived with the Comanches all those years," said Jimmy. "You are still glad we rescued you, right?"

"From the man named Ortiz? Yes, Mr. Jimmy," the young woman replied, yet then she hesitated. "But now I have traveled so far, just to finally find a home—and there is none."

"Come back with me to the Rim Rock," said Jimmy. "You can stay there." He paced back and forth in the room as WaShana considered the matter. Jimmy remembered what Pete Maxwell had said about WaShana downstairs. "How did you pay for this lodging?" he asked.

"Oh, I had a little money—from touring with Jane Edgarton. Most of it is gone, but the man—Mr. Maxwell—said I could stay as long as I needed. He said they can find work for me."

"No, no, you should not stay here!" said Gray, shaking his head. "I'll go down and settle your bill. Listen, girl, you are not simple-minded. You know what White men want. They'll make you give yourself up for money. Then your son will be mocked and scorned his whole life. Come back to the ranch with me. I will try to get Rodrigo back, I promise."

WaShana's mouth tightened. "I cannot be your woman, if that's what you're aiming for," she said.

"I'm not. Listen, I'm serious," Jimmy insisted. "This will work out. I even brought along an extra horse, hoping to sell it. All we have to do is buy or rent a saddle." The Tennessean grinned. "Maybe you need a side-saddle—since you've become a fine lady now, right?"

WaShana Nicole wiped her cheek and laughed. "Aho, I can still ride day and night, like a Comanche, Mr. Jimmy. Even without a saddle."

"So, we can do this?" Jimmy requested. The young woman nodded. "Great! So, pack your stuff up and we'll leave at first light. I'm heading' downstairs to settle up. You've got a fine baby boy there, WaShana. He's gonna have a home."

The next morning, the rancher arrived to find WaShana packed. Her infant son was tucked into a cradleboard, which she carried on her back as a papoose. WaShana wore an English tweed shooting jacket, given to her by Jane Edgarton. She also wore a pair of boy's denim trousers and had run a red ribbon through cut holes in her hat brim, to keep the hat from blowing away.

Jimmy Gray strapped the young woman's carpet bag behind the used saddle he had purchased. "Now, this mustang is fairly well broken, but you be careful, Miss," he said, holding the reins of the brown and white pinto filly. Jimmy looked down at WaShana's boots. Her calfskin boots were a remnant of her having dressed like a lady. "You look right nice, for a day trip out in the countryside," said Gray, "except them high-button boots will get ruined in the rough brush."

"I won't need them anymore at your ranch," said WaShana, stepping up in the stirrups and swinging herself atop the pinto. She adjusted the straps of the papoose. The infant, Trace Red Water, looked at Jimmy Gray and cooed. "Get on your horse, Mr. Jimmy," said WaShana, tapping her horse's flank with her heel. "And try to keep up, Sir."

Rather than taking the Trail, that led to La Vegas Grandes and Santa Fe, Jimmy Gray decided to veer west for the mountains. He wanted to avoid the rough towns of Loma Pardo and Las Vegas. Jimmy felt a desire to show WaShana Nicole the beauty of the Sangre de Cristo range. Spring had arrived in the foothills, the streams ran strong from snowmelt, wildlife abounded and aspen leaves shimmered anew in the sunlight. The weather was perfect for traveling.

By late afternoon, Gray and WaShana were climbing the crest of Aqua Fria Peak, over eleven thousand feet high. "See that other peak, the one with all the snow on it?" Jimmy pointed to a mountain that had turned rose-red in the brilliance of the sunset. "That's Angel Fire Mountain. Pretty, ain't it?"

"Yes, Sir," said the young woman, shielding her eyes to watch the golden-yellow sun grow larger, then flatten out and dissolve under the brilliant western horizon. WaShana held up her infant to see its final glimmer.

"It...it's," WaShana attempted to find the right words. "It is spectacular!" she said. "Look, Trace, it's beautiful!"

Jimmy Gray was distracted by the way the soft-rose light shone on the young woman's face, the gold of her hair and her exuberance. A cool, westerly breeze lifted the brim of her hat and she smiled.

The rancher pointed off to some smaller peaks off to the south. "That's the Rincon Mountains. After we pass them, we'll cross the Mora Valley and be close to our ranch. I say 'our', because Rodrigo has just as much a share in the property as me and Lew." The rancher regretted the mention of Red Water's name when he saw WaShana turn sad. "So, it's just as much your home, too, Girl. For both you and your young 'un."

WaShana was taking her own stock of the rancher that day. He was a lean, hard and undecorated man, who did not brag on himself. She remembered their first meeting, when Gray swore regularly and hardly paid attention to her at first. He mistook me for a boy, she recalled. Jimmy Gray was far different than Trey Edgarton. He was different than Rodrigo– and not talkative at all—until now, she thought. He was not like Dirt Bradshaw either.

"Can we camp here tonight?" WaShana asked.

"Too cold and windy after dark," said Jimmy. "Let's ease on down to the lee side and get out of the breeze."

Moving down the mountain, Gray found a spot where they could encamp. He quickly built a fire, using pinon and cedar; then he walked off to find more wood, while WaShana nursed her baby. When Jimmy Gray returned, dragging a tree limb, the blaze was crackling and popping. WaShana turned her back to the fire, hiding her bosom in the shadows out of modesty.

"That young 'un sure is feeding a lot. He is gonna get fat real quick," said Jimmy. He instantly wished he hadn't said this; it sounded too critical. Breaking off branches from the tree limb and adding rocks around the campfire, Gray tried to stay busy. "I'm sorry we haven't got much to eat ourselves, other than those biscuits we brought from the hotel," he said.

"It's all right. I'm used to not eating much while traveling," said WaShana. She pulled down her blouse and turned around.

"I'll get up early and shoot us a jackrabbit or sage hen," Jimmy promised.

"It's okay, Mr. Jimmy. That would take too long to cook. Honest, I can make it. Best to get an early start tomorrow," said WaShana. She nestled her infant upon her shoulder and patted his back. Trace burped loudly, and both adults laughed, breaking the awkwardness between them.

As they stared at the fire, WaShana felt a melancholy growing within her. It seemed every close relationship she had experienced with a man had ended badly. Perhaps it was best to just become friends, like she had with Dirt Bradshaw and Gregory Abramsen. She turned her gaze to Jimmy Gray. "May I ask you something, Mr. Jimmy?" WaShana wondered. "Is Rodrigo's woman ..at that reservation?" He did tell me about her. We had no secrets." When Gray hesitated, she added, "And I want no secrets with you."

The rancher knew he must not lie. WaShana had come all this way to find his friend, Red Water. "I was the one...who took Rodrigo there, to the Union Fort. He felt he had to go there." The Tennessean stood up. "Yes, it turned out she was there. I...I'm sorry."

"It is as it should be," said WaShana. She laid the baby boy back in his cradleboard. "Should I even go to your ranch? Is there work there?" she asked.

"There's a home there. I've built a house. You can stay as long as you want," said Jimmy. He was willing to go to any length to bring WaShana Nicole to the Rim Rock.

"I cannot do that. You are being too kind."

"Heck, I'll build you another house, if you can't find yourself to live in mine. "Jimmy began pacing restlessly again as he spoke. "You, me, your little boy—and Rodrigo Red Water—we can start a settlement!"

WaShana smiled at Jimmy Gray's wild notions. Still, such a thing was not unheard of in the West. "Aho, will you call it Jimmytown? Or Graysville?" she asked.

"Just Rimrock. It's got potential," said Jimmy. "Your man, Rodrigo, he once told me he had a vision, that I would become 'Father to a People'. A Señorita turned me down two years ago. Ha, so if I can't do it one way, I'll do it another. I'll build a town, full of half-wild gold miners, Indians, Mexicanos, brave women like you, and maybe even a reformed drunkard for a preacher."

"Sounds about right," WaShana laughed.

"Listen, I was worried about you riding that wild filly. She's tossed me a couple of times, but you managed her real well."

"Maybe 'cause I'm still a little half-wild myself," said WaShana.

Jimmy kicked a smoldering log on the fire to get it blazing again. "What I'm saying is, you seem good with horses. I'm thinking of turning the Rim Rock into a horse ranch, rather than cattle."

CHAPTER 46

Jimmy Gray and Shana Nicole were nailing up the last of the wood siding on the new ranch house, when Jimmy suggested they should go celebrate. "Pretty yourself up, Shana, and we'll head over to Las Vegas Grandes," he said.

"No, I am tired. Besides, who would watch my baby?" Shana replied. She had dropped her full 'WaShana' name in order to blend in with the people of San Geronimo. Jimmy had suggested she do this, telling her that Rodrigo had altered his last name to 'Rojos' when dealing with the villagers.

"We can leave him with Mack Del Rio's nanny," said Jimmy, taking a nail out of his mouth, while Shana held a sideboard in place. The rancher hammered the nail in with one stroke, then repeated the process at the other end of the board. "Me and Rosa Del Rio are on better terms now," Gray added.

"Then you go drink with HER," Shana Nicole told him. Anxious to get this work done, before the afternoon sun became too hot, she picked up another board. Her son sat upright in his cradleboard under a shade tree.

Jimmy Gray laughed. "You sound jealous," he said.

"Aho—I am not."

"Come on then, let's go. I'll buy you a bottle of wine," the rancher urged.

"Men tried to buy me drinks in Cincinnati and Chicago, but I would not do it and neither would Jane. She called not drinking 'Temperance'. Why don't you try that?"

Jimmy grinned. "I can take or leave it—whiskey, that is. Now, Big Lew, he could sock it away." Gray reached into a box and pulled out some more nails. "C'mon let's finish," he said, placing four of them in his mouth.

After nailing the last board, Jimmy made another suggestion. He told Shana Nicole she should have her son baptized. "You know, baptized. Since you decided on a name for the sprout, it seems right."

"Why? Why would we do that?" The young mother was still suspicious of the rancher's motives regarding the outside world. Although Jimmy Gray had been very kind to her, the former captive was still skittish about White men.

"It's what people do around here," said Jimmy. "You know, Christians. Most of them townsfolk are Catholic. It'll go a long way toward them acceptin' you."

"Let me worry about that. Besides, my parents were Lutheran. What are you? A preacher now?"

"Hell, naw. Most folks think I'm a rebellious heathern," Jimmy said, grinning. He walked over to the shade tree, where his Redbone coonhound sat, watching Shana's baby. Dipping a ladle into a wooden bucket of water, he took a good drink, then he re-dipped the ladle. "Dang it's hot. Guess I'll baptize myself." Gray removed his hat and poured the water over his head.

"You'll need more than that, Jimmy. With your low-down ways," Shana remarked.

"You're right. I'm gonna go jump in the creek and wash up. There's still a fire in the wood stove. You can go heat up some water if you want to take a bath. Because we are going into Vegas, dammit. It's Saturday," said Gray. "Put on a dress, brush your hair, and we're goin' to town, woman!"

Shana picked up her son and watched Jimmy walk away. The weight of responsibility for this new, helpless life felt overwhelming. She thought about the families she had lost; the Klausmanns and the Quehadis were gone from her life. Rodrigo was gone. The heartbreak and horror of

Trey Edgarton's death still haunted her. Shana remembered how the Comanche women thought WaShana was cursed, that any man who connected himself to her was doomed.

Looking into her son's eye, Shana prayed, "Great Spirit, Lord, help me forget this stuff in the past! Find a way that me and Trace can live safely, that our life can be good here."

When she went upstairs, to her bedroom in the ranch house, Shana looked through her wardrobe for something to wear at Las Vegas Grandes. *I have not dressed fancy since I was with Jane*, she thought. Shana held up the blue and white dress she had worn in Cimarron, at Maxwell's dinner party, when she first felt close to Trey Edgarton. "No, I cannot do it!" said Shana Nicole; she threw the dress on the bed.

Trace had fallen asleep, in a small cradle, which Jimmy Gray had bought in the village. Shana knelt down beside the cradle and watched him sleep, the way his little chest rose with every breath, his lips pursing, as if he was still taking nourishment from his mother.

Downstairs, the rancher had slicked back his wet hair; he buttoned a starched white shirt at the collar, then searched for his best pair of boots. A month earlier, when they had arrived at the Rim Rock, Jimmy had insisted that Shana Nicole take the upstairs room.

He had traded a steer and a cow in San Geronimo for two milk goats, an extra bed and the cradle. The rawhide rancher felt happy to have people in his home again. Although he often kept to himself, it felt nice to have someone in another room.

When Shana Nicole stepped down the stairs, Jimmy was surprised to see her still dressed in the same trousers and faded red flannel shirt she had worn while working on the house. "What's this?" he asked. "Why ain't you dolled-up, Girl? We are goin' off to Las Vegas tonight."

"We both know I can't ride off with a gown on, Mr. Jimmy," said Shana, standing two steps up from the floor with her arms crossed.

"Dog-dammit, did I just immerse myself for nothing? Get back up there and change. We're takin' the wagon," said Jimmy.

"You needed a bath anyway," Shana replied. "I don't want to go anywhere. Don't buy me no wine, I know you now, Jimmy Carl Gray. You can be hard as flint—rough like your hands. You think because my hands are soft that I am soft-hearted, like a woman's breast." Shana shook her head. "No, my heart is hard as a whetstone! From what I have seen, and who I have lost, I am more like you than you think!"

Jimmy Gray did not know how to answer this bold talk. He considered it for a moment. Upstairs, the boy-child cried out for his mother. This stirred something in the rancher's spirit. When Shana Nicole turned to go back up the stairs, he touched her wrist on the hand rail and urged her to wait.

"I am hard-scrabble too!" Jimmy told her. "I ain't got nobody. No family I can depend on. I was two steps away from living in a tipi myself this winter. You don't know it, but having you and Rodrigo Junior here is an answer to my prayers."

Hearing this, Shana Nicole's hard expression eased off. The former captive of the Comanches studied the thin, rough Tennessean and saw he was in earnest. Shana sat down on the stairs and cried everything out; she cried like a wounded animal as years of grief and hardship poured out of her.

Jimmy Gray sat down beside the young woman and placed his arm over her shoulders. After a few minutes, he said, "Let's go get young Trace and we'll go out on the porch and watch the sunset—maybe have a little rye to drink."

WaShana Nicole nodded. She wiped her face on her red flannel sleeve, then they both walked upstairs to comfort the child.

CHAPTER 47

Dirt Bradshaw and Charlie Larsen were tired of battles, but at least the Colorado Second Cavalry had the Confederates on the run. They had fought at Camden Point in Missouri, defeating Confederate guerillas under the command of C.S.A. Colonel J.C. Thornton and capturing ammunition, weapons and gunpowder.

In September 1864, regular Confederate forces under Major General Sterling Price had invaded Missouri with about 13,000 cavalrymen. From then on, the Second Colorado fought at Lexington, Missouri, the Little Blue River and Independence, where they were driven back toward the Missouri-Kansas state line A major battle took place the next day, at Westport, near Kansas City. Both the Union and Confederate forces incurred about 1,500 casualties and losses on October 23,1864. Sergeant Bradshaw and Lieutenant Larsen attacked across the iced-over Brush Creek at the start of the battle; they were forced to retreat when General Jo Shelby's Confederate "Iron Brigade" counterattacked. A see-saw battle was then fought over an open prairie, until the Union Army eventually gained the advantage.

After Westport, one of the largest battles west of the Mississippi River, the Confederates retreated south. The Second Colorado Regiment, under Colonel James Hobart Ford, then fought at Marais des Cygness and Mine Creek. On October 28th, the Confederates halted their retreat in Newton County, Missouri.

In mid-afternoon of that day, the Second Colorado lined up with the 16th Kansas Cavalry on their right and the 15th Kansas Regiment on their left. They faced Confederate General Shelby's men once again, north of a farm in Newtonia.

The battle began with an artillery exchange, but then Shelby's men attacked. The Confederates began to outflank the Union line on their left. Assisted by two mountain howitzers at their rear, the Second Colorado held on. Most had dismounted, yet Lieutenant Larsen stayed on his horse. "Hold the line, hold the line, men!" he shouted.

Crouched down behind a large oak stump, Dirt Bradshaw fired away with his Spencer repeating carbine. He had left his horse, Waukesha, back at the Ritchey farm, in order to keep close with his men. As he paused to reload, Dirt looked around. The two Kansas regiments were falling back! They had apparently seen the Federal artillery units retreating, which demoralized the troopers.

"Sergeant Dirt! Bring your men and fall back," Lieutenant Larsen ordered. "We will reform our line at the Ritchey farm!"

Bradshaw reluctantly complied, covering his group's retreat by rapidly firing his Spencer as he walked backwards. A bullet pierced the outer flap of his jacket and he lost his hat.

Dirt turned around to see some blue-uniformed soldiers lining back up back at the Ritchey farm. General John Sanborn's brigade had arrived on the field, after marching from Fort Scott. It was now approaching sundown. Bradshaw reloaded once again, then he spotted the rest of his unit over at the edge of a harvested cornfield. He saw his friend, Charlie Larsen, atop his horse, rallying his men to stage a counterattack.

Suddenly Dirt saw only the horse, galloping away from the cornfield. Dirt raced over to help his friend. Lieutenant Larsen had fallen among the cornstalks, not far from another wounded cavalryman, Private Marshall Barnes.

Charlie was shot in the chest. "Och, help...Barnes first..." he said, wheezing for breath. Dirt knelt down and lifted his lieutenant's head. He unbuttoned Larsen's cavalry jacket and saw bright red blood staining the shirt rapidly, before Dirt could do anything. With an abrupt inhalation and a ghastly long sigh, Lieutenant Larsen died. Dirt Bradshaw saw the light vanish in Charlie's eyes; next Dirt's own vision dimmed, as his eyes grew wet with tears.

The Federal artillery batteries were now reinforced and pounded away at the Confederates. Soon the enemy withdrew into the nearby woods. This fight would later be called the "Second Battle of Newtonia", a Union victory and the beginning of the end for General Price's Missouri Expedition—yet for Dirt Bradshaw, losing his close friend only stamped the event as a bitter loss.

Five months later, Dirt and Dave Bradshaw stood outside Camp Collins, on the high ground above the Cache la Poudre River. The Second Colorado was now protecting the Overland Stage Route from the Northern Chyenne, the Arapaho and the Sioux. Dirt had just recounted the details of Charlie Larsen's death.

"That was Charlie, for sure," Dave Bradshaw remarked. "In the midst of everything going sour, he always stayed steadfast and true—doing whatever thing he could do." The younger brother hung his head. Dave was dressed in a long, black wool coat, having left the military in January. He pulled up the collar to shield himself against the early March wind that blew across the flat prairie. "We are sure gonna miss him. Erica is taking it very hard."

Dirt Bradshaw kicked some frozen mud off his boots. A bugle sounded back at the fort. "The part that rankles me the most, Davey, is why did it have to happen in our very last battle with the Rebs?" Dirt sniffed and wiped his nose with his coat sleeve. He wondered if he was coming down with a cold. "Private Barnes died later from his wounds," he added, remembering another loss at Newtonia. "You know, years from now, men like us may boast about our battles—but right now, it's still just a crying shame. I wish I hadn't teased our Charlie so much, back when we three were all mining together."

"Aw heck, Dirt. That was just how we expressed our friendship. It's what men do," said Dave. "Back when we thought you had perished in that avalanche, Charlie actually told me that he missed your joking." He and Dirt began walking back to the stockade of Fort Collins.

Dirt Bradshaw now wore a Lieutenant's bars; he had been recently promoted, yet still thought of himself as a non-commissioned officer. It was almost noon and Dirt had invited his brother to have lunch at the officer's mess hall.

"Speaking of my exaggerated demise, how did all that legal stuff settle out?" Dirt asked. "You know, when I didn't show up at Miner's Court?"

Dave Bradshaw stayed silent for a moment, then he replied. "Maybe it's best you stay away from Denver, Dirt. Stay with the Cavalry. At least you'll eat better than most folks do, back in Denver City these days. Why don't you make a career out of the military?" Dave suggested.

Dirt stifled a laugh. They now stood outside the mess hall. "I only joined to impress a young lady," he said. "You may have heard of her—Miss Jane Edgarton, the lady abolitionist and writer."

"I met her in Lawrence, after her brother was killed in the massacre," said Dave. "Whatever happened to that girl who was with her—the one who helped you search for the gold? I couldn't believe she was the same person."

"I don't know. Jane stopped writing to me. Dirt and his brother now stood in line with other officers, waiting for their meal. "But in her last letter, Jane said she was not marrying Silas Soule."

"What about the rest of your search party? You sure had a strange bunch of compadres, didn't you, Dirt?"

Dirt grinned and nodded his head. The chow line was finally moving. "Well, last I heard, the girl, Nicole, was with Jane in Cincinnati. The Apache, Red Water, he was voluntarily going to that new reservation in New Mexico." Dirt filled his tin tray with biscuits, fried potatoes, sausage and bacon. "I'll pass on the beans," he told a cook who held out a ladle of the item. "As for Lew McManus, the big lug was going back to Tennessee."

"Hah, I was surprised all of you stuck together long enough to recover any of the gold." said Dave., as he poured some coffee into a ceramic cup.

The brothers found an empty table at the back of the mess hall. The hall was far nicer than the barracks kitchen that Dirt had used as a Sergeant. Elk antlers were formed into chandeliers, and stuffed game heads lined the walls. David waited until they were separated from the other officers before speaking more about the gold robbery. "What about that other wagon?" Dave Bradshaw asked.

"Funny you should mention that," said Dirt, dipping a biscuit into sausage gravy. "We took a boy prisoner, who was with the bushwhackers. He said the wagon, the one with gold coins as well as ingots, wound up south of the Red River, in Texas. After that, who knows?"

Dave glumly sipped his coffee. The army's failure to recover the second wagon was the main reason his own military career had stalled. Dave also felt resentment toward Silas Soule, who had up-staged him, by bringing the gold that was recovered back to Fort Leavenworth. "So, you said that Miss Edgarton was not marrying Captain Soule? That leaves the door open for you, doesn't it, Brother?'

Dirt grinned slyly, warming his hands around his coffee cup. "Indeed," he said. "Well, maybe, I reckon. I could still look up Mrs. Jones in Denver City."

Dave Bradshaw scowled. Of course, his brother was referring to Christina Russel Jones, the red-headed Union widow who had once caused Dirt a great heartbreak.

"You'd best leave that book closed, Dirt," Dave warned. "Besides, Mrs. Jones had drawn the interest of a big-time lawyer in Denver City. And like I told you, stay away from there. Silas Soule has been transferred to the Provost Guard in Denver. If he sees you there, you might get arrested."

Dirt asked why he should worry about Soule. His younger brother looked around and whispered, "We need to straighten out the deal with those bad stock certificates you sold. If Soule gets wind of your past shenanigans, you will wind up in jail. So you'd better stay out here on the prairie," Dave cautioned.

Feeling humbled, Dirt decided to change the subject. "You do look prosperous, Davey. How's the Badger Hole doing?"

Dave Bradshaw's mood brightened. "You won't believe it, Dirt! That avalanche you caused—and those floods this past spring—created a big gully on North Boulder Creek. A whole section of the slope was gone. Down in the creek, I found chunks of quartz glimmering in the water. When I took a pickaxe to it, I discovered a chunk of quartz, as big as a five-pound bag of sugar. Inside the crystal was a nugget, bigger than my damn thumb! I knew then, the Badger Hole Mining Company was back in business."

Dirt could hardly contain his own enthusiasm, yet he knew he had to suppress his brother's outburst. "Go easy, Brother," Dirt whispered, placing his palm on Dave's forearm. "Don't start another gold rush."

Both of the brothers glanced around the mess hall. Other officers had noticed Dave's enthusiasm, so he and Dirt hunched their shoulders and leaned forward across the table. "I've built a new flume and a woodpecker mill, to process the ore," said Dave. "And brother Nate is coming out West, as soon as the war ends. It won't be long now."

Dirt Bradshaw stuffed his second biscuit in his coat pocket and emptied his coffee cup. "Let's go outside Davey," he said.

Outside the fort's stockade, the sun shone bright on the distant snowed peaks of the Front Range. Dirt Bradshaw longed for the war to end, so he could once again experience the Rockies that summer. He yearned for previous days, yet they were gone.

"You know, the Union Army got Abe Lincoln re-elected," said Dave. "And people say that your victory at Westport was the 'Gettysburg of the West'. I'm proud of you, Dirt, for sticking with the Second Colorado. What are you going to do after the war is over?"

"Tell you what, Davey. You fought this battle too, when those Texans invaded New Mexico," Dirt told his brother. "Once the Second Colorado musters out, I will stay away from Denver City. I made good friends with the Ute Nation, over in the San Juan Mountains. Maybe I'll go there. There's also a high valley, just across the Divide. It would be a good place to build a cabin, maybe go look for a new strike. Or maybe I will ride down to the New Mexico Territory and see my strange friends again."

"Land somewhere, Dirt," said Dave, shielding his eyes from the bright glow on the Rockies. "After I clear things up legally, you can come back to the Badger Hole–and Denver."

Dirt shook his head, yet he grinned wide with expectation. "You gotta understand, Davey. I'd feel like a ghost, haunting Denver. It might get me drinking hard. I can go west—I could go east—after the war. Maybe I'll go see our folks in Wisconsin. And maybe I will go visit Cincinnati. Sure would like to hear Miss Jane play the violin again."

THE END

Printed in the United States
by Baker & Taylor Publisher Services